STONE HORSES

STONE HORSES

Sallie Gallegos

University of New Mexico Press

Albuquerque

All characters and events in this novel are fictional.
Any likenesses to real people and occurrences are purely coincidental.

Library of Congress Cataloging-in-Publication Data

Gallegos, Sallie, 1961–
    Stone horses / Sallie Gallegos.-1st ed.
        p.   cm.
    ISBN 0-8263-1666-2
    1. Hispanic Americans-New Mexico-History-20th century-Fiction.
I. Title.
PS3557.A41195S76   1996
813'.54-dc20   95-4394
                CIP

ACKNOWLEDGMENTS

I could not have completed this novel without help from the following people:

First, I am grateful to my husband, Matthias Guenther, because he supported us, which freed me to concentrate solely on writing. Most of all, though, I owe Matthias special thanks because he urged me to let go of the negatives that inevitably accompany work on a project of this nature.

Kathryn Jacobi-Dysart was the first to read early segments of *Stone Horses*. She recognized a spark of potential and encouraged me to work on. Her enthusiasm on behalf of this novel has remained constant over the years, so it is only fitting, and a real honor to me, that her own work graces the cover of this book. Apart from being an artist of exceptional talent, Kathy is the most positive and gracious person I have known; I am fortunate to have her friendship.

I am indebted to John Trujillo because he helps me keep dreams alive.

I am thankful to Dinah Lea Jentgen of Las Cruces, New Mexico, who proofread the entire manuscript before it was presented to the University of New Mexico Press.

Tom Mayer's straightforward advice and excellent creative writing classes at the University of New Mexico set me in the right direction.

David Remley, professor emeritus of the University of New Mexico, not only followed progress on *Stone Horses* but also recommended it to the University of New Mexico Press.

Finally, I thank all of the people at the University of New Mexico Press—those up front and behind the scenes—who had a hand in bringing *Stone Horses* to the point of publication. I am especially grateful to Barbara Guth, managing editor, for her support from start to finish, to Andrea Otañez, editor-at-large, whose patience and professionalism were unfailing, and to Karin Kaufman, copy editor, whose closing comments on my novel were exactly the words I needed to hear.

This book is for my father, Arnold Leopold Gallegos,
and all of the men and boys whose lives were interrupted,
irrevocably changed, or, at worst, lost in the terrible experience
of World War II. Like they and their loved ones did so many
years ago, pray for peace, pray for brotherhood.

ONE

Elena took baby Marcos out of the wooden box where he spent the day while the family worked in the garden. Snuggling the baby against her, she kissed his head and sat in the cool grass with her back against the trunk of a huge cottonwood tree to nurse him. Eduardo watched the black ball of his brother's head and the small hands that fingered the buttons of their mother's blouse.

Rosita, Eduardo's paternal grandmother, sitting beside Elena, saw her grandson staring at his mother and the baby; she put her hands on Eduardo's hips and pulled him into her lap. "Shall I tell you how it was when you were born?" she asked.

"Yes," answered Eduardo, still watching his mother and the baby.

"Very well. One year before you were born, your mother gave birth to a baby, a little boy. He was born here in Los Torbellinos, New Mexico, in your mother's bedroom. But the poor child became ill and died two weeks after he was born. Father Martínez baptized him before he died, and the child, your brother, is now a little angel in heaven." Eduardo was finally concentrating on the story. Rosita paused and asked, "Do you know what the child's name was?"

"Yes," said Eduardo; Rosita had been telling him this story since he could remember. "His name was Eduardo Ricardo Montez like my name."

"Exactly. His name was Eduardo Ricardo Montez, and he was born on January 29, 1925. In the beginning, he was a healthy baby. We sent for the priest who made the child's birth certificate and entered the child into the church ledger under the family name. Then suddenly the baby became ill. He could not keep any food

1

inside of him, and soon he could no longer take milk. The priest baptized him three days before he died. Your poor mother was sick with grief. We were all very sad. But one year later, on December 28, 1926, your mother was blessed with another child."

"I was the child," blurted Eduardo.

"Yes," Rosita laughed, "you were the child. You were handsome and strong and healthy. You helped us let go of the sadness. Your mother was happy that you were a boy so she could name you Eduardo Ricardo. She even used the same birth certificate that was made for the first Eduardo. Someday I'll show you that your birth certificate is the same one. Your mother changed the dates of birth, of course, but it is the original certificate that was made for your brother, God bless him. You, Eduardo, were a strong baby and you only cried when you were cold or hungry."

Eduardo was silent for a moment. He looked at his mother, who cradled Marcos in her arms. The baby kicked sporadically, exposing his chubby legs and tiny feet from beneath the hem of his white gown. "What did I wear?" he asked.

Rosita looked at Elena and Marcos and smiled. "You wore a white gown like all babies do. Perhaps the same white gown that Marcos is wearing."

"What did I eat?"

Rosita sighed and kissed Eduardo's cheek. "You nursed from your mother like Marcos is doing now. All babies need milk from their mothers because they don't have teeth," she laughed.

"But now I have teeth. Look," said Eduardo, opening his mouth wide.

"Yes, you have very fine teeth." Both she and Elena laughed.

Eduardo slipped off of his grandmother's lap into the space between her and Elena. It was a hot day with no trace of breeze. Eduardo felt his eyelids growing heavy and laid his head on his mother's lap; she put her hand gently on his head. He closed his eyes and listened. All around them grasshoppers were trilling their strange music, and far away his older brothers, Carlos and Roberto, were shouting and throwing stones at fish in the creek. He also heard the distant bleating of the sheep in the pasture. Elena ran her fingers through his hair and soon he was sleeping.

When he awoke, his mother and grandmother were gone; his head was resting on a folded coat. Eduardo sat up rubbing his eyes and began to whimper. Then he saw that his mother and grandmother were back at work in the garden. His father, Miguel, and his two brothers were there too. The family was harvesting ripe vegetables. Eduardo often tried to help by mimicking Carlos and Roberto, but they always scolded him for picking unripe vegetables or for ripping plants out of the earth. When the family worked in the garden, Eduardo was usually under the cottonwood tree with Marcos, who was more patient than Eduardo. He usually slept longer and, when awake, was content with waving his fat little limbs in the air.

Eduardo stood up, stretching. He yawned, walked behind the tree, pulled up his long shirt and peed in the grass. He walked over to the water pail, filled the dipper, and walked back to Marcos's box. He took a drink and looked down at his little brother who was still sleeping. Beads of perspiration stood on the baby's nose and forehead, and his hair was damp. Eduardo poured the rest of the water from the dipper out on the ground and carried it back to the pail. A grasshopper had landed in the bucket and was swimming frantically, trying to escape. Eduardo fished the large insect out and carried it back to Marcos's box. He thought of feeding it to Marcos, but Marcos was sleeping. If he woke the baby, he would be punished. Instead, he dropped the insect in Marcos's box and then, wiping his palm on his shirt, he noted with satisfaction that the grasshopper perched itself on the baby's chest.

Eduardo wandered into the garden to where his grandmother was working. When she noticed him, she stopped hoeing. "Ah, mi'jo, did you sleep well?" Rosita asked. Eduardo nodded. "Qué bueno." She leaned the hoe against her shoulder and wiped her hands on her apron. "Look, I have something for you." She reached in her apron pocket and took out a piece of folded newspaper. Inside were two biscochitos. Eduardo smiled. "Go ahead take them. I have to finish my work here." He thanked Rosita and took the cookies; he held one up for her to take a bite. She took a bite from the cookie and said, "What a good boy." Then she went back to hoeing. He stood beside her watching her work as he ate the cookies. He liked being with Rosita because she told him things. If she spotted a bird, she pointed it out to him and told him what it was called and all that she knew about it. She also told him the names of the weeds that she hoed out of the garden and why they were bad for the vegetables. But today she said little, so he grew bored and went back to Marcos's box under the cottonwood tree.

To Eduardo's dismay, Marcos was alone in the box, but at least he was awake. Eduardo knelt down. "Hello, baby," he said, cooing like his mother and grandmother did when they spoke to Marcos. The baby smiled and laughed. Eduardo stroked his cheek. He thought of stuffing a few weeds into Marcos's mouth, but the last time he did that his mother had spanked him. "Mamá, Mamá," yelled Eduardo, "the baby is awake."

"Alright," she answered. She was bending down picking squash. She stood upright rubbing her back. "I'm coming." She walked toward Eduardo and stopped at the pail of water to pour water over her hands. "Eduardo, do you want a cup of milk?" He nodded so she took the dipper that lay beside the pail, rinsed it, and carried it with her. She sat down by Marcos's box unbuttoning her blouse, but before she picked up the baby, she squeezed milk from her breast into the dipper. The stream of milk made a loud hissing noise against the metal as it filled the cup. "Here, sit down," Elena said. Eduardo sat beside her and took the dipper with both hands. "Gracias, Mamá." His mother did not let him have breast milk often because Marcos needed it more than he did. Although sometimes Roberto and even his father drank a cup, Carlos never drank breast milk. Eduardo drained the milk and gave the empty dipper to Elena. He wiped the sides of his mouth with the back of his hand and ran into the garden.

It was late afternoon. All of the vegetables that they had picked for the day had to be carried to the house and washed. After dinner, everyone would sit on the portal to slice and thread the vegetables onto long strings for drying. During this time of year, Eduardo and his brothers were allowed to sit up until their grandmother went home to her own house and their parents went to bed. Eduardo was alert and refreshed from his nap. He ran down the row toward the opposite end of the garden. He tripped and fell to his hands and knees. His father was standing near by and began to laugh. "Cuidado, mi'jito," he said. Eduardo stood, dusted his knees, and ran on. At the end of the row were baskets of squash and cabbage and pinto beans and onions and ears of sweet corn. He held his head over each basket and inhaled. The sweet corn smelled good but the onions and cabbages stank. Miguel came up behind Eduardo and hoisted him onto his shoulders. Then he stooped down and picked up a basket of corn and started walking in the direction of the house. "Carlos, Roberto," Miguel yelled, "let's take these baskets to the house." They followed with a half-filled basket between them. Eduardo could see everything much better from his father's shoulders. He twisted and watched Carlos and Roberto struggling with their burden. Behind them came Rosita and Elena carrying another basket. Elena carried Marcos in her free arm and Rosita carried gardening tools. As Miguel passed the orchard, the rich aroma of ripe fruit filled Eduardo's nostrils and his mouth watered. He held tightly to the crown of his father's felt hat, which had a wide sweat stain all the way around it. Miguel walked up to the well in front of the house and set the basket on the ground; he took Eduardo off his shoulders and headed back to the garden for another basket. The leaves on the trees in front of the house were already beginning to turn golden. The long-stemmed hollyhocks at either end of the portal were fading to yellow and drying out; their bright flowers were shriveled, and the stalks, no longer able to support their own weight, leaned wildly in all directions. Soon Elena would cut them down and collect the seeds.

Eduardo stepped onto the plank floorboards of the portal and looked up at the ceiling. Under the eaves of the porch hung long, colorful chains of dried apricots and squash. Ristras of chile hung by the kitchen door; they were already turning from green to deep scarlet. Eduardo realized he was hungry. His mother and grandmother were just arriving at the house with Marcos, and Eduardo hoped that dinner would soon be ready. He ran back to the well where Carlos and Roberto were drawing water and pouring it into a tin tub. Inside the tub were squash.

"Look, Eduardo," said Carlos, "help us wash these. You find one with mud on it and rub it off like this," he showed Eduardo.

Eduardo began to help; the clean squash went back in the empty basket. They left Eduardo and went back to help their father bring the rest of the vegetables to the house. From where he crouched, Eduardo could see smoke starting to rise from the kitchen stove pipe. That meant that his mother and Rosita were already cooking dinner.

After all of the baskets were brought to the house, his father and brothers helped him finish washing the squash. Then they sat in a ring on blocks of wood and began to husk the corn. The best husks were saved for making tamales, but the smaller, worm-eaten ones and the corn silk would be fed to the pigs and goats. Eduardo's hands were still too small and weak for husking corn. His job was to pile the discarded husks into a basket. Miguel, Carlos, and Roberto hardly spoke because they were tired and hungry. Elena came out of the house with a bar of soap, a wash pan, and a wash-cloth and towel. Eduardo watched her draw a pail of water from the well. "Eduardo," she said tiredly, "come here." She was already rubbing soap onto the washcloth. The white foam piled up on the cloth and her hands.

"No," retorted Eduardo. Suddenly his father's hand shot out and slapped him hard on the rear. Whimpering, Eduardo walked toward his mother, holding his hand on his stinging bottom.

Elena took his arms and unbuttoned the cuffs of his shirt. "Put your hands up," she said. He lifted his arms and she pulled the knee-length shirt off his back. His naked little body shivered in anticipation of the cold water. She pushed his hair back from his face and took up the soapy cloth in her other hand. He grimaced and pressed his lips tightly together. No matter how hard he tried the horrible tasting soap always got in his mouth and, even worse, in his eyes. "Close your eyes." He obeyed and whimpered louder. His mother scrubbed his face and pushed his head over the wash pan. Cold water splashed into his face, rinsing the soap away. Then she took the towel and dried his face roughly. He opened his eyes cautiously; this time they were not burning. He spit on the ground to rid his mouth of the soapy taste. Next Elena lathered her own hands well and washed his arms and hands. Finally, she rinsed the washcloth and wiped down his neck, back, chest, and between his legs. She dried him with the towel, shook his shirt out, and pulled it back over his head. He felt fresh and clean and his skin was still tingling from the cold water. Elena tossed out the pan of dirty water and refilled it. "After you have washed yourselves, come to dinner," she said to his father and brothers. They were old enough to wash themselves, thought Eduardo as he followed his mother into the house through the kitchen door.

The kitchen was always hot in the summer from all the cooking, and it always smelled of freshly baked bread. In one corner were a big wooden stove and the wood box. A long wooden table with six chairs, a cupboard, and a smaller table where they washed the dishes were the only other furnishings in the room. But the whitewashed adobe walls were decorated with brightly painted porcelain plates on which prayers were written. Eduardo sat down on the edge of the wood box. The table was already set. They were having beans and chicos left over from the noon meal, but now there were also freshly roasted green chiles, fried potatoes, and fresh tortillas. Rosita was rolling out the last tortillas and grilling them on the stove top. As usual, she had made a miniature tortilla for him. She smeared it with butter, folded it in half and passed it down to him. It was still warm, and gone in three bites. He wanted another one but knew he would have to wait. Elena lit two kerosene lamps and placed them on the table. Miguel, Carlos, and Roberto came in. Their faces were washed clean and they smelled like the horrible lye soap that he hated. Miguel hung his hat on a peg by the door, and they took their places at the table. Elena and Rosita served them, then Eduardo, and finally themselves. Miguel mumbled a short prayer; they all crossed themselves. Rosita took Eduardo's right hand and made the sign of the cross over his chest. "Like that, mi'jito," she said. "Now you can eat." They all laughed at him. He did not know why they were laughing but he laughed with them. He ate a whole tortilla and a large serving of beans and fried potatoes.

After dinner it was completely dark outside. Carlos and Roberto had to help Elena and Rosita wash the dishes, and Miguel went back out to lock the chickens into their hut and herd the sheep and goats into their sheds for the night. Elena gave Eduardo a stack of tin pans and told him to put them on the table on the portal. She carried lamps out behind him.

Eduardo hopped along the porch on one foot; he always looked forward to evenings in the summer and fall. Everywhere sat baskets of fruit and vegetables. The first stars were glittering in the sky, and crickets in the grass had started their music. Rosita came out of the kitchen carrying three paring knives; Carlos and Roberto followed with balls of thick thread and the large needles they used to string the long colorful chains of sliced apples, pears, and vegetables. Elena and Rosita sat at the table and began to peel and slice a basket of apples. When they filled a wash pan, they gave it to Carlos and Roberto, who sat on the plank floor and strung the sliced fruit on to the thread. Soon Miguel joined them; he too peeled and sliced fruit. Eduardo ate a few sliced apples out of the pan and then crawled onto Rosita's lap. He sat close against her body and stretched his short legs wide over her long, thin ones. She worked around him, paring fruit into a pan that he held between his legs. The adults drank coffee and talked of the next day's plans, the price of goods in the local mercantile, but mostly about the neighbors. Out in the wheat fields, fireflies danced and bobbed. Eduardo drifted to sleep trying to keep his eyes on one of these peculiar sparks.

TWO

Eduardo would remember his first encounter with los abuelos forever. It was Christmas Eve, four days before his fourth birthday.
Snow covered the ground, and the night sky was cloudless, a plain
of black sparkling with millions of crystal-white eyes. A band of
men, women, and children were singing in front of his family's
portal. Their voices were strong and clear, and steam gushed from
their mouths as they sang. Eduardo stood on the portal behind his
older brothers, Carlos and Roberto, watching. The melodies were
familiar to him. He was certain that he had heard them before,
but it seemed a long time past. After the singing stopped, people
swarmed onto the porch, the women and children heading into
the kitchen. Everyone smiled and talked festively while Rosita and
Elena served empanaditas, tamales, posole with red chile, panocha,
and apple pie. There was scalding hot coffee for the adults and hot
chocolate for the children.

Eduardo ate sitting on Rosita's lap and then wandered out of
the kitchen onto the porch. His father, Miguel, was there with the
other men, but they were not eating. They had a bottle, which they
took turns drinking from. Suddenly, a tall, handsome young man
with long black hair cocked his head and glared into the night as
if he had seen something off in the distance. With a jerk, he slung
his head back and let out a terrible howl. Then he poised himself
gracefully on his right foot, and clasping his hands tightly behind
his back, he brought his other pointed riding boot down in rapid
successions on the floorboards. He pivoted around and around on
his toe with expert speed. Some of the other men were clapping

in time and laughing. The smile on the dancer's face was beautiful but wicked.

Carlos and Roberto were playing just beyond the portal with some other boys. Eduardo crept toward them but stayed close behind like a shadow. All of the adults came out of the house and clustered on the porch; they encouraged the children to run and frolic in the snow. Eduardo heard his oldest brother, Carlos, whisper to Roberto in a strange excited voice, "They're here. I know they are; they're just waiting."

"What? Who is here?" Eduardo begged.

The children scattered in all directions. A bonfire blazing a few yards in front of the porch threw light in a wide arch. The children ran to the edge of the light, peered into the darkness, and with a shriek ran quickly back toward the fire. Eduardo joined in, laughing and hopping like a bucking colt into the dark. He had not yet made it back to the edge of light when Carlos and Roberto sprinted past him toward the fire.

"Aheee, aheee!" Two cries rang out like pistol fire. Eduardo froze and stared in the direction of the cries, but already they seemed to be everywhere. "Aheee, aheee!"

A woman on the porch shouted, "Oh my God, it is the old men! The old Grandfathers have come. Los abuelos, los abuelos! Run children! Run and hide!" Eduardo heard her and tried to run but could not. Los abuelos were coming from the river and out of the woods. Horrible things. There were only a few. No, there were many, too many. The sight of them sent a hot pain surging through his body; his joints ached but there was no time to think about the pain. He tried to move. His legs were stiff like ice.

"Run, Eduardo! Run! Run!" he heard Rosita call from far away. Then the abuelo came out of the forest's edge, moaning and grunting like a wild beast. He was stooped and dressed in rags; his steps were heavy and his head hung low over his chest so that Eduardo could not see his face. Eduardo still could not run; his mouth opened to release a cry but it caught in his throat and made his chest ache. He gasped for breath. The abuelo sank to his haunches in front of Eduardo and snapped his horrible head upright on his neck. The face was chalk-white with huge gaping holes for eyes and mouth; his hair was ropelike and filthy. "Give me two Hail Marys and an Our Father," his husky voice commanded. Eduardo did not respond. Suddenly the abuelo bolted high in the air, as agile as a fawn. He shrieked and danced around Eduardo. Then without stopping his jig the abuelo swept Eduardo up in his arms. There was never contact between the two bodies, and the hands that lifted Eduardo high in the air were powerful and large, as hard as stone. Eduardo's body was frozen. In a heave, the abuelo tossed him on the snow-covered ground and dashed after the older children. Eduardo rolled over and over and stopped. His eyes were open and his pants were wet. He saw more abuelos everywhere he looked. Carlos and Roberto ran with the other children calling for help and laughing wildly, but the abuelos never caught them. They only cracked their whips in the air and staggered theatrically until the children were finally taunting them.

Rosita stepped off of the portal toward Eduardo. One of the abuelos leapt at her. "Give me five Hail Marys," he demanded, cracking his whip in her direction.

"If you don't get out of my way, I'll give you a good slap in the face. That's all you'll get from me, you shameful bastard," she retorted, brushing past him. She took Eduardo up in her arms, and cupping the back of his head in her slender hand, pressed his face against her shoulder. She walked back to the portal but the abuelos did not go near her again. They were busy with a child on his knees in front of the porch; one of the abuelos twisted the boy's ear, forcing him to recite the Lord's Prayer. Eduardo began to cry; Rosita patted his back and kissed his cheeks.

On the porch everyone was laughing at him. His mother took him from Rosita and went into the house. She changed his wet pants, and told him to stop crying. When he did not, she slapped him hard in the face. He bit his lip and stopped whimpering, but tears were still rolling down his cheeks. "Those men out there are nothing but fools. They are only foolish young men wearing masks. On Christmas Eve they come to hear the children pray; they think it is funny to frighten children. They were here last year, but you were maybe too young to remember. Stop crying. They are only drunken fools wearing masks." Elena lay Eduardo in the bed that he shared with his brothers. She pressed her cool hand onto his forehead and told him to sleep. When she left the room and shut the door, he buried his face in his pillow to muffle his sobs. In minutes the door opened. It was Rosita. She sat on the bed beside him and stroked his hair until he was sleeping peacefully. It was Christmas Eve, and in a few hours they would be leaving for midnight Mass.

When Eduardo awoke, Rosita and Elena were hustling the children into heavy coats and wrapping them in quilts. The guests were gone. Eduardo refused to leave the house until Carlos picked him up and tickled him. "That, what happened to you, was only a game. It was only a game, a game that all the children play to see if they know their prayers," he teased.

It was cold outside, so cold that it hurt to breathe in the icy air. Miguel's figure was as dark as the night around him; he was slightly hunched against the cold as he sat high on the wagon seat. Elena and Rosita rode in the back of the wagon with the children. Eduardo snuggled between his grandmother and Carlos. His throat burned from the cold, but he did not cover his head; he was watching for los abuelos.

The church yard was crowded with wagons and a few buggies. Inside his family squeezed into one of the pews at the back of the church. Soon the building was so crowded that people stood in the aisles and crammed themselves into every corner. It was hot. Eduardo leaned his head against his grandmother, and soon he was sleeping again. But before long, she was nudging him awake to kneel. It seemed like hours before they were allowed to sit down, and his knees were tingling painfully. He was not able to sleep again because he was constantly being prodded to stand or kneel. Finally the Mass ended, and they filed out of the church.

The cold chased grogginess from his head. Above the sky glittered with silvery lights, and the hillsides were lit up with dozens of luminarios. As they drove home, they could see that more luminarios were being lit. Each fire began as a tiny yellow flicker that grew until it was pulsing with its own heat. Once Miguel stopped the wagon on the side of the road where a large fire had been built. They all climbed down from the wagon, joined by other families who had paused to warm their hands by the fire. Miguel had a bottle of corn whiskey, which he shared with the other men. Soon they were back in the wagon traveling toward home. Excitement rang in the children's voices. Carlos and Roberto said there would be stockings filled with treats when they got to the house. Rosita smiled and pulled Eduardo closer to her.

The boys hovered around the stove and laughed to keep from crying as the blood began to circulate warmth through their numb hands. They could still see the luminarios from the kitchen window. After eating they were each given a stocking filled with peanuts, oranges, and hard candy. Eduardo sat with his brothers organizing the bounty of goodies and trading away the ones they did not like. He was glad to be in the lighted kitchen watching the fires on the hillsides. He smiled. The abuelos were only foolish young men wearing ugly masks.

THREE

Except for Elena's sniffling and the clinking of silverware against dishes, it was silent at breakfast. Elena's elbows were resting on the table, and she held a handkerchief over her mouth trying to muffle her sobs. Her plate was pushed forward, untouched. She had been sad like this for days, and when she was not crying, she looked worried and tired. Eduardo poked at the fried egg on his plate with a piece of bread; he could not eat when she was like that. His mother wiped her nose. "Eduardo, finish your breakfast," she snapped. He stuck the piece of bread in his mouth and tried to chew.

After breakfast his father was leaving to work for monthly wages on a sheep ranch in Colorado. Eduardo knew his father's explanations for leaving by heart. At Christmas he had warned if he could not earn enough cash in his blacksmith shop he would have to leave Los Torbellinos. They had to have cash for the supplies from Mr. Lawrence's general store. Though Miguel was the only smith for miles, none of his customers had cash. Times were hard and people wanted to trade wheat or sheep for his work. But he could not buy goods at the mercantile with wheat or sheep.

Each time Eduardo's parents discussed Miguel's plans, Elena cried and asked him how he expected her to run the farm and look after two babies and two boys barely old enough to be of some help. So in a vain effort to save money, they had even boarded up Rosita's house, moving her in with the rest of the family. It was now late April 1930, and it had become clear that closing Rosita's house had not helped enough.

Finally the day had come. Miguel's horse was saddled and laden

15

with his gear. Eduardo looked out the window at the paint mare tethered to a post in front of the porch. She was stamping the ground nervously. Eduardo picked up a piece of egg and put it in his mouth. "Eduardo, use your fork," said his mother sharply. Miguel drank the last of his coffee. He stood up from the table, put on his coat, and took his hat off the peg where it always hung when he was in the house. Elena and Rosita also stood and collected the food they had packed in newspaper for Miguel's journey. Elena gave some of the bundles to Carlos and told Roberto to take Marcos out of his cradle. Eduardo slipped off of his chair and followed the family outside.

Miguel began packing the food into his saddlebags. Elena was sobbing loudly now; she took Marcos out of Roberto's arms and held him close. Rosita also had tears in her eyes. Miguel went to each of the children, embraced them, and kissed their heads. Eduardo ran to Elena and pressed his face against her. She put her hand on his head. Then his father picked him up and kissed his cheek. He put Eduardo down and laid his hand on Elena's shoulder. "Everything will be fine. You'll see," he told her. She said nothing. Finally, Miguel went to his mother, who took his face in her hands and kissed his cheeks. "Vaya con Dios. Buen viaje, mi'jo," she told him. Miguel mounted his horse and rode down the narrow driveway toward the main road. They stood and watched until he was out of sight. He would not return until fall to help with the harvest.

Elena's face was drawn and tired. She sent Carlos and Roberto to feed the animals, then she and Rosita set about clearing away the breakfast dishes. Eduardo was told to rock Marcos in his cradle. For sometime neither of the women spoke. At last Rosita sighed heavily. "Elena, mi'ja," she said, "if you're going to do it, you should tell him now." Eduardo looked at Rosita. There was a strange cracking in her voice that he had never heard before; it frightened him.

"I will tell him, Mother. I'm going to tell him today."

"Qué, Mamá? What? What are you going to tell me?" begged Eduardo.

"I'll tell you later," she said sharply. "Mamá," he whimpered, but she did not answer.

16

It was Saturday, and like every Saturday Elena set up the ironing board in the kitchen and heated the irons on the stove to prepare their clothes for Mass the next day. Elena led Eduardo into the bedroom that he shared with his big brothers and she began to take their Sunday clothes out of the wardrobe. Each of the boys owned a white shirt and a black jacket and trousers for church. Eduardo sat on the bed and watched as she laid out their Sunday suits. Next she collected the rest of Eduardo's clothes into stacks and began piling them on the bed. There were three knee-length shirts that he wore in warm weather, two pair of baggy trousers for winter, a night shirt, a stack of cotton underpants, a brown corduroy coat that used to belong to Roberto, and his boots for church and winter. Except for the Sunday suit and boots, she began to pack all of his clothes into a flour sack.

"Eduardo, tomorrow," she paused, "tomorrow after Mass, I'm going to send you to stay with Grandfather José for a few weeks," she said, packing the last of his clothes. Tears flooded Eduardo's eyes. His maternal grandfather, José Baca, lived two miles away in El Valle with Elena's mother and sister, Fidelia and Carmen. Almost every Sunday after Mass, Eduardo and his family visited his grandparents. Aunt Carmen was small and pretty like his mother, and she was warm and nice like Rosita. But he was afraid of Grandfather José and Grandmother Fidelia. They did not talk to children. They only talked about them as if they were not there. Plus Eduardo's father and brothers called El Valle the land of the owls. And everyone knew that owls were witches.

"You will only be there for a few weeks or perhaps a bit longer," said his mother. "Aunt Carmen will take good care of you. She likes you and you like her. Your grandparents will take care of you too. You should be happy to stay with them." She spoke gently, the way she talked to Marcos.

"No. No, Mamá," Eduardo sobbed. "I don't want to go. I want to stay with you and my grandmother Rosita. I don't want to go to El Valle."

"Your grandparents love you and they will take care of you better than I can," her voice was becoming louder. "Your father is gone now. He is gone." She began to cry again. "I can't take care of all of

17

you. I can't send Carlos or Roberto because I need their help here, and I can't send Marcos because he's still too small. In El Valle at your grandparents' you'll be well taken care of. Your grandparents have wanted you for a long time. You'll be happy there."

"No, Mamá. Please," he wailed.

Elena put her hands on his shoulders and shook him roughly. "Stop crying. Stop crying," she yelled. "You will go. Stop crying." She stepped away from him and took her handkerchief out of her apron pocket. She blew her nose, collected the Sunday clothes for ironing, and went into the kitchen. Eduardo lay down and curled himself into a ball. He cried until his tears were used up and the sobs turned into jerking spasms in his chest.

The next morning when Eduardo woke, Carlos and Roberto were already out of bed. He heard them talking to Rosita in the kitchen. Eduardo looked up at the ceiling and closed his eyes again. They were sore and swollen. He rubbed them and hoped for a moment that going to live in El Valle had only been a terrible dream. Opening his eyes he saw his sack that Elena had packed the day before. He began to cry again just as Rosita came into the room with a wash pan. "Buenos días, mi'jito," she said cheerily. "It's time to get up and dress for Mass. Don't cry, mi'jito. Don't cry," she said, taking him into her arms. After a few minutes, she stripped off his night shirt and washed him. She dressed him and combed his hair before they went into the kitchen.

Elena was nursing Marcos in her chair at the table; Carlos and Roberto were drinking coffee mixed with warm milk and sugar. On Sundays they were not allowed to eat breakfast until after Mass. Eduardo went to his place and Rosita mixed him a cup of coffee and milk. He had hardly eaten the day before and guzzled the drink from his mug. When he finished, Rosita gave him another. He started to drink the second cup, but tears welled into his eyes. Rosita took the cup from his hands. "Don't cry, Eduardo," she told him. She looked at Elena. "Mi'ja, there is no reason to send the child away. I cannot change your mind, but there's no reason."

"Please Mother," Elena said tiredly, "we've talked about this already. It's for the best . . . for his own good. My family will care for him better than we can. In El Valle Eduardo will be the only child. This is for the best," she sighed. "Come. If we don't leave soon, we'll be late for the Mass." Rosita shook her head and the two women began to clear the table.

Carlos, Roberto, and Eduardo put their coats on and went out on the portal to wait for their mother and grandmother. The three of them sat at the table on the porch. They were not allowed to play because they were wearing their Sunday clothes. Carlos was holding the sack with Eduardo's belongings. Eduardo rubbed his sore eyes.

The walk to church took half an hour. When they arrived at the plaza, his grandfather, grandmother, and Carmen were waiting for them. Greetings were exchanged and both families went into the church and settled into the pews. Masses were normally long and boring for Eduardo, but today it passed too quickly; he was crying by the end of the sermon. Soon they were back outside in the bright sunlight. Elena was leading him by the hand and they were all moving in the direction of his grandfather's buckboard. "No, no, no," Eduardo began to wail.

Carlos placed Eduardo's flour sack in the buckboard. Elena bent down to him. "Eduardo, now it's time for you to go with your grandparents and your aunt Carmen. We are not coming with you today, but we'll see you next Sunday at Mass. Stop crying and be a good boy. You'll see us next Sunday."

Eduardo threw his arms around Elena's skirts and held on desperately. "No, Mamá," he cried. "Please take me home with you. I don't want to go." Elena looked at her father and nodded. The burly old man stepped forward and whisked Eduardo into the air.

"No, no, no," Eduardo fought. "I want my grandmother Rosita. Rosita, Rosita," he cried.

"Venga, hombrecito," laughed his grandfather. "Why are you afraid? Do you think we are going to eat you?" The old man restrained Eduardo's furious fighting arms and legs. "Do you think I'm going to feed you to the coyotes?" he continued to tease.

"Mamá, Mamá," Eduardo screamed, but his mother and Rosita were walking away ushering his brothers around the corner of the church. Carlos and Roberto were trying to look back at him over their shoulders.

Eduardo sat on his aunt's lap on the ride to his grandparents' house. "Eduardo, you'll see your Mamá and your brothers and your grandmother Rosita every Sunday. Besides, we're not so far away from them. They live just up the river," she said.

Carmen looked like his mother and her voice was even similar to Elena's, which comforted him, but he continued to cry as she cleaned his nose with her handkerchief. "Don't cry, mi'jito. Don't cry." All of the fight was gone from him, though the tears continued to roll down his cheeks.

When they arrived at the house, Carmen carried him into the kitchen and up the narrow staircase to a bedroom he had never been in before. Seated on the bed crocheting was a woman. Carmen sat Eduardo next to the woman and said with a smile, "This will be your room." She smiled more than his mother. She touched his hair gently. "You'll share this room with Rafelita and me, and you are going to sleep right here in the bed with us. Won't you like that?"

"Hello, Eduardo," said the woman, his aunt called Rafelita. Her voice was liquid, songlike, and she was beautiful. "You have lovely, soft hair," she said, stroking his hair. "It's fine like the hair of an angel. I think you're going to like sharing this room with us. I have not been here long, but I like it. You'll see. You will like it too."

Eduardo stared at Rafelita. She was tall like Rosita but softer, with large breasts and smooth golden skin. Her features were sharp — high cheek bones and severely arched Spanish lips. She had rich black hair and wore it braided and arranged into a bun like all the women did. Her eyes were black and framed by thick, dark lashes. Strangely, she kept her eyes closed most of the time that she spoke to him, and she didn't face him while she talked. "It's a nice place . . . this room." She continued, "It is warm and safe, and when it rains there is beautiful music on the roof."

Eduardo looked around the attic bedroom. There was a wide dressing table in one corner. Its surface was covered with a crocheted doily, and there were hair brushes and ribbons and small ornate bottles arranged meticulously on top of it. Rosaries hung from either side of the mirror, and on the adobe wall beside the mirror hung a crucifix. They sat on a brass bed covered with a white throw and piles of dainty handmade pillows that spilled away from the headboard. There was a small wood heater in one corner of the room and a huge wooden wardrobe beside the bed. A treadle sewing machine was set up in front of the window; the floor was covered with colorful rag rugs and there were two chairs on either side of the door.

Carmen stood up and opened the wardrobe. She took Eduardo's clothes out of the flour sack and arranged them on a shelf. Eduardo started whimpering. "There's nothing to be afraid of. We're going to take good care of you, Eduardo," said Rafelita.

"Are you hungry?" Carmen asked. Eduardo nodded his head, still crying. "Very well. Then you need to stop crying and I'll take you down to the kitchen and we'll have breakfast. You need a good meal. Then you'll feel much better, and you'll see that you'll be happy here with us." Carmen moved down the narrow stairwell with Eduardo in her arms; over her shoulder Eduardo watched Rafelita run her hands lightly along the wall as she descended the stairs after them.

In the kitchen, José was already seated at the table, and Fidelia was busy putting the meal on the table. "Carmen," said his grandfather roughly, "I don't want you making a baby of that boy. I don't need a baby in this house." He rose and took Eduardo from Carmen and stood him on a chair. Eduardo stood still and straight. "Listen, Eduardo," he began, "I know you are strong because you fight very well; you fight better than a wildcat. And anyone who can fight so hard can also work hard. In this house, if you want to eat, you will work for your food. You are a strong boy and you are big for a four year old. You can earn your food. Do you understand?" he said, staring at Eduardo with his hands on his hips. "Do you understand?" repeated José.

"Yes," said Eduardo, nodding his head.

Carmen pushed past her father and sat down in the chair beside Eduardo. "Enough, Papá," she said. "Enough. He has had enough for one day. Go back to your chair. Sit down and eat but don't bother him anymore." The old man laughed and returned to his seat. "Sit down, mi'jito," she said to Eduardo.

"Hum," grunted Fidelia as she and Rafelita took their places at the table. José and Fidelia had been together for so long that they even looked alike. Their bodies were well filled out, which gave them the appearance of being younger than they were. They both moved with the same slow steadiness and their voices had the same raspy edge. Fidelia was taller and broader than her daughters, though not as tall or broad as José. Both Fidelia and José also had white hair. Fidelia wore her's pinned back from her face in a tight bun. But José's hair was thick like a beaver's pelt and stood up wildly on his round head. The whiteness of it was accentuated by the color of his skin, sun-browned as dark as a piñon nut.

Carmen served Eduardo a fried egg and fried potatoes and gave him a big slice of white bread smeared thick with butter and apricot jam. After he finished that and a glass of milk, he ate a big slice of apple pie and drank another glass of milk. His hunger made him forget the discomfort of being at his grandparents' table without his mother and family. They laughed at his appetite, and his grandfather joked, "A boy with an appetite like his has to be strong and healthy." Fidelia grunted, "Hum, it looks like he hasn't been fed for a week." Eduardo sat at the table finishing his pie while the women cleared the table and washed the breakfast dishes. His grandfather went out onto the portal to smoke his pipe.

When Carmen was finished with the dishes, she took Eduardo upstairs and changed him out of his Sunday clothes into one of his long shirts and a pair of baggy trousers. Then she and Rafelita took Eduardo for a walk by the river. Carmen looped her right arm through Rafelita's arm as they walked. Eduardo was on the other side of Rafelita and held onto her hand. He noted that her hands were soft and graceful; she wore lots of golden rings on her long fingers. They eventually came to a grassy clearing, where they stopped and spread an old blanket on the ground. The women sat down and Eduardo couldn't resist exploring a little. He picked flowers and took them back to Rafelita and Carmen. Rosita had taught him to take flowers to his mother; she had told him that all women liked to receive flowers from men. Carmen and Rafelita cooed with delight and began organizing the flowers into bouquets. At length Eduardo sat down between the two women and thought of Rosita and his mother and family. He felt tired and sad again. Soon he fell asleep.

When he woke, the sun was sinking on the horizon and he was hungry and cold. They folded the blanket and walked home. After a light dinner and the dishes were done, José and Fidelia went out on the porch. Carmen and Rafelita took Eduardo outside, where they all brushed their teeth and visited the outhouse before bed. Finally, upstairs in the loft bedroom, Carmen lit a lamp. She and Rafelita undressed and washed themselves and put on their nightgowns. Next Carmen undressed and washed Eduardo and put him in his nightshirt. He fingered the familiar cotton of his gown as Carmen turned back the blankets and told him to crawl in. The bed sheets were sweet and fresh, not like his bed at home. Eduardo grew drowsy as Carmen and Rafelita brushed and braided their long dark hair. Rafelita's eyes never watched the work of her hands. Eventually, Carmen blew out the lamp, and they got into bed on either side of him. Rafelita ran her fingers through his hair and kissed him good night. "Rafelita, he is as pretty as a little doll," said his aunt.

"Yes. I am so happy that he has come to live with us," answered Rafelita sleepily. Eduardo fell asleep listening to the whispering of Carmen and Rafelita as they prayed their rosaries.

FOUR

As usual Eduardo woke with Carmen and Rafelita at six in the morning, and after dressing they went downstairs together. José was at the table smoking his pipe and drinking his strong black coffee. His grandfather laughed when he saw Eduardo coming down the stairwell and pulled the chair beside him out from under the table. "Come here, jefe. Sit down beside me. Your tía will bring you your coffee, and you can tell me what I have to do today." Eduardo giggled and climbed onto the chair as Carmen mixed his cup of coffee. It was really only hot milk with a few teaspoons of coffee and sugar mixed in, though his grandfather liked to call it coffee. "That's right, mi'ja. The boss likes his coffee strong and black, black. It takes him through the day." The two of them sat at the table drinking from their mugs while they waited for the women to serve breakfast.

When breakfast was over, Eduardo went outside with his grandfather. José went into the fields to irrigate the wheat or repair fences, and Eduardo was left on his own. His job was tending the chickens, pigs, goats, and sheep. It took him all morning, and before lunch he only would return to the house to deliver fresh eggs from the chicken house or to fill the wood box in the kitchen.

Before he let the chickens out of their hut, he filled their feed bins with cracked corn and carried their water container to the creek where he washed it. Then he took the container back to the chicken pen and returned to the creek for a bucket of fresh water. After the food and water troughs were filled, he raked out the musty chicken house and collected eggs from the nesting boxes.

Locking the gate behind him, he started to the house with the basket of fresh eggs. On the way this particular morning, he stopped at the wood pile and hid one egg in the niche of a log.

Next he had to water the pigs, which took almost an hour. The pigs' water also had to be carried in buckets from the creek. He had to grasp the handles of the filled bucket with both hands. As he walked, his knees banged against the bucket, sloshing water out onto his legs and the ground. By the time he got to the pen, a fourth of the water was gone. But even worse, he was too small to pour the water over the top of the pen into the water trough. Instead, he had to heave the water bucket onto a high block of wood that José had placed beside the pen for him. Then he climbed onto the block of wood, lifted the heavy bucket, and tried to pour over the highest rung into the pig's water trough. There were only three pigs, but he had to make many trips to and from the creek to sate their thirst and leave their trough filled. Next he gave them their daily ration of cracked corn, which was not so heavy. With the bucket in one hand, he could still climb up the rungs of the pen and pour the corn into the feed troughs.

Eduardo never went in the pig pen. His grandfather told him that years ago a neighbor boy, a young boy like Eduardo, had been tending to his family's pigs and climbed into the pen for some reason. The boy was attacked by the pigs and half eaten by the time his father found him. Eduardo believed the story because the pigs always smiled at him and tried to bite his toes when he climbed on the rails of their pen.

The goats and sheep were easy to take care of and did not attack him like the rooster sometimes did and the pigs wanted to. The creek ran through their corral, and so he never had to carry water to them. He fed them their rations of corn and sometimes had to herd them into the pasture where they grazed.

His last morning chore was the hardest. He had to fill a basket with freshly cut weeds, grass, and alfalfa for the pigs and chickens. This took him more than an hour. He used a sickle to chop weeds and alfalfa from around the house and animal pens, but the sickle handle was big and awkward in his hand. When his grandfather cut weeds, it looked easy. José grabbed a huge bundle of grass in one hand and sliced it off neatly at the base. It seemed that one of José's handfuls nearly filled the basket. But even though his grandfather sharpened the sickle for him often, Eduardo could only handle a few blades of grass and alfalfa at a time. His grandfather told him that he was improving and working faster, but he could not tell. By the time he finished filling the basket, his hands ached and his back hurt from bending over. The pigs got most of the freshly cut grass, but he had to throw a few bundles in the chicken yard, too, because his grandfather said they would attack each other if they did not have fresh greens to peck at.

As Eduardo threw bundles of grass and weeds over the fence to the pigs he watched them fight for the choice offerings, pushing one another around with their snouts and heavy heads. He was sure that they could easily rip a child apart, but he still liked them. Sometimes he sat on the fence and scratched their backs with a long stick the way his grandfather had shown him. Eduardo started to climb on the fence with his scratching stick when he remembered the egg he had left behind the wood pile for José. He looked in the direction of the wood pile to make sure that his grandmother was nowhere in sight. She was not outside, nor could he see her at the windows of the house, so he ran to the wood pile and retrieved the egg.

Eduardo dashed up the trail to the end of the wheat field where he knew he would find his grandfather. Once in the cover of the wheat, Eduardo slowed to a walk. He had taken one whipping from Fidelia for feeding a moldy biscuit to the pigs and he knew he would receive the same treatment for stealing eggs, even though José coached him to do it. He ran a hand gingerly over his lower back and bottom. The welts from his whipping were finally disappearing.

Each day after breakfast, Fidelia took a tin canister out of the pantry and gave Eduardo and José two large biscuits to put in their pockets. They were to save these until they were hungry because they would not eat again until the noon meal. Eduardo liked the biscuits when they were freshly baked, but the women made them only once a week and stored them in the tin canister. After a few days, they became dry and tasteless, and by the end of the week, they had tiny spots of blue-green mold growing on them.

One day, as he passed the pig pen, the largest sow had sauntered up to the fence, grunting and pushing her dirty nose through the rails. He climbed up on the pen and took the moldy biscuits from his pocket. He threw the first one into the middle of the pen. The pigs rushed madly toward it, but the huge sow swirled and squealed so furiously that the two smaller pigs abandoned the race. The sow tossed her head back, swallowing the whole morsel almost without chewing it. "Qué cochina, qué cochina," Eduardo said to himself as he watched the pig sniff the dirt for crumbs. He tossed the second biscuit between the two smaller pigs, but again they had no chance. He was delighted as the sow rushed in and took the second biscuit. Then a hand had latched onto his ear, pulling him off of the fence. "I saw what you did," his grandmother scowled down at him. "What did you throw to those animals?"

"Nothing, nothing, Grandmother," but her hand twisted harder on his ear. "It was a stone, a little stone," he had cried.

"Qué muchacho malcriado. You throw food away to animals, and you are a liar too." Eduardo cried loudly as Fidelia dragged him by the ear to a tree and tore a large switch from it. She whipped him from his neck to below his bottom until he was screaming in pain. "You will never throw food away again. Do you understand? And since you think your food is so unimportant that you throw it to the pigs, you will eat nothing more today," she said, pushing him from her. Eduardo ran into the barn and cried.

Later that night, Carmen and Rafelita fed him and washed and salved the welts that covered his back. After that Eduardo always made sure that the coast was clear when he did something Fidelia might punish him for, such as stealing an egg from the chicken house.

The summer sun pounded down hot on Eduardo's head and shoulders as he walked toward the end of the field. At last he stepped out of the tall wheat and found his grandfather shoveling dirt and stones out of the irrigation ditch. José looked up surprised. "Qué tal, Eduardo?"

"Bien, bien, Abuelo. Look. Look what I have for you," smiled Eduardo, presenting the egg.

With a grin the old man pushed his shovel into the wet earth by the ditch and took a handkerchief from his pocket. "Qué suave," he said, taking off his hat and perching it on the handle of his shovel. He wiped the perspiration off his face with his handkerchief and ran it through his soaked hair. "Come. Let's take a siesta," he said, walking under the shade of a tree. The two of them sat down and José took the egg from Eduardo. "Did your grandmother see you take this?" he asked, staring Eduardo hard in the face.

"No, Abuelo," Eduardo answered, feeling important and secretive.

"Qué bueno, jefe. What a woman doesn't know won't hurt her," he laughed, taking his buck-knife out of its sheath on his belt. Eduardo watched as his grandfather drilled tiny holes at both ends of the egg with the tip of his knife. Then he returned the knife to its sheath and put his lips over one of the holes in the egg. In one terrific pull he sucked the contents of the egg into his mouth. His cheeks bulged for an instant. He swallowed once, twice, and the egg was gone. "Ahh," he said. "That was good. An egg puts the strength back into a man that the sun takes out." He handed Eduardo the empty shell to play with. Today he filled it with sand and then water; he emptied the shell and floated it in the irrigation ditch, finally bombarding it with sticks until it was crushed.

After José had rested, he stood up groaning, "Listen, jefe, are you finished with the animals?" Eduardo nodded. "Very well. Then go to the house and see if your grandmother has a chore for you. If not, come back here and keep me company." José put his hat back on and took up his shovel. Eduardo raced off down the trail, hoping his grandmother had no plans for him.

Fidelia was cooking lunch at the stove. She told Eduardo to fill the wood box. He carried five arm loads from the wood pile to the kitchen, and then swept the kitchen floor as he was supposed to after filling the box. "I am finished, Abuela," said Eduardo, returning the broom to the pantry. Fidelia patted him roughly on the head the way she did when she was pleased with him. "Fine, Eduardo. Go tell your grandfather that lunch is ready.

"Here I go, Abuela," he said, running out the kitchen door. Half way down the field behind the house he yelled for his grandfather, waited for his reply, and went back to the house to draw wash water from the well.

At lunch they had lamb stew that was filled with potatoes and carrots and seasoned with cilantro. Eduardo ate two servings and asked for another. He was always allowed to eat as much as he wanted. As Carmen placed his third serving in front of him, she said, "Our Eduardo has a good appetite because he works hard outside in the fresh air."

"Hum," grunted Fidelia. "Eduardo, after lunch, I want you to take your sack and collect wool from the corrals and sheep pasture." She had taught him to spot the tags of wool left clinging to briars and fence posts when the sheep brushed against them. He was to gather the tufts in a small burlap sack that Fidelia had given him. "After you finish in the sheep pasture," she continued, "go out into the llano behind the fields. There should be lots of wool on the sage out on the plain." She paused, "But you stay along the edge of the fields. You stay where your grandfather can see you." Her voice was becoming loud, almost shrill like his mother's sometimes did. "Did you hear me, Eduardo?" Eduardo stared at her. She went on, "José, you watch him. You watch him all the time."

José laid down his spoon and sighed deeply. "Fidelia," he said calmly, "that was twenty years ago. They live on reservations now. That can never happen again. That was twenty years ago."

"What, Grandfather? What? What?" asked Eduardo. "What happened twenty years ago?"

"Bueno, they were supposed to live on reservations then too. Renegados. Paganos," said Fidelia. "You never mind, Eduardo. Never mind what happened, but you stay near your grandfather. Do you understand me?" Eduardo nodded. "José, you watch him."

"Very well," said José. "I'll watch him."

After lunch Eduardo took his burlap sack and followed José out of the house. He waited until they were in the wheat field. "What is it, Grandfather?" he blurted. "What? Who is out on the llano?"

"Ay, mi'jito," sighed José. "If I tell you, you are never to talk of this around your grandmother. Never. Do you understand?"

30

Eduardo ran up beside his grandfather, "I promise that I'll never say anything. I promise, Grandfather."

"Muy bien, jefe. This was a long time ago. More than twenty years ago. Your mother was not even born yet. It was springtime, and I was plowing this field. Your uncle Juan, my first-born child, was with me. He was five years old. He liked to ride on the horse while I plowed, so he came with me into the fields nearly every day. Well, that morning he got tired of riding. I took him off the horse so he could play in the irrigation ditch like you do." José sighed and walked on. "I started down the field alone, and when I turned the horse, your uncle was gone. I ran back down the field calling his name. But no answer. I ran into the llano. I thought maybe he fell asleep or was hiding. I searched and called his name and still nothing, not even a footprint in the sand. An hour later, there were twenty men with me. We searched for miles in every direction and called his name, but nothing." José sighed heavily. "Then a man from up the canyon rode down with the bad news. A neighbor of his was found dead in the fields with an arrow in his back, and his horse and rifle were stolen. Finally, we knew where Juan was."

"Where? Where? What happened to him?"

"Apaches," José spat the word. "Renegade Apaches from the Jicarilla clan. I suppose I am lucky that they did not kill me too. Sometimes I wish they had rather than take my son. We tried to find them. Twenty of us from Los Torbellinos tried to hunt them down, but there was no sign to follow. Apaches are crafty devils, and they know these mountains better than any of us."

"But the child, Juan? What happened to him?"

"Juan was gone. I wanted to ride to the Jicarilla reservation to look for him, but my father said that the Apaches wouldn't be stupid enough to steal a Spanish child and then take him to the reservation where he could be seen by the Anglos or priests."

Eduardo was wide-eyed and stared out into the llano. "But what happened to him?"

"We did not know. We prayed that he was alive. Apaches often murdered Spanish and Anglo children, but since we never found his body, I hoped that he was still alive. It has also happened that the Indians raise the children of their enemies as their own. I prayed that my poor Juan was still alive. I thought of him always. And then eight years ago . . ." José stopped and took Eduardo by the shoulders, "If I tell you, you are never to speak of this."

"Never," promised Eduardo.

"Eight years ago my Juan came riding up to the house on an Indian pony." José chuckled and wiped his eyes. "He was with a group of ten of them—the Apaches. He told me that they were only riding through to the trade fair in Taos. He asked me to feed them. He said that they rode through every year. He told me that the old Apache who raised him had brought him to Los Torbellinos many times. They stood together at the edge of my fields, and the old man told him that he was taken from here when he was just a child. It was my Juan. He was a grown man, strong and handsome. I told him to come back to us, that we had missed him and prayed for him, but it was too late. He is one of them now. He doesn't understand our world, and he can hardly speak Spanish. He said they only wanted food from me. Nothing else."

José wiped his eyes with his handkerchief. "Of course, I fed them. There was a young girl with them and she had a baby. Juan's baby. Yes, jefe, that was eight years ago. He came back one time after that, maybe four years later, and by then he had two wives and four children. Four little Indios." José shook his head. "Your grandmother . . . it makes her crazy. The first time she begged Juan to come home to us. She can't understand that her son belongs with those . . . those Apaches. When Juan rode away, she was sick for weeks. The last time he came she refused to see him, and she will not talk about him. He is an Apache. His hair is long and wild like theirs; he dresses like them and speaks their language. He has two wives. Imagine that, jefe, two wives," José snickered. "But don't you say one word about your uncle Juan. Not one word to anyone," threatened José.

"No, Abuelo. Not one word," promised Eduardo as they walked on.

"Apaches," he said to himself. At his parents' home up the canyon, there were two Indian women who lived with the neighbors. They had dark skin and were small; they wore their hair in long braids that hung down below their waists. They were always barefoot or wearing moccasins. His mother hated these women and called them "las negras" and "las Indias." Once the neighbors had come to visit his mother, and one of the Indian women was with them. Elena would not allow her in the house. "And today, today are there still Indios out on the llano?" stammered Eduardo, looking at José with wide eyes.

José laughed. "Today, jefe, they only pass through the llano, but you don't have to worry. Today there are no more wild Indians. Who knows? Perhaps someday you'll get to meet your tío Juan, the Apache." They came to the end of the field. "Don't worry, jefe, there are no more wild Indios. Now go and collect the wool for your grandmother."

Eduardo hopped over the irrigation ditch looking out on the llano. All he saw were miles of sage and the black mountains beyond looming up on the western horizon. He looked back at his grandfather and decided to collect only the wool that clung to the bushes directly by the ditch.

That evening Eduardo sat on the porch with the rest of the family. Indoors, especially in the loft bedrooms, it was still too hot for sleeping. They relaxed in rickety chairs enjoying the fresh coolness of the night.

Eduardo stood beside Fidelia watching her card the wool that he had collected during the day. She sat by the light of a kerosene lamp but combed the tufts of wool so expertly that she could have done it in the dark. She gave Eduardo a handful of the fluffy carded wool. "You see, if you had not gathered this, it would have gone to waste. In the winter, I'll make something for you out of this wool. Maybe a pair of warm stockings, or if you bring me enough wool, or a vest. Would you like that?"

Eduardo thought of the wool vest that his father wore in winter. "Yes. I would like a vest," he said, squeezing the soft fibers.

"Very well. But remember," she said, taking the ball of wool out of his hand, "if you had not worked a little, there would be nothing. A little work, a little something. That's how it is in life, Eduardo."

José tilted his chair back on two legs and rocked gently, smoking his pipe. "José, you're going to fall," snapped Fidelia without looking up from her work. José sighed and brought his chair down on four legs. He refilled his pipe with the pungent Mexican tobacco that he bought from gypsy peddlers and in a few minutes he was rocking again.

The coyotes out on the llano began their howling. "Listen," said Rafelita. "Listen to them. They sound like babies crying . . . or laughing."

As the eerie wailing continued, the skin on the back of Eduardo's neck began to tingle. Rafelita closed her eyes and cocked her head to one side, concentrating. "Listen. It's more like crying and laughing at once," she said. The yapping stopped sharply. It was silent for a few minutes. Then it started again but came from another direction. "Now they are moving," she said, tilting her head toward the sound. The strange tickling started on Eduardo's spine again; he went to Carmen and leaned against her knees. She pulled him onto her lap.

José laughed at Eduardo. "Yes," he said, "they are out on the llano dancing under the stars tonight."

Later that night, snuggled into bed between Carmen and Rafelita, Eduardo fell asleep listening to the distant howling of the coyotes. In his dream a small boy like himself was being carried across the dark llano on the pony of a wild Apache.

FIVE

The tin roof and rafters creaked overhead from the heat of the midday sun, and though both windows were open, it was as hot as an oven in the loft bedroom. Wearing only a thin, cotton slip, Carmen knelt on a rug before Eduardo. He stood on a chair and turned slowly, very slowly, as his tía pinned up the hem of the dress that he wore. He stared down into her face. The tendrils of hair by her ears were damp with perspiration and beads of moisture formed a bridge across her nose and upper lip. The bodice of her slip was loosely laced; he could see the smooth, soft skin of her chest and the small mounds of her breasts.

"Eduardo, stand straight and hold your head up," she said, looking at him. He straightened up and stared at the wall in front of him. "Yes, like that. Now stretch your arms out in front of you." He did what she said. "Good. Now hold your arms over your head. Now out to the sides and turn around again." Carmen stood and stepped back from him. "Very good," she said, admiring her work as he turned on the chair.

"Tía," whined Eduardo pulling at the collar of the dress, "I'm hot."

"I know," she said, unbuttoning the back of the dress. She pulled it carefully over his head. "There. You may go now, but don't go too far away and don't get dirty. I'll need you to try this dress on one last time."

"Bueno, Tía," he said, sighing heavily the way his grandfather did. He hopped down from the chair and pulled on his trousers and shirt. "I'm going to the garden," he said, leaving the room. He found José hoeing weeds from the corn patch behind the house.

"Oye, mi jefe," grunted José, "bring a basket over here and collect these weeds for the pigs."

"Muy bien, Abuelo, but Aunt Carmen said I can't get dirty."

José began to laugh. "Oh. I see. She's sewing again and dressing you up like a little dolly? Is that it?"

"Yes, Grandfather," said Eduardo, frowning.

José shook his head and chuckled. "Then be careful not to get dirty." Eduardo began to collect the weeds into a pile. Carmen and Rafelita sewed clothing to sell sometimes to neighbors and sometimes to the owner of the store on the plaza. Whenever they had clothing for small children, they used Eduardo as a mannequin to make the proper fit. José was a few yards ahead with his back toward Eduardo. He began to laugh again.

"What? What is funny? What are you laughing at?" demanded Eduardo angrily.

"Aunt Carmen putting you in dresses like a little dolly."

"I hate it," snapped Eduardo.

José laughed again. "Don't be angry Eduardo. It's not so serious," José said.

Eduardo looked at the huge barrel-back of his grandfather, the stout shoulders, thick waist, bowlegs, and unbelievably thick mat of snow-white hair. Eduardo began to snicker. "Well, I'd like to see you in a dress then." They both laughed.

In a few minutes, Carmen began yelling for Eduardo. They looked up and saw her standing at the window of the loft bedroom. "Eduardo, come inside. I need you again."

"Here I come, Tía," he yelled scrambling to his feet.

"Buena suerte, mi jefe," said José as Eduardo raced indoors.

"Hurry up, mi'jito. Undress yourself," said Carmen excitedly. "Look. Isn't this a pretty dress. A pretty little dress for a pretty little girl." When Eduardo was undressed, she pulled the dress gently over his head and arms. She adjusted it on the shoulders and said, "Turn around." Eduardo turned and she buttoned it. She stepped away to admire. "Look at you. I can't believe it. You should have been a little girl," she said, pulling the dress perfectly into place.

Rafelita came to them and felt the ruffled collar and sleeves and the full skirt of the dress. "I told you this child is a little angel," she said, stroking his cheek and running her fingers through his hair, which they had not cut since he moved to El Valle. It hung to his shoulders.

"Rafelita," Carmen continued, "there is no little girl in Los Torbellinos who is prettier than Eduardo. I'm telling you, he looks just like a little girl."

"But I'm not a girl. I'm a boy," Eduardo interjected angrily.

"Don't get mad, Eduardo," said Carmen. She unbuttoned the dress and pulled it over his head. "Listen, would you like to come to the river to bathe with Rafelita and me?"

"Yes," he answered gruffly and stepped into his pants. The neighbors also bathed at the river; the women and children there made him think of Elena and Rosita and his brothers.

"But you have to promise that you will not cry," she said handing him his shirt. "You know how sad it makes me."

Eduardo shuffled his feet. "I'll try not to," he finally answered.

As they walked to the river, Rafelita was the first to alert them to faraway sounds. She told them there were other people at the river talking and splashing in the water. They walked on and soon Eduardo and Carmen also heard the voices. The young women greeted the neighbors as they walked into the clearing by the pool. Today there were only women and children at the river. Carmen and Rafelita undressed themselves and Eduardo. They sat on large stones in the river, soaped up, and waded into the deeper, colder water to rinse. Then Rafelita washed Eduardo's hair, and he dived under the cool water to rinse away the soap. Next Carmen and Rafelita washed their own hair and went to sit on the river bank on an old blanket, where they combed their hair and dried it in the sun. They talked with the neighbor women while Eduardo played in the pool with the other children.

On the walk back to the house, Carmen said, "Eduardo, Rafelita and I have been talking, and if you don't cry, we'll take you to see your family. Tomorrow is Sunday, and if you won't cry, we'll go to Mass tomorrow, and you can see them. But you have to promise not to cry."

"You have said that before," said Eduardo.

"Eduardo, you must not cry," said Rafelita. "You can wear the new suit that we made for you. And don't forget your new shoes."

"Tomorrow? You promise?"

"Yes, tomorrow, but it's only to visit," said Carmen.

The next morning Eduardo was the first to wake. Although he had lost track of the time, it had been months since he saw his family. He poked Carmen gently in the ribs. "Tía, wake up," he whispered. He poked her again. "Wake up. It's Sunday."

"Yes, Eduardo," she said sleepily.

Rafelita and Carmen washed him and dressed him. His white cotton shirt was ironed stiff and buttoned up high around his neck. His new jacket and trousers were of matching brown fabric, and on his feet were a new pair of shiny, black shoes. They were sharply pointed at the toe and laced up tightly around his ankles. "Tía," Eduardo said, looking down at his feet, "I'm going to show these new shoes to my mother today."

Carmen smiled and caressed his cheek. "You look like a real gentleman, Eduardo. Your mother will be pleased. Now go down and wait for us, and don't get dirty."

Eduardo walked onto the porch, watching his feet in the new shoes. It was going to be another hot, cloudless day. He sat down in a chair, dusting the tips of his shoes on the back of his calves. The women came out of the house with José, and they climbed onto the buckboard. All the way to the plaza Eduardo played with his hands and brushed them over his knees. When they arrived at the courtyard of the church, he began to search for his family. At last he saw them approaching from the far end of the church. He sprang to his feet pointing. "Look! Look! There they are."

Carmen and Rafelita laughed. "Yes, I see them, too, Eduardo," said Carmen, helping him down from the wagon. Eduardo stared at his family as they came closer. Carlos and Roberto were taller and thinner. And he expected to see Marcos in Elena's arms, or at least clinging to her skirts, but his little brother ran ahead of them all. Rosita and Elena walked side by side. Rosita's arm was looped through Elena's. His grandmother was thin and wrinkled. Fidelia and José were old, but their skin did not look like Rosita's. He also noticed that she walked slowly, leaning a bit on his mother's arm. Eduardo's feet felt rooted to the ground. José and Fidelia were already walking to greet his family. "Come on, Eduardo," said Carmen, pulling him by the hand.

"Eduardo, you have grown so much," said Elena. "Come here. Let us have a look at you."

Eduardo grinned but slipped behind Carmen. All of the adults began to laugh. He grasped tightly onto Carmen's skirts and peeked at them from behind her. Rosita stepped forward. "Come here, mi'jito," she said, putting her hand on his back. Now he stepped out from behind Carmen. "Look at you. You are not a little boy anymore. And you look so fine in your pretty new clothes," his grandmother said. Her face looked like an apricot that had been dried out by the sun. He looked away from her quickly and stared at his brothers. He recognized their same old Sunday clothes, but their clothes were the only familiar things about them. Rosita took Eduardo by the hand and they walked into the church.

Inside, it was dark and cool. Eduardo stared down the dark, tunnel-like aisle that led to the altar, where a warm glow of light flickered from the candles. As they walked closer to the altar, he smelled hot wax and incense. They sat down, and the pews around them began to fill with people. Finally Mass began; the priest looked small behind the pulpit, but his voice carried clearly through the church.

Eduardo's eyes poured over the high ceilings and walls where the fierce saints nested in their adobe niches. Their faces, set off by flowing robes of bright blue and green and red, were torn in terrible agony. On the altar behind the priest, there was a life-sized carving of Jesus Christ. His head was encircled with a crown of giant thorns, and streams of blood spilled from puncture wounds on his brow. Drops of blood fell over his eyes like tears. His head drooped limply toward his emaciated shoulder; every joint and bone seemed to show through the bluish skin. More blood rushed from wounds on his hands and feet, and a blood-smeared gash ran across his chest. But the figure's face was serene and peaceful, like the face of a sleeping baby's, not in anguish like the faces of the santos. Rosita sat beside Eduardo and nudged him when it was time to kneel or stand. All the time the wretched santos watched him.

Outside Eduardo squinted his eyes against the bright daylight. People were moving and smiling and chatting again. Eduardo took a deep breath and became conscious of Rosita's grasp on his hand. "Rosita, I am coming home with you." He pulled away from her and ran to his mother. "Mamá, I'm coming home today," he said, taking hold of her arm.

Elena sighed. "No, Eduardo. You will go home with your grandparents." He pulled on her arm and began to cry. Carmen picked him up and carried him to the buckboard. He watched his family over her shoulder; five blurred figures looking at him. "Eduardo, do not cry. You promised that you would not cry," said Carmen. His family was turning and walking away now. "Don't cry."

On the ride home Carmen gave Eduardo a peppermint stick that Rosita had given to her for him. Eduardo put the candy in his jacket pocket. When they got home, he stayed outside with José while his grandfather unharnessed the team. Eduardo took the candy out of his pocket and broke it in half. He handed one stick to José and began to suck on the other.

"Mi jefe," said José, shaking the peppermint stick at Eduardo, "this is your home now, and it will be your home until your parents decide to take you back to their house. There is nothing for you to do but accept it. If you cry every time you see your mamá, then we will not take you to see her. Do you understand?" Eduardo only sucked on his candy and looked at his shoes. José scratched his head. "I guess you don't understand," he sighed. "It doesn't matter." He stuck the peppermint in his mouth and started unbuckling the harness. "Hum," he took the peppermint from his mouth and examined it. "This is sweet, very sweet." Eduardo looked up at him and smiled.

That night Eduardo screamed in his sleep. When Carmen and Rafelita woke him, he told them that the santos were after him. "They are jumping out of the walls and laughing at me," he cried.

"You were only dreaming; it was a nightmare, Eduardo. Only a nightmare. Calm down and go back to sleep," Rafelita said drowsily. "We are here. Go to sleep."

But Eduardo could not sleep; he lay awake long after Carmen and Rafelita drifted off again. He only had to close his eyes to see the rich hues of the santos' robes blowing wildly about them as they flew off the wall. Their blue-white skin glowed, pulsed like light. The curving, scarlet lips gesticulated wickedly as the santos beckoned to him with their outstretched arms. One second serene and kind, the next cruel and hysterical, they had called his name, "Eduardo, Eduardo, Eduardo." Their eyes gleamed at him with unearthly intelligence. He did not sleep until he heard the first birds chirping outside the window.

Later that day while Eduardo tended to his chores, a man crept up behind him. Suddenly two strong hands latched onto his waist, spun him around, and swept him into the air. "No," yelled Eduardo, his arms and legs flailing before he recognized his father. Miguel laughed and swung Eduardo around and around. Before he set his son down, he held him close and kissed his head. "Eduardo, I see that you are learning to be a brave fighter. Are you learning these nasty habits from the witches?" he teased.

"Papá, Papá," was all that Eduardo could say.

"I've come to take you home with me for the day. But just for the day. Is that a good plan?"

"Yes, Papá. Yes," said Eduardo, nodding. "Let's go tell my grandfather."

Soon the two of them were riding up the canyon. Miguel held Eduardo in front of him on the saddle. Eduardo's mouth ached from smiling. Passing through the plaza, Miguel stopped at the mercantile store. "I have some business here. We need to go in the store." He got off the horse and helped Eduardo down from the saddle. Miguel went to the door but Eduardo lagged behind. He opened the door, "Are you coming in or are you planning to stand out here like a lost lamb?" Miguel said, holding the door open. His mother always made Eduardo and his brothers wait outside when they went to the store. His eyes widened and he rushed through the doorway. "Yes. Of course I'm coming in."

Eduardo followed his father to the back of the store. He wanted to touch everything. He stopped at the bins of grain and inhaled their sweetness. Walking past a shelf that was lined with hats and shoes and boots, he saw a pair of shoes exactly like the ones that Carmen and Rafelita had bought for him. There was another shelf lined with tin buckets and pots and pans.

Mr. Lawrence, the store owner, and Miguel were talking. Eduardo looked up on the wall behind them where three Winchester rifles hung on a gun rack. Below the guns was a glass case that held penknives and hunting knives and watches. He gasped at the sight of so much shiny metal. Then his eyes flashed over a toy pistol. "Look at this little pistol!" he shrieked.

Miguel looked down angrily. "Quiet! Where are you manners?" Eduardo ducked his head ashamed, but Mr. Lawrence smiled and took the gun from the glass case. He loaded some caps into it and pulled the trigger. The caps popped loudly and made Eduardo flinch. He could not take his eyes off of the gun. Mr. Lawrence pointed it at him and fired again. Bang, bang, bang. Eduardo flinched each time the cap popped. The men laughed. "Here, you can hold it if you like," said Mr. Lawrence, handing Eduardo the gun. Then he and Miguel continued talking. Eduardo examined the toy. He aimed it and pulled the trigger. The gun made a clicking noise; the caps were all used up.

Miguel took a large roll of money from his pocket and counted out almost every bill to Mr. Lawrence. The two of them shook hands. "Eduardo, give the toy back to Mr. Lawrence. We're leaving now." Eduardo handed the gun up to Mr. Lawrence. The shopkeeper took a long stick of candy from a glass canister and gave it to Eduardo. "Here's a little something for you, Eduardo," he said. Eduardo took the candy and thanked Mr. Lawrence.

Miguel did not talk on the ride up the canyon, so Eduardo thought about the toy gun and how it had sounded and felt in his hand. At the house nothing looked the same as it had in the spring when Eduardo was last there. Some of the leaves were just beginning to turn brown. Under the portal, firewood was stacked high along the wall; bright ristras of chile were already hanging by the kitchen door, and the colorful chains of dried fruit and vegetables were strung on the rafters. Miguel took Eduardo off the horse and his brothers came running up from the river. In seconds all four of the boys were heading back toward the creek and animal sheds; it suddenly seemed as if he had never left. He broke the peppermint stick in to fourths, and they sat on the corral sucking contentedly. Soon Miguel called them into the blacksmith shop and made a fire in the forge. All of them watched as their father sharpened and repaired tools. Carlos and Roberto took turns pumping the bellows while Miguel worked. After he finished with the tools, he measured all of their feet. They needed a good pair of warm moccasins because winter was coming. Their father made the shoes out of goat skin, and each of them chose if he wanted the hair on the inside or the outside. Carlos's shoes were finished first, but by that evening all of them had a pair of goat-hide moccasins. Eduardo asked to have the hair on the outside of his shoes so he could see it when he walked. The shoes were black and white and looked like little animals. They made queer treads in the dirt when he walked. Eduardo bent over and smoothed the hair until it lay in one direction. When he showed his moccasins to Elena and Rosita, they laughed and told him to pull up his trousers so they could see better. Rosita said they looked like little cats, the prettiest little cats she had ever seen.

That night they had roast mutton with gravy, potatoes, and carrots and fresh bread. Miguel told them about the sheep camp in Colorado and about all of the men he worked with. He told them of the big game he had seen and how one of the sheep dogs was torn apart by a bear. He said that the Colorado mountains were wild and beautiful like the mountains high up the canyon from Los Torbellinos. After dinner, they all went out on the portal just like they used to.

It was near midnight when they went to bed. Eduardo slept with Carlos, Roberto, and now Marcos. The double bed was crowded and the sheets scratchy, but Eduardo didn't care. He was excited and happy as the boys settled into bed giggling. They talked some, but soon his brothers were sleeping. Eduardo tried to stay awake as long as he could; he knew that he had to return to El Valle in the morning. But finally his eyelids closed and it was too much of a struggle to open them again.

SIX

Rosita Montez died in her sleep in the late hours of a wintery night soon after Eduardo's fifth birthday. At dawn Carlos delivered the sad news of her death to El Valle. Then he rode on, spreading the news to other families who lived farther down the valley.

José and Eduardo fed the animals and harnessed the team while the women prepared food and collected personal belongings to take to the Montez house. They would stay with Elena until Rosita was buried. By 7:30 A.M., the Baca family was in the wagon traveling up the canyon. Elena came out onto the porch to greet them; her face was pale but otherwise void of emotion. The neighbors were already at the house; they had arrived early that morning.

Eduardo stood by the wagon as the others rushed to Elena. They embraced her and his brothers. All of them were crying. Eduardo began to cry as well. One of the neighbor women stepped off the porch and took him up in her arms. She carried him into the house, crying and kissing his head while she repeated, "Pobrecito, pobrecito."

Rosita's body still lay on her bed in the sala. José and the other men went into the blacksmith shop and returned with two saw-horses. They placed these in the center of the room and lay boards across them to form a platform. After covering the boards with a sheet, José and two other men lifted Rosita's body and laid her on the platform. Then they led the children from the room so Elena, her mother, and sister could prepare the body for burial.

Miguel might not arrive for days. Elena had arranged to wire the news to him, but the telegram office was fifteen miles away

45

in another village. The rider would deliver the message by noon, and it would be sent to Antonito, Colorado, where another rider would have to go to the sheep camp to find Miguel. If he received the message in time, he could take the morning train to a village thirty miles northeast of Los Torbellinos. After that he would have to ride for a day to get home. But there was only one train a day. If he did not receive the message in time, he would have to wait until the following morning to take the next train. Nobody knew when he would arrive in Los Torbellinos, so they would have to keep Rosita's body frozen. The doors and windows of the sala were opened, and the embers in the corner fireplace doused.

The men began to chop wood and tend to the outdoor chores. They kept Eduardo and his brothers busy hauling wood and buckets of water to the kitchen. Elena and her mother and sister washed and clothed Rosita's body. Then they bathed themselves and put on their black mourning dresses with black veils and stockings. By noon they were prepared for the arrival of mourners. José drove his wagon to the plaza to fetch the priest. The alabados would be held for Rosita at the house every night until her burial.

Eduardo and his brothers did not go into the sala. They sat on the porch, and when they became too cold, went into the kitchen or the blacksmith shop where the men had built a fire. The dreadful waiting had begun. All day family members and neighbors came and went. Except to offer condolences, the guests said little. They sometimes embraced Eduardo and his brothers, and all of the women cried. If they were not crying when they went into the sala, they were in tears when they came out.

Neighbor women took over Elena's kitchen. They kept pots of hot coffee on the stove, and set out the food that arrived with each family. No cooking would have to be done during the time of mourning. Each family brought pies and cakes and plates of biscochitos and baskets of freshly baked rolls or stacks of tortillas. They brought pots of beans and posole and red chile. The guests shared in the bounty, but each family brought more food than they could eat.

By nightfall the villagers were still arriving and leaving. They went into the sala and kissed Rosita's cheek or placed their hand over hers and prayed. They gathered in the kitchen. No one smiled and most of the talk was speculation about when Miguel would arrive. The Montez family was never alone, and neither was Rosita's body. Relatives and neighbors would sit by her night and day to pray for her.

José kept the fire burning in the blacksmith shop where Eduardo and his brothers stayed with other children whose parents had come to mourn. Sleeping pallets were laid on the floor and Carmen and Rafelita kept them supplied with hot chocolate and sweets. Carlos and Roberto sat on their pallets, crying softly. Helpless to relieve their sadness, José sat near them hoping that at least his presence was a comfort. Eduardo stood beside his grandfather while the neighbor children stared at them expressionless between bites of their cookies.

Later, the sounds of grief sliced the cold night. The children peered through the flickering light at one another as the cries came from the house. Over and over they heard women crying, "Ay, Rosita, por que te fuites?" "Que haremos sin ti?" Carlos lay on his pallet covering his ears with his hands. Eventually Eduardo crawled on the pallet beside him and lay down close. Carlos put his arm over his younger brother, but each time a loud cry broke out, Carlos covered his ears and began to sob. "I wish they would stop. Why won't they stop?"

Late that night they finally fell asleep.

The next morning at dawn Eduardo woke as Carlos was squirming out from under the blankets. Eduardo stretched and felt the stiffness in his muscles from sleeping on the floor; he nestled back under the covers and looked around. There were three men sitting on the floor with their backs against the wall. They appeared to be dozing, and one of them was snoring loudly. José was gone and the other children were still sleeping. Carlos stood up. "Eduardo, I'm going to the house. Go back to sleep. I'll be back soon," he said tucking Eduardo in. Eduardo closed his eyes and went back to sleep.

A few hours later Carlos came back to the shop and woke his brothers. His face was scrubbed clean and he was wearing his Sunday clothes. "Get up," he said shaking them. "Wake up. You have to go to the house to wash and dress. Mamá told me to bring you to the house." They crawled out from under the blankets and went outside with Carlos. The sun was high, but it was freezing. Once in the house, Carmen and Rafelita ushered them into their bedroom. Carlos sat on the bed with his face in his hands while Carmen and Rafelita helped wash and dress the younger boys. "We are going to see your grandmother," said Carmen leading them from the bedroom. Carlos began to sob and Rafelita took his hand.

They passed through the kitchen, where people were gathered around the stove and sitting at the table. All of the women's eyes were ugly and swollen from crying. Some of them started sobbing anew as Carmen and Rafelita led the Montez boys through the room. "Poor darlings. Poor little darlings," one of them said.

It was cold in the sala. Chairs were lined against the walls where the mourners sat praying their rosaries. Elena was among them. When her sons entered the room, she turned her veil back from her brow. The black dress made her face and hands look especially white, and there were dark shadows under her swollen eyes. Elena took Carlos by the hand. "Mis hijos," she said, her voice hoarse from lack of sleep and crying. "It is time for you to say your farewells to your grandmother, and then we'll pray for her together. Come."

Rosita's body lay at the opposite end of the room. A small table was at the head of the platform, and on it were candles, a statue of the Virgin Mary, a crucifix, and Rosita's Bible. Elena and Carmen guided the boys toward the makeshift altar. Elena touched Rosita's cheek, then placed her hands over her mother-in-law's and whispered something inaudible to the rest of them. She moved aside and nodded to Carlos, who did the same and began to sob. Next Roberto stood beside Rosita with his hand covering hers. Carmen put her hands on Eduardo's waist and lifted him off the floor. From the floor, he had only been able too see the length of Rosita's body dressed in a dark dress and black stockings. His body stiffened when he saw his grandmother's face, for two dark coins covered her eyes like two gaping holes. Her mouth was stuffed with cotton, and her lips were blue and drawn back from her teeth. The skin on her face seemed deeply sunken at the temples and powder had settled into the wrinkles on her brow and upper lip. Her hair was pulled tightly, almost unnaturally, away from her face and her hands rested on her chest, her rosary entwined in her fingers.

Eduardo stared at Rosita's face. Then he noticed that her ears were also full of loose powder. His breath caught hard in his chest. He thought of long ago when she used to tell him the story of his birth. She had been so lively, graceful, and even beautiful. "Eduardo, touch your grandmother's hand. Don't be afraid," Carmen whispered in his ear. He was suspended over her body, his heart beating wildly in his chest. Numbly he reached out and placed his hand over hers. They were as dry and hard as the branches of an old tree and ice cold. He shuddered and Carmen set him on the ground. He rubbed his hand hard against his trousers trying to wipe away the age and the deadness. Elena, Carlos, and Roberto were already kneeling on the floor. Carmen pushed his shoulders gently and he knelt beside them. Carmen lifted Marcos up next, but when he saw his grandmother, he began to scream so loudly that one of the other women took him out of the sala. Then Carmen knelt beside Eduardo. All of the boys were sobbing. Carmen gestured toward the statue of the Virgin Mary, "My darlings, the Virgin Mary is now taking care of your grandmother," she whispered warmly. Eduardo glanced up at the pretty figure and felt suddenly reassured. Next Carmen and Elena prayed a rosary together. Finally, Eduardo and his brothers were excused from the room.

Carmen took them into the kitchen so they could warm themselves and have breakfast. They gathered around the stove. The guests were drinking coffee and eating slices of cake and toast with butter and jam. Carlos looked around the room and bolted out the kitchen door. Roberto and Eduardo followed him. Carmen moved to go after them, but Fidelia told her to let them be.

The boys followed Carlos across the footbridge. "How can they eat with my grandmother in the next room? How can they eat?" said Carlos, climbing onto the corral.

It was noontime but just as cold as it had been earlier that morning. The sky was flat gray and the air was so cold that it stung their cheeks and hands. The last snowfall had started to melt, leaving large patches of earth exposed. The trees were gray and barren and blended into the bleakness of the sky. "I hate the winter," said Carlos, and he began to cry again.

Roberto jumped off the corral; he pried a large stone loose from the frozen earth and hurled it at the creek. The stone landed and slid a few feet on the ice. "That, in there, in the sala, that is not what my grandmother looked like. That is not my grandmother," he said, tears welling.

"No. Don't remember her like that. It is too terrible," whispered Carlos.

The following day was just as cold and dreary. Time dragged on, and the agony of waiting for Miguel and finally laying Rosita to rest was nearly unbearable. The neighbors came and went, making sure the Montez family was never alone. There was always someone in the sala to pray for Rosita and the family and light fresh candles on the altar. And the women kept the house tidy while the men tended to all of the outside chores.

By the third day, Eduardo had lost track of time. The adults stayed up all night and slept a bit during the day, if at all. He ate with his brothers whenever they were hungry, and without regular meal times and daily routines, he didn't know if it was morning or afternoon. Sometimes he went in the sala with Carlos and Roberto to sit in the chairs along the wall. His brothers prayed or sang with the others, but Eduardo did not know the words yet. While the prayers and beautiful songs brought him comfort, he only wanted the miserable sadness to end.

On the fourth morning, it had begun to snow. "Thank God," José said. "It will cover up this miserable gray landscape." At dusk all the land and houses and trees were covered in a beautiful coat of white, and the snow was still falling. Miguel walked into the kitchen like any of the others who came to mourn. The collar of his long trench coat was turned up high around his face and his felt hat was pulled down low. His clothes were soaked. He had ridden all day. "I came as soon as I received the message," he said with a slur, his mouth and jaws stiff from the cold. "I could have been here earlier, but the storm. I could have been here sooner but . . ."

Elena went to him and took the hat from his hands. "Miguel, sit down and drink something hot. You have to get out of these wet clothes and warm yourself," she said, trying to push him into a chair.

"No. Where is she?" he said, brushing past Elena. He went into the sala and collapsed onto his knees at his mother's side. "Mamá, Mamá, Mamá," he cried like a little boy. "Ay, Madrecita, Madrecita!"

In time, Miguel left the sala. He sat in a chair by the stove and asked for whiskey. He drank two tumblers and then got up and left the house. It was dark in the blacksmith shop except for the dim light that came from the chinks in the stove. Eduardo and the others were still awake. When Miguel opened the door, they recognized his silhouette at once. He held a kerosene lamp in his hand, and for the first time they realized how much he resembled their grandmother. They rushed to him and he knelt and took them into his arms. "My sons, what will we do without her," he wept.

That night all the villagers came to mourn with the family for one last time. The clearing in front of the house was crowded with horses, buckboards, and buggies. Prayers were read and calming laments were sung late into the night. Comforted by the hopeful lyrics of the ancient songs, the heaviness in all of their hearts began to subside.

Early the next morning, five days after her death, Rosita's body was put into a coffin and taken to the church. The snow had stopped in the night and the sun was out, burning off the white blanket that covered the countryside. After the midmorning Mass everyone walked behind the wagon that carried Rosita's body to the cemetery. She was to be buried beside her husband, Antonio, who had been thrown from a horse and killed in 1918, the year Miguel was fighting a war in the Argonne Forest in France. The ground was softening and turning to mud and slush under the mourners' feet.

At the grave site, the priest offered another prayer for Rosita before her casket was lowered into the ground with ropes. Miguel took a handful of moist earth and dropped it into the grave. Elena did the same, and Carlos and Roberto followed her. Carmen pushed Eduardo forward; he took a handful of cold earth and threw it into the grave the way his brothers had. Then the villagers formed a line in front of the mourning family. People passed before him embracing him and patting his head.

Eduardo rode home to El Valle in the buckboard with his grandparents, aunt, and Rafelita. He sat on Carmen's lap and watched his family head toward their own home up the canyon. For the first time he was happy not to be going with them. The sadness and emptiness was still at his parents' house. The loneliness was everywhere. All around them people on foot were bogging up to their ankles in mud. The horses were slipping and tugging hard to pull their rigs; steam rose off of their backs and chests. "It's always so ugly and sad when the sun comes out and makes mud of the beautiful white snow," said Carmen. "I think I would prefer to have the snow forever than to have this dreary mess to look at." Eduardo looked around. Huge clumps of snow were falling from the trees and melting to slush on the ground. The road had become a solid strip of mud as far as he could see. The sun reflecting off the snow-covered fields hurt his eyes and he had to strain to keep them open. Eduardo ached for sleep, longing for the soft, sweet warmth of their bed in the loft. He turned to his aunt. "Tía, when we get home, can we go to bed until this day is over?"

Carmen smiled down into his face. Her lips were soft and pink, her skin smooth and fresh. She brushed the hair out of his face with a cool touch that reminded him of feathers. "Eduardo, that is the best idea I have heard in days. You look very tired, and I feel as though I could sleep until summer."

SEVEN

Late in January 1932, Diego Baca returned to Los Torbellinos from the racetracks in Kentucky. Diego was Elena and Carmen's younger brother and the last child born in the Baca family. He was five feet tall and weighed a constant one hundred twenty pounds, but he was firm and strong. People speculated that José and Fidelia's waning vitality accounted for his size, however, like many small men, what Diego lacked in height he compensated for in character. He had inherited his father's generous, dimpled smile and pretty white teeth. And above all, Diego Baca had a tender passion for women and horses.

By the time he was seven or eight years old, Diego was on the back of a horse at least two hours daily. Any horse would do, even a plow horse borrowed from the neighbors' fields. Fidelia had beaten him for wasting his time with "the stupid beasts," but he remained undaunted. A blistered rear never stopped him from his daily rides on the llano.

Diego returned to Los Torbellinos riding a fine thoroughbred stallion. The horse was a dark bay, sleek and fast. Without question, it was the most beautiful and valuable animal ever seen in Los Torbellinos. Diego said that he had won the bay in a poker game, which was, even though no one believed him, the truth. He and the stallion rode the train from Kentucky to Santa Fe and then eventually made their way north to Los Torbellinos.

Diego had gone to Kentucky a year earlier on a whim because he had read that the best racehorses in the world ran there. He found a job at the tracks as a stable boy and ultimately persuaded a trainer to allow him to ride one of the magnificent animals. Diego's talent impressed the trainer; there was not a horse in the line that did not respond well to Diego. Even the most high-strung horses straightened out for Diego. Soon he was appointed chief exercise boy for the trainer's line. It was not long thereafter that Diego became recognized as the jockey wearing the blue and green silk atop the saddle loaded with regulation weights.

When the race season was over, Diego stayed on as an exercise boy just so he could ride horses. But he left Kentucky after he won the stallion because he supposed its owner would be vindictive and make life difficult for him, or even worse, try to take the horse back. The horse was more dear to Diego than a career as a jockey. Besides, he wanted his friends and family in Los Torbellinos to see the prize stallion. He paid the fare to transport his horse to New Mexico the same night he won the poker game. The thoroughbred had a long, registered name, but Diego simply dubbed him Hero.

Eduardo and Diego liked each other immediately. Diego took Eduardo for long rides on Hero, and the little boy rode for hours without tiring; he was fascinated by the power of the horse beneath him and could see everything from the bay's high back. It was always too soon for Eduardo when his tío headed the horse toward home.

Diego had not been back for more than a week when he decided he should return to school. No one could remember the date of Diego's birthday, plus when Diego was a child, José had waited until his son was as large as the first-year school children before sending him off to school. Of course, Diego was older than the other students, but no one was certain by how many years. When he left for Kentucky, he had completed his freshman year in high school, so he returned to the Los Torbellinos High School as a sophomore.

Eduardo was awake the first morning that Diego prepared to return to school. He looked out the window of the loft to see his uncle saddling the stallion in the cold hours before sunrise. He ran down the stairwell and out into the freezing air wearing only his night shirt. "Take me with you. Take me with you. Please, Uncle." Diego carried Eduardo back into the house. With a stern nod, José decided that it was time for Eduardo to be enrolled in school. After all, he had turned six in December.

When Eduardo was dressed, Fidelia gave Diego two big tortillas with fried potatoes and chorizo rolled up inside for their lunch. Then Diego hauled Eduardo up into the saddle in front of him and the two rode off to enroll in school. When they arrived, Diego told Eduardo, "This is where you will come to school every day. It is not such a big thing to go to school. Once you learn English, it's nothing at all. The best part about it is the girls. There are lots of pretty girls here to look at. You'll see, and you'll like it here," Diego smiled. Eduardo smiled back and the two went into the office.

There was a plump, bald man sitting behind a big desk in the office. Diego spoke to him in English and the man took some papers from a desk drawer and handed them to Diego. Diego directed Eduardo to a chair, and he examined the sterile room while his uncle filled out the paperwork.

Soon they were outside again, walking toward a classroom near the office building. Diego sat on the steps outside the classroom door and pulled Eduardo down beside him. "This room is where you'll spend the day. At lunch time I'll find you, and we can eat together."

"No. I think I'm going to stay with you, Tío," Eduardo said, standing up.

Diego took him firmly by the shoulders. "You will go into this classroom and sit quietly through the lessons, or I'll never let you ride with me again. Your mother and Aunt Carmen only went to the third grade because when they were children my father thought women did not need school. Now they can hardly read and write. And they can't speak any English."

"But they can read. They read the Bible. My tía reads the Bible to me every week," Eduardo said defensively.

Diego sighed. "Yes. They read the Bible, but I don't think they really read it. They have memorized it. Anyway, it's like this: There's a big world outside of Los Torbellinos, New Mexico, conejo. And in that world, you have to read and write and speak English. And no one cares if you can read the Bible or not. You have to read other things like books and newspapers and magazines. Do you understand?" Eduardo stared blankly at his uncle. Diego continued more calmly. "I'll be in that building over there," he said, pointing to the high school classroom, "and I'll come for you at lunch." He tugged Eduardo's ears playfully. "But like I told you, you have to go to school. You're not a baby anymore. Do you understand?"

"Yes," Eduardo said crossly, pulling away from his uncle and rubbing his ears.

"For the first week you must watch the other children. And you must not speak. You're here to learn English, and the teacher will punish you if you speak in Spanish. You'll go inside and sit at a desk and watch the other children. It's easy. You sit there and pay attention. That's all. You'll see." Diego stood up and knocked loudly on the door. A heavy, frowning woman opened the door and glared down at them. Diego smiled at her. Her frown began to disappear. "Good morning. How are you, Ma'am?" said Diego cheerily. The woman nodded her head and almost smiled. "I enrolled this boy, my nephew, in school today. The principal told me to bring him here. He just turned six years old, and he speaks no English." The woman grunted and stood aside as Diego pushed Eduardo through the door. "Have a good day, Ma'am," said Diego still smiling. Then the door closed and Diego was gone.

The woman placed an unfriendly hand at the back of Eduardo's neck and guided him to the front of the room. The class was silent. All of the boys and girls watched Eduardo and the teacher as they walked down the aisle between the desks. The teacher shoved Eduardo into a desk beside another boy and stepped back. In Spanish she began, "I am Mrs. Sánchez and I am the teacher in this room. You will do as I say, or you will be sent to kneel in the corner. I will speak to you in Spanish at first, but you will speak no Spanish in this room. We speak English here. Now, what is your name?"

"Eduardo Ricardo Montez," Eduardo mumbled.

The teacher wrote his name in her book shaking her head, "You must learn to speak more clearly. You sound as though your mouth is full of pebbles." Finally she turned away from him and went to the chalkboard. She took up a pointer and aimed it at the large, white letters on the board. For the rest of the morning, the class recited the alphabet. Eduardo sat still and watched every move the teacher made. His stomach churned and his hands were shaking. After the first half hour, he began to memorize the chant A, B, C, D . . . , but then Mrs. Sánchez began to point to different letters and call on individual children to recite. He was lost again.

Eduardo was aching from a full bladder when the noon bell rang. He watched all of the children rise out of their desks and walk quietly to the back of the room. Once outside they ran off screaming. Mrs. Sánchez scowled at him so he rose and followed them out the door. In no time Diego was at his side.

"So how was your first morning of lessons?"

"I have to pee," Eduardo said, "and I hate it in there."

Diego led him to the outhouse. "From now on when you need to pee, raise your hand holding up one finger, and if you'll need more time, hold up two fingers. Then the teacher will permit you to leave the classroom to go to the outhouse. And conejo, I'm sorry that you hate it in there. But soon you'll start to like it. After all, it's much easier than working on the farm at home. You'll see; it's not so bad."

Eduardo and Diego ate their burritos and too soon the bell rang. Diego took him back to the classroom and left. For the remainder of the afternoon, the class recited numbers in the same fashion they had done the alphabet. Eduardo was no longer so afraid; the time passed quickly. When the bell rang again, he followed the other children outside and was relieved to find Diego riding over to pick him up.

That night he did not sleep peacefully, nor did he welcome daylight when Carmen woke him. For the first few weeks Eduardo had butterflies flitting in his stomach when he rose and dressed for school. He had seen what happened to children who could not recite the alphabet and numbers, or to those who talked in class. Mrs. Sánchez dragged them to the corner of the room by their ear and left them kneeling on the hard floor for hours until they began to cry. Then she told them to go back to their seats and called them stupid idiots and shameful children. With Diego's help, Eduardo practiced his lessons at home so that he would not be punished. Soon Eduardo learned that his classmates considered him privileged because he rode to school on a fine horse with his uncle. And each day at lunch time they watched enviously as Diego came and ushered his nephew into a crowd of grown-up boys. Sometimes Diego played a guitar and sang during the noon hour; all of the big girls would crowd around and smile and tease Eduardo. They asked Diego if Eduardo was his son, and Diego said, "No. He is not my son, but I would be happy to claim him if he were." Eduardo began to like school, and Diego had been right. It was easier than feeding animals and working in the fields and gardens.

At home Diego spoke English to Eduardo to show the family how quickly Eduardo was learning. Eduardo responded to his uncle in Spanish in the beginning, but after three months he began to use English. Diego was delighted because only José was able to understand some of what they said.

"Edward, what is the name of that cow-faced woman who is your teacher?"

"Her name is Mrs. Sánchez," answered Eduardo, smiling and rolling out all of the vowels.

"And what are you learning in school?"

"To speak on English and say the alphabet on English," he answered proudly.

In the evening, Eduardo practiced writing the ABCs and new vocabulary in his notebook while his tío did his own homework. They worked by the light of a kerosene lamp in Diego's tiny room, which was adjacent to the room Eduardo shared with Carmen and Rafelita. Diego checked Eduardo's work, and if the writing was messy, he made him rewrite it. In no time, Eduardo was being called to the board to write for the class.

"This boy has been here less time than any of you," Mrs. Sánchez scolded as she pointed at Eduardo's work on the board, "and see, he already writes better than any of you lazy fools."

However, Eduardo soon learned to use his newly acquired language with discretion because Fidelia was bitter about her inability to understand English. One afternoon he and Diego rode in from school to find Fidelia waiting for them outside. "Diego," she said, "I want you to ride to the plaza for me. I need some things from the store, and this time, you'll leave that shadow of yours at home. These days he has time for nothing except to ride on that horse with you and to be a school boy. I have work for him this evening."

"Please, Grandmother," Eduardo begged, "let me go with my tío. I can do the work when we return."

"Shut up and get off that horse." She stood with her hands on her hips muttering, "Muchacho malcriado."

Diego lowered Eduardo to the ground. "Don't worry, conejo, we will have many rides together."

"You're spoiling that boy. You treat him like a baby, and you're teaching him to be a fool for horses like yourself. Listen, we need sugar and coffee and candles, and if Eduardo needs a notebook and pencils, bring him some of those. Hurry home because I'm not saving dinner for you. Go."

Diego pulled Hero around hard and sped off toward the plaza. Before he was out of hearing range, he yelled, "Goodbye, goodbye, you mean, old woman. Don't work my school boy too hard." Eduardo began to laugh but stopped when he felt his grandmother's eyes boring into him. "What did he say? Heh . . . tell me what he said."

"I didn't hear, Grandmother," Eduardo said. "What shall I do?"

"Forget the chores for now, you liar!" She yelled, stepping closer to Eduardo. "This is not the first time you've lied. There is noth-ing worse than a liar, and you know that lying is a sin. You know what your tío said, but you lie and say you did not hear. Don't you ever lie to me again. Do you understand?"

"I understand, I understand, Abuela," Eduardo said.

"Bueno. First I want you to fill the wood box in the kitchen, and then I need you to help me feed and milk the goats. Now go to your work. Hurry. Go on."

Eduardo sulked off to the wood pile. First he collected a bas-ket full of kindling, and as he worked he thought of what Diego had shouted. He began to smile and then laugh. "You mean, old woman. You mean, old woman," he said aloud. "Mean, old woman!" Súddenly he felt a tingle down his spine. He turned slowly and not twenty feet behind him stood his grandmother with her arms folded over her breasts. She scowled. Eduardo's heart raced, and he felt his face growing hot and red. Fidelia's frown turned to a sneer; she only glared at him. He looked at her for a moment and then turned back to his work.

After hauling stove wood to the kitchen, he went to the pasture and drove the goats into their shed, where Fidelia was waiting with her milk pail. As usual, Eduardo went to the well for water to wash the goats' teats. After he had finished washing the first goat, Fidelia began to milk it. "You lazy boy. Look. Look in the pail. There is hair and dirt in the milk. Wash her again, and be more careful with the others, or you will get no supper tonight." Eduardo went back and knelt by his grandmother to rewash the goat. When he finished, Fidelia slapped him hard on the head. "Now don't forget what I said, lazy boy." Eduardo washed the other goats more carefully, and when Fidelia finished milking, they went in the house together.

Eduardo sat at the kitchen table to watch as Fidelia strained the milk through a cheesecloth into a large ceramic jar. His head was still stinging from the hard slap Fidelia had given him. The jar was sitting close to the edge of the table; when Fidelia turned away, Eduardo hesitated one second before his hand shot out and pushed the heavy jar off the table. It crashed to the floor splattering milk and clay shards all over the kitchen. Eduardo had barely enough time to appreciate the twin sensations of revenge and regret during the moment it took Fidelia to spin around and grab a stout piece of wood from the wood box.

His grandmother was on him in an instant. In one hand she held the empty milk pail, in the other the stick of wood. First, she hurled the bucket at him, hitting him in the head and knocking him off the chair. Then he felt the stick on his back and shoulders. Eduardo yelled with each blow. He heard himself begging, "Stop, stop, stop, help, help!" as he rolled under the table. But Fidelia was on her hands and knees with her piece of wood. Her face was red, raging, as she bellowed, "I'll get you. I'll teach you a good lesson that you'll never forget. You rotten child good for nothing but trouble." By that time, Eduardo was on the other side of the table scurrying to his feet and fleeing out the door. Fidelia let the stick of wood fly and hit him heavily between the shoulder blades. He nearly fell. Fidelia raged on, "Get out of here. I hope you go out into the night and the witches take you. You're not worth all the trouble you cause. Now I know why your mother does not want you."

Eduardo ran from the house to the river and onward in the direction of his parents' house up the canyon. He ran the first mile as fast as he could. Driven by fear and pain he ran blindly with Fidelia's words resounding in his ears, "Now I know why your mother does not want you. Now I know. Your mother does not want you." When he slowed, he felt his neck and back beginning to throb where he had been hit. His head had a large lump from the milk pail; when he pulled up his shirt to inspect himself, he saw dark ugly bruises already forming on his arms and shoulders. Eduardo began to cry, first softly and then harder. Unable to see for the tears in his eyes, he tripped over a rock and fell on the ground.

Darkness fell but Eduardo did not move. He thought of his real home. He thought about how the day had begun like any other day. Then things started going wrong. Little things, until finally, the beating. The ugly images flashed through his mind. "If Grandmother Rosita were still alive, I would go to her and tell her, and she would not send me back to El Valle," Eduardo blubbered aloud.

Hours later he heard the clacking of a horse's hooves against the stones of the riverbed. He recognized Diego's voice. "Conejo, conejo, where are you? It is late for little rabbits to be about. Where are you, conejo?" His voice was singsong drunk. "I am here, Tío," Eduardo shouted. In an instant the sleek legs of Hero were only feet away from Eduardo and Diego was by his side. At first Eduardo could only cry. Finally, between long sobs he said, "She beat me with a piece of stove wood."

Diego put his arm around Eduardo's shoulder. Eduardo could smell sweet wine on his uncle's breath and his clothes smelled of salt and alfalfa, like Hero. "Yes, Carmen told me what happened with the milk." Then he laughed. "But I see it as no great loss, conejo. I mean, what is a gallon of stinking goat milk after all? Now if it had been a few gallons of wine, that might have been cause for a beating." He held Eduardo close to his small body and laughed.

"Tío, feel here," Eduardo said putting his uncle's hand to the knot on his head.

Diego whistled, "That's bigger than a goose egg!"

"All over my body I have bruises."

Diego lit a match and pulled up Eduardo's shirt. He sighed and shook his head. He remembered one of the phrases that he had learned at the tracks in Kentucky, "Conejo, you look like a spotted-assed-ape." Diego laughed and Eduardo began to laugh, too. "You know, Eduardo, why do you think I am so small? That old lady hit me on the head so many times I quit growing. I tell you she beat the hell out of me until I was big enough to get on a horse and get the hell away from her. Probably she thinks that children can't grow up without beatings," he sighed. "But she's sorry; she's sorry for what she did to you." Diego lit a cigarette, and was silent for a minute. He stared blankly into the darkness. "Yes, she's sorry. She's crying in her room, and she even saved you a plate of food in the oven. I saw it. She saved you a big, fat chicken leg. It's as big as your arm," he said holding out Eduardo's arm. "Come on, conejo. It's time to go home now. I love you; we all love you. Your tía and Rafelita are worried. Let's go home."

Diego rose and went to the saddle for his jug. He took a big drink and said, "Here, conejo, take a little of this. It will calm you and help you sleep tonight." He held the jug for Eduardo who took a mouthful of the wine and swallowed. Diego tied the jug back onto the saddle after taking another drink; then he mounted and hoisted Eduardo onto the saddle with him. It was late spring and the night was warmer than it had been for months. Eduardo felt cleansed from crying, and he was secure and happy in the wiry strong arms of his uncle. He fell asleep listening to the drone of crickets and the clip of the bay's shoes against the rocks.

EIGHT

Rafelita stepped out the kitchen's back door holding a metal tub filled with freshly washed linens. She slid her right foot to the edge of the flagstones that served as a doorstep and stepped onto the ground. Diego watched her from the garden, where he was hoeing weeds with José and Eduardo. She wore a white summer dress that pressed tightly over her round breasts. She walked straight ahead with even steps. When she was nearly to the clothesline that ran between the house and garden, she stopped and shifted the wash tub against her left hip and stretched her right arm out in front of her. Slowly, she moved forward until finding the clothesline with her right hand. Then she set the tub on the ground and began hanging out the wash. Diego carried his hoe to the edge of the garden and leaned it against a tree. He walked up behind Rafelita, so close to her that he could smell the lavender water that she always wore.

"Diego? Where were you . . . where did you come from?"

"From the garden about forty feet right from here," he said, taking a pillowcase out of the wash tub. He shook it hard and hung it on the line.

"What are you doing?"

"I want to help you."

"As you like, but what about the garden?" she asked, putting a clothespin on the sheet in front of her.

Diego looked out into the garden. José had stopped hoeing and was watching him and Rafelita. Diego returned his father's glare, so José quickly went back to work. "The weeds will still be there when we're finished," he answered, still eyeing his father.

"Fine," she smiled. "But . . . your hands? Are they clean?" she asked as she reached over and took his hands in hers. Diego took a deep breath and closed his eyes as she felt them gently from wrists to finger tips. "Clean enough," she said, letting go of him and turning back to her work.

"Rafelita . . ."

"Yes?" She paused and turned her head toward him. Her eyes were closed as usual. "Well . . . ?"

"Where did you get all of those rings you wear on your fingers?" he asked stupidly.

"Oh these," she said, feeling the golden rings she wore on each hand. "These belonged to my grandmother. Perhaps they belonged to my great-great-grandmother before that, but when I turned eighteen, my mother gave them to me. She couldn't wear them anyway; her fingers were too plump. Why do you ask?"

"I thought maybe you got them from a . . . from a . . ."

"Do you mean from a novio? No, Diego," she laughed, shaking her head. "A blind girl doesn't have suitors. But do you like them?" she asked, displaying them for Diego.

"Yes, I like them," he said.

"I like them too. I never take them off. I'll never take them off." With that Rafelita bent down and picked up the empty washtub. "Thank you for helping me, Diego."

"Here, let me walk you back to the house," he said, trying to take the tub from her.

"No, Diego. I can find my way back to the house. Don't be silly. I can count. It's only eighteen steps. One, two, three, four, five . . . ," she said, brushing past him.

Later that afternoon, Eduardo and José sat on the corral watching Diego saddle Hero. Since the end of school in May, Diego had started training Hero for the races that took place every summer in Los Torbellinos and neighboring villages. The horse races were the highlight of the summer for the young men, and most of the villagers who enjoyed betting on their favorite horses. Every day after Diego finished his work, he saddled Hero and rode him to a sandy arroyo, where he loped the stallion for two miles. After the daily run, Hero was rubbed down and fed carefully measured amounts of oats and alfalfa to ensure that he would not become too fat and lazy.

While Diego was tightening the cinch on his saddle, José began to complain. "That poor horse is a bag of bones. Pure bones. If you don't feed him more, he's going to die before you ever find a race for him. You're going to starve him to death."

Diego shook his head, "Papá, this is how a racehorse is supposed to look. He's perfect. In top form. I know what I'm doing. Just wait. Soon you'll see him run and you'll see that I'm right."

"What makes you think anyone in these parts would be fool enough to match a horse against Hero? No one is that stupid. You're wasting your time. You'll never get a race for him. Never," José complained.

"You'll be surprised. Somebody will ask for a match. Maybe no one from Los Torbellinos, but news travels fast and someone will come up with a horse that is worthy of my friend here," he said, patting Hero's neck before swinging into the saddle. "Are you coming with me, conejo?" he asked, riding over to the corral where Eduardo sat beside his grandfather.

"What a question," said José as Eduardo jumped on the saddle in front of Diego. José climbed stiffly off of the corral and opened the gate for Diego and Eduardo. As they rode past the house, they met Carmen and Rafelita. Carmen held a basket with towels and soap and the old blanket that they took to spread on the ground by the river.

"Stop, stop," yelled Carmen. Diego pulled the reins and the bay came to a standstill in front of the well. "Eduardo, you need a bath. You're coming with us to the creek. Tomorrow is Sunday and I need to wash your hair for Mass."

"I'll bathe when we get back. I'll even wash my hair with soap. Please, Tía," begged Eduardo.

"No. You can ride with Diego tomorrow after Mass, but now you are coming with us. Get off that horse."

Eduardo swiveled in the saddle and looked up at Diego, but his uncle only shrugged his shoulders. He took Eduardo by the arms and lowered him to the ground. "And what about you, Tío?" said Eduardo, angrily looking up at Diego. "You need a bath too. Come with us and we can run Hero after we bathe. Please, you can play in the water with me," begged Eduardo.

"That's true, Diego," said Carmen coyly. "Why don't you come with us? I'm sure you could use a bath."

Diego put his heels into Hero's sides and sped away, blushing. "You shouldn't tease him," Rafelita said.

"It's good for him. Besides, lots of men bathe at the river with us, and Diego doesn't have anything to be ashamed of. I should know I changed his diapers when he was a baby," Carmen said.

"Carmen," scolded Rafelita, "he's still young."

"Hum . . . he's not so young as he sometimes acts," she said, heading off toward the river. Eduardo took Rafelita's arm and they followed Carmen.

After Diego was well away from the house, he slowed Hero to an easy lope. At the river, Hero waded into the water carefully choosing his own path. They climbed the river bank on the other side and resumed the lope across the llano to the mouth of the arroyo where Diego exercised Hero daily. Diego dismounted and rolled a cigarette.

"Why the hell did Carmen have to go and say that," said Diego, striking a match against his belt buckle. Hero watched and snorted loudly as a billow of smoke floated past his nostrils. "Why don't you come with us, Diego?" he said, mimicking his older sister. "Eduardo I can forgive; he's just a kid. But Carmen, she knows better than to embarrass me like that in front of Rafelita."

He took a long draw from the cigarette. If he bathed with them at the river, then everyone would know what happened to him each time he was near Rafelita. He only had to think of her without her clothes on and he became all hot and achy. It was bad enough just living in the same house with her. When he stood near her, his heart beat so wildly that he could feel it pounding against his chest. He wondered if she noticed the way his hands shook. The way his breathing became heavy and irregular when he was close enough to her to smell her perfume or to see the way her dark eyelashes curled away from her closed eyes. He wanted her to know, but she treated him the same way she did Eduardo. No. Eduardo could touch her whenever he wanted. He could climb onto her inviting lap and kiss her cheeks and let her touch his hair. "Qué conejo," said Diego, smiling. Eduardo went off to bed with Rafelita every night, and she scratched his back and told him stories until he fell asleep. Diego heard them from his room across the hall. "That doesn't happen to me," he said with a shake of his head.

Hero suddenly nudged him with his nose. Diego crushed his cigarette out against his riding boot. "OK, OK, here we go, boy," said Diego and mounted.

The bay trod into the deep sand. Diego lightly pressed his knees against Hero's sides, and the horse surged into a gallop. When Diego was with Rafelita, he could not think clearly. He said all of the things he did not want to say. And his voice usually cracked from desire when he spoke to her. It was frustrating for him to be near her, but it was torture being away from her. Nothing, not even riding Hero, could take her out of his thoughts. He had given up his old habits of riding with his friends and drinking wine until late at night in the foothills, because when he was away from home, away from Rafelita, he was miserable. He was hardly content these days, but at least at home, working with his father, he could see and hear her. There was no chance of being alone with her; there was always someone else around. But being near her, watching her, was better than the emptiness that came whenever she was out of his sight.

Hero galloped steadily on. His power never failed; his breathing was rhythmic as he drew and expelled air through his flared nostrils. The horse was covered in lather when they reached the end of the arroyo, though he could have gone on for miles. Diego dismounted, loosened the cinch, and led Hero down the arroyo until he was breathing normally again. Then he tightened the cinch and got back into the saddle. Hero was anxious to get home and be fed. He walked briskly, almost trotting. When they reached the river, Hero stepped into the water and waded through. Diego mechanically pulled him to a stop in midstream. The stallion stamped the water impatiently. Startled, Diego rode to the other side and dismounted. He tethered Hero to a tree and headed downstream on foot.

The pool where Carmen and Rafelita were bathing with Eduardo was less than a hundred yards away. He moved stealthily; no stones toppled and no branches cracked as he moved along the thickly wooded river bank. He had dreamed about her for too long. Diego did not hesitate long to moralize about his plan. Besides, tomorrow was Sunday, and whatever he did, he could confess it in the morning.

The pool lay ahead of him, but only Eduardo was still in the water. Diego crouched down and crept behind a fallen log that was overgrown with river-willows and tall grass. He could see the two women perfectly not forty feet away from him on the opposite side of the river. They were the only people at the pool this afternoon.

Both women were naked, lying outstretched on the blanket by the water. The late afternoon sun shone down on them. Carmen appeared to be sleeping, at least she was not moving. Rafelita lay on her back with her long, dark hair fanned out behind her to dry. She stretched her arms over her head and ran her fingers through her hair. Diego had never seen her hair loose. Her skin glowed golden under the sunlight. The mounds of her breasts rested high on her chest. Her rib cage was trim and tapered down to a thin waist, the curving sweep of her hips, and firm, shapely legs. She clasped her hands together above her head, stretched, and yawned. Then she turned on her side to face the water and leaned on her elbow. The curves of her body became more pronounced. She sat up and was facing him now. She leaned her head to one side the way she did when she was concentrating. Diego felt the skin on his neck and spine tingle as if he were the one being watched. Rafelita stood up and began walking toward the pool directly in front of him.

His heart was pounding harder and harder. Her serene, oval face with dark eyes and ruby lips. Her smooth throat. Her fair shoulders and slender arms. The expanse of golden skin. The fullness of her breasts and the slight curve of her stomach below her navel. The dark velvet below and her long beautiful legs. How could a woman be so desirable? Diego had seen and been with lots of beautiful, high-priced women in Kentucky, but none of them could compare to her. None of them had affected him the way she did. Rafelita walked to the edge of the water and leaned her head to the side for a few minutes. Then she straightened up and faced him. Her eyes were still closed but she began to smile. She bent gracefully down to the water and wet her hands. She pressed them against her face, throat, and over her breasts. She was still smiling, still facing him.

Diego pressed his forehead against the log and closed his eyes. "Jesus, Mary, and Joseph," he whispered. She turned and went back to the blanket.

"What is it?" asked Carmen sleepily as Rafelita sat down beside her. At that moment, Eduardo looked across the pool directly at Diego. He started to call out to his tío, but Diego immediately placed a finger to his lips indicating that Eduardo remain silent. Eduardo obeyed, glancing quickly over his shoulder at the women and back at his uncle, who was now shaking his finger threateningly. Dumbfounded, Eduardo turned to face the women, and when he turned back, Diego was gone.

"What is it, Rafelita?" he heard Carmen repeat her question.

"Oh nothing. I felt . . . I felt warm and went to the creek for water. That's all," Rafelita answered.

Eduardo reached into the water and splashed his face again and again. He knew better than to tell the women he had seen Diego lurking in the forest, though he could not imagine why his uncle wanted to spy on them in the first place.

NINE

At the end of June, Diego was approached by a man from a village twenty miles west of Los Torbellinos. He wanted to match his mare against Hero. Diego accepted the challenge without seeing the man's horse because he was positive that even the best horse in all of New Mexico was no match for his stallion. They arranged to meet at the Los Torbellinos racetrack the last Saturday in July. Within a week, everyone in Los Torbellinos had heard that Diego had found a race for his horse.

The racetrack was located at the southern end of town, where the mouth of Los Torbellinos valley opened, spreading out for miles in every direction. The llano was flat and sandy and vegetated by sage, desert grasses, cactus, and an occasional piñon tree. The track was a straight tract of land forty feet wide that had been lightly plowed and cleared of rocks.

On the race day, the early arrivals took choice positions on either side of the track near the finish line. Men clustered together to discuss their favorite horses, and women sat in the wagons gossiping and making their own speculations about the best horses and riders. All the people of Los Torbellinos favored Diego's horse and were ready to place bets on him. Drinking started early. Caution was forgotten and the stakes on Diego's horse rose.

The noon sun had reached its summit and was pounding down heat; a few billowy clouds floated along the hills but offered no respite. Around the track the air was thick with dust from the constant pounding of horses' hooves. Finally, at one o'clock, a match was set between two fiery mustangs. Three more races

71

helped diffuse the anticipation mounting before the big race. Diego watched his opponent's horse. She was tall and sleek and clearly of thoroughbred blood lines, but there was a trace of mustang in her, and he was sure she was no match for Hero.

At last, the final bets were collected. Diego placed $500, the remainder of his Kentucky earnings, on the race. All of the side bets on Hero added to $1,400, and an equal sum was collected by Diego's opponent. Diego's best friend, Fidel, collected the money bet on Hero and kept a list of who bet what.

Both horses were to be ridden bareback, as was tradition. José boosted Diego up onto Hero's back; a young man from the neighboring town would ride the mare. First, he and Diego loped gently down the track to loosen the horses' muscles and joints for the race. Both horses were impressive. Tension mounted as they loped past the spectators toward the start line marked in the sand.

At the line, the horses stomped their feet nervously. One of the judges announced, "Go on the count of three. Ready? One, two, three!" The horses yielded to their riders' commands, exploding into motion down the track. Diego and the bay stretched out easily in front of the mare. Diego knew that Hero was nowhere close to his peak speed; he slowed down so that Hero only led by one length. There was no need to let everyone know how fast Hero could move. He knew he had nothing to fear because his opponent was already whipping the mare to get the last speed out of her. She pulled and pulled for her rider but could not move ahead of Hero. In seconds they were over the finish line.

The spectators poured onto the track after the horses passed. Half of them shouted in jubilation and hugged one another and cheered Hero and Diego. The losers frowned, kicked at the dirt, and a few began to complain of an unfair start. Diego pulled Hero to a stop and slid to the ground. He smiled proudly and rubbed the bay on the shoulders. "What a good horse," he said, still breathing heavily. "I never doubted you for one second." José took Hero by the reins just as Diego was lifted into the air by the crowd. Cheering and smiling, someone offered him a bottle of wine. "I'm rich!" he shouted, holding the bottle aloft. "We're all rich," cheered someone else in the crowd.

Fidel walked over holding the winners' pot, which he had just collected from the owner of the mare. He was smiling. "Oye, Diego, that pinche cabrón tried to say that the start was unfair, but the judges disagreed."

"Everyone could see it was a fair race," yelled another man in the crowd as Fidel began calling out names and passing out cash to the winners.

"Of course, it was a fair race," said Diego, "but it wouldn't be a race in Los Torbellinos if the loser didn't say the winner cheated!" He took a long drink from the jug of wine. "Besides, you didn't hear him asking me for a rematch did you?" After an hour or more of celebrating, the crowd began to disperse. Wives were anxious to get their drunken husbands home before the inevitable brawls broke out between the winners and disgruntled losers.

Diego's friends were ready to move the party to their favorite spot up the canyon. They had bought wine for the occasion and even arranged to have girls meet them at the designated spot. One of them had secured a fat lamb that was already dressed and waiting to be roasted over an open fire. But Diego told them he was going home with his family.

"What's the matter with you, hombre?" said Fidel in disbelief. "I don't know what your problem is, but you haven't been yourself lately. No time for this. No time for that. No time for your friends. You've been acting like a woman," he complained, leading the group away from Diego. "He's being whipped by someone, someone or something? Or maybe he's so cheap that he doesn't want to share his good fortune with us," laughed Fidel. "That's for sure," they all agreed and rode off to celebrate without Diego, shaking their heads and making jokes about him.

That night the family had a lazy dinner. They lingered after the meal for a long time, drinking coffee until finally, Fidelia made the first move to clear the table. José and Diego, with Eduardo in tow, moved out onto the portal with a bottle of wine and five glasses to wait for the women to finish their chores.

After the last crumb was swept off the floor and the last polished dish set in its place in the cupboard, the women came out to the porch. The sun was dropping behind the mountains on the western horizon; levels of yellow and orange light swirled and blended into burning crimson and finally sank in a faint glow of violet. The women took their seats at the rickety wooden table while Diego poured glasses of wine for each of them.

José filled his pipe, held it familiarly in his hand, and lit a match to the tobacco. "This is not a day to complain of," he said proudly, puffing out a cloud of smoke.

Still smiling, Diego rolled himself a cigarette and passed the papers and the tobacco to Rafelita, who expertly rolled three neat cigarettes, one for herself and the other two for Carmen and Fidelia. The adults were content, relaxed, and satisfied to drink their wine and enjoy the peacefulness of the evening in silence, but Eduardo would have none of it.

"Abuelo, tell us a story," he pleaded. However, the conversation had already moved on to the day's events at the racetrack and on to other topics that Eduardo found boring. He wandered to Carmen's chair and leaned against her sleepily. She collected him onto her lap and soon he was asleep. Carmen motioned to Diego, who rose, took Eduardo off her lap, and carried him upstairs to bed. He returned and poured the last of the wine into their glasses.

Presently José rose stiffly from his chair. "Ah, qué trabajo," he sighed, emptying his pipe in the ashtray on the table. "I need my sleep like Eduardo does. If I were a little bit younger, maybe I would stay up later, but I'm a tired, old man," he grumbled. Fidelia stood up too. "Yes, it's late for old people like us."

"You two shouldn't complain so much. You're not that old or that tired," said Carmen. "I'm the old, tired one in this family." She stood up stretching then collected the empty glasses in one hand, and caught up the empty bottle in the other. "It was a long day, a long hot day under the sun. I'm tired. Are you ready for bed, Rafelita?"

"Yes. I could sleep now," she said, also rising. They all bid Diego good night and left him alone.

"You'd think they were all one hundred and one years old," he said to himself in English. His parents had taken the kerosene lamp off the table and shuffled down the porch and into their bedroom next to the sala. He heard Carmen and Rafelita talking as they went through the kitchen. The stairwell creaked as they went up to their room. He heard the window in his parents' bedroom being opened to catch the night breeze.

Diego sat in the dark completely alone and empty. Despite the wine and his win at the tracks he was sober, restless, and unhappy. The coyotes had been yapping sporadically out on the llano for hours, and now they broke into a prolonged wail that made him feel more empty, more lonely. He concentrated on their howls, trying to forget everything. He heard the single hoot of a an owl from the cottonwoods along the river.

"To hell with this," he said, standing up. He started for Hero's shed, but the thought of riding up the canyon to join his friends wasn't appealing either. Instead, he turned around and went upstairs to his room.

He opened the window and stood beside it, breathing in the cool night air and listening to the distant hoot of the owl. After a few minutes, he took off his shirt and belt and laid them across a chair. Next he sat on the bed, pulled off his boots, and dumped them heavily on the floor. He lay back on top of the quilt with his arms folded behind his head and tried to sleep. But he was hot, not in the least bit sleepy. When he closed his eyes, images of Rafelita burned like a fever. Quiet, beautiful, mystical Rafelita. She lay in the next room less than twenty feet away from him, but as untouchable as ever. He felt like putting on a real drunk; a numbing drunk would be better than the way he felt now. Maybe he would go find a girl to caress and lie with, to take away the emptiness for a few hours. There were girls at Fidel's party; Diego had to get out of the house and away from his pathetic longing. He made himself sick. He would get smashing drunk and take the first girl he could find. He pulled himself to the edge of the bed and picked up a boot off the floor. Then he heard the door across the narrow hall open. Someone stepped onto the landing, shut the door carefully, and started downstairs.

Diego's heart began to race. It was too quiet to be Eduardo, and he was almost certain that it was not his sister. Hope returned. He waited, not daring to breathe until whoever it was opened the kitchen door and walked out onto the porch. He dashed to his window and saw Rafelita step into view from under the eaves of the portal. She wore a white nightgown and her hair was free, hanging down her back. She walked toward the well. Without waiting to pull on his shirt or boots, Diego whispered, "Now," and followed her as quietly as possible downstairs and outside into the night. He stopped just off the porch to watch her draw a pail of water from the well. She closed the lid of the well and set the bucket on top of it. Then she found the tin cup that hung from a nail on the well house and filled the cup with cold water. She lifted it to her lips and drank. Through the darkness, the line of her white nightgown glimmered faintly like a beautiful feather.

Keeping his eyes on her, Diego approached her. "Rafelita, don't be frightened. It's me," he said softly, stepping up behind her.

"Diego, I thought you were asleep. I heard you go into your room earlier."

"Yes, but I couldn't sleep." She turned to face him. He had never been so close to her before. His face was inches from hers.

"I couldn't sleep either. It's still so hot in our room, and I had such a thirst from the wine. I had to have a drink of water." She reached out in front of her and was startled to find Diego so close. Her hand touched his bare chest and she withdrew it quickly as if she had touched fire. "I . . . I should leave now . . . go back to bed."

"Don't go. Stay," persuaded Diego gently. "Stay here with me, Rafelita. Please." He reached out and caressed her cheek softly; he let his hand slip behind her head under her dark, rich hair. He ran his fingers through her hair and brought it forward over her shoulder. Its silkiness fell over his arm and slid down his bare chest and stomach like a cool, delicious waterfall. He brought a handful of it to his cheek and inhaled it's rich sweetness. She did not move. He detected a slight heaving across her breasts, or did he? "You're beautiful," he whispered almost too quietly for her to hear.

"Diego, it was you. You were the one watching us at the river. It was you wasn't it?" There was a tinge of doubt in her voice.

"Yes. The first time about a month ago, and since then every time. I'm always watching you, Rafelita. Always."

"I know . . . but don't say that. You shouldn't say that. You don't know what you're saying. I'm so much older than you."

"Do you think I care?" He took her face in his hands and caressed her cheeks with his thumbs. "Do you think I care? Do you think I want a silly young girl who doesn't know if she wants to laugh or cry? Who doesn't even know what she wants. That's not what I want."

"You don't realize the consequences. You're crazy, Diego."

"Crazy for you."

"You don't know what you're doing. If we do this, there's no return. You'll never be the same again and I . . ." He floated his fingers lightly over her lips. She kissed them softly.

"Shh, you're beautiful. You're the most beautiful woman I've ever seen. I know what I'm doing, and I know what I want. And you?" he whispered into her ear. "Do you know what you want? Do you?" He touched his lips against hers. She kissed him lightly. "Well, do you? Do you know what you want?"

"Yes," she said. "I know what I want now. Don't let me think about tomorrow."

Diego kissed her softly; her lips were cool and fresh. Then he took her by the hand and led her past the horse stalls and into the alfalfa meadow beyond. He unbuttoned her nightgown and pushed it off her shoulders. It fell in a billowy ring around her feet. He kissed her naked shoulders, throat, and firm breasts. He sank onto his knees kissing her stomach and navel. He encircled her waist with his arms and pressed his cheek against her. "Do you still know you want?" he asked.

"Yes, yes, yes," she whispered. Diego pulled her gently down to him in the cool green sea of alfalfa.

TEN

José's orchard was one and a half acres of paradise located on the southwest boundary of his property; here, the corner of his alfalfa field dropped abruptly down a twenty-foot embankment to a verdant flat of ground bounded on the north, south, and west by ravines. Above these ravines rolled the arid llano with its sparse vegetation. José's orchard was an oasis at the edge of the desert.

The Baca family had devoted four generations of loving attention to their fruit trees ever since the orchard had come into existence in it's haphazard fashion, almost by a quirk of nature. In the beginning, when José's great-grandfather first possessed the land, the entire one and a half acres had been covered by wild plum trees that grew so densely together, like river rushes, that it was difficult to walk between them. The scrubby trees produced sweet, dark purple plums that ripened in late summer. In those early days the grove of plum trees produced even more fruit than the birds and half the inhabitants of Los Torbellinos could use. So on a whim, and taking a tip from nature, José's great-grandfather had uprooted some of the thorny trees and in their place planted apple and apricot trees. It was a battle to keep the hardy wild plums from reclaiming their ground, but in the end, the apple and apricots established themselves and thrived in the rich earth.

The next generation and the next went on in this fashion until, when the property came into José's hands, the plum trees had been pushed back to the perimeter of the property, where they still flourished in a thick belt, like a fortress wall, encircling the other varieties that now claimed the center of the grove. There were apples and apricots and cherries. Two massive pear trees bore a strange, round fruit no bigger than a small plum. Three beautiful peach trees were one of José's contributions to the orchard. He had acquired these in the 1880s when a group of Mormons became disenchanted with their attempt to farm a section of the Los Torbellinos valley and left. José dug up the parched saplings, transplanted them into his orchard, and coaxed them to life. José had also strewn timothy grass seed in the orchard that spread into a rich carpet of grass and clover in the moist, cool ground under the trees.

Perhaps because the orchard was surrounded by the walls of the ravine, or perhaps because José willed it, his trees were rarely blighted by late frosts. There was never a year that he was completely without fruit. But even if the opposite were true, José would have tended the trees the same, for this lovely orchard was his pride and joy. He pampered the trees like children. Any time dark troubling thoughts disturbed him, he had only to visit his orchard to recover his positive perspective on life. The trees whispered to him; so simple, so clear, so true was their wisdom. It was not in church, but here, in his orchard, where José saw and felt and understood God. It was here that he asked for and received answers, and he knew that in this orchard he would someday hear God calling him and he would go without regret.

At the break of dawn one morning in August, José and Eduardo walked through the alfalfa fields and down the steep path to the orchard. It was José's turn to use the ditch water to irrigate his garden and fruit trees. The water came from Los Torbellinos Creek, whose source was high in the mountains above the valley. Though it was late summer and the water in the streambeds had dwindled to a trickle, a trickle was all José needed to sustain his gardens and fruit trees. Under the water-rights system established generations before by the first Spanish settlers into the valley, José had access to the water in the ditch for two days and two nights; then it would be turned over to his neighbors. The system ensured that all landowners received adequate water for the cultivation of their crops.

José and Diego had directed half of the ditch water into the vegetable garden, which Diego was tending, and the other half would be used to flood the orchard. For the next two days, José would not leave the orchard. His meals were brought to him, and he would doze at night under the stars, waking every hour to move the irrigation water to a dry section of the orchard.

It was still dark, cool, and fresh when José and Eduardo walked through the orchard toward the ditch at four o'clock in the morning. The sharp fragrance of pine sap carried down from the sierra on the morning breeze warned of autumn. Eduardo watched his grandfather slide a sturdy plate of wood into the head gate in the mother ditch; the trickle of muddy water advanced down the parched feeder ditch, bringing with it an earthy smell reminiscent of the first raindrops after a long dry spell. After José opened the water onto a thirsty section of ground, he and Eduardo walked slowly around the orchard inspecting the trees. José placed his hand on the branch of an apple tree. "I climbed in this old tree when I was a boy," he said affectionately patting the branch. "It's getting old now, but its apples are still the best we have." He plucked a ripe apple off the tree, rubbed it clean on his shirt, and cut it in half with his buck knife. He gave half to Eduardo and ate the other half himself. "If you take care of these trees and love them, they love you in return. You have to talk to them and listen to them, and give them what they need—water, pruning, and love. You respect them and they you. That's how it is, mi jefe," said José, moving on to examine a peach tree that was already picked bare of fruit.

Eduardo hoisted himself onto a low saddle branch of the apple tree and, munching his apple, watched José walk around the peach tree. Then he heard a shuffle in the branches overhead and looked up. A fat raccoon was curled up in the crook of a branch, sleeping contentedly after a night of gorging on ripe apples.

"Abuelo, Abuelo," Eduardo shouted. "Come here. There's a fat raccoon in this tree." José walked slowly back to Eduardo, frowning. The raccoons were a problem in the orchard. Left unchecked they could harvest more than half of the fruit from the trees. They had to be shot because there was no way to keep them from creeping into the trees at night. But José found it difficult to shoot these strange creatures, as he found it difficult to shoot or kill any living thing. In the fall, it was with a heavy heart that José slaughtered the cattle, sheep, and pigs he had nurtured. And in earlier years, his most unpleasant arguments with Fidelia had been because of his reluctance to shoot the raccoons that climbed into their fruit trees. José marveled at the human-like dexterity of their miniature black hands; besides, why didn't they have as much right to eat the fruit as he and his family? But Fidelia had another opinion of the pesky raccoons and had ended their discussions one morning long ago by waltzing into the orchard with José's old Winchester and blasting five fat, unsuspecting raccoons out of the trees. Her aim had been none too spectacular and José was left the task of finishing the maimed animals. Since then, he had destroyed the animals himself, but if no one else had seen them, he tried to ignore them and hoped they would slink back to their nests.

"Look up there," said Eduardo excitedly. "It's a big fat one."

José peered up through the foliage and spied the big raccoon. "Qué lastima," he said shaking his head. "It's an old female. Look, you can see her teats; she's got a nest of little ones somewhere. Qué lastima. If she doesn't move on before lunch, we'll have to shoot her," José said sadly. "If she's not gone by noon, you tell Diego to bring the rifle. But hopefully she'll leave before then."

Their talking had awakened the coon and she was looking down at them. "Will her young die if we shoot her?" asked Eduardo still staring at her.

"It's difficult to say. I think they should be old enough to survive on their own now, but it depends on when they were born. If they were born late, of course, they'll die without their mother."

"Maybe we can chase her out of the tree with rocks, or I can climb up there and poke her with a stick," Eduardo suggested.

"We can try, but they are stubborn creatures. They feel safest up in the trees and almost nothing brings them down, nothing but a bullet."

Eduardo set about collecting stones, which he and José threw at the fat coon. None of the stones hit her but she retreated to the end of the branch. Finally, her weight became too much for the tip of the branch and it collapsed, dropping her to the ground. She landed heavily on all fours and waddled off into the plum thickets. José chuckled. "It doesn't look like she's hurt. Besides, a little fall is better than a bullet." He tried not to think of her young that she would eventually bring to the orchard to feed.

Eduardo was proud of his work. "Híjole, I wish those animals would stay away from here," he said importantly. José mussed Eduardo's hair, "I only hope we don't find any more here this morning."

As José walked back to move his irrigation water, a white owl flew out of one of the huge pear trees and rose heavily into the air. "An owl at sunrise means bad luck," prophesied José to himself. Eduardo went to work raking up all of the windfall fruit from underneath the trees. What was not edible would be fed to the pigs and goats.

By noon José and Eduardo were hungry and ready for a break. José walked over to where Eduardo was still raking sour apples into piles and sat down in the grass with his back against the tree. He picked up the water canteen and took a long drink. Using a bandanna to wipe the perspiration from his face and neck he said, "Oye, mi'jo, it's time for a rest. Your grandmother said she would pack a lunch for us before she went out and leave it in the kitchen. Why don't you go up to the house and bring it. Tell your uncle to come down here and have lunch with us. He's been under the hot sun in the garden all morning. It's nice and cool here. He can have a rest with us."

"Here I go, Grandfather," said Eduardo. He leaned his rake beside José's shovel and sprinted across the orchard and up the path to the alfalfa field. His stomach was churning from hunger, and he began to salivate thinking about what the women might have prepared for them. He jogged easily all the way to the edge of the garden where he expected to find Diego. Not seeing him, he went around the house to the well where he thought Diego might have gone for a fresh pail of drinking water. But he was not at the well either. Eduardo walked across the portal and opened the kitchen door. He blinked to adjust his eyes to the dimness. The lunch pail was sitting on the kitchen table; Eduardo pulled the pail to the edge of the table and lifted the tea towel that covered the bucket. Instantly a whiff of warm tortillas and green chile floated up to his nostrils. Fidelia had neatly packed half a dozen plump burritos of stewed beef and green chile. There were also boiled potatoes and boiled eggs and some ripe tomatoes. Eduardo took the salt shaker off the table, dropped it in the pail, and tucked the tea towel back into place. He grabbed the pail by the handle and started for the back door; maybe Diego was between the rows of corn.

As he reached the door, a creaking racket startled him; it was coming from upstairs. It sounded like bedsprings going crazy the way they did when he sometimes jumped on the bed. He set the lunch pail on the floor, walked to the narrow stairwell, and listened. It was definitely someone jumping on the bed in Diego's room. Confused, Eduardo started up the stairs. The women were at the neighbors, but why would Diego be jumping on his bed? At the same time Eduardo laid his hand on the door knob and opened the door, he started to call Diego's name, but when the door opened, all that came out of his mouth was a suffocated croak.

Diego was on his bed, but he was not alone. He lay on his back naked, and Rafelita, also naked, was sitting on him. Her legs were straddled wide over his pelvis and she was moving her body down on top of Diego, causing the old bedsprings to go wild. Diego's hands were on her waist, and she was caressing her own hair with her head thrown back. Her freed hair trailed down her naked back and brushed across Diego's legs. Eduardo took in this scene for a split second before Diego and Rafelita turned toward him. Rafelita slid off of Diego crying, "Oh my God." Diego reached for his pants and commanded angrily, "Shut the door!"

Eduardo slammed the door and stood on the landing stunned. He was trembling and feared the worst from Diego for having opened the door without knocking. He heard rustling in the bedroom, and Rafelita kept repeating, "Oh my God, what should we do?" Then Diego said, "Don't worry. I'll go talk to Eduardo. Don't worry." Eduardo fled down the stairwell and collapsed into a chair at the kitchen table. Would Diego beat him? He began to cry.

Diego came down the stairs wearing only his mud-flecked trousers. He was rubbing his fingers through his hair. Eduardo looked at him through his tears and continued to cry dumbly. "Eduardo," Diego only called him Eduardo when he was angry, "you know that you're supposed to knock on a door before you open it."

"I was looking for you. Grandfather told me to find you so we could have lunch together. He said you were alone. He said the women were not here. I didn't know," sobbed Eduardo.

Diego's tone lightened. "OK, OK. Stop crying. Here's what you do. First, go outside and wash your face, and then you go back to the orchard with the food. You tell your grandfather that I'll be there soon . . . that I had to finish moving some water in the garden." He took Eduardo's chin in his hand and looked him hard in the face. "You go back there and you don't say a thing about what you saw. You don't tell anyone. No one, not ever. You understand, conejo?"

"Yes," Eduardo sobbed.

"Stop crying. I'm not mad at you, but you don't tell anyone what you saw. Now go wash yourself, and remember I was in the garden and I'll join you soon."

Eduardo rubbed his eyes. He stood up and headed slowly for the kitchen door to wash his face at the well outside. "Remember, tell your grandfather that I'll be there in a few minutes, but don't wait for me to start lunch. And stop crying," yelled Diego as he ran back upstairs to his room.

After washing, Eduardo took the lunch pail and walked slowly back to the orchard. He cleared his throat countless times to take the crying from his voice. Then he panicked. What was he supposed to say? He could not remember. The images of them in Diego's room flashed continuously through his mind. Why were they doing that? Why wasn't Rafelita with Fidelia and Carmen? Why did he have to see that? He felt shaky and weak. What was he supposed to say? He took a few deep breaths and thought hard. He was to tell José that Diego was still watering and would join them soon. They should start lunch without him. When Eduardo reached the steep path, the scene flooded vividly back into his mind. Opening the door to Diego's room had been like opening an oven door. A wave of heat had blasted him in the face, and Diego and Rafelita had both been drenched, their bodies gleaming shiny and slick. Eduardo stumbled and regained his step just in time to rescue their lunch from tumbling down the ravine. José watched Eduardo and chuckled. "Cuidado," he yelled from under the apple tree. Eduardo trudged over to the tree and set the pail on the ground without looking at José. José watched him carefully, and then came the worst, the inevitable. He knew something was wrong. "What's the matter with you? You look . . . sick." What is it?"

"Nothing," blurted Eduardo too hastily.

"Nothing. What do you mean nothing? You look like you've been bitten by a rattlesnake."

"No. I'm fine," said Eduardo, terrified. Uncovering the lunch pail, he pulled out burritos, potatoes, eggs, and tomatoes and began piling them into a pyramid on the grass.

"Wait, wait, wait, mi jefe," said José, taking the burritos off the ground and placing them back in the pail. "Do you want to feed our lunch to the flies and ants?" Then it all clicked in José's mind. "Ay Dios," he sighed. "And your tío? You saw your tío?" He watched Eduardo closely.

"Yes," said Eduardo, concentrating hard on peeling an egg. "He said he's coming soon. When he finishes with the water."

"Bien, bien, Jefe, and was your tío alone . . . was anyone else at the house?"

"Yes . . ." Eduardo flicked the last bits of eggshell off the egg onto the ground.

"Yes, he was alone, or yes someone else was at the house?"

"I don't know," said Eduardo, shoving the egg into his mouth. "I can't remember," he added around a cheek packed full of boiled egg.

"Muy bien, mi jefe," said José, patting Eduardo's shoulder. "It's fine. Forget about it. Don't worry, you don't have to say anything. Forget about it and eat your lunch. Ay, Dios mío," sighed José, biting into a burrito. "I feared it would come to this."

Twenty minutes later Diego appeared on the trail at the top of the ravine. "Ay, Dios mío," mumbled José as Diego walked spryly down the hill toward them.

"What's happening, hombres," he said, nonchalantly flashing his bright smile.

"You tell me," said José, taking a bite of his boiled potato.

"What do you mean?" Diego smirked, staring at José and then Eduardo.

"Nothing, son. Sit down. Eat." Diego sat down. "Su mamá y las chicas? Are the women at the neighbors?"

"Sure," Diego shrugged, "Mamá and Carmen are, but I guess Rafelita didn't go with them. I guess she had a headache, or something, I don't know."

"Bien," acknowledged José; they ate their lunch and made small-talk for the next half hour. Finally, José brushed off his hands and took a deep breath, "Eduardo, I want to talk to your tío. You take my shovel and go check on the water. Hurry up." Eduardo stood up and left carrying a half-eaten burrito in one hand and José's shovel in the other. He walked slowly across the orchard; he knew that Diego thought he had talked to José.

"Well, my son," began José, "tell me . . . what are your intentions with Rafelita?"

Diego had expected the worst but was still taken aback. He ran his fingers through his hair and coughed, "What are you talking about?"

"You know what I'm talking about," said José steadily.

"What did Eduardo tell you?" accused Diego.

"Wait a minute, Eduardo didn't tell me anything. You have no right to be angry at him. That boy worships you. He didn't have to tell me anything, but I know he saw something; it was written all over his face. He was turning green he was so scared that he'd say the wrong thing. However, this is not about Eduardo. This is about you . . . you and Rafelita. I guess I've seen it coming, but I tried to close my eyes," said José, playing with a blade of grass. He was as embarrassed as Diego. "And if I know it, it won't be long before your mother knows, if she doesn't already, and Carmen? You can't hide something like this from the people you live with. What are your plans? Are you going to get married?"

Diego stood up and paced nervously. "Married, married," he said sarcastically. "Don't think I don't want to. Don't think I haven't tried."

"Well, what's the problem?"

"The problem," said Diego laughing ironically, "the problem is 'what would the people say?' What would the good people of Los Torbellinos say if I married Rafelita. What would the good people say?" He walked around the tree raking his fingers through his hair again.

"Son, come here and sit down. Sit down and explain what is happening. What's this with the good people?"

Diego sat down. Almost whimpering he began, "You know, Rafelita is afraid people will talk about us. I'm almost eight years younger than she is; she's blind; I'm still a kid. What will people say about a twenty-six-year-old blind woman marrying me. Maybe I'm even too short for her. Hell, I don't know," said Diego as tears flooded into his eyes. "I just want to take care of her. I don't care what anyone says or thinks."

José put his hand on Diego's shoulder. "Calm down, my son. Calm down." He was pained by Diego's grief and confusion and because he knew Rafelita's worries were well founded. "It's true that people will talk. At least, they'll talk until they have something more juicy to talk about. But you know that's how it is here and that's how it's always been and always will be. People talk because they don't have anything better to do. But talk is only talk."

"You try telling that to Rafelita," said Diego more calmly. "I told her I'd take her away from here where she wouldn't have to hear the gossip and the dirty remarks, but she won't have that either. She's afraid to leave this . . . this 'good town.' "

José was silent. The idea of Diego leaving Los Torbellinos again was no more satisfactory to him than it had been the first time. "Maybe she doesn't love me," Diego raved on. "Maybe I'm not man enough for her. Maybe that's the truth."

"Diego, don't be a fool. Rafelita is a good woman, a kind woman. She is not the type to play with a man; don't paint her as a witch in your mind to make yourself feel better. Calm yourself. Maybe she needs more time."

"Maybe," said Diego regaining control. "Maybe you're right."

"You know," chuckled José, "when your mother and I were young, life was not so complicated. One Sunday after Mass, my father told me to get in the wagon, that we were going to get a wife for me. Well, we went to visit your mamá at her father's house. Old man Manzanares was a devil. He used to whip your mother and the others outside so every one who passed by could see. He made them hold onto the corral so they wouldn't fall when he was whipping them. I had seen that with my own eyes. I was scared of him, and I wasn't sorry when we buried him two years after our marriage. No one even cried at his funeral. But anyway, we went over there and they told us, 'Children you're going to be married next month.' I was seventeen and your mother was fourteen. It was that simple, and in one month we were married. Today you young people have it much more difficult. Times are changing."

"Yes, times are changing," said Diego, "but not in Los Torbellinos. Here people are still so bored they live for gossip. They pick at people's hearts like vultures pick the eyes out of a sick animal before it's even dead. I don't care. I don't care what they think, but Rafelita. She . . ."

"Be patient. Rafelita needs some time." José paused and cleared his throat. "But if you two are not more discreet, it won't be long before the whole family and everyone in the valley knows about you. And then I can promise you that people will have some talking to do. You know how it is."

"Si, Papá, I know how it is," said Diego tiredly. He stood up again. "I guess I'll go talk to Eduardo. You're right, he's not looking very good."

José watched Diego walk over to Eduardo. Diego made some kind of joke and he heard the two of them begin to laugh. Then Diego put his arm around Eduardo's shoulder and they continued to talk. José put a hand on the tree and stood up slowly. Supporting himself against the tree he watched the youngsters. He loved them both so much. Watching them brought tears to his eyes. He loved everyone too much. That was his problem. José stretched his tired limbs.

"Ay, Dios mío, poor Diego has not chosen an easy path for himself," he whispered to the trees. "God willing, everything will be fine."

ELEVEN

Two Sundays before school was to resume, Eduardo made his first Holy Communion and confessed his puerile sins for the first time. The same day, his infant sister Feliz, who was born in May, was baptized by Carmen and Diego in a private ceremony. The baptismal ritual freed her young soul from original sin, promised her a righteous upbringing and a passage to the eternal kingdom. Miguel had come home from the sheep camp in Colorado to witness these events, as well as to help with the fall harvest.

A photographer had been summoned to Los Torbellinos to make portraits of the children who had gone through the sacred rites of their first Holy Communion. Under clear, blue skies and the bright sun of early autumn, first the little girls, all in white lace and veils, went one by one before the camera holding their bouquets and candles like stoic miniature brides. Then with his baggy suit, white collar, and tie, glossy head of hair, and candle in hand, Eduardo at last stood for the camera. The photographer adjusted his lens, and with a click Eduardo's stern face was captured on film. Afterward the Baca and Montez families left the church courtyard and traveled together up the canyon to Elena and Miguel's house to celebrate the day's events.

That afternoon, when Miguel finished giving the blessing for their meal, Eduardo and his brothers were allowed to take their plates and sit on the porch to eat. Elena followed them and presented a fifty-cent piece to Eduardo.

"Mi'jito, this is your reward for having learned your catechism," she said, patting his shoulder. "Carlos and Roberto were also rewarded, and you, Marcos," she said to the littlest boy, "will be rewarded when you make your first Holy Communion." She went back into the kitchen to join the adults.

"Híjole!" exclaimed Eduardo happily. He placed the coin by his plate and watched it while he ate; it was the first money he had been given.

Later Miguel, José, and Diego joined the boys on the portal to have a glass of wine and a smoke. Diego was moody and quiet. He swallowed a glass of wine in one gulp, finished smoking his cigarette, and rode off on Hero before the women had time to serve dessert. The children went to play after their dessert, and the adults sat on the porch drinking wine, smoking, and discussing crops. José saw that Rafelita had stiffened when Fidelia asked why Diego was gone, but he hoped no one else had noticed.

An hour before sunset José and the women left for El Valle in their buckboard, but Eduardo stayed with his parents as he often did when Miguel was home. At night, as usual when at home, he had a hard time falling asleep. Sharing a bed with Carmen and Rafelita had spoiled him. His brothers tossed and fought for the quilts, kicking and talking in their sleep. Twice Eduardo woke and went to the window for fresh air. And then once again he had gotten out of bed to trap a cricket that was trilling under the window and making more noise than Carlos and Roberto together; he caught it in his hand and dropped it out the open window, remembering that José said it was bad luck to kill a cricket.

The household woke early as usual, and the boys went out to do their morning chores before breakfast. Eduardo accompanied Roberto to help him tend to the chickens. As they were collecting the eggs, Roberto asked, "What are you going to do with that money that Mamá gave to you? Have you decided yet?"

Eduardo took the coin from his pocket to examine it again. "I don't know," he said. "Maybe save it, but probably I'll buy something nice with it down at the store."

"I think it's better to spend it on something nice," encouraged Roberto. "That's what Carlos and I did, but will you buy something nice to eat, or something nice to keep? That's the question."

Eduardo played with the coin for a moment. "Oh, I think it is much better to buy a thing that one can keep than to buy a thing that one can eat. Don't you think so, Roberto?"

"Of course," Roberto agreed. "We'll go to Mr. Lawrence's store today, after we finish breakfast. If Carlos asks Mamá, she'll let us go. She always listens to Carlos. You watch, it's like that. Then you'll find some little thing at the store that is nice to keep."

The boys hurried with their breakfast and ran most of the way to the plaza. They burst into Mr. Lawrence's store panting and sweating.

"What have we here?" Mr. Lawrence's voice boomed.

"He," Carlos said pointing at Eduardo, "my little brother, he has some money to buy something."

"Oh, I see," said Mr. Lawrence. "Well, I have lots of dulces that boys like to eat."

"No sir," Roberto said, "we don't want anything to eat. We just finished eating."

"Then I can show you some other things, but how much money do you have to spend?" Eduardo took the coin out of his pocket and held it up for Mr. Lawrence to see. "Come I'll show you some knives for fifty cents. You'll like those." The boys followed him to the glass case at the back of the store. The case contained an assortment of penknives; next to them was a small toy gun like the one Eduardo had held the first time he went in the store with his father.

"That toy pistol," Eduardo asked without hesitation, "how much is that?"

Mr. Lawrence removed the cap gun from the case. "This sells for fifty cents with two boxes of caps included." Eduardo looked at his brothers and they nodded their heads. "I want that pistol, please," he said holding up his coin. Mr. Lawrence showed them how to load the caps into the gun before he handed it over to Eduardo. They all grinned, thanked Mr. Lawrence, and said goodbye.

Outside they clustered around Eduardo and took turns holding the gun and aiming it at imaginary targets. Then instead of taking the road home, Carlos led them up the river to an alcove where a small stream branched off from its main course and kept the grass cool and green. "Here is where we will play banditos," Carlos announced. "Eduardo will be the sheriff first because he has the pistol. The rest of us must find sticks to use as guns. The one who kills Eduardo first gets to become the new sheriff and use the pistol."

They slithered through the grass on their bellies. Terrible cries rang out as imaginary bullets knocked them to the ground. The pistol exchanged hands again and again. They splashed through the streams and sank dead into the moist coolness of the grass, forgetting all of their responsibilities at home. They played until Marcos began to cry because he was always the first one to be shot and had never gotten the chance to play sheriff. Finally, they gave him the pistol. Bang, bang, bang. He shot all three of them, and when they fell to the ground clutching at their wounds, he laughed until he wet his pants.

As they headed home, their empty stomachs told them that it was well past noon, and the sun was traveling toward the western horizon behind the sinister, black mountains. Their boyish chatter subsided as they left the sanctuary of the woods. Passing the blacksmith shop, they heard men's voices and saw smoke rising from the chimney. They peered through the door and saw Miguel with some of their neighbors. He was preparing to shoe draft horses. One of the men had a bottle of mula and was already drunk. The others were taking turns sipping from the bottle.

The boys left the shop and found their mother behind the house scrubbing a tub of dirty laundry. She ignored them at first; then she rose and looked them over scornfully. "And where were you all day?" She demanded, wiping her hands on her apron. She directed the question to Carlos.

"We were down the river," he replied sheepishly.

"Down the river. Is that all? You were down the river."

"No. We were playing," he confessed.

"So you were playing down the river. I thought you said you were going to the plaza to buy something at Mr. Lawrence's store."

"Yes, we did. We went to the plaza and Eduardo bought a toy. Then we went up the river to play with it."

"Eduardo bought a toy with the money I gave him, a toy!" an angry frown spread over her lips.

"Look Mamá," Eduardo held the gun up and smiled nervously.

"It's a pistol that makes noise almost like a real gun." He pulled the trigger and popped two of the remaining caps.

"Dios mío! You bought a stupid toy with the money I gave you. What a foolish waste. A stupid toy good for nothing. Surely I thought you would have found something more useful, Eduardo," she yelled at him. Eduardo ducked his head ashamed. She improvised a pistol by shaping her fingers. She pointed at first one child and then another. "Bang, bang, bang," her voice was becoming higher and hysterical. Her face was growing red like Fidelia's did when she became angry. "You are a foolish pack of children. And you are as filthy as pigs! Look! Look at Marcos! You let Marcos piss on himself! Go to the creek and wash yourselves, and you, Carlos, you make sure that Marcos takes off those filthy pants and you scrub them before you come back to the house," she screamed.

The boys turned and left. Their father was standing close by leaning against a tree laughing drunkenly. "Bang, bang, bang," he said as they passed him.

"Si, muy chistoso! Of course, you think it's very funny, Miguel. It's all very funny to you because you have been drinking with the neighbors, and now you are drunk so everything is all very funny." She pushed a strand of hair from her face and bent back over the tub of clothes.

Miguel walked toward her. "Elena," he said, "why are you so serious all the time? The children must play sometimes. They are not men yet. There is no harm in a little play."

"Easy for you to say," she snapped. "You're not here to see that your sons are cared for and to see that they mind me. If I allow them to play foolish games all day, who will help me do the work? Who will tend the garden and all of the animals? Who will see to it that three meals are always on the table, and who will see to it that the children are always safely in their beds at night? Not you, Miguel. You're rarely here to help me, and when you come home . . . look at you," she began to cry. "When you come home, you drink with the town drunkards." She wiped the tears off her cheeks. "No, Miguel, you don't know what it is like to worry for them when they're not home, or to worry if they will always have enough to eat every day, every week, every month. You don't know what that feeling is like, Miguel, and you never will," she sniffled.

Miguel turned and went back to his friends in the blacksmith shop. By dusk the last of the neighbors had headed toward their own homes. Elena was in the kitchen preparing dinner; curls of smoke billowed out of the chimney. All four boys were at the wood pile splitting and stacking logs.

Miguel left the shop slightly staggering. "You . . . you, muchachos . . ." He belched, swayed, and suddenly collapsed on the ground in front of them. Embarrassed, the children giggled nervously at the helpless form crumpled before them. Slowly he pulled himself to his hands and knees; his body rocked back and forth before a long stream of vomit shot out of his mouth and formed a sickening puddle on the ground in front of him. The boys turned their heads in shame and disgust. Carlos put down his ax and went to his father's side. He placed his hands firmly under Miguel's armpits and heaved him to an upright position on his knees.

"Bien borracho," he whispered shaking his head. Miguel lurched to his feet pulling himself free of Carlos's grasp, and in an attempt to balance himself, crashed backward against the wood pile. He cursed loudly, spat, and charged off in a reckless course to the blacksmith shop.

The boys huddled together listening as their father crashed about in the smith. "Bien borracho," Carlos repeated. The others nodded their heads. Within seconds, Miguel stepped back into sight at the doorway of the shop. In his left hand he held the sleek steel of a .22 rifle. Clumsily he loaded cartridges into the rifle and then charged back to where his sons stood.

"You cabroncitos," he snarled. "You like to play war? I'll teach you how to play war. I was there . . . in the war . . . in the filthy trenches with the rats . . . in the Argonne Forest. I can teach you what it's like, I know what it's like," he said, his glazed eyes set intently on the darkening forest around them.

"It was quiet sometimes," he continued as if talking to himself, "like it is now. I didn't even hear it at first, the terrible sound of the gas shells hissing through the air and landing softly in front of the trenches. I was on watch duty, but I didn't know what it was. They tell you what to expect, but it's not the same, no it's not the same," he laughed madly. "No. There was hardly enough light to see those ugly clouds of yellow gas rising up off of the ground and expanding. I watched too scared to move. I just watched," he began to cry and then started laughing. "But then another sentry farther down the line called the alert. 'Gas! Gas!' Finally I screamed, too. Gas! Gas! Gas!" He screamed and covered his face momentarily with his hands. "My eyes, my eyes," he yelled clutching at his face. "My eyes. I can't see. I can't see. My nose . . . my nose is bleeding; it's bleeding," he screamed, wiping at his nose with the back of his free hand. "Look! Look!" Miguel shouted dangling his hand in front of their faces. "It's bleeding!" he screeched. Horrified, the boys watched him. Miguel shook his head and began to laugh again.

"If you want to play war, I'll teach you," he said, pushing Carlos roughly. "Go over to that plow blade and get down behind it on your stomachs. I'm going to teach you what it's like to be shot at." His eyes were wild as he pointed to the plow that was near a shed about a hundred feet away. The boys stood still, baffled. "Go on," Miguel ordered. "Are you deaf? You heard what I said. Go and crawl behind that plow, and I'll show you. Now move."

Blindly all of the boys except Marcos hustled toward the shed. They scurried behind the blade with their heads pressed against the metal and their bodies stretched out behind them.

"What's the matter with him. Is he crazy?" said Roberto weakly.

"I don't know," whimpered Carlos. "Maybe so." Instinctively they covered their ears with their hands.

"Don't move," Miguel commanded. The rifle cracked and the first bullet plowed into the metal. Crack, crack, came two more shots from the rifle.

From the kitchen, Elena heard the gunfire. She looked out the window and saw Miguel standing at the wood pile firing the rifle at the plow. Marcos was sitting on the ground covering his ears with his hands and crying. She ran from the kitchen, grabbing a broom as she went. The first blow hit Miguel behind the knees, dropping him to the ground. Then blows fell on his head and shoulders as she screamed, "Are you crazy? Have you lost your mind? You are going to kill them."

The rifle fell from Miguel's hands; Elena shoved it with her foot and sent it sliding through the dirt. She kicked at Miguel who was now covering his head stupidly with his hands. After one more heavy blow to his head with the broom, she walked away and picked up the rifle. She dropped the broom and grabbed Marcos's arm, pulling him to his feet. Dragging him behind her, she walked toward the plow calling to the boys. Still dumbfounded they lay in the dirt near the plow. Finally they followed Elena into the house trying not to look at their father, who was still crouched on the ground rocking back and forth with his head in his hands.

Once the boys were inside the house, she returned to Miguel, where he knelt in the same position. "Get to your feet and find somewhere to sober up. If you ever drink whiskey here again, I'll shoot you myself. I will," she threatened. "You could have killed my children. You drunken bastard," she cried, slapping his head. "Get up and go wash yourself. You're a disgrace to me and your sons." She left and slowly he rose to his feet and walked off to the creek to bathe his face in the cold water. His head was already aching from the whiskey, but that would go away. The shame and pain in his heart never would.

Miguel waited until dinner was over and the lights were off in the house before he dared venture inside. He went first to the boys' room and stood in the doorway listening to their breathing. He shook his head; shame was with him, always with him. How, he asked himself, how could he have done that to his sons? How could he and the others have done what they did in France? He had seen too much. It was with him now and forever always on the fringes of his thoughts. Sometimes, like today, center stage in his mind and actions. But always in his dreams. Why? He wiped his eyes and nose. When was the last time he had slept peacefully like his sons were sleeping? He walked softly up to their bed; his hand hovered longingly over their dark forms. Perhaps he should wake them, try to explain. "No," he whispered. Hopefully he had not already ruined their dreams by his outburst. Finally he went to his wife's room. "Elena," he whispered.

"Shh . . . the baby is asleep. Come to bed. And don't speak of this day ever again. I want to forget this disgrace. I want to forget that it ever happened."

Miguel undressed and got stiffly into bed beside his wife. He lay on his back staring at the dark ceiling with his hands clamped tightly over his chest. He too wanted to forget; he only wished he could.

TWELVE

The last Saturday in September, José, Diego, and Eduardo set to work chopping wood after morning chores. As Diego paused to remove his shirt, in the warm sun, he looked up and whistled in wonder.

Pointing toward the fields behind the house, he said, "I'll be damned. Look. Look at that." Eduardo and José stopped their work and looked. Coming slowly down the field off of the wagon trail that led onto the llano was a ragtag company of Apaches. One man drove a buckboard pulled by two mules. The other nine rode potbellied mustangs, many of which were pintos. There were also four spotted mongrels loping beside them. Eduardo hopped on his chopping block to get a better view. They all had long black hair and wore the same kind of clothes. Only one of them was wearing a hat, a felt one like José and Miguel wore. All the others had wide strips of cloth tied around their heads to keep their hair back from their faces. These headbands were placed low on their foreheads, nearly covering their eyebrows and giving their black eyes a menacing appearance. As they rode closer, Eduardo could make out more details of their attire. His heart was pounding.

"Would you look at that," exclaimed Diego again.

"Es Juan," said José, beginning to smile. "It's my son."

The group rode past the house and directly up to the wood pile. Their dogs began to bark but stopped when one of the men yelled at them. Eduardo glanced at the house and saw that his grandmother, Carmen, and Rafelita had come out on the porch. They must have seen the Apaches even before Diego had. Juan came forward by himself. He was in the lead and slid easily off of his mount. His long, dark hair was streaked with white. Beside him were two young boys, maybe thirteen and ten, who rode double on a paint mustang. Juan motioned for them to dismount, and they slipped off the horse's back. José stepped forward and took Juan's hand in both of his. "Mi hijo," he said, his voice cracking. Juan stared at his father stonily, but José continued to pat Juan on the back repeating, "Welcome, my son." Juan spoke to the two young boys in Apache and they stepped closer to him and José. "Mis hijos," said Juan, "Utímio y David." José placed his hands on the boys' shoulders and smiled at them. "My grandsons," he smiled. They nodded and continued to look nervously first at José and then at Diego and Eduardo. Eduardo stood fast on the chopping block, but Diego had stepped up beside his father, smiling mischievously.

"You remember your brother Diego?" said José. "He was maybe as old as Utímio the last time you saw him." Juan nodded and accepted Diego's hand. José pointed to Eduardo and they directed their gaze on him. "This is Eduardo. He is the son of your sister Elena. He lives here with us," said José. Juan and the boys nodded. The rest of the company remained on their horses appraising Eduardo, José, and Diego as well as the house, sheds, and corrals. The old man driving the buckboard spoke to Juan in Apache. Then Juan said in slow, strained Spanish, "We want food. We haven't eaten in two days."

"Of course, of course, right away," said José, motioning for them to dismount. "Diego, show them where to put the horses." Then Juan spoke to his sons in their language, and they began to collect the reins of the horses as the men dismounted. Diego put on his shirt and took some of the horses toward the corral. Utímio and David led the rest. Only two of the horses were wearing saddles; the others had blankets spread over their backs.

Eduardo hopped off of the block of wood and followed Diego and the two boys. In the corral, Utímio and David pulled the blankets off of the horses and unbridled them. While they did this, Diego climbed over the corral rails and began pitching hay from the haystack into the corral. The mustangs kicked and bit each other to get at the food. Utímio and David began throwing the blankets over the rungs of the corral. Fascinated, Eduardo watched. Neither of the boys was as dark as some of the others, and their eyes were larger and more round, but their hair was long and wild just like Juan's and the other men's. They wore simple pullover shirts made of cotton flower sacks that were brightly colored in floral designs. Their baggy trousers were of a thicker, canvas-like cotton that had once been white but was now dark and mottled with oily stains. Their pant legs were tucked into hide moccasins that came up to their knees. The older boy had bands of leather tied around his wrists, and like the others, both of them wore wide headbands tied behind their heads. When they finished with the horses, they stared back at Eduardo. The older boy said something to the younger in their language. Then the older asked, "Do you speak English?"

Eduardo was shocked but found himself answering in English. "Yes. A little. I'm learning."

"We too, me and him," he said, pointing at his brother. "We are learning on the reservation at school."

"What's your name again?" the younger boy asked.

"Eduardo," he stammered.

"Eduardo, Eduardo," both boys repeated his name. Utímio continued, "We have a brother like you, about the same size. How old are you?"

"Almost eight," said Eduardo, relieved to see that Diego was rejoining them.

"So you speak English," said Diego, smiling his bright friendly smile.

"Yeah, we are learning," said the older boy. Both boys smiled warmly at Diego.

"Do you know some Spanish?" Diego asked.

"No . . . maybe only some words. No Spanish. Only my father speaks it."

"I wish I could speak Apache," Diego smiled.

"We can teach you," said the older boy.

"That's a deal," said Diego, still smiling as they joined the others back at the wood pile. Some of the men were sitting on blocks of wood, but most of them were crouched low to the ground on their haunches or sitting cross-legged in the wood chips. Utímio and David unharnessed the two old mules and took them to the corral. José had gone into the house to talk to the women about a meal. One of the younger men had a long buck knife that he was throwing at the ground. He held it by the tip and flipped it hard out of his hand, sinking it deep into the same spot on the ground at every throw. Eduardo watched the man, awed by his quick, steady aim. Finally the man glared at Eduardo and sheathed his knife in a strap on his knee-high moccasin.

Diego had seated himself on the ground by Juan so Eduardo joined them. They were sitting beside the old wagon that was held together in places by twine and wire. Some of the cracked spokes were splinted together with sticks and twine. The bed of the wagon was stacked high with deer hides and hand-woven baskets. Diego pointed at the wagon and asked in Spanish, "Where are you going with these things?"

"To the trade fair in Taos," answered Juan.

"You go there every year?"

"Yes, every year."

"What do you trade for?"

"We need salt, sugar, flour, cloth, blankets, and bullets."

"And do you make a fair trade?"

"Not like before, but we get enough."

Diego nodded and they were quiet for a few minutes. "Why are you so far south?" he asked. "If you're going to Taos, you're about sixty miles out of your way. It's a lot faster from the Jicarilla Reservation to Taos than from here."

"Yes, we were in Santa Clara two days ago. We traded baskets and dried venison for some clay pots. Pots bring better trade at the fair. Now we'll trade the pots in Taos. But we have no food. No food since two days before in Santa Clara."

"I understand," said Diego, looking toward the house where José appeared on the porch. Diego could see that his father's face was strained as he walked toward them. "The women were cooking when you came, but they are frying more potatoes and making more tortillas now. The food will be ready in a half an hour," José said to Juan and Diego. Juan translated to the rest of the group.

They nodded and began to speak among themselves. José sat on a block of wood and began talking to Juan.

Soon Carmen appeared on the porch, "Papá, Diego, Eduardo," she yelled, "I need you to help me bring the food out." The three of them went in the house and Carmen directed Diego and José to the heavier dishes and skillets. Eduardo took up the mountain of warm tortillas that were wrapped in a tea towel and headed for the door.

"Eduardo," yelled Fidelia, "come here. You're not going back out there. You stay here with me. Come back here." But he ignored her and broke into a run. At the wood pile he looked back at the house. Fidelia was standing on the porch with her hands on her hips shaking her head. He looked away from her and watched Rafelita coming toward them carrying two apple pies. He went to her and took one of them. Carmen began to serve the food. She took a bowl and ladled beans and chile into it, putting a large serving of fried potatoes and a thick slab of salty ham on the side. The men were standing in front of her, eyeing the food hungrily. She handed the first bowl to the man with the knife on his moccasin, but he shook his head and pointed at the apple pie. Carmen took up a piece of pie and placed it in the bowl on top of the beans. He took his bowl happily, picked up a tortilla, and walked away to eat. Raising her eyebrows, Carmen served the others.

Diego had brought over buckets of water and a wash pan and soap for washing, but these were ignored. The men took their bowls, sat down on the ground, and using their fingers like spoons, scooped food into their mouths. Their finger nails were dirt-caked and their hands black with dust and horse sweat from the long ride. Eduardo absorbed the spectacle unaware that he was staring. The older boy walked to Eduardo holding his bowl. He touched Eduardo's shoulder. "Eduardo, you come eat with us," he said. Eduardo went to Carmen and she served him a bowl of beans and chile. He took a spoon and went and sat on the ground by the boys and Juan. "What, you do not like this sweet food?" Utímio asked, pointing to his own piece of apple pie.

"Yes, I like it," said Eduardo, "but I will eat some later."

"Now, or later, no difference," shrugged the boy, smiling his friendly Baca smile.

One man picked up a spoon and dangled it under his ear lobe. He spoke in Apache and they all laughed. Juan smiled slightly and said, "He says it makes a good decoration for his ear." Eduardo, Diego, and the others grinned.

Carmen asked Utímio and David questions, which Diego translated to English for her. She was troubled by the way they spoke with full mouths and ate ravenously with their fingers, but she tried to hide her shock. José was the only one who did not stare at their guests. He ate little and talked to Juan, asking him about his family and life on the reservation. Juan answered his father's questions but offered no unsolicited information. He asked no questions of José or the others. No one mentioned Fidelia.

The meal over, Carmen began collecting the empty bowls, pots, and pans. When she walked onto the porch with the first load of dirty dishes, Fidelia met her in the doorway. "Don't even think of bringing those dishes in my kitchen. First, you make Eduardo help you scrub them outside at the well, and then I'm going to boil them. Who knows what kind of filth and disease those Indians carry."

"Bueno, Mamá," said Carmen wearily. She set the dishes on the porch. After she and Rafelita had gathered the last of the dishes, they went into the kitchen where Fidelia was pacing restlessly in front of the stove. She had already set two caldrons of water on the stove to boil. "After you wash the dishes with a lot of soap, I want every one of them scalded in these pots. Did you hear me, Carmen?"

"Yes, yes, Mamá," said Carmen. "I will. I promise that I will scald every last one of them." She sat down at the table and buried her face in her hands. She looked up at Fidelia, "Mamá, I think you should go see Juan."

"No!" screamed Fidelia. "He made his choice. He prefers those . . . those filthy heathens to us. Let him have them. Let him have the filthy, uncivilized bastards."

"But mother, the children, two of his sons are with him. Who knows, maybe they'll never come here again. Don't you want to see the children, your grandchildren?" asked Carmen, looking her mother boldly in the face.

Fidelia reached out and slapped Carmen once, drew back her hand to hit again but stepped away crying. "Those are no grandchildren of mine; don't you call them my grandchildren. Don't you understand? Those are thieves . . . Apaches . . . filthy Apaches. Heathens," she said rushing out of the door and along the porch to her room. Carmen and Rafelita heard the door open and slam shut.

"This is very difficult for her. You have to try to understand that, Carmen," said Rafelita.

"Yes," sighed Carmen, rubbing her cheek, "I try to understand, but why does she make it worse for herself? She makes everything much worse than it is. Why does she have to do that?"

"Try to think how you would feel if Eduardo disappeared and you didn't know if he were dead or alive. Every time someone mentions Juan's name, or when he suddenly shows up, she has to relive all those years of pain. He was her first child. No one can give those years back to her. No one can take the pain away, and nothing will ever bring Juan back to her. His visits only remind her that he was once a part of her. Perhaps it's easier for her to hate. It's all she's had during these years of suffering."

"Perhaps you're right, but he is still her son. I think it would have been easier for her if Juan had died."

"Don't say that and don't judge her so harshly. It's not our place to judge her. She cares, but it's hard for her to show people that she cares. She finds other ways to show it. She helped prepare all of that food, didn't she? And don't forget, it was your mother who brought me here to live with you after my parents died. No one made her do that; she has a good heart."

"I don't know," sighed Carmen, getting up from the table. "Come. I think we have some shirts that will fit Utímio and David." Rafelita followed Carmen upstairs to their room.

By 3:00 P.M. Juan and his group were making ready for their departure. They and their ponies were well fed and rested and José had given them provisions for the rest of the journey. He had offered to let them spend the night, but Juan said that they wanted to travel to Los Ojos before nightfall. Then they would only have a two-day ride to Taos. They were standing by their horses ready to leave when the man who wore the knife on his moccasin spoke to Juan in Apache. Juan asked for liquor and José sent Diego to the cellar for two gallons of apple wine. After that the party did not linger long over goodbyes. Juan and his sons shook hands with José, Diego, and Eduardo; Carmen gave each of the boys a white shirt and crying, kissed their cheeks. The group mounted and set off with a nod of thanks to their hosts.

Diego was the first to break the long silence after the band was almost out of sight. "Phew," he snorted, "they smelled like a herd of billy goats."

"Bueno, they've been traveling for a long time," added José dryly.

Diego wisely changed the subject. "I have to say that Juan looks good." He grinned, "I guess having two wives and ten children agrees with him. Did you see, Carmen, Juan looks exactly like Papá. He's going to have the same white hair before long. And those boys of his, Utímio and David, they're handsome."

"That's true. Anyone should be proud to have such handsome children," smiled Carmen. "And Papá, Diego is right. Juan looks more like you than any of the rest of us." José smiled and put his arm around Carmen's shoulders.

"All of those Apaches are good looking people, with the exception of that one ugly bastard with a crushed-in face . . . the one who kept playing with his knife. I didn't like him at all," said Diego.

"He scared me," said Eduardo "but I liked Juan and Utímio and David."

"I like them too, conejo," said Diego, ruffling Eduardo's hair. "Maybe you and I should grow our hair long like theirs. What do you think?" Eduardo giggled with Rafelita.

"Don't even say that, Diego. Mamá would shoot you both," said Carmen.

"Well," sighed José, "now they're gone. Maybe for good. Who knows, but I'm glad they visited. Now I know Juan is alright and his family is also fine. It did my heart good to see him and the two boys. It's a pity that your mother won't see them, but now it's over, and we've still got some hard work ahead of us," he said, nodding toward the wood pile. Diego and Eduardo collected their axes and went back to work beside José.

Carmen and Rafelita went to the well and drew water to scrub the dishes as they had promised Fidelia. They poured water into a wash tub and scrubbed the dishes with mounds of soap. After they finished washing and they carried the dishes into the kitchen for scalding, Fidelia joined them in the kitchen. First she dropped the spoons and ladles into one caldron and left them to boil. Then she submerged the tin soup bowls in the boiling water and after ten minutes fished them out with a wooden spoon. As she worked over the boiling pots, the anger began to subside. The purification of her dishes lightened her anguish. When the dishes were done, Fidelia was hit with a manic burst of energy and she set to scouring the entire kitchen. Hours later, she collapsed onto a chair at the kitchen table and rolled herself a well-earned cigarette. Puffing, she proudly admired the polished windows, the spotless counters and cabinets. She had climbed on a chair to dust the vigas with a moist rag, and now she was waiting for the newly scrubbed linoleum under her feet to dry. She had purged Juan from her thoughts; he might try to return like the dust and cobwebs to her kitchen, but she would wash them away again. Keeping her house in its immaculate state was one element that she controlled absolutely. She finished her cigarette, stood up, and wiped down the table top and cupboards for the fourth time, erasing the invisible dregs of life.

Later that night, long after the others had retired, Rafelita and Diego lay on a blanket in a field that had already been shorn of its crop. The night sky was clear and starry. The silhouette of the house loomed before them and the farm slept. They held onto one another, shivering in the cold night air. Neither of them spoke; their talks had never brought resolutions. They clung to each other, desperate to draw that which no one has, but everyone craves.

THIRTEEN

Diego was on the bay waiting for Eduardo when the last bell rang to release the students for the afternoon. The tremendous horse snorted impatiently, pounding the ground with his hooves. A thick cloud cover had settled over the valley and it was warm for late November, almost balmy, as sometimes happens before a heavy snow fall. The children—awed by the pending storm—left their classrooms quietly. It was cold enough that their breath turned to a smoky vapor when they exhaled.

Eduardo walked to Hero's shoulder and looked up at Diego; they grinned at each other and Eduardo stroked the bay's neck before he stretched up to be hoisted onto Hero's back behind Diego. "It'll be snowing soon," Diego commented, almost to himself as they rode out of the school yard. The bay broke into a swift, steady trot on the dirt road that led to the plaza. Riding through the main and only street in the town, they saw a group of men huddled under one of the sheds behind Mr. Lawrence's store. The men had built a fire in a large barrel to warm themselves while they talked.

"What's this important meeting for?" Diego shouted.

Fidel, Diego's best friend, was in the group. He had quit school years ago, though he was younger than Diego. "We're celebrating for you escueleros and this beautiful sunny day," he yelled. "Get down from that horse and join us."

Diego and Eduardo stabled the bay in a shed opposite the store and joined the others around the barrel of fire. Fidel greeted Diego with a slap on the back. Fidel had strong Indian features, and his teeth flashed a bright contrast against his smooth dark skin. "And you Eduardo," asked Fidel, "what's new?"

Eduardo smiled and kicked at the ground, "Everything's the same as ever," he said looking up at Fidel.

"That's safe," nodded Fidel, dragging on his cigarette. Diego found an empty milk crate and turned it upside down to sit on. The men were drinking whiskey; some of them smoked and others chewed tobacco. Eduardo knew that they would be staying for a long time, so he squatted on his haunches at Diego's feet and listened to the men talk. Tiny flakes of snow had begun to fall.

Mano Agapito, a bent and shriveled little man with a tongue like a parrot's, was complaining that one of his cows had died the previous night for no visible reason. "I saw her just before I went inside for the night, and she was fine. She was eating hay and nursing her calf. There was nothing wrong with her."

"Where did you keep her?" a man named Albino inquired.

"Why, in the pasture with all of the others," the old man explained excitedly. "There was nothing wrong with her, I tell you."

"Impossible," said Fidel, "there had to be a sign. Maybe you didn't examine the carcass well. There has to be a sign somewhere. She was sick, or she ate something like a piece of wire, or maybe someone . . ."

"Like I say," interrupted Mano Agapito, "I checked her for everything. There was no sign. Nothing. She wasn't even weak or sick and then suddenly dead. I don't understand it," he said, shaking his head.

"Mano," said Fidel, "did you cut her open?"

"No. Why should I cut her open?" snapped Mano Agapito. "I already said that there was no sign, no slobber, no sign of bloat, no blood. Why should I cut her open?"

"Well, Mano," said Fidel picking at a callous on his hand, "it sounds to me like maybe someone got rid of that cow for you."

"What are you talking about, 'got rid of her for me?' " demanded Mano Agapito.

Fidel sighed, "Well, what you said about not finding any signs on her reminds me of something a man I know once told me." Fidel smiled. "This man told me how one could kill an animal without leaving a sign on the carcass."

"What are you talking about?" said Mano Agapito angrily.

"Naturally, I would not know if this is true," said Fidel still smiling, "but I was told that if the animal is shot straight in the rectum, there is no sign left on the body. Which is not to say that's what happened to your cow, Mano," consoled Fidel. "Nevertheless, your story is very curious."

Mano Agapito was red in the face and working his toothless mouth, but no words came. "Calm down, Mano," said Diego, trying to disguise a grin. "You don't know if your cow was shot up the rectum. Besides, if you want to make sure, you just have to cut her open. You'll be able to see if her guts were shot. Maybe you could even find the bullet."

"Fidel is right," sputtered Mano Agapito, licking his dry lips with his round dry tongue, "that cow was shot, and after I make sure, I'm going to get the bastard who did it. Give me time and I'll fix him, you watch."

"Yes, it's a sad thing that men cannot trust their neighbors. Alas, we all know that it's the nature of men to be jealous of what others own," said Diego sympathetically. "But Mano, you can't be sure that your cow was killed. You make sure before you get yourself too excited, or before you go out and try to shoot your neighbor."

All of the men were trying to contain their amusement, but Mano Agapito was now determined. "The bastard. I'll fix him. You watch, I'll get my revenge," he promised, sucking on his pint of mula.

Diego coughed to keep from laughing. "There is no end to it, Mano. Who is ever the first man to seek vengeance? When is one's innocence truly spoiled, and in the end, is there fairness or happiness in retribution? Who knows? I don't know," he said as he took a drink.

"That's true," said someone else, and they all drank and watched the snow fall.

"Take conejo here," Diego continued, "to my knowledge he has yet to spoil his innocence, but perhaps today . . . perhaps tomorrow. Who knows? One day, or another, eventually it happens to all of us, and then there's no return to innocence. Jealousy, anger, lust, greed, vengeance, and hatred, they spoil men's lives. We are all victims; there is no escape."

The men were silent. They stared at the snow, which was pelting the ground in smooth even sheets. Diego sent Eduardo into the store to buy some chocolate bars. When he returned to the shed, he noticed that in the short time he was gone the snow had become deeper, and it continued to fall in heavy layers. He sat on a block of wood near the warm barrel and ate his chocolate bar that was turning white from having been on the shelf for so long.

"What Diego said is right," began Albino. "There is no end to it . . . the jealousy, the hatred, the vengeance. But I confess that I have taken it upon myself to repay a certain man for his wrongdoing to me. You see, I have a fine stallion. You all know him. Anyway, this neighbor of mine has three mares. Never once has my neighbor asked to use my stud to breed his mares, but on many occasions I have found my stud grazing happily in the field with those mares. Of course, not once has he been cut or scratched, as he would be if he had jumped a fence to get into the pasture. Naturally, I suspected what was happening, but I had no proof."

Albino spit a brown line of tobacco juice against the barrel of fire; it sizzled and burned away.

"Finally, late one evening I got my proof. I was standing in a grove of trees at the end of my fields cleaning an irrigation ditch when I saw my good neighbor hopping the fence into my property. I watched as he walked up to my stud with a bucket of grain and coaxed him through the gate into the pasture with those mares. I didn't try to stop him, but I decided it was time to collect my stud fees for those colts. After all, by now his mares have had five foals from my stallion, a good stallion. That miser owes me stud fees, but I've never seen a dime." Albino kicked the barrel of fire, and a spray of sparks flew into the darkness. "Of course, I confronted him and told him that he has five horses from my stud. I told him I wanted ten dollars for each horse, which is nothing, but he only laughed. And you won't believe what he said. He told me, 'Compadre, I got these foals off a stud from over the hills. What are you talking about?' I told him I had watched him coax the stallion into his field, but he laughed and denied it. Then I vowed to myself that I would seek revenge."

Albino paused and chuckled, "I took my time because time is all I have. The thing passed, and I was even friendly with my good neighbor. We talked and drank a bottle of wine together from time to time. I waited and waited and waited. Then a few years later my neighbor bought a fine bull. It was a big strong bull, and it kept all of the cows with calves. My neighbor, he was very proud and very happy with his bull. He even told me once, 'Compadre, for a fee I'll let you put my bull to your cows, and since we're friends and neighbors, I'll even give you a good price.'" Albino chuckled again, "Can you believe that? He was going to give me a good price. I said, 'Very well, compadre, one of these days I'll use your bull and I'll pay you your good price.' And I waited." Albino laughed long and hard. "Then the next spring my good neighbor found his fine bull standing alone in the corner of the pasture. It was spring time and of course that bull should have been in the middle of the herd chasing the cows, but he was standing alone in the corner very sad and ashamed because his testicles had been cut away in the dark of night," Albino grinned. "A prime breeding bull castrated in the prime of his life."

Mano Agapito licked his thin lips. "And your neighbor, your neighbor," he said quickly, "what did your neighbor do?"

"Mano Agapito, what could my good neighbor do? It's certain that he never collected more calves or breeding fees off of his fine bull; it was much too late for that, and what could he do?" said Albino proudly. They all laughed.

"That's very funny, primo," said Diego, rolling a cigarette. "But now you probably can't sleep at night wondering what your good neighbor will think of to get his revenge against you."

"Against me? Who said that I castrated that bull?" said Albino, smiling.

"Of course, who said that you castrated that bull, Albino. And you, Fidel, who told you that story about shooting the cows up the rectum?" asked Diego.

Fidel made his toothy smile. "Hombre, I'm not telling you nothing," he said in English. "Let's just say my good neighbor told me about it."

"Well, if you ask me, I say it's all absurd," said Diego. "None of it makes any sense. I stab you in the back so you stab me in the back and then I have to stab you again and it goes on like that forever. It's ignorant."

"I don't know if it's ignorant, Diego. I mean someone has to even out the odds," said Albino.

"What are you talking about, even out the odds?" asked Diego.

"Well, for example, let's say my neighbor has fifteen cows and I only have four. Well, then it makes sense that during the summer, when those cows are up in the mountains on the summer range, maybe two or three of my neighbor's cattle will be poached when I might not lose a single cow."

"That's where you're wrong, friend," said Diego. "I can promise you that your good neighbor will poach a cow from you, or someone else, for every one he lost. You think just because he has a few more cattle he's not going to try to replace the ones that someone stole from him? It doesn't matter whose cow it is, a cow is a cow, qué no?"

"That's true, Diego," Mano Agapito piped in. "There's no law that says a rich man has a pure heart. Besides, Albino, how do you think the rich get rich in the first place," he said, shaking a finger. "I'll tell you how. If they don't inherit everything they have, then they get it through a lot of hard work and a lot of dirty work, and that's how it is," he said. "And it takes a lot of hard work and a lot of dirty work to keep a rich man rich. That's what my father always used to say. God bless him."

"You tell him how it is, Mano Agapito," laughed Fidel.

"Look, like I already said, it makes no difference if someone has ten cows or one hundred cows. That's not the point. The point is that if all of the good people in the valley would butcher their own animals, then everyone could stop stealing from their neighbors to try to make up for their losses," said Diego. "And you all know that's the truth, but it's never going to change."

"Yes, it often happens," agreed a quiet man named Simon, "that a man becomes jealous of what another man owns, so he takes it upon himself to make things more even. But whatever he does will come back to him just like Diego said and just like it says in the Bible." They watched the snow falling beyond the arch of light that was cast by their fire. Mr. Lawrence came out of the store and locked up for the night. He said good night to all of them and walked into the darkness in the direction of his home.

Finally Fidel broke the silence. "What's all this serious talk about right and wrong? Diego, when did you become so holy?"

"Hey, you don't see no pair of wings on my shoulders or no halo around my head do you? I didn't say I was above vengeance. I only said it doesn't make sense." He took a swing from the bottle that Fidel passed to him. It was silent under the shed except for the crackling of the fire in the barrel; they passed the bottle without speaking. "If the snow falls like this all night, there will be more than three feet in the morning," one of them noted.

"Bueno," Diego remarked, "I should take Eduardo home before long, even though they'll probably close the school tomorrow. Eduardo, go for the horse and we'll leave."

Eduardo unfolded himself from the ball he had tucked his body into to keep warm. When he left the canopy of the shed, the snow flakes covered him and turned to water on his cheeks. The snow was well above his ankles now, and after he took a few steps, the snow made its way up his pant leg and chilled his skin. He was anxious to be on Hero, where at least his feet would not get wet. And he welcomed the thought of something warm to eat and then getting into bed under the thick quilts that awaited him at home. He hoped that Fidelia would not be too angry with Diego for keeping him out so late. With luck she had gone to bed hours ago.

In the shed, it was dark and silent. Eduardo made a clicking noise with his tongue, but Hero did not make his usual snorting, stomping response. It was too quiet. Eduardo hurried along the wall of the shed until he found the rope that secured the bay to the post. The line was taut, and a few feet from the wall Eduardo felt the stallion's head suspended by the tether where he had gone down. Eduardo whirled screaming, "Tío, tío, tío! Something is wrong. Something bad has happened to Hero." His voice was shrill and strong and carried clearly to the others.

The men met Eduardo between the sheds. Diego ran past Eduardo, and Fidel followed carrying a torch from the barrel. The burning stick of wood illuminated Hero's crumpled body. His forelegs and haunches were sprawled and he had apparently kicked frantically. His long neck was stretched out, hanging from the tether line. A thick froth coated his mouth and drooled down, frozen to his chin. The bay's body was still warm but lifeless and undignified. Diego ran his hands gently over the horse's nose and muzzle and over the slender ears, as he had done so many times before. He tangled his fingers in the mane. Trembling, he felt his heart constricting. The heaviness traveled into his limbs and numbed his mind to everything except the raging pain within him.

The others stared at Diego; Eduardo had begun to cry. Fidel went forward and put his hand firmly on Diego's shoulder. "Calmate, calmate, hombre," he soothed.

Diego wrenched himself free and cringed against the wall. His eyes burned wildly. "Calm myself," he said. "I am calm."

"It looks like poison," Simon said. "Look at the slobber and the way he kicked. This is a bad omen. All this talk of vengeance it comes to no good. Why would someone poison this horse?"

"Jealousy, why else?" added Albino. "I'm surprised it didn't happen sooner, but why here? Why tonight? We didn't hear or see anyone or anything. This is strange."

Mano Agapito waggled his jaws for a few seconds without forming words. Then he licked his lips. "I don't like this. I don't like this. I'm going home." Once more he repeated, "I'm going home now," and then staggered out of the shed into the falling snow.

"Diego, come on, let's go. You can't do anything here, especially not tonight. We'll come back in the morning. Come on. Albino and I will take you and Eduardo home," said Fidel, putting his hand on Diego's shoulder again, but Diego pushed Fidel's hand away. The others stared at Diego and then Fidel. "Very well, Diego, at least, I'll take Eduardo home. Don't worry about him." They all turned to leave. Eduardo lingered. He looked at the dead horse; the big round eyes were open and staring but the light was gone from them. Eduardo looked at his uncle leaning against the wall like a stone man. Before he left the shed, he went to the bay and stroked its mane. Then he pulled out some of the coarse hair, curled it around his finger, and tucked it into his breast pocket. He went to Diego and embraced him tightly around the waist; Diego did not move, but he mumbled, "The good people of Los Torbellinos." Still crying, Eduardo turned and raced into the storm to find Fidel.

FOURTEEN

A string of bad luck is worse than a year of bad luck, or even seven. A string of bad luck might continue forever. And a string of bad luck was exactly what Fidel had predicted the night the stallion was killed.

"You watch," Fidel had cautioned Eduardo the night he took him home after they found Hero dead. "You watch, if it isn't true. A string of bad luck always follows when an animal dies on the night of the full moon." It had been a full moon on that night years ago because as they were riding home a strange thing happened; the snow had stopped and the clouds spread allowing the glowing orb of the full moon to show itself eerily for a few minutes before the storm resumed. And it was precisely then that Fidel had cursed and crossed himself and made his prediction.

Eduardo had never doubted what Fidel had said. First of all, the bay was gone. Eduardo had loved Hero. He used to take apples and sugar out to the barn and feed them to the stallion when no one else was around. He stayed with the horse for hours, stroking his chest, rubbing his ears, and talking to him. He even used to say, "I love you, Hero," and he knew that Hero loved him too from the way the big horse nuzzled him with his soft nose and nipped him gently on the neck and shoulders.

Of course, after his horse was poisoned, Diego was never the same again. He was bitter and gone most of the time. When he came home, he was either drunk or acting crazy, trying to make people believe that he was a brujo. He said cruel things to all of

121

them, but especially to Rafelita, who finally moved away to live with relatives in Santa Fe. There was an uncanny emptiness in the house and in their hearts after she was gone. It seemed that Diego drank even more once Rafelita left. So naturally Diego and Fidelia fought constantly, and beside the heavy emptiness, there was always tension and anger.

Then the worst happened. Fidelia became ill with cancer. Even in his most frightening nightmares, Eduardo never experienced an event as horrible as her disease, and he saw how her illness changed them all. The cancer sapped the life out of the family just like it did Fidelia.

For months after the doctor told her she had cancer, Fidelia seemed undaunted. She carried on with her scrupulous house-keeping, cooking, and gardening as always. At first, it did not seem like the cancer could break her courage, but gradually she slowed and was later confined to bed with the will but no energy to fight. The final months before her death had been miserable for the entire family and agonizing for Fidelia. The doctor could only prescribe morphine to deaden the pain that ate away at her chest. And when Fidelia was not in a stupor from the heavy doses of morphine, she only prayed for death.

Eduardo was twelve when they buried his grandmother. He moved back to his parents' house up the canyon soon after her funeral because he never felt whole in her house after the long illness. After Fidelia's death, José could not bring himself to move back into the bedroom he had shared with his wife for almost a lifetime. When Fidelia had become bedridden, he set up a cot in the sala, where he slept when not tending to his wife. And even though they burned all of Fidelia's clothes and the mattress and curtains and rugs and had scrubbed the room, repainted it, and aired it for weeks, José never slept there again. He continued to sleep in the sala. Eduardo understood how his grandfather felt because neither could he bear to be near the room where she had lain dying for almost a year.

But Eduardo left that behind him in El Valle; he worked hard to purge the experience from his memory. Besides, perhaps the move back to his parents' would break the string of bad luck. He felt certain that nothing could be as terrible as that last tragic year of Fidelia's life.

By the time Eduardo moved into the house, his little sister, Feliz, was almost six years old. Pedro had been born a year after Feliz, and now there was also Simonita, the youngest of the Montez children. There were eight of them living in the two-bedroom adobe house. Feliz and Simonita slept in the bedroom with Elena, but when their father was home, they slept on a foldaway bed in the sala. There were two double beds and a twin bed in the boys' room. The house was crowded and life was hectic, which was exactly what Eduardo needed to help him forget. He was happy to be home, where he was surrounded by noise and life and the obnoxious influence of Roberto.

Roberto was the desperado of the family. His deviousness was as much a part of him as the coarse, black beard that had forced him to begin shaving at age twelve. Almost daily he caroused the neighborhood searching for the slightest opportunity to sow havoc, although he himself was uncertain whether the drive came from the act of making mischief or the challenge of evading punishment for his terrible crimes. When Carlos was too busy for him, Roberto exerted his corrupting leverage over Eduardo and Marcos. The two became his cohorts, not because they too lacked conscience, but because they lacked the will to resist him. However, if they had not been there to follow, Roberto would have managed his sinister feats alone.

Most of Roberto's deeds were spontaneous impulses, such as the time the neighbor's yellow tomcat wandered into the garden where the three boys were working. The cat began to rub against Roberto's legs, purring contentedly, so he bent down and collected the friendly animal into his arms. Cuddling it, he bluntly commanded Marcos to run to the house and fetch matches and a jar of kerosene. Later, like a doctor cleansing a wound, Roberto doused the cat's tail in the kerosene, explaining that the show was much more lively if only the tail were ignited. Otherwise, the creature would expire too soon. Roberto laughed with glee when the cat set out screeching across the meadow with its tail aflame. Eduardo and Marcos laughed, too, but only in grim horror and guilt. They might as well have been the ones to light the match because from the instant Roberto cuddled the cat in his arms they knew its luck was out.

The incidents of that summer eventually became enduring, unspeakable boyhood secrets etched vividly into Eduardo's memories. At any time in his later life he could envision each scenario as if it were happening before him on a screen. *Ah . . . there they were, luxuriating, lolling, rolling, swimming through the lushness of Mr. Lujan's corn patch. They left the cool sea at midnight under a spray of stars, and the damage behind them could not have been equalled by a herd of wild horses set free in the field for a week.*

What now? Three figures run clumsily with their heavy burdens and stop at the river bank to spill stolen pumpkins out of gunny sacks. A trill of wicked laughter slices the silence as the first pumpkin is smashed. The pumpkin battle begins. Aim. Bull's eye! Laughter. Pain. Run. Aim. Bull's eye! Revenge! More laughter. The last pumpkin is gone. Their battle ground is strewn with the remains of Mr. Trujillo's pumpkin crop. Their bare chests are slick with sweat and mush, their pants coated with goo. Their hair is sticky, clumped together. How will they explain to their mother? A huge clump of orange pulp slides off of Eduardo's head. A seed is clinging to Marcos's ear, and Roberto's eye is beginning to swell. Hysterical laughter ensues.

Off again, boys? Sh . . . the three are crouched behind a wood pile trying to steal a big, fat, white hen out of the Trujillo's front yard. Quiet. Here she comes. Quick as lightning she is snatched up and tucked under Roberto's arm. Her beak is closed tight with his free hand. The three of them race across the creek where the Trujillos keep their starving pigs inside a rickety pen. Whoosh . . . the white hen is up in the air, almost flying, flapping her wings in desperation. For an instant she is suspended over the gruesome, upturned faces of the pigs. Oops. The pigs snatch the poor hen out of the air and render her to pieces. Chomp, chomp, chomp. A flash of red and white splashes across the boys' field of vision. Then even the piercing screams of the pigs stop. They are smacking, grunting and sniffing through the dirt at the remaining feathers. Time to move on, muchachos.

"Oh no! it can't be. Mrs. Vigil was not supposed to be home," mumbles Roberto over a mouthful of apricots. Corpulent Mrs. Vigil is coming toward them with her sturdy broom in hand. They are treed in Mrs. Vigil's

orchard. Their pockets bulge with evidence. Eduardo and Marcos look to Roberto for directions. He spits the fruit out of his mouth. "On the count of three we jump," he instructs. "She's too fat. She'll never catch us. Uno, dos, tres," and they all jump. Eduardo and Marcos hit lightly on the ground and run. Roberto trips and falls over himself. Half of his shirt is still up in the apricot tree. Mrs. Vigil is on him in a heartbeat punishing him with her broom.

Eduardo and Marcos wait loyally at the edge of the orchard while Roberto takes his beating. At last, they are running together again, the three of them. "Cabróna," Roberto pants, "Qué cabróna. I will have to visit her again. Wait until she tells Mamá of this. Qué cabróna. I will visit her again." They catch the beating of their lives at home, but soon resume their travels about the neighborhood. Then suddenly the summer and boyhood had stretched into a corner; school began the following day.

Their days in the classroom lagged into dull, endless hours that were too boring to remember with definition. Carlos had graduated from middle school the previous spring and now he would attend the new Los Torbellinos High School located near the plaza. Roberto, Eduardo, Marcos, and the rest of the Montez children walked to the schoolhouse located a quarter of a mile up the canyon from their home. Their teacher was Mr. Vigil, the very husband of the neighbor who a few weeks earlier had treed the Montez boys in her orchard. Mr. Vigil was a robust, short man with a shock of close-cut black hair and loose red lips that waggled when he spoke. Mr. Vigil had only completed the ninth grade himself, but he could read, write, and speak English, and he was entirely responsible for the boredom the students experienced in his classroom.

The schoolhouse was a square, tin-roofed adobe structure built in the 1920s. Inside, a wooden partition ran down the middle of the building separating it into two classrooms. Students aged six to nine sat on one side; the older students sat on the other. Mr. Vigil took turns working a few hours with the younger group and then a few hours with the older group. Each school day began the same; after they recited the Pledge of Allegiance outside the schoolhouse, Mr. Vigil rang the hand-held bell and classes began. In the morning, Mr. Vigil disappeared behind the partition to work with the younger children while the older children practiced their penmanship. Through the partition they heard Mr. Vigil begin his lesson. "Rat, rat, rat, tat, tat," he said, pointing to words on the chalkboard. "Rat, rat, rat, tat, tat," the little children recited. Miraculously most of Mr. Vigil's pupils learned to speak English and to read and write.

Of course, Roberto did what he could to disturb the peace, but the schoolhouse was Mr. Vigil's domain. The man's title, his reputation, his pride in being a schoolteacher were invincible to insult and immune to injury. Year after year he had subdued the rebellious elements in his schoolhouse—the likes of Roberto —through passive resistance. The pain of the straight pins that Roberto planted in Mr. Vigil's chair never seemed to phase him, for he did not so much as flinch when he sat down on them. He slightly grimaced as he stood to extract the pins from his rear, but without a curse or a reprimand he lined the pins up on his desk. The plump bull snake that Roberto tucked into his teacher's desk drawer may have brought a slightly better reaction, still the deed was hardly worth the effort. Roberto's wicked endeavors flatly failed to rouse Mr. Vigil's anger, and there was no sport without a good show of anger.

Determined to see some kind of reaction on Mr. Vigil's expressionless face, Roberto crept into the schoolhouse one night and sawed half way through the legs of his teacher's chair. The next day when Mr. Vigil took his seat at the head of the class, his chair held up for about four minutes before the legs collapsed and sent the teacher's thick rear heavily to the floor. Slowly Mr. Vigil rose to his feet. He dusted off the seat of his pants and dryly ordered some of the boys to clear away the debris. The bland expression on his face killed the laughter in the classroom almost immediately, and as ever there was no trace of anger or any other emotion. He was that boring.

"He might as well be dead," Roberto mumbled. And in the end, in defeat, the boy attacked his studies and became a good pupil. It was that or die of boredom. They read, they wrote, they did mathematics, and they studied American history. "It's killing my spirit," Roberto said calmly every day at lunch as he tore into his tortilla and bit off a chunk of his boiled potato. "It's just so damned boring that it's finally killing my spirit."

It was no great shock to Eduardo and Marcos when Roberto hooked up for good with Carlos and his friends from the high school. Perhaps they were even relieved, though they could not quite shed the shadow of their deeds. Roberto had to find new ground to conquer, but they were stuck with his legacy.

One Saturday in the late fall, the four Montez boys finished their chores early, so Carlos and Roberto announced that they were going to the waterfalls with some other boys from the high school. Eduardo and Marcos followed them secretly, but soon one of the older boys spotted them. Carlos sent them home, saying they did not want kids tagging after them.

"Well, at least we're finished with our work for the day," Eduardo said, trying to console himself and Marcos.

"Yes," Marcos agreed. "But what do you think those high school boys are doing with Roberto?"

"It's more like what is Roberto doing with those high school boys. Roberto," Eduardo spat the name in disgust.

"Yes, Roberto," Marcos reiterated.

"Listen, Marcos, I saw a fancy tray of biscochitos with jam and peanut butter and fresh bread set out in the kitchen. Feliz told me that they are for the Trujillo sisters. They're coming over later to visit with mother."

"Sugar cookies with jam and peanut butter and fresh bread?" Marcos noted with interest.

They found the tray in the kitchen with a tea towel spread over it just as Eduardo had described. They could hear their mother and the girls cleaning the sala. Marcos picked up the jar of peanut butter and loaf of bread and walked out the kitchen door. Eduardo shrugged, filled his pockets with cookies, and followed Marcos out of the house.

FIFTEEN

Eduardo and his brothers stood at the back of the church on Ash Wednesday solemnly watching a group of men who had arrived at Mass early. They were the Brothers of Light, a sect of the most devout Catholics. These men had become members of the brotherhood by making a personal vow to keep the commandments of God. The Penitentes, or Brothers of Light, aimed to imitate Jesus Christ by perfect observance of the duties of a Christian and sought individual empathy with the Savior through physical suffering. Penitentes practiced their ritual most righteously during Lent, going far beyond the acts of penance customary for a good Catholic. For Penitentes the holy season of Lent was not only a time to forsake all vices but a time to relive the passion of Christ's crucifixion.

The Brothers of Light were all ordinary men of the community, but tonight, as they sat close to the altar, they seemed more elevated than the rest. Their faces were void of all emotion. Perhaps they were enthralled by the words of the priest, or perhaps they were contemplating the grim, holy vigil they were to undertake during the next forty days.

After Mass, the Penitentes had their foreheads smeared with ashes and took confession like everyone else. Then in a procession they walked to their own place of worship, the morada. Fermín Velásquez, the hermano mayor, led the brothers in song and prayer as they marched. Despite the cold, many members of the congregation, including the priest and the Montez boys, joined in the night walk.

Once inside the small, adobe building the hermano mayor conducted the prayer and after an hour all but the hermanos rose to leave. The brothers would now convene for hours in private. Only the Brothers of Light who had gone through the rigorous initiation rites and secret vows knew what occurred during these meetings. And they were sworn to secrecy.

As the Montez boys walked home, Carlos explained what would happen. "They are going to hold meetings every Friday until Holy Week. Then they'll stay at the morada all the time from Tuesday night until daybreak of Holy Saturday."

"But during Holy Week, they pray and serve penance with the most severity," Roberto said.

"Yes, remember, it was last year during Holy Week that we prayed with them at the cross outside the morada?" Carlos added.

"Yes. It was cold, beginning to snow, and still they had their shirts off, whipping themselves," Roberto grimaced. "I think they have to be a little crazy."

"Roberto, the hermanos are the holiest men in Los Torbellinos, and you call them crazy. What's the matter with you?" Carlos scolded.

"No one could pay me enough to do that to myself," Roberto retorted.

"That doesn't surprise me," said Carlos sarcastically. "You don't have the faith or the courage or the strength that they have, Roberto."

"Well, I don't see you jumping to take their vows, Carlos," Roberto laughed. They walked on.

"Are you going to pray with the Penitentes again this year during Holy Week? Will you come with me?" Eduardo asked.

"I will," Carlos said. "We can join their procession during Holy Week, and we can pray with them at the cross later at night."

"I'll go too, but I'm warning you, Eduardo, you're going to freeze your cojones off just to watch a bunch of guys whipping themselves," Roberto said, already beginning to shiver. "Man, last year it was a week before the ice in my balls melted."

"OK, it's cold and it's not pleasant to witness," Carlos said, glancing scornfully at Roberto, "but watching the brothers makes one aware of the suffering of Christ. If you've forgotten, Roberto, Christ died for our sins. The least we can do is acknowledge his suffering and so what if we have to suffer a bit ourselves. Maybe a little suffering will do you good."

"Of course, your holiness," said Roberto, crossing himself and laughing. "I'll even try to remember to put some big, fat stickers in my underpants before I go to bed tonight."

Carlos ignored Roberto and went on. "First they receive vertical cuts on each side of the spine; these wounds are made in privacy by the picador. He cuts them with a flint. That's what makes the scars you've probably seen on the backs of the hermanos. After they receive the cuts, they begin to flog themselves with the disciplina, a whip made of coarse rope."

"They say the hermanos used to practice other forms of penance that were more harsh, but they don't do that anymore, at least, not in public," Roberto said.

"That's true," Carlos added eagerly. "Father told us that they used to whip themselves during the public processions. He used to walk with them when he was a boy, but the church decided the Penitentes should no longer practice penance in public. Now all of the Brothers of Light are supposed to serve penance only at the morada, or in privacy. Still they've always had secrets. Father said that years ago in Taos they actually used to nail a man to the cross, but that, too, was outlawed. We're lucky that they still allow us to pray with them. You wait, Eduardo, soon you'll understand their devotion."

"Two years ago Juan Trujillo died soon after Easter because the penance had been too much for him. His son told me," Roberto said happily.

"What happened? How did he die?" Eduardo asked.

"A fiber from the disciplina got embedded in one of the wounds on his back. Then an infection developed and he died. At least, that's what I heard from his boy," Roberto said. "Some of them must die each year. If not from the wounds or the weather, then from starvation."

"Some do," Carlos agreed, "but that proves their true devotion. I mean, if they die, they become martyrs . . . like Christ. Each year when they begin penance, they don't know if they'll survive. That's a sign of their faith. Wait until you see it, Eduardo. It is something to witness," Carlos concluded, and the three of them walked home in the dark.

Friday before Holy Week the meeting at the morada was proceeded by a long procession through the streets of Los Torbellinos. Fermín again led the procession of hermanos followed by the rest of the congregation. The brothers carried a heavy wooden statue of Christ, which was passed from one hermano to the next. Many also carried huge timber crosses.

The procession began at the Catholic church on the plaza and, again, the Montez boys joined the Penitentes in their march. Their song became chantlike as the marchers fell into rhythm with the hymns. The walk lasted hours, but the group never faltered in song or pace. The hermanos went on, seemingly mindless of fatigue from bearing the heavy timber crosses. Blood stained their shirts where the heavy crosses had rubbed their shoulders and backs raw.

The procession traveled miles before they returned to the morada. As they entered the building, the hermanos stacked the heavy crosses in a pile on the ground and everyone was invited into the hall to continue the song and prayer. Finally the open meeting came to a close, and the Montez boys and the others were asked to leave. Outside it was dark and below freezing.

"Now the brothers will ask the picador for the wounds of Christ and he will cut their backs. Then they will begin the march around the giant cross there," Carlos said, pointing to a huge wooden cross that loomed through the darkness behind the morada. Those who wished to continue the vigil with the Brothers of Light stood silently outside and waited.

After an hour, the door swung open and an eery beam of light escaped into the dark. The hermanos stepped into the cold air in single file. Their hooded heads were bent and they looked neither left nor right as they marched slowly toward the cross. Each man wore only a pair of white cotton leggings and a black hood. As they walked barefoot over the frozen ground, a few of them stopped at the stack of crosses and selected timbers to carry before they continued toward the giant cross behind the morada. The Montez boys and the others followed the hermanos to the back of the building but stood at a distance.

The hermanos knelt at the base of the cross and recited a short prayer before they began to march in a wide circle around it. As they marched, they wailed in unison. Their ghastly cries were accompanied by the dull rhythmic slapping sounds made each time they cracked the disciplina over their bleeding shoulders and backs. With each slow step they swung their knotted whips first over the right shoulder and then with the next step over the left. For more than an hour they marched, flogged themselves, and continued the terrible wailing. Blood stained the buttocks of their white cotton pants. It was impossible to distinguish one ghostly figure from another because of the black hoods each wore. At last Fermín broke the circle and trudged toward the shelter of the morada; the others followed and shut the door behind them.

"Now they will cleanse their backs with rosemary water and continue to pray through the night. Perhaps they will resume their march around the cross. Who knows," Carlos said tiredly. "But they'll probably stay inside since this is the first night of Holy Week. They can't continue penance hour after hour. Let's go home. We'll come back tomorrow night."

"Eduardo, now you've seen the beginning of their penance, but wait until the close of Holy Week. Then you'll see the true zeal of the Penitentes," added Roberto enthusiastically.

"And on Good Friday we'll attend the tinieblas in the morada at midnight," Carlos said, laughing strangely. "They darken the morada and create madness with devilish sounds. Then they invite the ángel de las tinieblas, the Prince of Darkness, into the morada, and supposedly he comes to steal the soul of those whose faith is weak. But for those whose faith is strong, there is enlightenment. I promise that you'll never forget the tinieblas."

On Good Friday, the Montez boys returned to the morada for the final meeting of the Penitentes before the end of Lent. The tinieblas were the most feverish of all the meetings. The ritual began at midnight when the hermanos entered the morada singing. The room was dimly lighted with candles. Through the flickering light,

Eduardo surveyed the drawn exhausted bodies of the hermanos. The three boys sat on a long bench with many other people facing the altar. Tonight there were more people in the hall than on any of the previous nights.

The hermano mayor began speaking. "In this grim hour we will call on the spirits of the dead to rise up and walk the earth. These are the spirits of the unfaithful; the wicked who will never find peace. Pray with us and show your faith . . . your belief in the resurrection of Jesus Christ, or lose your soul forever to the sinners and their leader, the Prince of Darkness." One by one the candles were extinguished until the hall was completely black. It was silent just long enough for total darkness to settle around them. A powerful voice commanded the spirits, "Rise, rise up, lost souls!" Instantly a deafening rattle of heavy chains, sticks and metal, began. At the same time the hermanos wailed terrible cries of grief and agony.

The uproar pounded all else from Eduardo's mind. He felt as if he were in a void floating away from the morada and away from the terrible racket. He was enjoying the drifting sensation when the woman next to him took his right hand in hers. Instantly, he was back in the morada and became aware of the ache in his ears. Trembling, he sought Carlos's hand with his left hand, and he began to pray harder than he had ever prayed in his life. At once the clamor stopped, and Fermín began a prayer. When he finished, the strong, low voice commanded again, "Rise, rise up, lost souls!" and the terrible racket commenced. Eduardo's ear drums were throbbing, and soon he was drifting again.

His mind went reeling back through the years to a scene in his boyhood that he had forgotten about until this moment. He was a small boy. He could remember the clothes, even the shoes he had on. He was sneaking into Diego's room in the loft at his grandparents' home in El Valle. The time was months after Diego's stallion had been killed. He knew that it was summer because his uncle's room was like an oven from the summer heat; perspiration actually broke out on his face, neck, and back. He heard the leaves of a large elm tree brushing against the glass of the bedroom window.

Eduardo stood in the doorway and looked around the room quickly before he went to his uncle's bed and knelt down beside it.

Under the bed he found a half-empty gallon jug of red wine along with several empty bottles. He pushed them aside and had to lie flat on his stomach to reach what he was looking for. He pulled out three shoe boxes that were bound with twine. Eduardo worked quickly to open the boxes; he already knew what he would find in each of them because he had done this before. The first box was full of bits and pieces of small and large bones and tiny rodent skulls. Eduardo probed the contents with his finger; every detail was clear to him down to the dry brittleness of the bones. Methodically he took up the second box and untied the twine. This box was full of feathers, all kinds of feathers. There were soft, downy feathers from the chicken coop and beautiful, colorful feathers from wild birds. A musty odor rose out of the box and tickled his nostrils. Setting the feathers aside, Eduardo opened the last box, which was filled with different tags of hair. Some of the hair was animal and some human. Diego kept the tags separated by looping them and tieing them fast with thread. Eduardo pushed the loops of hair back from the corners of the box. He wanted the coarse tag of reddish-brown hair that he had removed from Hero's mane the night the great horse died. The hair was still wound into the tight loop he himself had formed when he wrapped it around his finger that night; Diego had secured this tag of hair with thread as he had all of the others in the box.

Eduardo laid the horse hair on the flat of his palm and his thoughts drifted farther back to when he had given it to his tío a few months before. Eduardo had kept the hair for a long time because Diego did not come home for weeks. When he finally did return, he was a drunk practicing witchcraft. It was late and the family was asleep the night Diego crept in, but in the morning, as Eduardo had done for weeks, he looked in Diego's room. There he was, piled up on the bed asleep, reeking of wine. He slipped through the doorway and went to Diego's side. Stepping closer to the bed, Eduardo saw that Diego was unshaven and had lost weight. Eduardo thought of trying to wake him but changed his mind. Instead, he took the horse hair out of his pocket and placed it on the pillow beside Diego's head hoping that his uncle would find it when he woke. Then Eduardo looked around the room and saw the beginnings of Diego's collection. Confused, Eduardo looked over the bones and feathers and hair that were scattered over the top of the dresser. Then he left the room quietly and went to school without saying anything about Diego to his grandparents or Carmen.

Eduardo finally closed the boxes, put the twine in place, and shoved the boxes back under the bed. He vaguely heard the racket in the morada and barely felt the pressure of the woman's hand squeezing his own. He did not wish to remember any more; he wanted to drift, not think, but the memories continued to flood through his mind. Now he was going downstairs and outside. It was Sunday morning and everyone else was at Mass. Eduardo had lied about having a stomachache so he could stay home. He walked somberly to the barn and crawled onto the haystack in front of the stall where Hero used to be stabled. As he sat there, he saw Diego approach the house and enter it through the back door; as usual, Diego staggered drunkenly and carried a bottle. Eduardo did not try to talk to his tío anymore because when he tried, Diego only laughed like a maniac. Nevertheless, Eduardo was comforted that his uncle was upstairs sleeping off his wine.

Soon the others came in from Mass. "Why aren't you in bed? I thought you were sick," were the first words out of his grandmother's mouth. Then without giving Eduardo time to reply, she asked, "Is he home? Did he drag himself in yet?"

"Yes, he just came in. Drunk again," Eduardo answered.

They all frowned and shook their heads. Eduardo saw the pained expressions on their faces. "Qué cochino, el Diego," Fidelia continued to rave. "He has become a disgrace to us." She climbed from the wagon without waiting for José to help her and hurried toward the house.

Eduardo ran after her. "Abuela," he begged, "please leave him alone. Please let him be." Fidelia ignored him and rushed onward to the kitchen door. She charged up the narrow stairwell to the loft. "Leave him alone, Grandmother," Eduardo continued to beg, still following her.

"Shut up, Eduardo. I've already had enough," she yelled. Now at the top of the stairs she began to bang on Diego's door. Eduardo was standing behind her half way up the stairwell. "Open this door. Open this door immediately," Fidelia screamed, her face becoming a deeper and deeper red.

There was rustling in Diego's room. "Go away," he yelled. "I'm trying to sleep."

Furiously Fidelia kicked the door again and again until the lock gave. Diego was at the doorway in seconds. "Get out of here, old woman," he bellowed. "Get out of here and leave me alone."

"No, no, no," she retorted. "It is already enough. You are drunk again. You are a shame to yourself and to your family. You are crazy to pretend you are a brujo. What's the matter with you? You've lost you senses. You are sick, a drunk," she raged.

From his position on the stairs, Eduardo had full view of Diego. He was slight and somewhat stooped in the doorway, but his voice boomed back as loud as Fidelia's. "I am telling you now to leave!"

"You are insane. If you really think you are a brujo, then make me disappear," she continued. "Go on and make me vanish. You take down the crosses above our doorways so you can enter our house, and you play with little bones and feathers. Diego, you are not going to do anything with your foolish toys, and you are not a brujo. You are only a fool and you are disgracing yourself and your family. You are nothing but a harmless fool and all of the people know it and all of them talk about you and they laugh. Do you hear me? They laugh," she screamed, stepping toward him.

"Enough," Diego yelled and pushed his mother from the doorway. He shoved her to the edge of the stairwell. "Now leave me," he blubbered.

At first Fidelia backed down the stairs, maybe two steps. Then she made the wrong choice. "No Diego, let's see your toys. What did you find last night to make people laugh at you more?" she asked, starting back up the stairs.

Diego stood fast on the landing at the top of the stairwell. "No," he screamed as if exhausting the anger and frustration of a lifetime. Then he raised his foot and kicked her hard with the tip of his boot. The blow landed solidly against her left breast and sent her tumbling backward down the stairwell.

Eduardo threw himself against the wall when his grandmother

fell and only barely missed being knocked off his feet. First he glanced at Diego standing in shock at the top of the stairwell; the tortured expression on his uncle's face burned itself into Eduardo's memory. Then Eduardo turned and went to his grandmother. Her forehead was scratched and bloody. She moaned when Eduardo helped her to her feet, and she was holding herself where Diego kicked her.

Then Diego was gone again for a long, long time. And within a few weeks, Fidelia had developed a lump on her left breast where the blow landed. Each year thereafter the lump became larger and caused her more pain. Finally, José forced her to see a doctor. The doctor told them the lump was cancerous. Eduardo remembered the long illness. Fidelia was dying before their eyes; they did not need a doctor to tell them that. Now, too, he clearly remembered the hours that he had spent at her bedside, holding her hand while she suffered. Helpless to relieve her pain, he cried with the same breath that he prayed for her end.

At last the racket in the morada ceased and Eduardo felt himself returning to the present. On the bench in a daze he noticed the candles were being lighted again. Eduardo felt drained in a peaceful way. Colors, shapes, objects and peoples' faces had a new distinctive freshness and purity about them. Next he heard his name being called, "Eduardo, Eduardo." The voice was coming from everywhere. He recognized the voice of his Grandmother Fidelia. "Mi'jo," the voice continued, "do not worry anymore. Your prayers for me were kind, full of love." Her voice was soothing, free of pain. Eduardo felt light, as if he could float. Tears of joy flooded his eyes. At last he understood, remembered what had happened all those years ago, and his grandmother had freed him from the heavy guilt he had suffered since her death. He was free.

The hermanos exited quickly into the private quarters of the habitation. Everyone else sat in the morada with serene smiles on their faces. The silence was strange after the deafening, hellish noise.

People began talking to one another in whispers. "Tonight their penance will be wretched, much worse than before," Carlos whispered to Eduardo, who was still trembling. "It has to be, for tonight they will express the final grief, the final agony of Christ. Come. Let's go to the cross to watch the final procession from the morada."

Outside the sky was clear. The stars cast down a dim light that illuminated the landscape. The boys stood shivering in a huddle with the others. Soon a crack of light appeared at a back door of the morada and the Penitentes emerged. As before, they were clad only in their light trousers and black hoods. They moved slowly toward the cross. Many of them limped over the frozen ground as if each step caused great pain. They knelt at the cross and prayed before they began their grim march anew. With each methodic slap of the disciplina, blood trickled from the puckered, pulpy flesh of their backs. Tonight the wails that had seemed theatrical on the first night were now racked with pain. After they had marched for an hour, the hermanos fell to their knees at the cross and prayed again.

"They look like skeletons," Eduardo whispered.

"They've fasted most of this week. They take only bits of bread and some oil and vinegar with water. The weather, too, and the penance have reduced them," Carlos said. "Also, if you look closely, you can see that tonight some of them have twined barbed wire into their whips to make their penance more severe. They haven't left the morada all week, except to serve penance at the cross. What food they eat is delivered to them by their helpers, the wives of the Penitentes. Perhaps tomorrow some of them will return to their homes, but most of them remain within the morada until Mass on Easter Sunday. Then they attend Mass with their families, and after that they will hold a feast in the morada."

"How do they have the energy to feast after an ordeal like this?" Eduardo asked, but before anyone could reply, the Penitentes were rising stiffly to their feet to continue their path around the cross. Their pace seemed to slow, but the slap of the disciplina into the liplike wounds on their backs sounded at the same regimented intervals. After the first few hours, one and then another of the hermanos collapsed on the ground. For a few minutes, they remained anchored to the ground by their own weight until somehow they pushed themselves to all fours and then staggered to their feet. One man too weak to rise to his feet continued around the cross on his hands and knees. The others marched on, whipping themselves and wailing.

At last, as the sky began to glimmer with the thin light of daybreak, the brothers made their retreat into the morada. They passed close to the small gathering where the Montez boys stood. They could see the sickening splatter of the hermanos' lower backs as they passed into the morada.

The community did not see the Penitentes again until Mass on Easter Sunday. The brothers looked gaunt and exhausted, but they were reunited with their families; once again jovial, ordinary men of the village. They had fulfilled their spiritual devotion for another year, and like Eduardo, had found individual enlightenment.

SIXTEEN

Since turning thirteen in December, Eduardo had not been co-operating with himself. His gangly arms and legs smashed into things so often that his knees and elbows were usually shrouded in black and blue. His hair, which had always been light, was turning darker, almost black, and worse, stiff hair was sprouting out of his skin where it had always been smooth. Soon he worried he might look as grisly as his grandfather, or even Roberto. But most shocking of all was an unpredictable sensation that began as a tingle in his stomach that spread warmly up his spine and into his thighs before flooding hotly into his groin, making him want to sing and cry at once. He also recently had become ambivalent toward games, sights, and sensations that once brought him pleasure. He could not depend on the familiar anymore. Everything changed. He was changing. The energy that raced nonstop through his mind and body were transforming him into another person.

Each morning when he woke, the strength of the summer day drew him out of bed while his brothers slept on. He dressed silently and left the house even before his mother was up. Yawning and stretching, he went outside to brush his teeth and wash at the well before he rambled over the footbridge and down to the animal pens near the creek. The one thing he was still certain of was his mother's apathy toward him. It picked at him constantly, and he planned to earn Elena's recognition.

This ambition gave him an outlet for his excess energy. First thing after washing, he opened the gate to the chicken yard, and before releasing the flock from their adobe hut, he scattered cracked corn on the ground and filled the old dented wash pan with clear creek water. Then he unlatched the door and stood aside as the birds rushed into the yard, pecking frantically at the corn. He ducked quickly into the musty hut to collect the eggs and carried them up to the house, where by now his mother was preparing breakfast. As he deposited the tin can filled with eggs on the kitchen table, he and Elena exchanged a brief glance and said good morning to one another before Eduardo left the house again.

Next he milked the goats and led them to pasture to graze for the day. Then he cut bundles of green alfalfa for the pigs and carried fresh water to them before he returned to the house for his own breakfast. By the time he arrived at the house, the rest of the family was already at the table because Elena would not tolerate anyone sleeping past seven o'clock in her house. When Eduardo sat down at his place, Elena never acknowledged that he had entered, or that he had not been present earlier. The first heaping plate was always handed to Carlos, the second to Roberto, the third to himself, and so on down to the youngest. This was typical in most houses but irritated him anyway.

Eduardo and the others gulped down their fried eggs, bread, and frijoles. Then they filed out of the house to attack whatever task Elena had planned for their day. There was enough work around the farm to keep four strong boys busy all the time. They were responsible for tending the gardens, caring for the livestock, and hauling wood. All of these chores required long hours of hard labor, and there was also the general upkeep of the corrals and sheds. Their mother, being meticulous like her mother had been, would not allow them a moment's peace until every stray weed was beaten back and every corral and animal shelter was raked clean. On the rare occasions when they caught up with all of their work, Elena deliberately planned a tedious project to keep all four boys working for days.

Nevertheless, as boys will, each found time for himself, usually in the early evening just before dark. Roberto often excused himself and Carlos by announcing with a wink that their mother only thought she could keep them out of trouble by working them to death. And then he and Carlos were off. Eduardo and Marcos sometimes spent their free hours together, but in the past months, Eduardo craved time alone.

When he had been eight years old, Diego had helped him build a miniature ranch. They had collected thin willow twigs and tied them carefully together to make two corrals. Then he and Diego had spent hours along the creek bed searching for beautifully colored stones to serve as horses; for the cattle they had selected plain gray river-washed stones to fill the miniature corral. As a small boy Eduardo had played with his ranch set for hours at a time. He knew exactly how many cattle he had, and had given names to all of the stone horses, which were beautiful. They were the only things that had not changed over the years. He could rely on the stone horses, for their timeless beauty was the link to his destiny.

From the first day he played with the corrals and stone horses, Eduardo vowed to himself that someday he would have a fine ranch of his own. He wanted cattle, lots of cattle, and beautiful horses. Eduardo stored the stone animals in a leather pouch that Diego had given him. When he had lived in El Valle, he kept the miniature corrals in a corner of the bedroom he shared with Carmen and Rafelita, but after he moved home, he hid the corrals and stones in the hollowed trunk of a huge cottonwood tree because he did not want his brothers to know that he still kept toys. He had not played with the corrals and animals in years, not like he used to. But the stick corrals filled with the shiny stones still comforted him and helped him envision his future.

It had been weeks since Eduardo had visited the secluded clearing where he kept his ranch set, so after the chores were finished, he crept away from the others to daydream for awhile. He walked into the shade of the huge tree and knelt in the grass before the hollow tree trunk. First he only looked at the delicate stick corrals and the leather pouch containing the stones, but soon he carefully removed the corrals from the niche. Next he took the stone animals out of the pouch and separated the plain gray stones into the larger corral and the beautiful stone horses into the smaller corral. He crouched on his haunches and examined his work; it did not excite him the way it once had. Staring at the twigs and stones, he realized that a ranch of his own was what would give his life meaning the same way the farm in El Valle had kept his grandfather happy.

Exhausted and still thinking about José's dedication to the land, Eduardo fell into the grass. Crossing his hands behind his head, he gazed up into the branches of the cottonwood tree. The crickets were beginning their familiar evening music. It had been a hot day and he and his brothers had worked hard. Eduardo was glad to be relaxing in the cool grass under the shade of the tree. He watched as a robin flew up into the branches overhead with an insect in its beak. Then he saw the nest. This gave him something to do. He hurried to his feet and climbed easily up the trunk of the tree and out onto the branch where the nest was perched. He was close to the nest and could see the red, featherless baby birds. Slowly his hand stretched toward the nest and hovered over it for an instant. This is something Roberto would do, he thought. Shaking his head, he drew his hand back to his side. Eduardo sat motionless in the tree and watched for a long time while the mother bird flew to and from the nest with food for the nestlings. She was undisturbed by his presence.

After his discovery of the bird's nest, Eduardo returned to the cottonwood tree each day. Sometimes he laid on the grass beneath the tree to watch the mother robin fly to the nest to feed her young, but most of the time the wee chirps high in the tree compelled him to climb up and sit near the tiny birds.

One afternoon, as Eduardo approached the tree, he saw a dark spidery figure arched over in the tall grass. It was Jesús Trujillo, a neighbor boy who was a few years older than Eduardo. Jesús was poised and waiting; he held a slingshot in his hand.

Jesús was taller than Eduardo, but Eduardo did not think of that when he burst into the clearing screeching like a hawk. Jesús sprang into the air screaming with fright. He had been so intent on targeting birds that he had not seen Eduardo approach. Eduardo was in front of Jesús in an instant, "What are you doing here on my father's land?" he demanded in a manly voice that surprised both of them. Jesús still had not collected his own voice; he did not understand the fury in Eduardo's eyes. With an apologetic smile, he stammered, "I . . . I'm only killing birds. See," he said, handing his bag to Eduardo. "I've already killed five."

Eduardo snatched the bag away from Jesús and emptied the limp, feathery bodies on the ground. He shut his eyes and sighed relief when he saw that the mother robin was not one of them. Jesús stared at him dumbfounded. Dramatically, Eduardo threw the bag on the heap of dead birds and clenched his fists. "Go away, Jesús. Go play your little games somewhere else. This is private land."

Jesús shook his head as if to register what had happened. He dropped to his knees and crammed the birds back into the sack, keeping his eyes on Eduardo. Eduardo stood his ground. Jesús rose cautiously to his feet backing away from the clearing beneath the tree. He turned and walked slowly toward the barbed wire fence; he glanced at Eduardo as he crossed the fence. Then he walked off a few paces before he turned to face Eduardo. In a girlish teasing voice, he yelled, "Eduardo Montez you're really crazy you know that? You're crazy, crazy, crazy." Finally Jesús turned and sped away.

The dark scrub oak on the other side of the fence seemed to absorb Jesús. Eduardo reached to the ground and collected a few stones. In rapid succession, the stones flew into the forest where Jesús had disappeared. They ripped through the forest. Finally, satisfied that Jesús was no longer lurking in the bushes, he climbed the cottonwood tree and sat on the limb where he had a plain view of the baby birds. They were solid gray balls of downy feather now. Their brilliant yellow beaks protruded from their fluffy heads as they bobbed and begged to be fed. Eduardo crossed one arm over the other and buried a proud, babyish grin in the crook of his arm.

That summer the crops in the Montez garden promised to produce an abundant harvest. Still Elena nagged her sons to work harder, and like every year, she predicted grimly that the entire family would starve if they did not harvest a good crop. To quiet her, the boys poured all of their energy into the garden. They destroyed every weed and carefully pulled the dirt around the tender vegetable stalks where the last watering had washed it away. They cleaned a quarter mile of ditch line from their garden to the mother ditch so that the irrigation water would flow unobstructed to the garden. Finally, except to wait for the crops to ripen, no more work had to be done in the garden to assure a rich harvest. Nevertheless, for at least a few hours each day, the Montez boys took their gardening tools and trudged dutifully into the garden where they scraped off the heads of minuscule weeds that dared to pop above the earth. Their effort, although unnecessary, humored Elena and so made life more pleasant for all of them.

Carlos, Roberto, and Marcos worked at a leisurely pace taking frequent breaks and vanishing during the hottest part of the day. Eduardo, on the other hand, was always the first to begin work in the garden and the last to quit for lunch or at the end of the day. And while his brothers rested at the garden's edge in the shade of the cottonwoods, he worked on. He had seen his mother walking near the garden while his brothers rested and he had been working. He knew she had seen. And again near dusk of each day, when Elena walked up and down the rows inspecting their work, Eduardo knew that she had seen him collecting the garden tools from where his brothers had abandoned them. She had to have noticed his efforts.

At the end of one such long, hot day, Eduardo went to the cottonwood tree and his nestlings. It had been two days since he had last seen them so he climbed up the tree. They had filled out and become more active since his last visit. Their gray down was replaced by stiff flight feathers. They were changing fast, already hopping onto the edge of the nest and testing their wings. It troubled him to think of the birds not being there anymore, or maybe he was only exhausted. He climbed down from the tree and walked heavily back to the house. He knew that it would not be long before the baby birds left their nest forever.

Eduardo found his brothers drawing buckets of water from the well to heat for their baths. They were joking loudly and splashing on each other. Eduardo was too tired to want their company. He went into their bedroom and found clean clothes, his comb, and toothbrush. He took a towel and went to the creek to bathe by himself. The cool water revived him and soothed his aching muscles.

The next morning when Eduardo entered the kitchen after collecting the eggs, Elena told him to catch the horses because she was going to the plaza to buy supplies at Lawrence's store. Eduardo went off to harness the team. Usually Carlos was the one to drive the horses when they needed something from town, or when they hauled firewood. But when Eduardo went in the house after harnessing the horses, he said, "Mamá, I want to go with you to the plaza. I can drive the team."

Elena looked at him as if she were considering his suggestion. "No," she decided. "You've never driven the team before. I'll take Carlos with me because he knows the horses. Your father taught him to drive the team, and they can be difficult. I'll take Carlos; it's not worth the risk."

"Alright," was all Eduardo could think of to say, and he left the house quickly to hide his disappointment. After breakfast, Carlos and Elena drove away in the wagon. He watched them bouncing along the dirt road. Carlos was grown-up and handsome. Eduardo went to the tool shed and found an ax; he carried it to the wood pile, where he began to chop stove wood at a furious rate.

When Elena and Carlos returned from town, Eduardo had chopped a pile of wood almost as tall as himself. Elena looked over at him and the pile of wood but said nothing. Carlos and the other children helped carry the supplies into the house. Eduardo ignored them all and continued to chop wood. In half an hour, Carlos walked out to the wood pile where Eduardo was still working. "Eduardo, Papá sent a letter with money in it."

Eduardo quit chopping. Drops of perspiration were rolling out of his scalp and dripping off his face and hair. "When is he coming home? Did he say he is coming home soon?" he asked.

"No, he didn't say, but come inside. Mother sent me for you; it's time to eat." Eduardo raised the ax and let the blade fall into the chopping block. He followed Carlos as far as the well, where he drew a bucket of fresh, cold water and poured it over his head and washed his face and hands and towel dried his hair before going inside to lunch.

During lunch, Elena was talkative. She smiled frequently without complaining about anything, and then when lunch was nearly over, she did not give out instructions to each of them as she normally did, the rare cue that the rest of the afternoon was theirs.

All of the children dispersed in different directions, happy to have some free time. Eduardo walked out on the portal and sat down in a chair. He could not think of a thing he wanted to do. He could not even get excited about the chance to visit the nestlings. He looked down at his shirt and saw how filthy it was from his work that morning and decided he better go in the bedroom and change. While he was changing shirts, he heard Carlos and his mother talking in the kitchen. He went to the door and listened more carefully. They were not saying anything interesting, just casual talk. Carlos started to excuse himself, and Eduardo heard him push his chair back from the table to get up and leave. Then Elena said, "Oh, wait a minute, mi'jito, I almost forgot. Today when I was in Mr. Lawrence's store, I bought you a regalito, some chocolate bars." She rustled around in the cupboards. "Here. Here they are. But don't say anything about this to your brothers and sisters. Remember . . . shh," she reminded him again.

"Gracias, Mamá," Carlos said cheerfully. Eduardo heard him whistling as he left the kitchen. For an instant, Eduardo continued to fumble with the buttons on his shirt. Then he felt a scarlet flush of humiliation surge into his cheeks, and a flood of tears rushed uncontrollably into his eyes. His vision clouded, and he fled from the bedroom dashing his palms against the heavy door in the sala to push it open. Recklessly he ran over the bridge and away from the creek, stumbling toward the cottonwood tree.

Eduardo fell on his knees in the clearing beneath the tree. He tore the fragile stick corrals out of the hollow and then stood up and, one by one, tossed them in the air and kicked them to pieces. Then he took up the heavy leather pouch and poured a few of the stone animals into his hand. These he threw in a wide arch into the forest and let the pouch drop from his hand into the grass. He took a robotic turn toward the trunk of the cottonwood tree. He watched his brown, muscled arm extend toward the trunk. Both hands clasped the tree, and his feet eased onto the wide trunk. His body rose up off of the ground; like so many times before, he rose up the tree, finally straddling the branch where the robin's nest rested on a thin branch above his head. He wiped at his eyes to clear the blurry vision and raised his head to peer into the nest. The nestlings were gone. His breath caught in his chest. He had been clear about his intentions to mutilate the robins, but the birds had flown from the nest. Eduardo felt at once ashamed and elated. He sighed and, beginning to laugh, climbed down the tree. Leaning against the trunk he laughed more and wiped the childish tears from his cheeks. He was glad the nestlings were gone . . . testing their wings in the forest. They had escaped him, and he hoped they would also escape the likes of Jesús Trujillo and other treacheries that surely awaited them in the forest.

Eduardo sat down and his hand slipped onto the leather pouch that contained the remainder of the stone animals. He poured them in a heap between his legs. One by one he plucked up the gray stones and with lightning speed fired them into the forest. Now all that remained were the brightly colored stone horses. He began to free them into the forest. He no longer needed them; his dreams were part of him now.

SEVENTEEN

At dusk, Eduardo left his grandfather's house, jogging at a brisk pace up the canyon toward home. He felt lighthearted after having spent the day with José. Just like old times, they were outside all day irrigating the orchard and tending to other chores around the farm. Each time Eduardo visited his grandfather, he was reassured to see that José was as lively and active as ever. He had not seemed to age a day from Eduardo's first memories of him. Still burly and round with a full head of scruffy white hair, he was a man who lived for the outdoors.

When he was about a quarter of a mile from his parents' driveway, Eduardo could see the silhouette of a man standing in the middle of the road struggling to hold onto the reins of his horse. The animal was panicked and shying away from him. Eduardo hurried and soon recognized the man as Fernando Romero, an elderly, wealthy neighbor whose property bordered the Montez property on the north. Eduardo was close enough to hear Fernando talking to his horse, trying to calm him. "Calm down, calm down, Cochise," the old man repeated gently. At a distance of twenty feet, Eduardo slowed to a walk and approached carefully so as not to spook the horse further. "What's the problem, Mano Fernando?" said Eduardo, still behind the old man.

"Eh, who's there?" Fernando's voice came in static, excited puffs.

"Eduardo Montez, Miguel's son. What's wrong with your horse?" Eduardo answered and asked at once.

"Some locoso cabrón threw an empty wine bottle on the side of the road. My horse stepped on it and it splintered. He's cut his right front foot. I think there's a piece of glass wedged into his flesh just below the fetlock, but he won't let me get near him. He's frightened," panted Fernando. Eduardo glanced down at the horse's front hooves and saw that blood was gushing out of a cut close to the hoof.

"Here let me try to help," said Eduardo, stepping up beside Fernando and taking hold of the reins. As if relieved, Fernando let go of the leather and stepped away from Eduardo and the frightened animal.

First, Eduardo loosened the tension on the reins by backing up with the horse calmly and slowly instead of pulling against him. "Whoa, boy. Whoa, boy," he crooned gently. Within seconds the horse was at a standstill, trembling but no longer pulling away from Eduardo. He continued to talk soothingly and eased his hand up slowly to let the horse sniff him. Soon Eduardo was stroking the animal's neck and shoulders and was able to see that there was a shard of glass still wedged into the wound. The horse was now favoring his injured foot by holding it off the ground. Finally, Eduardo cupped his left hand over the raised hoof and in one swift movement pulled the broken glass out of the wound. The horse bolted and stood a few paces from Eduardo stamping his stinging leg. Eduardo looked at the piece of glass to see if perhaps part of it had broken off in the horse's wound, but it was a solid strip of glass pointed at the end like a knife. "Look at that, Mano," said Eduardo as Fernando came up to him, "it's a good two inches long."

"That's an ugly bastard," said Fernando taking the piece of glass out of Eduardo's hand. "You know what, Eduardo, every crazy idiot who throws bottles should be shot. Yes, they should be shot."

"That would take care of the problem for good," agreed Eduardo, now amused at the old man. "But your horse is going to be fine. That piece of glass came out clean; it's going to take some time but he'll heal."

Fernando walked over to his horse to examine the cut. "You're right. It's not as bad as I first thought. What luck that we weren't too far from home when it happened. He's not going to have to walk far on that wound, qué no, Cochise. I'll dress it as soon as I get him home," said Fernando, thinking aloud.

"I'll come along to help you," offered Eduardo.

"If you're sure it's no trouble, I'd be glad for the help," Fernando admitted.

"No, it's no trouble," said Eduardo, collecting the horse's reins, and they set off toward Fernando's house, a ten-minute walk from the main road. They went directly to Fernando's long wooden barn. While Fernando searched for a flashlight and the necessary items for dressing the wound, Eduardo unsaddled the horse and switched him from bridle to halter. Then he went to the creek for a bucket of fresh water to rinse the wound, and when he returned, Fernando was standing by Cochise holding disinfectant along with salve and strips of an old sheet. Fernando directed the beam of light on the wound so Eduardo could work. First, he poured the cool water over the cut to rinse away dirt. Next Eduardo squeezed a stream of disinfectant into the cut; Cochise stamped his foot angrily for a few minutes and then settled down so Eduardo was able to apply the salve. Finally, he wrapped the bandages into place.

"There we go, boy," he said, standing up and stroking the horse's shoulder. "That's all we can do for you tonight."

"Yes, he'll be fine now. I'm going to have to keep him in his stall until that wound closes, but he'll be fine. I've seen much worse," said Fernando. The old man fetched a ration of grain for Cochise and told Eduardo to follow him to the stall. Except for two milk goats that bleated beseechingly in the stall next to Cochise's, there were no other animals in the huge barn. Cochise went happily into his stall and began to devour the grain from his feedbox. Eduardo was holding the flashlight now and he directed the beam of light into the darkness. "This is some barn," he noted, looking around.

"Yes, it is; it's only a shame that it's so empty. Cochise here and those silly milk goats in the next stall are the only animals I keep anymore." They shut Cochise into his stall and left the corral that encircled the barn. Eduardo helped Fernando put away saddle, bandages, and cans of medication; then Fernando closed the door to the storeroom.

"Eduardo Montez," he said, "you come up to the house with me and we'll have a cup of coffee and something to eat."

"Well . . . alright . . . why not," Eduardo shrugged his shoulders and followed Fernando to the big dark house. Eduardo and his brothers had always been curious to inspect the mysterious, dark rooms of Fernando's house, which even though run-down, was still one of the largest and finest houses in Los Torbellinos. Fernando opened a rickety wooden gate that led into the yard and orchard, and they walked up the path toward the big house. It was a long L-shaped house with doors and windows of every front room opening onto the airy portal that ran the entire length of the house. The matching doors, door frames, and windowpanes were painted dark blue, as were the wooden pillars that supported the portal. The house had a pitched, tin roof, and the massive adobe walls had been plastered in cement and painted white. As they walked the length of the portal, Eduardo was compelled to peer into the tall, dark windows. The blackness in the rooms made his stomach twitch. At the far end of the portal were two large rooms that formed the foot of the L shape, and it was toward these rooms that they walked.

Light from a kerosene lamp emanated from one of these windows. As they drew nearer, a short, corpulent Indian woman opened the door and stared at them. "It's me, Juanita," said Fernando, as a second Indian woman stepped into the doorway beside her. "Hello Florinda," said Fernando to the other woman. Both women looked to be in their forties and appeared to be identical twins. They were born in the house and had lived here since. They stared mutely at Eduardo. "You know Eduardo Montez," said Fernando, "one of Miguel and Elena's sons." Smiling, Eduardo said hello to them and they nodded.

"Why are you so late? We were worried about you," said the woman named Florinda.

"I'm sorry," said Fernando. "Cochise cut his foot out on the road on a broken bottle. Thanks to God, Eduardo came by and helped me bring him home and dress the wound. Now I want to give Eduardo a cup of coffee and something to eat."

"I see," said Juanita, "and is Cochise very bad?"

"No, no, nothing that won't heal in a few weeks."

"Well, Florinda made enchiladas and left the pan warming in the oven. There's also a fresh pot of coffee on the stove, but Champo, remember, when you drink too much coffee, you don't sleep well."

"Don't worry about me and my sleep," snickered Fernando.

"Well, you call us if you need anything, alright, Champo?" said Florinda.

"We'll be fine. Both of you go on to bed now," said Fernando.

"Good night," said both women, stepping back inside their room. Fernando and Eduardo said good night and went to wash at the well, which was only a few feet off of the portal. Fernando finished washing first and went inside the room next to the women's room. He lit one kerosene lamp on the table and another on the shelf over his big cookstove. Next he began setting another place for Eduardo at the round oak table where Juanita and Florinda had already set out his plate, coffee cup, saucer, and silverware. Eduardo stepped onto the portal and stood in the doorway outside the screen door feeling awkward for the first time that evening. Fernando looked up from setting the table. "Don't be timid, son. Come in, come in."

Eduardo went inside. The delicious aroma of piping hot enchiladas awakened his appetite, though he had eaten a few hours before with Carmen and José. "Come in and sit down," said Fernando, pulling out a chair at the table. Eduardo took a seat and looked around the huge room while Fernando busied himself with preparations for their meal. The room was easily thirty feet long and fifteen feet wide. The ceiling impressed him most of all, for it was ten feet high and formed by huge vigas that spanned the width of the room. Boards were nailed on top of these to form the actual ceiling, and the thick adobe walls were freshly whitewashed. The room was divided into kitchen and living quarters. In the corner behind Eduardo's chair was the wood stove, and to its right was a bulky buffet. Above the buffet hung a cupboard with glass doors that contained dishes and other kitchen utensils. Beside the buffet was a pastel-green kerosene icebox that hummed and rattled steadily. At the far end of the room were Fernando's double-wide brass bed spread with a patchwork quilt, an ornately carved wardrobe with matching dresser, and a comfortable-looking armchair upholstered in blue mohair. On the wall opposite Eduardo were two pane-glassed windows that were as tall as himself, and in the middle of them hung Fernando's gunrack holding two rifles. The room was orderly and comfortable, and someone, perhaps Fernando but more likely one of the women, had collected a beautiful bundle of wild sunflower blossoms, which were arranged in a ceramic vase at the center of the table. He glanced around the room again. "This is a nice room . . . a nice house," Eduardo said.

"I'm glad you like it," said Fernando, setting a blue-and-white speckled coffee pot on an iron plate in front of Eduardo. "If you want to come back tomorrow, I'll show you all of the rooms. This house is like a maze. We'd get lost at night," he chuckled, "but if you'd like, I can show you the house tomorrow."

"Yes, I'd like that," said Eduardo, burning with curiosity. He had sensed upon entering this one room that the old house was even more intriguing than it appeared from outside.

Eduardo watched Fernando move easily around the kitchen. He was now calm and controlled, so unlike the frightened, frail man he had seemed an hour earlier. Eduardo thought of how Fernando had shown concern for his injured horse, how he had politely invited Eduardo to dinner, and how gently he had spoken with Juanita and Florinda. Fernando struck Eduardo as dignified in the same way the old house was dignified. Eduardo felt growing respect for this kindly old neighbor who set a bowl of ripe tomatoes on the table, and at last, opened the oven and placed the hot pan of enchiladas in front of him. Fernando sat and held out his hand for Eduardo's plate, which he filled with a generous helping of enchiladas. Finally, he served his own plate and poured them each a cup of hot coffee. "I think that's everything," he said. "Enjoy your meal."

"These are very good," said Eduardo, sampling the enchiladas.

"Yes, the girls are wonderful cooks. They take good care of me. You know, I don't know what I'd do without them," said Fernando, wiping delicately at the corner of his mouth with his little finger. "Wonderful girls," he said, as if Juanita and Florinda were five years old. "They're only half Navajo; their father is someone from here, but I've never been able to figure out who, and they don't seem to know either. Whoever it is was a sly fox. You see, their grandmother was my wet nurse; my grandfather took her off of the Navajo reservation on the Arizona border, and named her Rosinda. Well, Rosinda raised me beside her own daughter, Tilla.

Then after I married and had my first child, Tilla was suddenly pregnant with Juanita, and not a year after Juanita, Florinda was born." He chuckled, "No, I never could figure out who the daddy was. It wasn't my business anyway, but I love those girls like my own. Of course, Rosinda and Tilla died years ago, not long after my wife died," he said wistfully.

"Your daughters used to visit my mother years ago when Grandmother Rosita was still alive. I remember that Juanita and Florinda used to come to our house with your daughters." Eduardo also remembered that his mother never allowed the Indian women to enter her house, but he did not mention that.

"Oh yes, that was quite some time ago, when my daughters were home to visit more often, but now they rarely visit. Christina, the oldest, she lives up in Denver with her husband the banker. And María lives down south in Santa Fe with the mailman. Yes, my sons-in-law, a banker and a mailman," sighed Fernando. "City men through-and-through."

"Have you been to Denver and to Santa Fe to visit your daughters?" asked Eduardo, uncomfortable with the disappointment that suddenly shaded Fernando's mood.

"Oh, why yes. I visit both of them. They've both tried every trick they know to pack me out of Los Torbellinos forever. They'd love to see me sell the house and land tomorrow, and then I guess I'd spend the rest of my life warming rocking chairs in their living rooms, or the train seats between Denver and Santa Fe. They'd pass me back and forth and feel like they were doing me a favor. No señor, I don't care for the city. I don't understand the city and I don't understand the people who live there. Christina and her husband live in a little wooden house. It's painted light blue with white window frames and white doors. I think their whole house could fit inside this one room; the rooms inside that house aren't big enough to turn around in. The ceilings are so low that I'm always afraid I'm going to bump my head when I stand up. I feel claustrophobic every time I walk in that house, like I'm suffocating. They do have a kitchen and bathroom with running water, and my Christina, she's proud of that house. She's got a tiny yard, smaller than my chicken yard, where she grows roses and some other pretty flowers that I've never seen before. She washes her windows about twice a day, and she's as happy as can be taking care of her little yard and that matchbox house. I was up there once in November when a storm blew in. It was a nightmare. The house rattled and shook every time the wind blew, and I could feel the cold air blowing right through those paper-thin walls. So what did my son-in-law do?" chuckled Fernando. "Why he simply turned up his gas heaters. No, I've got no business sitting in a little matchbox house all day. I don't care for that life."

"What about Santa Fe? Do you like Santa Fe better?"

"Naturally. Santa Fe is a good town. In Santa Fe there are a lot more people . . . you know, our people. People who speak Spanish. And María, at least, her husband owns a real house, an adobe house. The rooms are big enough to live in, and they heat it with wood like we do here. Of course, she's got a fancy kitchen and bathroom like her sister, but her yard is a yard. For example, it's big enough to keep chickens and a dog, and they have some fruit trees, too. Nonetheless, there's nothing for me to do down in Santa Fe either. No, there's no place for me in the city, but do you think I could drag my daughters with their city husbands and city children back to Los Torbellinos? No señor, not with a team of twelve angry oxen." Fernando noticed that Eduardo had by now finished his first serving. "Pass me your plate, son." Eduardo gladly handed his plate over for a second serving. Fernando had talked so much that he had not made much progress with his own meal but had finished two cups of black coffee.

"So your grandchildren don't like the country either," Eduardo said, trying to imagine what it might be like to grow up in a city, trying to imagine what a city was like.

"I have five grandchildren. Christina has a boy and a girl who are about your age, I guess. When they visit, I can't get either one of them to take a ride on my horse. You know what my grandson does all day? He sits inside, or out on the portal, reading stacks of comic books. It's not normal, and the little girl, well, she just complains all the time because she has to use the outhouse instead of an indoor toilet like they have at home. And then of course, neither one of them understands more than a handful of words in Spanish.

Now María's children all speak Spanish, but they are all girls and they don't like Los Torbellinos any more than their cousins from Denver. You know, I once tried to show the land to my grandson. Well, he agreed to walk out into the fields with me, and I tried to explain the property boundaries to him and to tell him how long this land has been in the Romero family, but he didn't say much. Then before we had even seen half of the property, you know what he said? Try to guess," laughed Fernando, "go on, try to guess."

"I don't know. I have no idea," said Eduardo, beginning to smile because Fernando was rocking with laughter.

"Alright, he said 'Grandfather, my socks are full of stickers. Can we go back to the house?' " Fernando and Eduardo both laughed. "Can you imagine that? I can promise you that my sons-in-law don't mind walking through the property, though, because they're big land speculators. They are calculating how much they can sell the land for and how much that will leave each of them to split down the middle and stick away in a bank. But I'm not dead yet, and I've made it clear that no one is selling this land before I'm ready to sell, and when it's time to sell, I decide who I will sell it to because it has to be someone who appreciates the land for it's real value, not for how much paper it's worth."

Eduardo thought of Juanita and Florinda and before thinking blurted, "But what will Juanita and Florinda do if you sell the land?" He felt ashamed for having asked, but Fernando did not seem to mind.

"That's one problem I don't have to worry about. My daughters have already tried to haul them off to live in the city. When I'm gone, they will go to live with my daughters. I told them to go now; life would be easier for them in the city, but they refuse to leave me," Fernando said proudly. "You see, they are really more like my blood than my own daughters . . . both of them are angels. I don't know what I'd do without them. I only pray that they will like life in the city more than I do." With that said, Fernando stopped talking long enough to finish his first serving of enchiladas. Smiling, he served Eduardo again and then himself. "It's good to see a boy with an appetite. That grandson of mine eats about enough to keep a mouse alive. The only thing he'll eat is butter bread with jelly, but enough about me and my family. Why don't you tell me about yourself."

"About myself . . . there's not much to say," Eduardo blushed self-consciously.

"Oh, I don't believe that. For example, you know horses. That's easy to see. Tell me how you learned about horses."

Eduardo was a bit stunned. He had never been given such a compliment and never had considered himself skilled at anything. "Well, I guess I learned mostly from my grandfather and, from my uncle I . . . I love horses. Horses are my favorite animals. Someday I want to have lots of them."

"That's a clever ambition," said Fernando contentedly. "Horses are respectful animals and they deserve respect. Here, pass me your cup." As Eduardo passed his cup over for a refill, a cat began meowing outside the screen door. "Ah, there's Gatita. Would you do me a favor and open the door for her." When Eduardo opened the door, a silky gray cat brushed past him indifferently and went to Fernando's chair, where she began to purr and rub against his legs. "What have you seen today, Gatita?" said Fernando as he spooned a small serving of enchiladas onto his coffee saucer and set it on the floor for the cat.

"The chile doesn't seem to bother her," Eduardo noticed, taking his place back at the table.

"This cat, she eats everything," said Fernando. "I guess she knows what's good for her. It makes no sense to worry about a cat; cats they can take care of themselves just fine, and they don't do anything they don't want to do. I admire that," he said, stroking the cat's head. "But let's get back to you. How old are you, and where do you fit in between your brothers? You're daddy has so many children it's hard for me to keep track of you all."

"I'm thirteen and I'll be fourteen in December. Carlos is the oldest. Then there's Roberto, myself, Marcos, my two little sisters, Feliz and Simonita, and our youngest brother, Pedro."

"That makes seven children, correct?"

"Correct, and there were two who died soon after birth, both before I was born."

"Imagine that, nine children, and that second brother of yours, Roberto, he's the one with the blue beard, right?"

"Yes," said Eduardo smiling. "He's the one with the blue beard." Eduardo saw that the cat had finished her plate of enchiladas and wandered over to the stove behind him, where she began to meow again.

"Eduardo, she wants in the oven. Will you turn around and open the oven door for Gatita?"

"What? Open the oven door?" asked Eduardo, not sure he understood Fernando.

"Yes, open the oven door for her." Shaking his head, Eduardo turned and opened the oven door. Without hesitation, the cat pounced into the oven and turned to stare at Eduardo with her head cocked to the side as if waiting. "Now go on and shut the door." Before Eduardo shut the door he placed his hand in the oven; it was not hot but very warm. The cat continued to stare at him as if he were stupid so he closed the oven door still puzzled.

"Will she be alright in there? I mean it's awfully warm in there." Eduardo said doubtfully.

"Don't worry about Gatita. Like I already told you, a cat doesn't do anything it doesn't want to do. That hot oven is one of her favorite places; she'll come out when she's ready." Eduardo shrugged his shoulders and grinned. Closing Fernando's gray cat into the oven suddenly seemed no more unusual than any of the events that had transpired that evening.

"I was asking you about your brother Roberto. You know, more than once we've seen him lurking around here at odd hours trying to peek inside the windows. Once it was before daybreak, another time before dark, and then at midnight, and so on. What the hell do you think he's looking for anyway?" said Fernando with a broad smile.

Eduardo did not even have to close his eyes to conjure up the image of Roberto creeping around the big, dark house, desperate to see something, anything. He began to laugh with Fernando.

"That's a good question," said Eduardo. "I don't think he even knows what he's looking for. Roberto is just a rascal. Don't pay any attention to him, Mano. He's harmless . . . at least, most of the time he's harmless," Eduardo said. Then the oven door sprang open and Gatita flew out, landing on the floor about six feet in front of the stove. The racket startled Eduardo but caused him to laugh. Gatita looked at him disdainfully and tiptoed over to Fernando, who stooped and collected her into his lap, where she curled up purring contentedly.

"This cat somehow she reminds me of that brother of yours," Fernando snickered.

"You're right," Eduardo agreed, "I know exactly what you mean."

After about ten minutes, Gatita jumped off of Fernando's lap and walked to the far end of the room where she jumped onto the armchair and went to sleep. Eduardo helped Fernando clear the table. Then they drank the last of the coffee.

"Mano Fernando, I should be going now. It must be late." Fernando pulled a silver pocket watch out of his vest pocket, snapped it open, and squinted down at its face.

"Yes, it's after midnight, but you don't need to leave on my account. I stay up late every night. The girls say my coffee is guilty, but I don't sleep well even when I don't drink any coffee. Anyway, you go on home and get a good night's sleep and don't forget to come back tomorrow. Remember, I promised to show you the house."

"I won't forget, but what time should I come?"

"Oh, I guess about lunch time would be good. You can have lunch with us, and then I'll show you around," said Fernando. They walked out onto the portal together. "And Eduardo, thank you for your help. I'm grateful," he said, extending his hand to Eduardo.

Eduardo blushed. "It was nothing," he said modestly. "I'm glad I could be of help. Thank you for dinner and good night."

"Good night, Eduardo Montez," smiled Fernando, and he watched as the boy walked down the path and disappeared into the night.

EIGHTEEN

The next morning after breakfast, Eduardo went about his chores as usual, though quite excited about touring Fernando's majestic old house. At noon, without a word to anyone, he slipped off to the fence that separated his parents' property from Fernando Romero's. He looked once over his shoulder to make sure no one was watching before climbing the fence and sprinting across the alfalfa field. Eduardo found Fernando by the corral tying Cochise's lead rope onto a post. "Hello, Mano Fernando," Eduardo called loudly as he approached. "Oh, hello Eduardo," said Fernando. "You're just in time to help me with Cochise. I want to let that wound air. Then I'll show you the house like I promised."

"Fine," said Eduardo, and he went to work unwrapping the wound. They staked Cochise in the orchard, where he could graze while the fresh air worked on his leg.

"Well, now I'll show you around the place and after that we'll have some lunch. What do you say to that?" smiled Fernando.

"That sounds good to me," answered Eduardo, and they set off toward the house. Fernando took a heavy ring of keys out of his trouser pocket.

"We'll start in these front rooms, and then I'll show you the rooms behind my room . . . the big sala, or dance hall as we call it, and the rooms behind it on the west side of the house."

The first four rooms were nearly as large as the room where Fernando lived. The sole entry to each room was through the doorways on the portal. Every room had four tall, matching pane-glass windows, and each had either a small wood-burning stove or a corner fireplace. The ceilings were high, spanned by huge timber rafters. As they entered the rooms, Fernando lifted the orange shades to let sunlight filter through the windows. The light exposed a thick layer of dust that covered the floorboards and everything else in the rooms. Fernando told Eduardo to hop up on a chair and poke at the boards between the vigas with a broomstick. When he did, dust poured through the chinks like flour through a sifter. Fernando explained that the ceiling of every room in the house, with the exception of his and the room Juanita and Florinda shared, was decked with a two-to-three-foot layer of dirt. "You know, before we had tin roofs, dirt was the only roofing available. It kept moisture out, and it's good insulation . . . cool in the summer and warm in the winter. However, it's a mess to live with, especially since the boards between the rafters up there are old and starting to rot. Now that I have a tin roof on the house all this dirt above the vigas is a nuisance. Years ago we busted out the boards between the vigas in my room and the girls' room so we could remove all of that dirt and put down new boards between the vigas. It was a miserable job, raking out those layers of dirt and dust, something I never want to experience again. But in my father's day and his father's day and so on, they used to pile new dirt on the roof each year. Now it's all got to come down. Otherwise, these rooms are useless. No one can live in this dust that falls like rain from the ceilings. Look," he said, shaking a sheet that was draped over an old sofa. A thick layer of dust dispersed into the air. Eduardo sneezed. "You see what I'm talking about," laughed Fernando. "God only knows how many tons of dirt are up there. Yes, it's got to come down, but I won't be the one to do it."

Before they left each room, Fernando lowered the shades again and locked the door on the way out. Dust or no dust, Eduardo was intrigued by the spacious rooms that were filled with mysterious wooden crates, ornately carved wardrobes, and other pieces of furniture that were draped in old sheets.

"Who used to live in all of these rooms?" asked Eduardo as they walked down the porch.

"Well, different people at different times, but all of them were either Romeros or married to Romeros. Then, of course, there have always been Indians in this house, and they've had their rooms just like the others. Did you know that my house is one of the oldest in Los Torbellinos? Parts of it are even older than the church on the plaza. Most of it was built by Indian slaves. This next room I'm going to show you, the sala," said Fernando, selecting a big key from the ring, "was used as a meeting room, a dance hall, and long ago as a refuge during Indian raids."

Fernando fidgeted with the key in the keyhole of a double-wide door built of thick, cumbersome boards. Finally the door handle turned and the heavy doors creaked on their hinges as Fernando pushed them open. Eduardo whistled in surprise at the size of the room. It was forty feet long and twenty feet wide: long, tunnel-like, and dark. There was only one narrow window at the far end of the hall, which was more like a slit in the adobe wall than a window, not wide enough for a man to crawl through.

"You say this was used as a refuge during Indian attacks?" stammered Eduardo.

"Oh yes, I suppose the last time was when my grandfather was a young boy. In those days the Apaches were a great menace. They raided the valley often, especially in the fall to take their share of the harvests and animals. Of course, they were vicious and killed when they could. Men, women, children, they weren't particular. Naturally, the people of the valley had to defend themselves, and in numbers, they had a better chance to survive the attacks. When the Apaches came, the people of Los Torbellinos gathered here, in this very room. The warriors couldn't come through the window, nor could they come through the door because there were men on the roof with rifles. And as you can see, the walls are three feet thick."

"But how did the people know when they should come here? How did they know when the Apaches were going to attack?"

"That's the sad part. They didn't always know, and many people died because of it. However, during those times the villagers kept a constant watch out for the Apaches. There were sentries who scouted for Indian war parties. At the first sign of trouble, these sentries warned all of the villagers and they gathered here as quickly as possible. Later, during my grandfather's time, they worked out a warning system using the church bells. That way they were able to alert all of the villagers at once, and those who were lucky made it to this shelter. They kept barrels of fresh water and venison and hardtack in storage here because starvation was the greatest threat during an attack. And look here," said Fernando, pointing to an alcove built into the wall. In it sat an aged, porcelain statue of the Virgin Mary. "This figure of Our Lady was here before my grandfather was born. She watched over the people and protected them from the Apache warriors. Those must have been terrible times, and I'm glad that I never had to live through such an ordeal. My grandfather did, and he told me that it was horrifying. But later," smiled Fernando, "in better times, this sala was used as a dance hall during fiestas and for weddings. Everyone who came to a dance here had to bring a hanging lantern, and we hung those lanterns up on the vigas and danced until daylight. Yes, dances were held here until the bigger and finer dance hall and community center was built down on the plaza. Since then, this old sala has been empty. Now the only thing we use it for is curing jerky," said Fernando, indicating the wire racks that were scattered about the huge room. The floorboards under their feet creaked as they walked across them. Eduardo tried to imagine all of the history that had passed in this dark, lonely hall. The Apache raids intrigued him most of all. "I wonder," he said, "I wonder how many times the Apaches attacked here."

"You're just like my son," Fernando laughed, "he couldn't hear enough about the Apaches either, but I can't answer your question. However, I'm sure that the Apaches raided this village no more than the Spanish raided the Apache and Navajo camps. You see, it was a violent time, and after the Apaches raided one of the Spanish villages, all of the men from all of the neighboring villages organized into bands. These bands hunted the offenders down, and when they couldn't find the guilty party, it seems any group of Indians they came across would do. They killed the men and stole the women and children. Yes, in those days almost every Spanish family had one or two Indian slaves. Rosinda, Juanita and Florinda's grandmother, was such a captive. Some families treated their Indians better than others, but there were some vile Spanish men who made their livelihood from trading and selling Indian flesh. These men raided the Indian camps regularly to steal the young children whom they later sold in Santa Fe. Those unfortunate children were taken into Mexico where they were forced to work in the mines. My grandfather was party to such raids on the Navajo reservations and others. He said that the children between seven and twelve were snatched up off of the ground by the hair on their heads. Then the men tied their long hair onto their saddle horns and transported the children in that barbaric manner. There was so much cruelty on both sides," sighed Fernando, "unforgivable cruelty."

Eduardo wandered up to the niche that housed the figure of the Virgin Mother. Her skin was yellowed and cracked, her face serene. Eduardo noted that two dusty altar candles stood on either side of the statuette and wondered when they had last been lit. Finally, they left the sala, and walked to the west side of the house, where they entered a large room that led into two adjoining rooms. "These three rooms were the first built," said Fernando. "They are the oldest in the house, and then the sala was added behind them. Years later the front rooms where we live were built onto the east side of the sala. It was put together one room at a time; the same way the Indians added onto their pueblos. The entry door there, the only one leading into these rooms, used to be four feet tall, and it was so narrow that a wide person had to turn sideways to step through. The windows were also like the one in the sala, not windows at all, only slits in the adobe to let a little light in. We opened up the door and these windows when I was young. I remember when we chipped into the adobe walls my father was hopeful that we would find a pot of golden coins. Of course, we never did. All we found were some old chicken bones," laughed Fernando, "but I'm not saying that means there isn't a pot of gold somewhere in this house. There are lots of walls, lots of rooms. Who knows?"

Eduardo began counting on his fingers and then shook his head, "How many rooms are there in this house. Too many for me to keep track of."

"Including the sala, ten. Nine regular rooms and the sala."

Eduardo whistled, "Ten rooms. My parents' entire house could fit inside your sala." He laughed, "And there are eight of us living there, nine when my father is home from the sheep camps."

"And that's how a house should be, Eduardo. Full of life, full of children. I find it very sad, tragic, that this big house is so empty and closed down. It brings tears to my eyes when I think about how empty it is, but what am I to do. My daughters will have nothing to do with the place."

They went outside into the bright sunlight. As Fernando locked the door behind them, Eduardo looked hard into the old man's face. It was a handsome, brown face with strong, sharp features, high cheekbones tinged with a healthy red glow, a distinctive, arched nose, and warm dark eyes. Fernando wore a mustache, which was white and neatly trimmed like the remaining hair on his head. His face was long and thin like the rest of him, and his hands were large and strong with long, slender fingers. He still wore his gold wedding ring, which was pressed into his ring finger like a part of his body. As every time Eduardo had seen him, Fernando wore a freshly ironed, white cotton shirt with the collar buttoned all the way up to his neck. He wore a dark vest with the chain of his watch hanging out of the left breast pocket, a pair of baggy, beige trousers, and black boots. On his head was a cream felt hat that had a wide, white silk band around it. He smelled pleasantly of soap and freshly ironed cotton. Eduardo thought of the night before, of how he had first pitied Fernando Romero as he had struggled futilely with the powerful horse. But now Eduardo realized that Fernando was somehow too noble for pity; he commanded respect.

On the way to the front of the house, Eduardo looked around. "I can't understand why your daughters and their husbands and children don't want to live here. I can't understand it," he said, shaking his head.

"I can't understand it either, but as I told you, city people are difficult to understand. They have different needs and values."

"Yes," continued Eduardo excitedly, "but one only has to look around at the beautiful old fruit trees there," he said, pointing at the trees in the orchard off the portal, "and this fine house nine rooms and the big sala, and the sunny portal facing south. What more could a person want!"

Fernando laid his hand on Eduardo's shoulder. "I'm glad that you appreciate the place," he said, "but my daughters and their husbands don't see the beauty here, don't realize the value of the land. Or should I say that they think of it's value often, but always in dollar signs. It's a shame." Fernando left Eduardo for a few minutes and went into the kitchen. Eduardo heard him talking to Juanita and Florinda. When he returned, he told Eduardo that lunch was not ready and invited him to walk across the creek and into the alfalfa fields with him.

It was late August but the alfalfa in Fernando's fields had not been harvested. Eduardo knew that Fernando leased his land and cattle permits to a man named Juan Valdez. Juan Valdez owned two hundred head of cattle and leased another one hundred permits from Fernando. The cattle were still on the summer range high in the sierra, but in another month they would be rounded up and brought back to the valley to winter. It had been a moist summer, so the feed in the fields was high and thick; the feed might carry the cattle through the winter, but Fernando was doubtful.

"Juan Valdez is a miser. He's too greedy to pay a crew of workers to come in and harvest the hay off of these fields," he complained. "Instead, he turns the cattle in to pasture with all this feed still on the ground. Of course, the cattle are fat and happy for a few months, but when they need the alfalfa most, in the cold winter months, it's all gone. Then those poor animals start wasting away, and many of them die of starvation before spring ever arrives. Then when the animals die, he leaves the carcasses to rot in the middle of the fields. I told him to drag them out into the chamisal behind the fields. Every year he promises that he'll have his Mexicans tend to it, but of course, they never do. I only allow him to winter one hundred head on my property. He runs the rest farther south on his own land, but it's the same down there. Every spring when he pushes the herds back onto the range it's a sorry looking pack, and he leaves enough carcasses behind to feed the coyotes for the entire summer. Somehow he continues to operate."

169

"My father says that Juan Valdez's cattle are so hungry that they eat fence posts and trees."

"That's the truth," agreed Fernando shaking his head disdainfully. "Then by February and January the cattle are so starved that they start busting through the fences to go out and feed on the chamisal. I told him I wanted the fences repaired so he sent out his Mexicans to patch up the breaks with twigs and rusty wire. They did pathetic work and now all the fences are in terrible shape."

"Well, Mano Fernando, if . . ." Eduardo hesitated, "if Juan Valdez misuses your land, why do you lease to him?"

"The answer is that I don't have any choice. There is no one else in Los Torbellinos who can afford to lease the land and cattle permits. I don't know how Juan makes his money, but he does, and he pays me regularly once a year for the use of my land and permits. That money keeps my daughters happy. And when they're happy, they don't nag me to sell, sell, sell. Oh, Juan Valdez is a crooked swindler. For example, during dry years, he's tried to make me lower the lease on the land. I told him the price wasn't changing and he could take it or leave it. Of course, he quit trying to barter after that, but he knows that I don't like him." Fernando chuckled, "I'm certain that the banker from Denver has had private conversations with Juan Valdez; they think they are going to sell my place to that snake. I know so because fat Juan came sniffing around asking for a price about two years ago." Fernando snapped a dry twig off of a tree and cracked it in half. "I told him the land and cattle permits were not for sale. The bastard smiled his evil smile and said, 'Compadre, time, time is more stubborn than any man.' And he laughed in my face. Yes, he was angry at me, sour, and he still is. No, Juan Valdez is not ever going to own one acre of my land."

They walked into a grove of oak trees near the end of one field, and Fernando pointed out fresh bear signs. He said that bear and porcupine loved the oak grove and had occupied it in the summer every year since he could remember. Fernando sat down on a log in the cool shade of the oak trees. "It's a paradise for bears. They come to feed on the acorns, and those porcupines like the oak too. If we looked long enough, I'm sure we could find a fat porcupine up in the branches of one of these trees." Fernando sighed and took his hat off. "I don't blame them for coming here; it's a nice place to be."

Eduardo sat down beside Fernando. "How many acres do you own here in the valley?" he asked.

"On this side of the river, the east side, I've got three hundred and fifty acres, and on the west side, one hundred and fifty including the land that the house and the orchard occupy."

Eduardo fidgeted with his hands. "My father only has fifteen acres," he said feeling ashamed, "and only fifteen cattle permits."

"But your father's land is a good piece of land and it's well cared for. And your cattle are not sickly, half-starved creatures. One healthy cow is worth more than half a dozen sick ones. You people keep everything on that property in the best condition. That's important. Your family has a fine piece of land."

"Yes, but fifteen acres and five sons. I'll never own any of that land. You know how it is, Mano," Eduardo said.

"Yes, that is a problem," Fernando agreed sympathetically, "a problem that the Lord took out of my hands. You see, my only son, Alfonso, was killed in combat in France in 1918. So there is no question about inheritance; everything will be divided between my daughters."

Eduardo stared at Fernando. "Your son was killed in the war?" he asked in disbelief. "I didn't know. Until today I didn't know that you had a son. I mean when you told me he liked to hear about the Apaches. I'm sorry, Mano Fernando. I didn't know."

"Yes, Alfonso volunteered just like most of the young men did. My son went over in 1917, on the same ship with your daddy, but they were in separate regiments and never fought together in France. Alfonso was killed in October of 1918, only one month before it all ended. One month, can you imagine that? I received a telegram that said my son, Alfonso Fernando Romero, had been killed in action in service to his country on October 2, 1918. He was killed near Verdun. My only son killed in his best years in a foreign country, fighting a foreign war, and buried in foreign soil. I pray that he was, at least, buried. President Wilson was promising to keep America out of that mess over there. I guess those crazy Germans had to be stopped, but for me and other parents like me, the price was high. Now I fear the same thing is happening again. It won't be long before Europe is at war again, and then it won't be long before America is right in the middle of it."

Eduardo was still thinking about the dead son, Alfonso, and though he had never thought of it before, he realized how it could have happened to his father just as easily. The horror of it all caused his skin to crawl. "That's terrible about your son. He could have had a good life here. He could have had so much."

"Yes, but he's gone now, and I'm too old to run the place alone. I never was able to find hired help who did the job the way I wanted it done. And the first time I met my sons-in-law, I knew that they were hopeless." They sat listening to the grasshoppers making their cracking noises out in the tall alfalfa and watched as magpies swooped down, disappearing momentarily in the grass to catch them. Then Fernando continued more cheerily, "But you like my land and the house don't you, Eduardo?"

"Who, me?" said Eduardo surprised. "Do I like it? Of course, I . . . I've dreamed of owning a place like this since I can remember. That's all I've ever wanted."

"Good, very good, then I'll sell my place to you," said Fernando lightly.

"To me?" Eduardo was not sure that Fernando was serious. "But how? I . . . I'm only thirteen and I don't have any money. How could I buy your place?" he jabbered.

"Don't get so excited, son. I know you're only thirteen, but you'll be a man sooner than you think. I like you. You're a good boy, and it doesn't matter to me if you are thirteen or thirty. Time doesn't make a good boy bad or a bad boy good. You are now what you will always be, and you are the only person I know who I want to sell my land to. Like I said, don't get too excited. Think about it, and in five or six years, we'll make a deal. I'll sell you this land and the house and the land I own up in the sierra too."

Eduardo noticed himself laughing nervously. He still wondered if Fernando was teasing him, yet he was talking with a straight face, serious and calm like always. "But Mano Fernando, I don't have any money, and I don't know how to earn enough money to pay for a ranch."

"Don't worry about the money. Remember, my son-in-law is a banker. We'll work out a deal. You see, I'll take out a loan from the bank on this land. Then my daughters and their husbands can take that money and stick it in the bank, or run their fingers through it day and night for all I care. But you, well, it will be your responsibility to pay the bank back. To start with you'll have one hundred cattle permits to work with. You're young, if you start thinking now, you'll come up with a plan to pay off the bank, and then after you have freed yourself from the bank, all of this will be yours." Fernando laughed and examined his felt hat. "Ha, I can hardly wait to see Juan's face when he finds out that I sold my land to Eduardo Montez." Eduardo was trying to absorb all that Fernando had said. He could find no reason to laugh. "Don't look so serious," said Fernando, patting Eduardo's shoulder. "Sometimes problems in life are so simple that we don't see the solutions, but we have found ours. I want my land to go to a man who has some heart. I trust you and I've never been wrong about a person. I either like them and trust them from the beginning, or I never do. And I can see that you appreciate a sturdy house, rich land, and living creatures. The solution is simple. All one needs is a plan, dedication to the plan, and faith. That's all. So what do you think? Shall we make a deal?"

"Yes, of course, if . . . you think so. If you trust me. It's your land."

"It's my land now, but the question is do you want it to be your's someday?"

"Of course, like I said, I've always wanted a place like this."

"Then when you're eighteen, and if you have discovered a way to pay the bank, which I know you will, I'll sell you this land, as God is my witness. Is it a deal, Eduardo Montez?" asked Fernando, smiling broadly and holding out his hand to Eduardo.

Eduardo took Fernando's hand firmly in his and they shook. "It's a deal," said Eduardo.

"Good," said Fernando happily, "let's keep it between the two of us for awhile. Five years pass more quickly than you'd think, and I trust that you will come up with a good plan between now and then. Let's go back to the house for lunch. I have a good appetite. In fact, I feel better than I have in years."

NINETEEN

The Lepage family moved to Los Torbellinos in May 1939 to run Mr. Jaramillo's small dairy farm. Mr. Jaramillo had property and relatives in Los Torbellinos but lived in Santa Fe, and while his dairy did not earn a big profit, it paid for itself and gave him an extra income. That is, extra income when he could find a tenant reliable enough to tend the farm and cattle. He only wanted tenants on the land, which made his propositions impractical for the locals who had their own farms to run. On various occasions Mr. Jaramillo had procured the services of the town winos, but all of those arrangements had been fruitless. The winos were interested in milk only as an exchange for booze, and whenever they could exchange enough milk for enough booze, they ceased milking the cows.

But Mr. Jaramillo was a persistent man. He spotted the Lepages in Santa Fe and immediately recognized the gaunt look of desperation on the face of Mr. Lepage. The family originally came from Arkansas. They were drifters like so many who were forced to leave their land because of foreclosure. They followed Mr. Jaramillo to Los Torbellinos in a rattling Ford truck, all of their possessions packed securely on the flatbed. Mr. and Mrs. Lepage and their six-year-old son, Jim, rode in the cab. The Lepage daughters, Lydia and Darlene, rode in the back with their long, sun-browned legs dangling over the edge.

When they arrived at the dairy, the current tenant was nowhere to be found, though he had thoughtfully turned all of the cows and calves out to pasture. Mr. Jaramillo noticed with satisfaction, as he showed the Lepages around the farm, that Mr. Lepage rattled loose fence posts and shook his head in disgust at the piles of manure that covered the floor of the barn and barnyard. "There's a god-awful amount of work to be done around this place," he drawled, "but it ain't nothing that we can't handle." Finally, Mr. Jaramillo drove out of Los Torbellinos certain that the Lepages were not going anywhere.

When he returned to the farm in mid-June, Mr. Jaramillo hardly recognized his dairy. The sheds and fences had been repaired. The barn was, at last, clean, and Mr. Lepage had plowed and replanted the pastures. A sound schedule of feeding and milking had all of the cows producing at maximum capacity. The dairy was finally turning a steady profit, and Mr. Jaramillo allowed Mr. Lepage to keep one half of all the money they made. Even the adobe house on the property showed signs of hard work and gratitude, and the family had planted a large vegetable garden as well. Of course, Mr. Jaramillo was careful to show little enthusiasm for all of the improvement, though both men knew more work had been done on the dairy in the last month than in the last ten years.

Lydia and Darlene Lepage were tall, lithe creatures, both of them growing so fast that they were all lean and no fat. They had fawn-like brown eyes, and their hair was the color of wild honey streaked with gold from the sun. They were tanned deep brown from hours of work outdoors, and their cheeks held a rosy, healthy glow. All summer the villagers had seen Mr. Lepage and his daughters busy about the dairy, and everyone had to agree that without the support of the girls, Mr. Lepage would have killed himself working. Lydia and Darlene were strong and nearly as capable as their father. And though the villagers of Los Torbellinos were skeptical of Anglos, they had to admire the Lepage family for their determination and hard work. Also, the family was more readily accepted into the community because they were Catholic and attended Mass regularly, even though the Masses were given in Spanish.

Lydia and Darlene began school in the fall. Neither had been able to attend public schools for the past two years because their family had never settled in one place after the loss of their land. However, their parents had forced them to continue reading and writing and figuring while they traveled around the Southwest looking for work. Lydia was fifteen and started at the high school as a freshman; she was a classmate of Roberto's. Darlene was thirteen and put in Mr. Vigil's eighth-grade class with Eduardo.

When Darlene wandered into Mr. Vigil's classroom, a treat he had been expecting, he called her to his desk, appraised her, smiled, tugged at his testicles, and entered her name in his class roster. By the end of the first day, she was his classroom aide. He hauled a student desk directly parallel to his and told Darlene that she would sit by him permanently.

Before school started, Eduardo had only seen Darlene Lepage from a distance. Of course, he was as curious about the Lepage family as the rest of the locals, and during the summer he had been given ample opportunity to watch the family, as the dairy was next door to Fernando Romero's, where Eduardo now spent all of his free time. Nevertheless, glimpsing Darlene from a distance could not compare to seeing her two feet away. When she stepped timidly through the door of the schoolhouse wearing a flour-sack dress and worn leather loafers with her socks turned down neatly around her ankles, Eduardo thought that his heart was going to explode. That now familiar hot sensation raged through him as he noted how the fabric of her dress was only slightly interrupted by the firm mounds of her breasts and hung loosely over the flatness of her stomach. He noted the muscular curves of her arms and how she carried herself erect with her head high and her arms swinging gracefully at her sides. His eyes caught on the stretch of slender legs between the fold of the socks and the hem of the faded dress. He was dazzled by the pretty face, red cheeks, soft smooth skin, and thick hair. Eduardo shuffled restlessly in his seat and took a deep breath.

The first months of school were a whirlwind of adjustment for both of the Lepage girls. In the beginning, they were ostracized by their classmates because they were Anglos with heavy Arkansas accents, and of course, they physically stood out from the rest of their Hispanic classmates. But eventually, the Lepage girls became popular at school.

As a freshman, Lydia took classes with five different teachers. Except for Miss Vásquez, the English teacher, all of her instructors were men. Miss Vásquez was forty-five and had never married.

She was petite with black hair, full lips, and a somewhat timeless physique. Over the years she had developed an unsavory predilection for her handsome male pupils. However, with Lydia in the classroom, Miss Vásquez's flirtation with her male students seemed pathetic even to herself. The first day of school, she decided that she did not like Lydia because Lydia reminded her too much of what she could never be again. But in the rest of her classes, Lydia was received well by the male teachers, even assigned to front-row seats close to the teachers' desks.

"This town is not bad, and most of my teachers are nice," Lydia told her little sister, as they were herding the cows in from pasture after school. "But I hate that old witch named Miss Vásquez. And you can believe me when I tell you that she hates me. It's as plain as day. She's always picking on me when I haven't done a thing. 'Lydia, why do you squirm in your seat like that? Do you have ants in your pants?' Or 'Lydia, turn around and stop talking.'" Lydia mimicked her teacher in a high, whining voice. "It's the same thing every day, and she's always making fun of the way I talk. She even said that I don't speak proper English. But I have some of the best grades in the class, though she tries hard enough to mark me down for the littlest thing." Lydia tossed back her pretty head and laughed a clear, unaffected laugh. "But who cares. All of my other teachers like me just fine, thank you. They're always gawking at me, and I smile as pretty as you please, like I don't know what they're gawking for."

"It's the same way with me and Mr. Vigil," said Darlene. "He's always teasing me and telling the whole class that I have roses in my cheeks on account of all the milk I drink at the dairy. And he says the same thing about my being nearly as tall as all the boys in the class. He says it must be because of all the milk I drink. And he's always gawking at me . . . but he's as nice as can be," added Darlene, laughing.

"They think we're as fresh as tomorrow's dew. But mind you, Darlene Lepage," Lydia's face turned grave, "don't you say a word about any of this to Mama and Daddy. They're likely to keep us out of school like before when we were always on the road. You know how Daddy is, and I like school. You promise, Darlene? Cross your heart and hope to die," Lydia said, staring her sister hard in the face.

"I cross my heart and hope to die," Darlene said, as she crossed her hand over her heart. "I like school too. Guess what!" Darlene continued. "Today I had to whip the feathers out of Pedro Lucero for the second time this week. See, it was recess, and I was minding my own business talking to the other girls. That's when little Pedro walked up, and right smart, he says, 'Darlene, are you going to milk your paw's cows tonight?' Then he pulled hard on my braid and ran away. Well, I was for ignoring him till he ran off a pace and started moo-mooing at me like a old cow."

Lydia was laughing hard. "Silly pea-brain. First, it's an old cow, and second, he's sweet on you. That's why he's teasing you."

"I . . . I know it." Darlene sputtered, "but that moo-mooing! That was what got me! And I'm not sweet on him . . . for your information. But anyhow I went after him, and he let me catch him! I could tell. But I tossed him on the ground belly-up. Then I sat right on top of him, and I was going to beat him good. I was really going to do it . . ."

"Darlene Lepage!" Lydia exclaimed. "Someday you're going to have to start acting like a lady."

"I know it," Darlene went on, "but guess what! Pedro, he liked it. He made these little smooching noises, and he said a bunch of junk in Spanish. Since I could tell he liked every bit of it, I just got up and let Pedro go because anyway I saw Mr. Vigil standing off a ways, staring. He never said a word, not a word. He was just watching."

"Well, Darlene, you grow up. You're thirteen going on fourteen, and someday, just someday, you're going to have to start acting your age."

"Well, I won't either," said Darlene in defiance.

Mr. Vigil had been watching. He had seen Darlene's attack on Pedro from start to finish. He watched as Pedro taunted Darlene, and when she could no longer ignore him, he watched her sprint after him and catch him by the back of the collar. Then she squeezed him roughly about the shoulders with both arms and pulled him into her chest. At the same time, her leg shot between his tripping him with expertise. In nearly the same instant, Darlene was solidly straddling Pedro, threatening him with a clenched fist. Mr. Vigil only watched with an idiotic grin on his face. He had seen Darlene's sweater slip off of her shoulder. He had seen her undergarments at one point in the struggle. Then when she sat on Pedro, he watched the hem of her dress peel back over her lovely thigh, and he licked his droopy lips and pulled at his crotch.

Eduardo had also been watching, in disgust at Mr. Vigil, and in wonder at Darlene. In fact there was hardly a time during the school day that Eduardo was not watching Darlene Lepage, or at least, not uncomfortably aware of her presence. Ten times a day he was shocked to discover that he had been so absorbed in staring at her that he was totally unaware of what Mr. Vigil was droning on about at the head of the class. Before Darlene, Eduardo's thoughts boiled incessantly with schemes for earning the money to buy Fernando Romero's ranch, but since Darlene, he now had to contend with a double fixation. His desire to be a landowner was still as strong as ever, but now there was also Darlene Lepage. In his thoughts, Darlene Lepage walked home with him and followed him around while he did his chores. At the dinner table, he had no appetite and had to force himself to eat to avoid a scolding from Elena. But sleep often gifted him with vivid dreams, and these he cherished.

In the morning, his impetus for getting out of bed was to see Darlene Lepage. On Saturdays and Sundays he visited Fernando as often as possible and volunteered to do chores outside where he had a wide view of the Lepage house, barnyard, and pastures. His heart raced at the slightest glimpse of her.

At school Eduardo never talked to Darlene. He thought sometimes that even before he was looking at her he glanced up to find her staring at him. Perhaps that was only coincidence because he could not believe she might be interested in him. At least, she never talked to him, and she was friendly with other boys in the class. Still, he wondered constantly if she had been looking at him, or if he had only imagined it. He could hardly trust himself anymore, but he did pray. He prayed with more determination than he had ever prayed for anything that he would get the chance to be alone with Darlene Lepage.

Eduardo was given his chance. One Saturday afternoon in January Eduardo walked down to the river and began to follow it with no particular destination in mind. He had already walked past the dairy twice in the morning; there had been no sign of Darlene or anyone else. His chores were finished for the day. So there was no distraction to prevent his mind from indulging in the fantasies that after months had become a burden. Ultimately all the daydreams ended and left him with a racing heart, a pervading sense of his loneliness, and no satisfaction. It was already happening; before he even reached a bend in the river, his mind was flooded with thoughts of Darlene Lepage.

He walked on to the bend in the river and sat on a big fallen log facing the setting sun. It was warm there with the late sun shining on him and reflecting off of the snow-covered ground. He closed his eyes. When Darlene actually walked around the bend, Eduardo was faraway romping through summer pastures with her; they were playing chase and tumbling together into the tall grass. Darlene saw and recognized Eduardo and came to an abrupt halt. His eyes were closed; she could turn around and run, but instead her foot shifted and rattled a few stones along the river bed. Instantly Eduardo's eyes snapped open, and there stood Darlene no more than ten yards in front of him. She looked as startled as he felt. Sagging around her frame, she wore a man's heavy overcoat that was gray and patched and ridiculously large on her. Her feet were encased in a pair of boy's work boots that were coated in cow manure and mud. The overcoat hung down almost to the rim of the boots. Her hair was braided as usual, though tousled. They faced each other for a few seconds that ticked away like hours. Eduardo swallowed. It seemed impossible. What now? His mind was a total blank; his tongue ached with dryness.

Darlene shifted her feet and self-consciously smoothed the loose tendrils of hair into place. She spread her hand awkwardly over the front of the coat. "Mama won't let me wear my school coat on Saturday, not when I've been helping Daddy. I hate this old coat," she said, shrinking inside of it.

Eduardo dug his fingers into the rotten log. Please, please, please, he begged, and then his mind was clear. "Well, at least, maybe it's probably warm," he said, himself shocked at the feigned calmness in his voice.

"Yes," she smiled. "At least, I suppose it's warm enough." She giggled nervously.

"What are you doing out here?" Eduardo asked.

"Well, walking. I come here all the time. Only I never seen anybody here before, and I wasn't expecting to see anybody here today either." She looked down at the coat and the boots and color rushed into her cheeks. "Hey, you won't tell anybody about this. I mean you won't say anything about it at school will you?"

"About what?" Eduardo was puzzled.

"You know, about seeing me all straggly like a old . . . a old scarecrow."

"I won't say anything, but what's a scarecrow?"

"Never mind. There aren't any out here anyway. I've never seen one single scarecrow out here. But you promise now. Promise you won't say a thing," she was moving toward him almost smiling.

"Okay, I promise," Eduardo smiled.

"Cross your heart and hope to die?"

"What?"

Darlene shook her head and walked directly in front of him. "You know, cross your heart and hope to die," she said, crossing her heart. "It's a oath. It means you won't break a promise." She took his right hand and crossed it over his heart. "See, like that." She giggled. "I guess it's really a kids' game." She dropped his hand, looked up at the sky, around at the forest, whistled, giggled, and then pushed him backward off the log. He landed on his back in the snow. Darlene was dashing away, laughing as she ran. Eduardo was on his feet in an instant chasing her, feeling lightheaded, not at all sure if Darlene was really a few feet in front of him. He caught her by the waist and toppled her onto the ground. Yes, it was really happening. Now what, he thought. They were both breathing hard and looking one another straight in the face.

"In English . . . in English," she puffed, "in English your name is Edward. Right?"

"Yes," he said, relieved.

"Oh. Well, I thought so. That's a nice name. That one's easy to

figure out. From Spanish to English, I mean. Edward. I like it."
She had raised up into a sitting position and was leaning on her
palms.

"Thanks," Eduardo said, removing his grip on her and settling
next to her on the ground. Most of the time he was not sure he
understood what she was saying through her thick accent.

"Well, Edward, my daddy told me and Lydia all about boys," she
said. "He says no good ever comes from a girl being too friendly
with boys. I guess he's really talking to Lydia, though. She's my
big sister, and the big boys are crazy about her. They even follow
her home from school," she continued. "But I don't think there's
any harm in me being here with you because you're just like a
little old lion cub." She had collected a handful of snow and now
threw it directly in Eduardo's face. She scrambled to her feet and
ran. They chased each other around in the snow finally settling on
the log to regain their breath. It was nearly dark.

"They'll be worried about you," Eduardo said reluctantly. He
hesitated, "If . . . if you want, I can walk you home. At least, as far
as the road."

"That's sweet but let's wait just a minute. It's so nice out here.
And do you know that I'm surprised to hear you talk," she said
coyly. Then she smiled again, "I mean you never talked to me before." Eduardo only shrugged his shoulders. "Besides," she went
on, "you never told me why you came out here all alone. Were
you waiting for somebody?"

"Yes," Eduardo answered, shocked at himself.

"I knew it. For who? Some girl probably," she frowned.

"You. I was waiting for you," he blushed, still stunned at himself
and everything that had happened in the last half hour.

"For me . . . really and truly?" Now there was a puzzled looked
on her face, like when he had first opened his eyes to see her standing in front of him. "You wouldn't tease me would you?"

"No. Really. I was waiting here for you." He reached over and
took her hand. "Really. I was. I was thinking of you and hoping
you'd come here."

"That's sweet. I believe you, Eduardo. Hey, I don't have any
good friends here. I mean we could be friends, if you want. Could

we . . . well, could you maybe meet me here tomorrow at about the same time?"

"Yes, I'll be here."

"Well, I better go, or my daddy, he'll be real mad. I can make my way home fine by myself." She stood up. "Promise you'll be here tomorrow."

Eduardo crossed his heart with his right hand, "I promise," he smiled.

"You're funny." She giggled again, boxed him playfully on the shoulder, and ran toward home.

Eduardo sat on the log in a daze. He had not known it was possible to feel so happy. He remembered every word of their conversation. He replayed the scene in his mind again and again. Only this time it was real.

TWENTY

Since their first encounter in January, Darlene and Eduardo met every weekend, and sometimes during the week after school. Now it was the first Saturday in May, and Eduardo was sitting near the creek below Fernando's barn, skipping stones over the water while he waited for Darlene. Eduardo still spent lots of time at Fernando's, and after Fernando had begun to pay him for his labor, Elena no longer complained when he headed across the fields toward the old man's house. But Eduardo would have helped him even if he was not paid because Fernando respected him and treated him like a man.

Today Eduardo planned to introduce Darlene to Fernando and the sisters for the first time. Then Fernando had promised to lend Cochise to Eduardo so he and Darlene could ride out into the foothills and arroyos.

When Eduardo sighted Darlene running down the hill toward the creek, he glanced at his watch and saw that it was noon. Today they would have more time than usual because Darlene's parents had driven into Española for the day. Eduardo stood up to greet her. They embraced lightly and she kissed his cheek.

"They just left about ten minutes ago. They'll be gone till after dark," she smiled.

"Good. Let's get started. Mano Fernando is waiting for us to show you the house. Then I think that Juanita and Florinda have made something for us to eat; they always bake sweets when they know I'm coming over. After that we can go riding."

"I'm nervous," said Darlene.

Eduardo stared at her puzzled. "Nervous? Why?"

"You know, about meeting strangers and everything, and I can't even talk to them."

"Don't worry," Eduardo laughed, "they're all very nice. Juanita and Florinda are always teasing me and each other; they're funny. And don't worry I'll do all the talking, but if you want me to tell them something, just say so. It won't be a problem, you'll see."

"I hope you're right, Eduardo," Darlene said as they walked up the hill toward Fernando's. When they neared the house, they saw Fernando sitting on a bench on the portal waiting for them.

"Hello, Mano," Eduardo called cheerfully. "Look, I told you I would bring Darlene to meet you." Fernando stood up and walked toward them.

"What should I say," whispered Darlene.

"Just say hello," Eduardo said. "Mano Fernando, this is your neighbor Darlene Lepage," Eduardo said proudly. Darlene extended her hand to Fernando and said hello.

Fernando took her hand and smiled warmly. "Hello, Darlene Lepage," he said. Then he spoke in Spanish and Eduardo smiled.

"Mano Fernando said for me to tell you that you look like a doll."

Darlene blushed and covered her face with her hands, "Oh my gosh," she said, as the two of them stared at her smiling. When they toured the house, Darlene was as awed as Eduardo had been. Then they went into Fernando's living quarters where Juanita and Florinda had already set the table for coffee and were now setting out an apple pie and a plate of freshly baked biscochitos. When they walked through the doorway, both women rushed up to them wiping their hands on their aprons. Juanita pinched Eduardo on the cheek.

"You, Eduardo, finally you think we're good enough to meet your girlfriend," she said teasingly in Spanish. Eduardo smiled and introduced them to Darlene. They shook hands and smiled at one another.

"We speak a little English," said Florinda, "but not so good."

"I . . . I wish I could speak Spanish as good as you speak English," said Darlene, blushing self-consciously.

Florinda put her arm around Darlene's shoulders, "I like this girl, Eduardo," she said laughing.

Darlene felt more at ease, and they all moved to the table and sat down. Florinda served the coffee while Juanita served each of them apple pie. Then they began to speak in Spanish at once.

"So when are you going to marry this pretty girl, Eduardo?" asked Juanita smiling. And "What will your mamá say about your blonde girl?" chuckled Florinda. Now it was Eduardo's turn to blush; Darlene was begging to know what they had said, but before Eduardo could translate Juanita was on to the next subject.

"You, Florinda, think about what pretty babies they'll have," she said, elbowing her sister in the ribs, and both of them laughed heartily. Darlene was smiling and looking from one person to the next bewildered by all of the chatter in Spanish.

"What did they say?" she pressed Eduardo. But Eduardo was blushing and refused to tell her.

"Don't worry," said Florinda, "we only say he better marry you fast, tomorrow." They all laughed and Darlene and Eduardo blushed together.

"Alright, that's enough," said Fernando. "We're forgetting our manners. These young people are our guests, and look, they haven't even been able to take a bite of their pie," he scolded. "You girls let them eat in peace."

"True," said Juanita in Spanish, "they need to eat. They need to build up their energy," she winked at Florinda and the two were laughing wildly again.

"I wish I could understand them," said Darlene.

"No you don't," Eduardo replied, shaking his head.

At last, Juanita and Florinda settled down and busied themselves with serving up coffee and pie and were not satisfied until Eduardo and Darlene had eaten three pieces each. After they were stuffed, Eduardo and Darlene thanked the women. Juanita invited Darlene to visit again whenever she wanted and promised that they would fatten her up. They said good-bye, and Fernando walked out onto the porch with Eduardo and Darlene.

"You kids have fun," he called as they walked toward the barn.

Eduardo saddled the tall buckskin and mounted. Darlene stepped

187

up to Cochise's side and Eduardo took her hand and helped her swing up behind him. They rode across the river, through the alfalfa fields, and out into the chamisal. Eduardo headed Cochise to a wide sandy arroyo, which was one of his favorite places to ride. He was thinking of telling Darlene of his plan to buy Fernando's place. Then Darlene pinched his sides and bit his neck playfully.

"Why are you so quiet?" she asked.

Eduardo sighed, "I was thinking of telling you something, but you'd probably laugh."

"Maybe and maybe not. Tell me and let's find out," she teased.

"Well . . ." he paused.

"Well?"

"Well, it's about Mano Fernando's place. I mean what do you think of it?"

"I think it's the finest old house I've ever seen or been in. I've never been in a house as big as his. I wish our house was that big. Then each of us could have a room all to ourselves," she said.

"Yeah, I like it too, and . . . and I'm going to buy it someday. I'm going to buy the house and the barn and all of the land, too," he blurted.

"Now that's something to dream about," Darlene said cheerily.

"It's not a dream, Darlene," Eduardo said hotly. "I'm going to do it. Mano Fernando already promised me that he'll sell to me. He wants me to have his place. I know he's not a liar; you know he's my best friend."

"Why are you so angry? I told you it's a great idea. Why are you angry?" she repeated.

"I'm not angry but I thought you were laughing at me."

"No, I'm not laughing. I wouldn't do that. Everybody has to have a dream," she said hastily, "but . . . I mean, how will you get the money? I mean, a place like his has to cost a lot of money."

"I know," Eduardo admitted. "That's the problem, or it's a problem, and it's not a problem. What I mean is that Mano Fernando says he'll get a loan from the bank for the value of the place. See, his daughters want him to sell the ranch, so he'll give them that money from the bank and they'll be happy. The problem is that I have to get monthly wages somehow to pay back the bank loan. Then the place will belong to me, but how am I going earn monthly wages in Los Torbellinos?" he said, disgruntled.

"I see what you mean, but there's a way I know of for a man to earn good money. Of course, you'd have to leave here to do it. My mother's younger brother, Tony, he's a sailor. He wanted to see the world so he joined the navy right after he finished high school. If you listen to him, there's nothing better. In the navy, his food is paid for, and he doesn't pay rent because he lives on a ship. His uniforms are all paid for too, and best of all he gets a monthly pay check along with all of that other stuff. Since he doesn't spend much money to live, he can save a lot. Besides that, he's traveled everywhere. He's been to Alaska and every city on the West Coast and of course Mexico. He's been to Hawaii and even to Japan. He brought me and Lydia the prettiest silky, pink pajamas from Japan. Uncle Tony says that a sailor's life is the best life there is. No, he wouldn't change it for nothing. Maybe it would be right for you, too, Eduardo."

"My father was in the army. He fought in the war in Europe. He was in France. I guess I could join the army, or the navy, like you said. I wouldn't do it forever maybe like your uncle wants to, but just long enough to pay off the bank." Eduardo smiled, and kicked Cochise into a gallop. "I don't know why I never thought of that before."

Darlene yelped and held him tightly around the waist, "There is one thing about it, though. I mean, if you're a sailor, or in the army, that's all you can do. You can't have a family," she giggled. "I mean, what would you do with a family? You couldn't take 'em out to sea, that's for sure. Uncle Tony says that's the best part. He says he never wants to be tied down to a family. I think he saw how hard a family can be. He saw what happened when we lost the farm. He saw what my father went through. No, Uncle Tony says it's good enough to have a girl in every port, which I believe he does because he's a handsome devil. He says he won't ever get married and throw his freedom away."

"Well, my father was in the army and he has a family now, but I wonder how much the monthly wages are," Eduardo said, slowing Cochise to a walk again.

"I don't know exactly, but it's steady money, and remember, you can save that money because you don't need it to survive. I'm sure you'd earn enough to make payments for Fernando's place, if that's what you really want."

"That's what I really want, Darlene. I've always wanted it," he said.

Since his discussion with Darlene, Eduardo decided that enlistment in the military was his best option. He was reluctant to tell Fernando what he was thinking because Fernando had lost his son to the military and was unhappy that the draft had been reinstated at the beginning of 1940. Fernando predicted that this was the first step, and that before long America would again be involved in the war in Europe. Eduardo did not want to worry Fernando and felt it best not to tell him of his plan yet.

On the bright side, Eduardo noticed that after he had confided in Darlene about his dream to own a ranch, they had begun to talk more. Before when they were together, they had kissed and petted and played, and that was fine, the best. But now it was also good to have someone to talk to, to really talk to. And since they had begun to talk, Eduardo could no longer remember the loneliness that used to plague him because now that he had Darlene he had forgotten the anguish of loneliness as easily as one forgets the anguish of physical pain once it is gone. He liked to talk to Darlene, but he liked listening to her most of all. He was enchanted by her smooth, dreamy drawl, and her stories were always interesting. Talking and listening to Darlene was one of the best parts about being with her. They talked about themselves and their families and made discoveries that they never could have made alone.

After Eduardo confided in her about his wish to own Fernando's ranch, Darlene opened up to him. She confessed that she had felt like a nobody after they were forced to leave their land in Arkansas. Everywhere they went they had been unwelcome, and she had heard too many of the cruel remarks that people made about her family and others like them. Those people had laughed and called them "drifters" and "white trash," names that hurt her deep inside. She said she knew that the cruel remarks had hurt her mother and father, too, only they pretended not to hear, not to notice. When they were on the road, Darlene said she used to go off by herself to cry and that she had cried more for her parents than she had for herself.

In Arkansas, no one was cruel to them. They were not poor there. They had once owned a big farm and a lazy old farm house that had been in her family for three generations. She even had horses to ride and dogs and cats, and she adored animals. She said her father had been well respected in their community. And her mother used to help the teachers at their old school and often taught catechism classes in the summer. Then it happened; they were on the road, and she had watched a part of her father die when they were forced to leave the farm. Overnight he looked ten, twenty years older.

Darlene told Eduardo it had been the miracle she prayed for when they got the house and dairy in Los Torbellinos, and it almost reminded her of home. Her father said the difference was that it was not their land. And though Darlene thought she knew what her father was talking about, the dairy was heaven for her because their house was roomy and clean; it felt safe to have a roof and a bed and a home again. There were lots of pretty calves to pet and play with. She also had a new puppy, and she told Eduardo that she stole milk every day for a herd of wild cats that she had tamed. A herd of cats? And even she had laughed at herself when she said that. Best of all was that now she had Eduardo to love. And even though she said the strangest things, and sometimes was rough and giggly when he wanted to be gentle, Eduardo loved Darlene. And she was tender when she wanted to be, and when Darlene was loving, he could barely keep from yelling his happiness to the entire village.

One late afternoon, while he and Darlene were wading in the creek, Eduardo started talking about his mother. He told Darlene that he knew his mother did not care about him. Darlene's love, Carmen and Rafelita's love for him, and even José and Fernando's love for him proved that. He said he had tried all his life to show his mother how he cared, but it was as if his love was met by vast emptiness, nothingness. He told Darlene how he had been sent away from home when he was young, and he did not know why. Finally, when he returned, he could tell that his mother did not feel anything special for him. If he had never come home, it would not have mattered the least to her. He tried to make his mother happy. He tried to be a good son, but his efforts always met the same cold indifference.

Carlos and Pedro seemed to be Elena's favored sons. It did not seem to bother Roberto or Marcos, or he could not tell if it did. But he did not understand why his mother felt that way. If he could just understand why it was that way, he thought it would not bother him so much. But he had no idea.

Darlene didn't know how a mother could love one of her children more than the others and said it was terrible that he had been sent away from home. Eduardo told Darlene that his mother's indifference had only bothered him when he was younger, but Darlene looked him straight in the eye and insisted that he still cared. Always afterward Darlene was more gentle with him. He noticed that she was less like a tomboy each time they met, although she did have a strong wild streak in her. She reminded him of a pretty foal when she suddenly jumped up and did something silly for no reason. He loved her. And he often told her so, which stopped her from being silly for a while. Eduardo did not know anyone else like Darlene; he knew there could not be anyone else like her, and the last months had been the happiest of his life.

At last, there was only one week of school left. Darlene and Eduardo had many plans for the summer. Eduardo promised to show her all of the beautiful places he knew about in the valley and beyond. They had so much to look forward to. After school on Monday they arranged to meet at the bend in the river where they had met for the first time so many months ago. Both of them had to go home and do chores after school, but it was now late May and the days were much longer.

It had been a beautiful spring in Los Torbellinos. The hills, forests, and pastures were fresh and green, dotted with colorful wild flowers. Eduardo decided he would surprise Darlene with a bouquet of flowers like he always knew he would someday. He collected the flowers along the way, a big, bright bunch of them. The weather had been beautiful all day, but a sudden darkness rolled over the sunny landscape. Eduardo looked up at an ominous cloud that was blotting out the light of the sun. It seemed alive, as it swirled and billowed and turned in on itself. Then a huge clap of thunder opened the writhing cloud and sheets of water fell from the sky. Eduardo dashed under a tree and tried to shelter the flowers from the rain. The rain pelted the branches of the trees. A strange hiss arose from the surrounding forest as the water beat against the young leaves.

Eduardo's heart sank; he was sure that Darlene would not come out in this weather. He had left early to pick the flowers, otherwise, he would not have come out either. Now he was stranded in the rain. He decided to wait until it let up before he heading home. The flowers were drenched like he was and he was about to lay them on the grass under the tree when he saw her standing by the creek. She could not see him through the rain. There was a look of despair on her face.

"Darlene, Darlene," he yelled, his heart thumping faster and faster. She turned toward him and the bewildered expression vanished from her face and she smiled brightly. They ran to each other and embraced, both of them laughing and aching with happiness and life and the sensation of rain pouring down on them. Eduardo held the drenched, sagging flowers up to her; their bright heads drooped. Darlene took them and smiled beautifully, the girlish look completely gone. He took her face in his hands. Her wet cheeks were slick and alive under his fingers. Water gushed over her face and his hands. He was almost hurting from the way her beauty made him feel. Darlene dropped the flowers and cradled his face in her hands.

As she touched him, the rain stopped magically as if it had been sliced off with a knife. The last drops fell in one terrific sheet. The dark cloud rolled away from the late afternoon sun and the brilliant blue sky was itself again. Absolute silence reigned for a few seconds before the birds filled the forest with their music. Darlene and Eduardo stood still in awe of what they had just witnessed, had just been a part of. The leaves glistened with wetness. They were both soaking wet, cleansed like the forest. The flowers were scattered around their feet.

"That was so strange," Darlene whispered. Eduardo bent his head and kissed her on the lips, really kissed her, and she kissed him back like never before. They stopped kissing, both of them dizzy. Darlene shook her head and dashed off inviting a chase, the other Darlene now. It was fine. It was fine to run, to use his body, to feel every muscle stretch and pull with so much life. Finally winded, she plopped down in the wet grass. He shook his head at her, smiled, and plopped down beside her. Their chests were pounding, pounding. They waited until their breathing slowed to regular rhythms, and they embraced so tightly Eduardo could think of nothing else. There was nothing else.

TWENTY-ONE

The gray gelding stood under a tree at the far end of the meadow, barely visible through the thin light of early morning. Eduardo walked up the meadow toward the horse carrying a can of dried corn in his left hand and a rope in his right. The horse regarded him with disinterest and shifted its weight from one tremendous haunch to the other. When Eduardo was only yards from the gelding, he clicked his tongue and rattled the corn. "Hola, caballo," he coaxed, offering a handful of feed. The horse turned his head from Eduardo and exhaled a long breath before plodding stiffly into motion up the meadow from Eduardo.

"Cabrón," Eduardo cursed. For a moment, he watched the swaggering rump as the gelding trotted off. Eduardo had hoped to be on his way before full daybreak, and now the sun would be up high over the hills before he caught and saddled the horse. Almost weekly during the summer the Montez boys rode into the sierra to check their fifteen head of cattle; the cows were grazing and had to be rounded up frequently so newborn calves could be branded and the mother cows inspected for health. Sometimes all of the Montez brothers rode up together, but this time Eduardo volunteered to go by himself. He wanted to be alone. He loved to ride into the sierra, into the solitude and beauty of the high country. Since Darlene and her family had left Los Torbellinos nearly three months before, he had no reason to stay home. There was no one he wanted to be with. He was trying not to think, not to feel the emptiness. "Damn," he mumbled, as he followed after the gelding. At the opposite end of the field, the horse made no further attempt to evade him. Eduardo took a handful of corn and held it out on his palm; while the gray gobbled the corn, Eduardo stroked the horse's nose and slipped the rope easily over his neck. "I guess you have something to prove, too," Eduardo said, smiling faintly. It felt unfamiliar, or unfair, to smile. He patted the gelding's shoulder and set off toward the barn.

After saddling the horse, Eduardo tied the gelding to a post and went into the kitchen. Elena had filled a sack with jerky, dried apples, and tortillas. Eduardo gulped his breakfast, anxious to be on his way, and grabbed the sack of food. He tied a canteen of water to the saddle horn and stuffed the food into the saddlebags. Elena stood in the doorway nagging him to eat enough, to find a safe place to sleep, and to build a big camp fire. Though he had not told her, he would be spending the night in Fernando's old cabin. In fact, Fernando was riding up into the sierra later in the afternoon to join him. "Yes, yes, Mamá," he replied with irritation. He mounted and said good-bye. He sighed with relief as he kicked the gelding into a trot and moved briskly down their long driveway to the main road. Feeling strong and rested, he looked forward to his work for the next two days.

After traveling north up the canyon for nearly an hour at a quick trot, Eduardo and the gelding were approaching the last two houses that were situated in the bottleneck of the valley. The road here was less traveled, and these two families who lived at the fringes of the irrigable land were strange, reclusive people. Except to attend Mass occasionally and shop at Mr. Lawrence's, neither family mingled with the rest of the community. Only some of the younger children attended Mr. Vigil's one-room schoolhouse, though they never seemed able to learn English or read and write. The Valdez children were always clean and neat, and their parents worked hard to keep their house and small pastures in excellent condition. But some of the children in the Valdez family were prone to frightening as well as embarrassing outbursts. The youngsters went into fits, pulling their hair and screaming obscenities. Nothing could subdue them.

But the Valdez family was less often the topic of town gossip than the other family, the Perezes. Eduardo was not even sure how many there were in the Perez family, but somehow the lot of them crammed themselves into a slovenly little house that was itself a spectacle. From the outside, which was all anyone besides the Perezes had ever seen of it, the house was a bewildering patchwork of tins and boards and wash pans. Wash lines full of clothes, gunny sacks, farm equipment, stovepipes, deer antlers, animal skins, and even animal bones hung from the walls and rafters of the porch. It was more a heap of junk than a house; though, oddly at every visible window, there were bright masses of red geranium blossoms. The flowers seemed to thrive on chaos.

Elena had forbidden the family to speak to the Perez children. In fact, Eduardo had heard his own mother say some of the worst things about the Perezes, and he had heard plenty of rumors. Roberto, out of his undying curiosity, or in defiance of his mother's order, had verified all of the terrible tales by befriending one of the younger Perez boys and pumping him for information. No one in Los Torbellinos could think of anything redeeming to say about the Perez family.

Eduardo rode quickly past the shambled house. Smoke was rising from one of the sundry, crooked stovepipes, and one of the girls was standing on the porch staring at him. Eduardo nodded a greeting toward her. Enthusiastically, she waved and grinned at him. She was short, squat and looked old and haggard, though she was probably no older than Carlos. It looked as though her belly sagged with a child. Eduardo coaxed the gelding into a lope. He knew that when people said the Perezes slept together they really meant the Perezes had sex together, or as Roberto put it, they bred like animals. It was too grotesque, and Eduardo wondered if all of the gossip were really true. It seemed possible, but he wondered how people came to know these things. If it were true about the Perezes, then it might also be true what people, including Carlos and Roberto, said about Lydia Lepage. Eduardo did not know what to believe anymore; he did not trust anyone. He loped the gelding until he was well past the Perezes.' He felt ashamed that he had not smiled and spoken to the lonely, life-beaten girl. He looked over his shoulder and saw her still standing on the porch looking after him, smiling. He felt ashamed that he did not turn around and take her away from that vile house. If everyone knew about it, why had nothing been done to help those girls, to help Lydia Lepage?

It was true that Lydia Lepage had been raped by Mr. Salazar, her math teacher from the high school. Darlene told him that the last time he saw her. The rape happened on the last day of school before their summer break started. Every year the high school students were bused to the Los Torbellinos waterfalls for the end of school picnic. There was a deep man-made cave in one of the cliffs that formed a wall to the waterfall; few people knew about the cave. Mr. Salazar knew about it, though, and he had forced Lydia Lepage into that cave on the day of the picnic, and he had raped her. That was Darlene's story. Eduardo believed Darlene, but he was confused by all of the different accounts he had heard after the Lepages disappeared from Los Torbellinos overnight.

Eduardo had been the only one who even knew they were leaving. He watched them go. By the next day, the entire village was talking. Even Carlos and Roberto said that Lydia was a flirt. Maybe she asked for it. She was overly coy and obliging toward all of her male teachers. That made Eduardo think of the way Darlene smiled at Mr. Vigil, but he knew she did not mean anything by it. Still, he could not understand why Lydia would go to the cave alone with Mr. Salazar. Carlos and Roberto said she had been clinging to Mr. Salazar's arm since the buses arrived at the falls because the boys were catching the girls and tossing them in the river. They wanted to throw Lydia in, too, but she held onto Mr. Salazar's arm; he would not let them touch her. After that, the boys ignored Lydia for the rest of the day because they said she was acting superior. After lunch she still had her arm looped through Mr. Salazar's arm, and some of the boys were already making jokes about them. Then Lydia and Mr. Salazar disappeared. People did not put all of the pieces together until the next day. No one was even sure how the word got out about the rape. Maybe someone saw Lydia go into the cave with Mr. Salazar, or as Darlene told Eduardo, saw Mr. Salazar force her into the cave. Eduardo certainly never told anyone what he knew.

Darlene told him that they had to leave Los Torbellinos because her father said people would talk. They would tell lies about what happened, and Lydia could never hold her head up in Los Torbellinos again. Mr. Lepage had been right about that. People did talk, but of course the school tried to keep the whole thing quiet. They protected Mr. Salazar. He was young, only thirty-two, and a good math teacher. He was handsome and had a wife and two children. He and his family lived on the high school campus in the modern houses built for teachers; they were respected in the community and attended Mass every Sunday. Carlos and Roberto did say that Salazar flirted with all of the pretty girls, and that he stared at girls in an ungentlemanly fashion, like Mr. Vigil did. Eduardo could make no sense of it, did not want to think of what happened, but he could not clear it from his mind. Lydia should not have gone to the cave with Mr. Salazar, but no one deserved rape. Now the Lepages were gone and his Darlene was gone with them. He knew that Darlene was innocent, and her sister probably equally so.

By noon, Eduardo and the gelding were high in the mountains. The aspen and scrub oak were tinted with faint colors of gold and rust and a delicate chill in the air warned of fall's arrival. The wind whipped and whispered mournfully through the treetops, filling Eduardo with sadness. The howling wind blotted even the clipping of the horse's hooves on the rutted wagon road. To break the sound of the eerie whispering, Eduardo patted the gelding's broad neck and talked loudly. At the base of a mountain pass, Eduardo was grateful to find the cattle trail covered with fresh tracks. It gave him something to concentrate on. The trail began at the base of a hill, where a spring filled a muddy pond with water; the path winded up into the mountains to the west. Eduardo's horse climbed the steep trail for two hours. At the top of the plateau, the terrain spread into rolling, grassy hills that gradually curved down to the other side of the mountain. The tall, coarse grass lay wind-beaten, close to the ground. Grazing a short distance from the trail were the cattle he had tracked. Eduardo spotted four of his father's cows in the pack.

The gelding was soaked and puffing from the steep climb, so Eduardo rode to a stand of aspen trees to unsaddle his horse and stake it to graze. Then he ate some jerky and dried apples and took a long drink of water. He walked back to the place where the cattle trail made its steep descent down the mountain. Far below were the houses in Los Torbellinos. The distance seemed too great for him to have covered in less than a day's ride, and beyond his valley, he saw the purple mountain ranges of Santa Fe. The sky was cold blue against the dark shapes of the mountains on the horizon. Surely by now Fernando was on his way to the cabin that was situated not far from the base of the cattle trail down in the canyon. He looked forward to seeing his old friend; perhaps riding into the sierra completely alone had not been a good idea after all.

Eduardo gazed off the mountain peak for a long time. Slowly he became aware of the incessant whispering of the wind again, and it brought back the emptiness. He had not stopped thinking of Darlene. Looking out over the panoramic vista, he was at least comforted by the sight of the mountains near Santa Fe where he knew she now lived with her family. When he turned away from the view below, the gelding was still grazing. There would be enough time for him to search for more cattle later, so he lay in the grass. He shut his eyes and thought of Darlene and this new loneliness that was empty and cold like the sky. Eduardo was below the chill of the wind now, and the sun was hot on his face and body. He settled down comfortable, warm, and relaxed.

With his eyes closed and his body resting peacefully, his last meeting with Darlene began to reel through his mind like it had hundreds of times before. It was Friday after the last day of school. Carlos and Roberto had come home a bit later than usual because of the high school picnic. They were happy and laughing about the fun of the day. They did not know what had happened at the picnic, not yet. Of course, neither did Eduardo. He and Marcos were chopping wood at the wood pile when their older brothers walked up. Eduardo listened to their adventures without feeling jealousy the way he might have before Darlene came into his life. They were all in a good mood because school was out for the summer, but Eduardo was especially happy because he would be meeting Darlene in a few hours. Finally, Carlos and Roberto went in the house; Eduardo and Marcos remained at the wood pile chopping and stacking stove wood. Then they were joined by Pedro, and the three of them went off to clear stones from a field they had recently plowed. That was when Eduardo had felt a tingling sensation down his spine, as if someone were watching them. He turned and saw Darlene standing in a clump of trees. She had never been near their farm before; he knew something had to be wrong to make her come there. She was motioning frantically for him to follow her, and he could see that her face was distorted from crying. He turned quickly to see if his brothers had also seen her, but they had not. He made up an excuse that he could no longer remember and darted off. Darlene had already left the thicket.

Eduardo ran wildly through the forest. Branches slapped him in the face and pulled at his clothing. He jumped logs and dashed around trees, oblivious to the obstacles in his path. When he raced into the clearing and saw Darlene kneeling on the ground slumped over by grief, he knew that the fear inside of him was real. Slowly he walked up to Darlene and knelt down in front of her. She looked at him and tried to mouth words, but only strangled sobs came out. He took her face in his hands. "It can't be so bad," he said, trying to convince both of them. "Tell me what's wrong?"

"We're leaving. We're leaving tonight," she choked. The shock of her words muted Eduardo.

"Daddy says we have to go. He's . . . he's already started packing our things," she cried.

"No!" Eduardo shouted.

"Oh, it's too terrible. What happened. Today . . . today at the high school picnic," she stammered, "Lydia's teacher, Mr. Salazar, he . . . he," but she could not finish, and began to sob uncontrollably again.

Eduardo thought he knew, but he was not certain. "What Darlene? What is it?" he urged.

"He raped her," she blurted. "I heard it all. Lydia was a mess when she came home. Her clothes were dirty and torn, her hair a mess and one of her eyes is turning black and blue. She started crying when she saw all of us. Then she was out of her head. I guess Daddy knew it right then. He made me leave the room with Jim, but I listened anyway. She says Mr. Salazar took her to see a cave; she says when they got there, he started squeezing her and trying to kiss her, you know, and she told him to quit, but . . ." Darlene had not stopped crying and it was difficult for Eduardo to make out the words. "But then he slapped her and made her go in. He said she knew what she was doing all the time. He made her go in and . . ."

Eduardo understood. He held Darlene to him. "But you can't leave. Don't leave, Darlene," he begged.

"We have to. Daddy says no one will believe Lydia's story. I never seen my daddy cry before, not even when we lost the farm, but when he came to tell me to start packing, he was crying. I'm so scared," she whimpered.

"Where will you go? I can come there. I can still see you."

"I don't know where we're going. I guess, Daddy doesn't know himself. He says we have to leave here. Eduardo . . . I have to go now. Right now," she moaned with the tears streaming down her face.

"No Darlene," he said, holding her. "No."

They held each other tightly. "I have to. Now. My father went off to find a doctor to get something to make Lydia rest. That's why I could sneak away. I had to tell you."

"No," was all he could say, but it was too late. Darlene was already wrenching herself free.

"Eduardo, you know I love you. I always have," she cried. Then they embraced for the last time. They kissed and she pulled away. "We're leaving tonight after dark. As soon as we pack up. I'll write to you, Eduardo. I promise I will," she said.

"I love you," he whispered. They kissed one last time, and then she was gone.

What could he do? He was a stupid kid. He felt as helpless as a baby. He watched her go with tears flooding down his face, more tears than he knew he had. His beautiful Darlene slipped away into the forest, and he had done nothing to stop her.

After Darlene left him, Eduardo went home. Like always, he was able to fool his family. They never suspected a thing. That night after dinner, when he was certain his mother was in bed, he crept out of the house and ran toward the dairy farm. He ran as fast as he could, and then suddenly came to an abrupt standstill near the main road. The Lepages were pulling out of their driveway. Where he was standing, he knew they could see him in the headlights of the truck, but he did not care. All of them except Darlene would think he was some hooligan wandering around in the night. He tried desperately to see Darlene, but he was blinded by the headlights. As the Lepages pulled off down the road, he could see that their belongings were tied to the flatbed of the truck. Eduardo watched the jalopy until the last glimmer of light disappeared far down the road. He felt weak enough to faint; it was as if all of his strength vanished with the light. Helpless, he ran like a madman down the driveway to the house the Lepages had vacated only minutes before. He had no idea what he hoped to find there. He tried the kitchen door and it opened. He went inside, and his skin began to prickle from the silence and absolute emptiness of the dark house. He groped along the shelf of a cupboard until he found matches and the nub of a candle. After lighting it, he roamed from room to room. The place had been left neat and clean. There was some old furniture that had probably been there before the Lepages moved in, and everything personal had been taken. Eduardo found the room that had to have been the girls.' There were two newly built twin beds against one wall, but of course, there were no mattresses or blankets left behind. There was nothing tangible to help him remember. Still, he lingered there until he was overcome by fear or dread or something worse aching inside of him, and he rushed out of the house.

The days of tasteless food and dull sadness ensued. For weeks after the Lepages left Los Torbellinos, Eduardo thought that he would never hear from Darlene again, though she had promised to write. If she did write, Eduardo did not want his family to see the letter, so he visited the postmaster and briefly explained the situation. The friendly old man assured Eduardo that if a letter came he would set it aside until Eduardo came to pick it up. Eduardo had visited the post office twice weekly after Darlene left town, and by the fourth week, he had begun to give up hope that Darlene would ever write. But the last week in June, he walked into the post office hopeful. Then the postmaster smiled and retrieved an envelope. Without glancing at the writing on the envelope, Eduardo tore into the letter and read:

June 15, 1940

Dearest Eduardo,

I promised you I'd write so of course I am. I wouldn't think of not writing. Things are better than I thought they'd be. We live in Santa Fe on the northwest side of town. It's in the country not like in a city at all. Thank God for that. My father got work with the railroad. He's gone from home most of the time now but he makes good money and we have a nice house.

My mother works for a rich family. She does housework and sewing for them and sometimes Lydia and me help her there. The people are real nice.

Lydia is better now. Thank God.

I still have my pup, Spots, and there's lots of room here for him and my little brother to play. As I hope you know I miss the dairy and Los Torbellinos and of course most of all you. It's not as pretty here as it is in Los Torbellinos, and I don't know anyone here except the people we work for. As you can tell it is pretty isolated out here.

Please, please, please don't forget about me but you can't write me yet because of how my father is especially since you know what. But I'll find somewhere for you to write to me. PLEASE don't forget me. I'll write again soon as I can. I love you, I love you, I love you, I love you, Darlene

Since then Eduardo had received other letters, which helped but did not ease his miserable loneliness. But her letters were better than nothing. He was relieved that, at least, Darlene was only sixty miles away instead of six hundred; most of all he was bolstered by the fact that she was secure in their new home. Reminding himself of that, Eduardo jumped to his feet smiling. Darlene had not forgotten him, and he would not forget her, not ever.

TWENTY-TWO

It was late afternoon when Eduardo started down the mountain with five cows and four calves. At the end of the trail, he left the cows in the meadow, where he would pick them up in the morning, and headed south toward Fernando's cabin. After ten minutes, Fernando's property and cabin came into view. Eduardo surveyed the lush, green meadows along the river by Fernando's cabin, and as he rode closer he was relieved to see Cochise grazing nearby. Though Fernando was nowhere in sight, he had already built a fire that smoked lazily in the pit outside, and Eduardo suddenly realized how happy he was that he would not be spending the night alone.

At the south border of Fernando's property line, another small cabin or hut was located almost adjacent to the barbed-wire fence that separated the two pieces of land. The hut and land belonged to a man named Nicolás Martínez, who was a distant cousin of Fernando's. At one time, the two families had been the wealthiest in the valley, and some people still believed they were. Nicolás was an eccentric old man, the last survivor in his family, which owned a big house in El Valle plus the lovely stretch of land in the high country. Nicolás, however, lived in Santa Fe and scarcely visited his family home in the village; in fact, the big house was vacant and boarded up.

When Eduardo dismounted to open the gate, he felt the tiredness in his body. Surely Juanita and Florinda had not sent Fernando into the sierra without a feast. Closing the gate behind him, he remounted stiffly and rode to the cabin. The fire in the pit had burnt down to a pile of embers. Eduardo dismounted, and wondering where Fernando might be, threw a couple of sticks of wood on the fire. Next he unsaddled his horse, hobbled it, and turned it loose. Cochise ran up to get acquainted with Eduardo's horse, who ignored him and lay down to roll not five feet away from the fire pit. After a good roll, the gray managed to get back to his feet despite his hobbles, and he hopped off toward the river after Cochise.

It would still be light for another hour. Eduardo gathered his saddle and gear and went to the cabin door. He pushed the creaky old door and stepped inside. Everything, right down to the musty odor that rushed to his nostrils, was exactly as it had been the last time he was there. He put his gear in the corner next to Fernando's saddle and then peeked into the flour sacks hanging on hooks from the rafters. There were a number of burritos and tamales as well as fried pies—probably apricot, his favorite—and an assortment of apples, boiled eggs, a tin of crackers, and sardines. Eduardo closed the bags, looking forward to a good meal. He took a bucket off a hook on the wall, located his bar of soap and toothbrush from his saddlebags and went to the creek, where he removed his shirt, boots, and socks. He splashed his face and body with cold water, washed, brushed his teeth, and combed his fingers through his hair. Finally he slipped into his clothes and filled the bucket with water before returning to the cabin.

Eduardo built up the fire and made a pot of coffee. His skin was still tingling from the coldness of the water; he felt refreshed and wide awake now. The air was chilly, so he went into the cabin and untied his thick blanket from the back of his saddle and draped it around his shoulders. Outside again he was beginning to grow concerned about Fernando, so he wandered back toward the river. At the same instant that he put his fingers to his mouth to whistle, he spotted Fernando coming down a steep trail on the east side of the river. Fernando saw him and waved. The old man picked his way carefully across the stones in the creek and walked up to Eduardo smiling.

"Hello, son," he said, cheerily patting Eduardo on the back. "How did you do today? Did you find some of your daddy's cows?"

"Yes, I left them grazing up the road a ways."

"You'll find the others tomorrow. I bet you're tired, tired and hungry."

"A little," Eduardo admitted.

"Well, the girls packed us enough food to last a hundred years. Lets go up to the fire and have something to eat."

Back at the fireside, Fernando fetched their food and two coffee cups and they settled around the fire. Then they heard the clipping of horses' hooves and the rattle of a wagon on the road above. Eduardo stood, looking up toward the main road. The wagon was bouncing down the hillside behind two pinto horses, Grandfather José's team. There were two figures jostling on the seat of the buckboard, but Eduardo could not recognize them at such a distance. Whoever they were, they were definitely heading toward Fernando's cabin. One of the men hopped off the wagon seat and began to open the gate. "Who is that?" Mano Fernando said, squinting into the waning light.

Eduardo's heart raced. It did not seem possible but it was his Uncle Diego. Eduardo had not seen him in nearly two years, but there he was opening the gate for Nicolás Martínez, who was driving the team. "It's Tío Diego and Nicolás Martínez, but what are they doing up here?" said Eduardo, beginning to smile.

"What? Nicolás?" chuckled Fernando. "I haven't seen my primo in months."

Diego was back on the wagon seat now and they were bouncing down the hill toward the cabin. Even though Eduardo felt a bit awkward, he began to wave energetically. Diego had done some crazy things since Eduardo was an adoring little boy, but so had he. So had everyone he knew. When Diego recognized him and began to smile and wave, Eduardo felt relief and elation. His uncle looked clear-eyed and sober, unlike the last times Eduardo had seem him at José's.

Before Nicolás drew the team to a halt, Diego jumped spryly off his high perch and ran toward Eduardo. "Hey," he said, "look who's here. Is that you, conejo? Sonofagun! Well, sonofagun!" Diego stretched out his hand to Eduardo and the handshake ended in a masculine embrace. Diego felt like a twig between Eduardo's arms; Eduardo could feel his uncle's sharp shoulder blades through the fabric of his jacket. They stepped back from each other. "Son-ofagun, conejo, what the hell they been feeding you?" he said, appraising Eduardo. "Last time I saw you, you were already taller than me. Now you look like a goddamn giant, Hercules."

Eduardo blushed and shrugged his shoulders. Diego was thinner than before, and his black hair was turning white like José's. Also, the cockiness and the twinkling eyes that had always been Diego's trademarks were gone. Even when Eduardo had seen Diego drunk, that liveliness, that spark of the devil, had never vanished completely. How could two years of life change a person so much?

While Eduardo stared dumbly at Diego, Diego stepped up to Mano Fernando, shook his hand, and began speaking to him in Spanish. Then Diego turned back to Eduardo.

"Conejo, come over here and meet Nicolás. He's the best man in the world," Diego said, pulling Eduardo toward the wagon. Nicolás had driven the team up beside the cabin and brought it to a stop. He pulled up hard on the brake and stepped heavily to the ground. "Nicolás," Diego went on in English again, "look here. This is my nephew. He's my sister's boy, but I practically raised him," he said proudly. "Mr. Eduardo Montez, meet Mr. Nicolás Martínez."

Nicolás extended his hand to Eduardo. He had a friendly smile. Eduardo took his hand. "Pleased to meet you, Eduardo."

"Likewise, sir," Eduardo said. Nicolás had graying hair and rosy cheeks, sparkling, black eyes, and a jovial quality about his face. He was heavyset in a muscular, youthful way that reminded Eduardo of José.

"What brings you up here?" he asked.

"I came up here to check my father's cattle. I found five today. I'll look for the others tomorrow."

"I see. How many cows does your father have?"

"Oh, only fifteen." Eduardo answered.

"Well, it's wise of you to keep an eye on them. Everyone will be pushing their cattle down the canyon in another month. If you don't keep an eye on them from time to time, you won't know where the hell to look for them before winter," he said, still smiling in a friendly way. Nicolás and Fernando greeted each other and began to speak in Spanish.

"Listen, conejo," Diego said aside to Eduardo, "you help me with these horses. Then we'll all go over to your fire and get reacquainted."

"Yes, of course," Fernando said, overhearing them. "Both of you will spend the night in the cabin with us tonight. There are four cots and we've got plenty to eat. There's no need for you to go crawling into that hut of yours, Nicolás, when there are good beds in this cabin."

"Yes, yes, of course, we'll spend the night here with you," Nicolás said.

Eduardo and Diego unharnessed the team while Nicolás unloaded a few boxes from the back of the wagon. Diego turned the two pintos loose, and they ran up to Cochise and Eduardo's horse nickering. Diego laughed, "I see you hobbled that gray elephant-looking horse of yours. What? He doesn't like you much?"

"That horse," Eduardo said smiling, "that horse doesn't like nobody."

They went back to the fire where Nicolás was opening cans of beans and pouring them into a pot. "I hope you're both hungry because we got plenty of food in them boxes," he said first in English and then translated to Spanish for Mano Fernando. Nicolás did not have a trace of a Spanish accent when he spoke English. Then it dawned on Eduardo that Diego and Nicolás always spoke in English to one another. Both of them had lived away from Los Torbellinos for many years and seemed more comfortable speaking English than Spanish.

"Dios mío," Fernando laughed, "don't open all those beans. Like I told Eduardo earlier, I have more food here than we can eat. I hope you're all very hungry," he said.

"I'm always hungry," Eduardo said.

Soon Diego was frying bacon, and Nicolás was chopping squash and onions. When the bacon finished cooking, they fried the squash and onions together in the pan where the bacon had cooked. They also had a big loaf of store-bought bread. After the squash cooked, Nicolás dished up a plateful of squash, beans, and bacon for each of them. Still complaining about there being too much food, Fernando passed around the burritos and tamales.

Eduardo now realized how hungry he felt and noticed that the others were also putting away their share of food. Even Fernando, who usually ate sparingly, was polishing off his meal. It had been a long time since Eduardo had enjoyed food so much. Finally, Eduardo and Diego took the dirty dishes to the river and washed them.

Later Eduardo built up the fire while Diego and Nicolás walked off to the buckboard. Each of them returned with a heavy quilt draped around their shoulders. Diego carried his old guitar, the same one he used to play when he and Eduardo lived in El Valle. Nicolás carried a bottle. The two of them resumed their places around the fire, and Diego began to strum melodies that evoked memories for Eduardo. Nicolás uncorked the bottle and held it up to the firelight, as if to admire it. Then he took a drink. "Ah! That's good whiskey," he said, passing the bottle over to Eduardo.

Eduardo did not hesitate. He had never tasted whiskey before but was anxious to. He drank and passed the bottle to Diego. Then he sat back relishing the sensation of the liquor and thinking about how pretty the fire was. It was peaceful in the sierra.

Diego drank and passed the bottle to Mano Fernando. "So, Eduardo, what have you been up to these days since I seen you last?" Diego asked, without looking up from his guitar.

"Me? Oh, you know, school, working. The same old things."

"Really. Well, what about your family, your mamá and papá, your sisters and brothers?"

"They're all fine. Yeah, they're all fine. My father is still working in Colorado. But everyone is fine."

"We stopped by to visit old José and sister Carmen today," Diego said, strumming. "Both of them are still full of the devil. Anyway, what grade you going into this year? You were always a pretty good student. You keeping your grades up?"

"I start high school this year. I guess I'm doing OK. I always make my grades." Eduardo was bothered by his uncle's monotonous, subdued tone. This was not the uncle he remembered. Maybe he even preferred the wild man Diego had become after Hero died so many years ago. Nicolás passed the bottle over. Eduardo drank.

"So you're starting the high school," Nicolás laughed. "Damned if I didn't think you was about to graduate high school."

They all laughed. The laughter, or the whiskey, seemed to rouse Diego out of his doldrums. "Oyes, conejo, so what about the girls? Las muchachitas," he said, lifting his eyebrows. A sly grin spread over his face. He was looking directly at Eduardo now, interested. His eyes were nearly twinkling like they used to. "What about it?"

"Yeah, I guess so," Eduardo said shyly.

"What do you mean, 'you guess so'? What kind of a goddamn answer is that?" Diego prodded. Now his eyes were absolutely sparkling.

"Yeah, I mean, there was a girl, and nice, too, you know. I guess, she was my girl. But she had to go away with her family."

"Damn! I knew it," Diego said, slapping his thigh. "A good-looking kid like you, well, it just figures. Who was she? What was her name?"

"Her family was from Arkansas. Her name was . . . is Darlene Lepage."

Diego whistled. "So you had yourself a little gringita," he laughed playfully.

"Yeah," Eduardo smiled. "She's real pretty and a real nice girl. But she's . . . they went away about three months ago."

"It sounds like you miss her," Diego said.

"Yeah, I do."

"Why did they go away?"

"Ah, some trouble. You know, lies. Something bad happened, and then someone started a pack of lies." Eduardo stopped. To say anything more felt like betrayal. There was silence.

"Hum, I know all about lies," Diego said. He started strumming the guitar again. Eduardo was relieved that his uncle was not going to pry any further.

"Lies. Lies of other people pained me all the time when I was younger," Nicolás said. "I wasted my youth worrying about the lies people told about me. Now I'm an old man. Of course, at last, I learned not to give one goddamn what people say about you. Sure, I finally learned the secret, but now I'm too old and ugly to live

211

a beautiful life," he cackled. They all took another drink. Eduardo was feeling happy and lightheaded; drunk but not too drunk. He wanted to ask Diego about his life since he had left Los Torbellinos, but he decided that Diego would talk if he wanted.

"You know, muchachos, we're being rude talking in English," Nicolás said in Spanish. "We're forgetting our comrade, Mano Fernando, here. You see, mano, we were just talking about lies." Fernando nodded but said nothing so Nicolás went on, "Years ago when my brothers passed away some locoso down in Los Torbellinos started the rumor that I did it." He was talking loudly now. "May I remind you all that I was half way across the country when Pablo died, but I came home to bury him. Then about a month later, when I was already back in California, poor Baldino accidentally set himself on fire. I shouldn't have left him alone because he never was very smart. Then, let me tell you, everyone down in the valley was certain I did them in . . . for all that family money," he laughed bitterly. "Jesus Christ, there was no money. Why in hell would I be working out in California if I were a rich man? When I got back to bury Baldino, well, I knew what people were thinking. You wouldn't believe it."

"Sure, I'd believe it," said Mano Fernando, laughing ironically, "Don't forget that I'm supposed to be made of money myself."

"Of course, you too, qué no, primo. I guess there used to be money in our family, maybe a hundred generations ago," Nicolás sputtered. "Nothing can compare to the lies that are bred in little towns."

"Take it easy, hombre," Diego said sleepily. "I thought those lies didn't bother you no more."

Nicolás was silent, angry. Diego continued to strum his guitar seemingly unconcerned.

"Hell, you're right," Nicolás laughed. "You're right. I guess I'm just getting drunk. But I still got nothing for small towns. I'd sell the house tomorrow if I could." He laughed his friendly laugh again. "But the trouble is that no one will buy it. They all think it's haunted, or cursed."

All of them laughed and Eduardo felt relieved. Diego played a piece of lively music. Then he tapped the guitar. "Well, men, I'm going to sleep. Good night, good night, gentlemen." He stood up stretching. They said good night and he went into the cabin with his guitar.

Eduardo threw some wood on the fire. "I was wondering, do you ever get up to Santa Fe?" Nicolás asked.

"No. I've never been out of Los Torbellinos, except to the neighboring towns and once to Española with my father," Eduardo admitted.

"Ha, ha. That reminds me of myself when I was your age, but now I've been just about everywhere in the country. Anyway, Santa Fe is a good town. If you ever get up there, you look us up. See, your uncle, he lives at my place in Santa Fe now. About two years ago, I saw him in a local bar. He was drunk and trying to make trouble, actually he was only making a fool of himself. I recognized him because I know your grandfather very well. Anyway, I guess Diego reminded me of myself some years ago," he said. "It's usually the case that we have pity on those who remind us of ourselves," he laughed. "So I told him to calm down, and for some reason he listened to me. I told him he could stay at my place for the night; he's been there since. Now he gets odd jobs, and he doesn't drink too much anymore. I guess, he's like the son I never had. He's about the right age, too, to be my son."

"Eduardo is like that to me," smiled Fernando. "I mean like the son I lost. But what brought you two up here, Nicolás?" he continued.

"Whenever I can force myself, I come up to check the old house in the valley. Kids love to go in there and snoop around. Every so often I have to come up from Santa Fe to nail up the doors and windows where they busted in. Little bastards. I'd like to catch some of them and scare the piss out of them," Nicolás laughed.

Eduardo cleared his throat. He was guilty. Two summers before, Roberto had coerced he and Marcos to break into the old Martínez house with him.

Nicolás went on. "At first, Diego said he wouldn't come with me. Then for some reason he changed his mind. Yesterday and this morning we boarded up the house, and we visited with José and Carmen for a few hours. Then we parked my car at José's and borrowed his team to come up here to do some fishing. Your tío says he came along to fish, but I know he wanted to see your grandfather."

"He used to take me fishing with him when I was a little boy. I never could catch a fish, but I used to dig all of his worms for him, and he told me to put them on his hook for good luck. He's a pretty good fisherman."

"He's a good man, your uncle." They stared at the fire. At length as if thinking aloud, Nicolás said, "You know, even if I find a buyer for the house down in the valley, I'll never sell my place up here. It's too beautiful and peaceful; there's no amount of money that would make me think of selling my place in the sierra."

"How many acres do you have up here?" Eduardo asked.

"About forty-five. About the same as my primo here. How many is it you have left up here, Fernando, forty-five or fifty?" he chuckled.

"Fifty, only fifty," Fernando answered flatly.

"Did you know, Eduardo, that the entire valley from here north all the way up to the T where the road divides west and east used to belong to Fernando's family? That's right. They owned the richest land down here along the river and up the ravines west and east from the river as well. They owned miles and miles of the richest country from this point north, and my family owned about the same amount of land from the fence line there and south for miles and miles. Did you know that?" Nicolás asked again.

"No. I didn't," said Eduardo, looking at Nicolás and then Fernando.

"That was a long time ago, Eduardo. That was in my grandfather's day. Before the 1860s, half of that land that belongs to the Pierce family today, well, it used to belong to my grandfather."

"What happened? Why did he sell?" asked Eduardo.

"He didn't sell, and my grandfather didn't either," Nicolás answered bitterly. "That was the time of the gringo and the time of the great land swindles. You see, this Pierce, whose grandsons own the land today, he came in here with a set of deeds for my family's land and for Fernando's too. Of course, they were false deeds, but in the end they held up in court. As if he were God himself, Pierce appeared one day out of nowhere and informed our families that our deeds were invalid. He showed them the false deeds and said that the land now belonged to him. Our grandfathers went to court in Santa Fe, but that was an Anglo court. After about four or five years, the courts approved Pierce's deeds, and he came into possession of the Romero and Martínez land. They left us this land, where the hut and cabin are, I suppose as a sort of consolation. But it ruined our grandfathers, ruined them," he said shaking his head.

"No, that can't be," Eduardo said in disbelief.

"That's what our grandfathers and fathers said at first, too, but as impossible as it sounds, that's how it happened," Fernando reassured him. "The same thing was happening all over the New Mexico Territory in the 1860s. Characters like Pierce came up with false deeds, or found ways to invalidate the original ones. The courts supported them and the rightful owners lost the land that had been in their families for generations. There was much land fraud during those years."

"What did your grandfather do?" Eduardo asked.

"He went to court, but from the beginning, the odds were against him. Then . . . then when Pierce took over the land, it was too much for my grandfather. He had a favorite meadow up the river there," Fernando said pointing north, "about three miles from here. Three months after Pierce and his men took over we were forced to clear the sheep off the land to make room for Pierce's cattle. It wasn't long after that when my grandfather went to this place up the river and shot himself in the head. That's all that was left for him to do. I was ten; my father and I were the ones who found him, but that's what my grandfather did. He shot himself," Fernando repeated.

"My grandfather, he didn't kill himself," Nicolás added, "but he might as well have. He lived like a walking corpse for about ten years after they lost the land, and finally he gave up on life and died, a miserable man at the time of his death."

"Just like the that, Pierce came into all this land without paying anyone a penny?" Eduardo asked.

"Just like that," said Nicolás.

"I don't know," interrupted Fernando. "We don't know all the facts. I'm sure he had to pay someone for those false documents, and then he probably had to pay off a corrupt judge or two, but

215

he surely never paid the amount the land is worth, and he surely never paid our families a penny."

"As I said, it was the time of the powerful gringo and the rule of crooked laws. It still is," Nicolás laughed.

"It ended not only my grandfather's life, but my family's way of life. We used to run more than eight thousand head of sheep in this valley. After we lost the land, we had to cut the heard drastically, by three-fourths," said Fernando. "At the time, we were still allowed to run the sheep on public domain." Fernando chuckled and shook his head. "Then in the 1900s the Bureau of Land Management closed down public domain to open grazing so we had to cut our herd again. The Bureau of Land Management issued us permits to graze one thousand head on public lands, but the wool prices were sinking, and the cost of shearing and transporting the wool of one thousand sheep made the herd unprofitable. That's when my father decided to trade the sheep permits for cattle permits. Nearly everyone in Los Torbellinos did the same thing. The rate of trade was ten to one. We could exchange ten sheep permits for one cattle permit. That's what we were left with, one hundred cattle permits, which I suppose is better than nothing because beef is still bringing good money on the market. But that's how it all happened . . . just like that," said Fernando.

"That's not fair," Eduardo protested.

Fernando shook his head, but Nicolás laughed cheerily, drank from the bottle, and passed it to Eduardo. "You tell me, Eduardo, what is fair?" Eduardo shrugged his shoulders, for he had no answer. Then Nicolás went on, "You know, I never trust a person who doesn't cuss a bit, drink strong coffee, or a little whiskey now and then. A few vices are humbling. Eduardo, I haven't heard you cuss, but you take a little whiskey, and if it's true that your uncle raised you, then I figure you know how to cuss, too. So you remember to look us up when you get to Santa Fe."

Nicolás stood up stiffly, stretched and yawned. "I'm going to sleep now, men. Good night," he said, walking off to the cabin. Eduardo and Fernando said good night to him, and shortly afterward Fernando followed.

Alone now, Eduardo gazed into the fire, thinking about how

content he was in the company of the three older men. None of them had lived easy lives, but they were survivors, all three of them. And all of them had the courage to defend their individuality. The bottle of whiskey was at Eduardo's feet. He took another drink. Diego had come into his life long ago only to disappear one day. But now he was back for a while. Their paths would cross again in the future. Eduardo was confident that more than coincidence governed the way people moved in and out of his life. The thought comforted him, for he knew that someday he would see Darlene again. Then he forgot everything and watched the fire glowing and dancing before him.

TWENTY-THREE

The first day of the 1940-41 school year, Eduardo woke with butterflies in his stomach. He left the house with Carlos and Roberto at 7:10 A.M.. The walk to the south end of town where the new high school had been built five years before took about forty-five minutes; there was no bus service for the students who lived in Los Torbellinos, though students who lived in the neighboring villages were bused in daily.

Los Torbellinos High School was one of the first boarding schools in the state of New Mexico. The modern campus consisted of large, appealing buildings and lovely, well-kept lawns, the only lawns ever seen in Los Torbellinos, and the school was supposedly one of the best in the state. Nearly six hundred students, some from faraway New Mexico towns and out of state, attended the boarding school. Most of the teachers lived on the campus in modern houses built especially for them, and most of the teachers were Anglos, as were many of the students.

As usual, the first day of school began with a general assembly in the gymnasium. The principal introduced himself and his staff and welcomed students to another school year at Los Torbellinos High. Afterward the students went through the hectic process of registering for their classes, which only took half the day, and at noon they were permitted to go home. Classes would begin the following morning.

The next day Eduardo and his friends wandered from class to class, too nervous to absorb the content of the lessons and intimidated by the ordered structure of the lessons as well as the automatic bell systems. All of their teachers lectured at lightening speed. And the vocabulary! Half the time Eduardo was not sure that he understood them at all, but he was relieved to find out that his friends were equally baffled.

After lunch, Eduardo had two regular classes before he went to gym, his last class of the day. Carlos and Roberto, as well as most of Eduardo's freshmen friends, took P.E. the same hour. The gymnasium was the most beautiful and expensive building on campus. Inside were two large locker rooms, a basketball court, a large room used for boxing, a weight room, storage closets, and the coaches' offices. The building was big enough to get lost in. The first day of class the coach had taken them on a tour of the gym. Eduardo and the other freshmen had gazed in awe at the high ceilings, water fountains, modern showers, and toilets. The coach had taught at the school long enough to know that many of the boys had never used modern plumbing before, so he gave a mock demonstration of how to use the toilets, sinks, and showers. A few of the city boys started to snicker, but Coach Hansen cut them off with a mean glare.

When the tour was over, Coach Hansen looked at his watch. "Put on your P.E. gear and be out on the gym floor in six minutes." The boys rushed into the locker room. Eduardo and his friends stuck closely to Carlos and Roberto and watched everything they did. They all undressed hurriedly, shoving their clothing into wire locker baskets on the wall. Next they put on their T-shirts and trunks, and since many of the boys did not own gym shoes, they went onto the basketball court wearing socks.

Coach Hansen was pacing the floor outside the locker room glancing at his watch. When they were all assembled in front of him, he blew his whistle loudly and shouted, "Settle down and listen up. This gymnasium is my domain, and my job is to train your bodies as well as your minds. I'll tell you right now that I hate quitters. I am going to push you until it hurts, and I don't want to hear about your aches and pains." He strutted up and down the lines surveying his class. He wore an immaculate white sweat shirt that fit tightly over his barrel chest and huge arms. His slacks were black and his white gym shoes were spotless. "I hate to hear, 'I can't do

it.' And if I tell you to do something, and you tell me you can't before you even try, I'm going to run your ass into the ground. Now
I'm going to introduce you to my boxers." He blew his whistle.
"I want boxers up here," he said, pointing to a black line on the
gym floor. The boys on the boxing team stepped out in front and
formed a line facing their classmates. "This is my team," he went
on. "They are boxers because they are the best. They all worked
hard to get here and they work even harder to keep their places
on the team." Carlos and Roberto had both been on the team since
they were freshmen. "This is Manuel," the coach said, placing his
hand roughly on the shoulder of a tall, well-built senior, a local boy
whom Eduardo and his friends knew from around town. Manuel
stood in the middle of the line, sneering. "He's the captain of my
team, and he is also my athletic assistant. If he tells you to do something, it's as good as if I told you to do it, so you do it. Understand?"
The boys eyed Manuel and nodded their heads. Hansen went on,
"This year I have six positions on my boxing team. We hold tryouts in one month. If any of you boys think you have what it takes
to join my team, I suggest you start preparing today. Next Monday
there will be after-school practice for those of you who would like
to try out. But for today Manuel is going to lead you in calisthen-
ics, and then I want you to give me thirty laps around the gym."
He blew the whistle and Manuel took charge.

Later in the locker room, the upperclassmen undressed casually
and went into the showers. Eduardo and his friends were reluctant
to follow, not knowing exactly what to do.

"Don't stand around like a bunch of women," Carlos cautioned
them under his breath, "or these guys will make it tough on you.
Take your clothes off and go shower up." Eduardo and his friends
undressed and went awkwardly to the showers, too nervous to enjoy the luxury of the modern plumbing.

A local, fat boy was the last one off the court. Some of the best
athletes were already getting dressed when he came panting into
the locker room. His face was red and sweat was pouring off of
him. When he undressed and walked toward the shower, one of
the senior boys snapped his towel at the boy's rear. The wet towel
stung viciously, making him cry out. "Pura manteca," said the boy

who hit him. Some of the others started laughing and continued to tease the chubby boy until Carlos told them to shut up and mind their own business.

On Wednesday in gym class, the coach sent around a sign-up sheet for those interested in trying out for the boxing team. Eduardo signed his name on the paper and dressed out for P.E. The class went through the regular warm-up routine again, and then they started a program in the weight room. Finally the coach blew the whistle. First, he announced that the seniors and freshmen would not be meeting for P.E. class the next day because the annual freshman initiation would take place. Then he told everyone to hit the showers. When Eduardo's friend Victor came out of the shower, some of the older boys began to taunt him. "Goddamn! You look like a drowned rat," one of them said. Victor ignored them and put on his pants. "Ratoncito, let's me and you wrestle on the mats," another boy said, gesturing toward a pile of mats in one corner.

"No. I have to go home," Victor said meekly.

"It won't take long," the other boy persisted. "What's the matter? Is your mamá waiting for you with cookies and milk? Come on," he said sternly. Victor found himself walking over to the mats. The older boy joined him, and before Victor was able to touch the other boy, he was thrown roughly on his back. All of them laughed; then before Victor could get up, someone yelled, "dog pile!" In seconds, sixteen boys hurled themselves on top of Victor. Eduardo and Carlos were sitting next to one another on a bench pulling their clothes on; they watched Roberto rush over to be the last to jump roughly on the squiggling heap of bodies.

"That happened to me every day of school for the first four weeks when I was a freshman," Carlos said with a frown. "And it'll probably happen to most of the new guys this year. It always does. They picked on me until I made the boxing team," he said in disgust.

"Really?" Eduardo said, helplessly watching the squirming bodies. He was shocked for Victor's sake, but also because he thought that Carlos had never suffered through any kind of humiliation. He suddenly felt more kindly toward his brother. In fact, in the last few days, Eduardo had begun to develop more respect for Carlos because he was not cruel and immature like so many of the other seniors.

"And Roberto? What about him? Did they pick on him, too?" Eduardo asked.

"Well, they weren't so hard on him because I was already here, and well, you know, Roberto is a joker and pretty strong. I mean, a lot of the older guys already knew him through me anyway. They won't bother you because you got both of us, but the new guys who are little and shy really catch hell. It's the same every year," he said, shaking his head. He stood to go help Victor.

But at that point, Manuel walked into the locker room. He looked at the bodies on the mat and began to laugh. Then he blasted his whistle and went over to the mat and began to pull the boys up by their arms. "Okay. That's enough. It's over. Get up," he said, blowing the whistle again. One by one the boys rose to their feet, panting and laughing. At last Victor was able to stand. He was red in the face and tears were streaming down his cheeks, but he would not cry aloud. The rest of the boys were laughing. Then one of them said, "Maybe again tomorrow, Victor."

The next day, the seniors and freshman assembled in the gymnasium to begin the annual auction of freshmen slaves to senior masters. Shortly after the auction, senior and freshman classes would be excused for the day to repaint the huge, white letter M that had been laid out in stone on one of the tallest foothills on the east side of town. This huge letter M, which stood for Mustangs, the school's mascot, could be see from miles away. At the beginning of each year the freshmen students, under the direction of their senior masters, climbed the hill to give the M a fresh coat of whitewash.

Carlos had promised Eduardo that he would purchase him to spare him possible humiliation, but in the end, Manuel bought Eduardo because Carlos used up most of his money buying one of the freshman girls. He couldn't top Manuel's bid.

Soon masters and slaves walked from the high school to the base of the hill where the letter M was situated high above. Sacks of lime and buckets had been transported by truck to the base of the hill, but the lime and buckets of water would have to be carried up the steep hill. Eduardo was appointed as a water boy. While other students carried the sacks of lime up the hill, his group ran off to the river to fill the buckets. When they returned to the base of the hill, Manuel and another senior were sitting in the shade of a tree waiting to direct the detail up the mountain. Manuel stood up with an exaggerated yawn.

"Alright, you boys make a line and climb very carefully because we don't want you wasting any water. Now lets go in single file. Up that hill," he commanded. The boys queued up and began the long, steep climb, each carrying two buckets of water.

After they climbed less than a hundred yards, Manuel began to bark again. "Hey! You boys need to be more careful. Can't you see that you're spilling the water. We can't mix the lime without water so don't spill it all unless you feel like making another trip to the river. Go on keep climbing. You'll be to the top in another twenty minutes. Keep climbing! Climb, climb, climb," Manuel ordered. Eduardo grimaced and stepped more carefully, trying to still the splashing water in the two buckets he carried.

"To hell with you, cabrón," he mumbled under his breath.

Finally, at the top of the hill, Eduardo set the buckets down and stretched his aching arms. Manuel came up behind him. "Alright, you don't have all day. Take that water over and help them mix the lime. Remember, no spilling." Eduardo ground his teeth and picked up the buckets again. "That's good," Manuel said condescendingly.

"Sonofabitches," complained one of the boys. "Just wait till we're the seniors and it's our turn."

"They're all a bunch of idiots, like babies," Eduardo said.

They mixed the whitewash and carried it in buckets to the freshman girls who were painting the huge rocks with old brooms. Most of the girls' faces had been painted clownishly with bright red lipstick; even a few of the boys had to succumb to the indignity. But the humor of the makeup had worn off hours ago; now there was something absurd about the rosy-red cheeks and the huge smiling lips.

As long as the seniors let them work in peace, it was not so bad, Eduardo thought. There were more students in the freshman class than there had been in the entire building at Mr. Vigil's schoolhouse. All of them were his age, and more than half of them were girls. Eduardo eyed María Archuleta, whom he had not seen, except in church, since he had lived in El Valle with his grandparents. She was the most boisterous of the flock of girls. Her long black curls flounced over her shoulders and ample bosoms. Her body was an endless wave of movement. He could not help comparing her to Darlene. They were both attractive but absolutely different. Eduardo felt a twinge of guilt for making the comparison. He shook himself out of the reverie, but it was too late. María had seen him watching her and her eyes gleamed. Her lips parted over her beautiful teeth.

"Eduardo Montez, is that you?" she screeched loudly so that attention was drawn to them. "I remember when you started school in El Valle in Mrs. Sánchez's classroom. Wasn't she always pulling you around by the ears?" she laughed, and everyone laughed with her. Eduardo's face burned scarlet and he turned away from the girls. Was she always that loud and obnoxious?

At noon they paused for lunch. Eduardo and his friends from Mr. Vigil's school went off and sought what shade there was at the base of a piñon tree. Perched noisily nearby sat María and her friends. The boys began to eat, but soon small pieces of bread were landing in their hair and in their laps.

"Ignore them," Eduardo said. "Pretend you don't even notice."

They continued to eat their lunches, though somewhat annoyed. Then a half-eaten apple flew over and hit Victor hard in the back of the head. Immediately the girls broke into shrill, wicked laughter. María, of course, was the loudest of all. Victor turned and glared at the girls. Eduardo turned, too. There was María laughing with those bright eyes of hers staring directly at him.

"If you girls don't stop, I'll start throwing things back," Victor threatened angrily.

"Oooh," mocked María. Her girlfriends cackled madly but stopped throwing food.

After lunch they put the finishing touches on the job. Manuel and some of the other senior boys walked around the huge letter with their hands on their hips, inspecting it.

"Move that stone over." And "You need more paint here," they ordered. But at last the job was completed to the seniors' satisfaction.

Eduardo and his friends were the last to walk down the hills toward the village. They took their time and watched the others swirling down the path like a troop of ants. Manuel was walking with María Archuleta, sometimes offering her his hand when they came to especially steep slopes. Eduardo and his companions watched them.

"That Manuel thinks he's really something special," one of the boys commented.

"Yeah, he thinks he's a real stud," Eduardo said, watching Manuel.

The following Monday after gym class, Coach Hansen summoned the sixteen boys who wanted to try out for the boxing team. Once assembled, the boys left the gym and followed Coach Hansen in his jeep to the main road.

"OK," he shouted from behind the wheel, "you're running three miles to the C.C. camp and three miles back. Anyone who doesn't make it, don't bother staying for practice tomorrow." He drove off and the boys followed him.

The run to the C.C. camp was downhill, and no one lagged behind. The return, however, was all uphill. Coach Hansen drove behind the pack and yelled at them. "Keep your pace. Pick up those knees and move your arms."

Eduardo kept up with the best runners at the head of the pack. Back at campus one boy came in far behind the others, but no one stopped running. At the gym, Eduardo bent over and drew hard to regain his breath. Coach Hansen walked up to him. "Montez, that was some good running. You've got the wind alright. Stand up and walk. Keep breathing. Tomorrow we'll see if you can box anything like your brothers," he said.

The month before the actual tryouts passed quickly. Three boys dropped from the competition; the others ran eighteen miles a week, lifted weights two days a week, and practiced sparring three days a week, not including three hours on Saturday. Finally, when the day of tryouts arrived, Eduardo felt confident. After all, he had been boxing with his brothers since they had joined the team.

Eduardo knew he could box better than most of the boys in his weight class. The boys were paired for two matches each according to their weight classification. When it was over, one junior, three sophomores, and two freshmen were selected as the new members of the boxing team. Eduardo won both of his matches easily. Eduardo and another freshman boy from out of town were selected as bantamweight substitutes, which was as good as they had expected. Most important was that they made the team and would get to travel everywhere the team did.

TWENTY-FOUR

On his way home from school, Eduardo stopped at Lawrence's store to buy a newspaper, a sack of oranges, and four Hershey chocolate bars. At the beginning of the week he had promised Fernando that he would pick up the paper and translate the headline articles for him, as he often did. The oranges were a gift for Juanita and Florinda and the chocolate bars a gift for Fernando. Eduardo knew Fernando loved chocolate bars and had seem him eat as many as six at one sitting. Elena would be furious to know that Eduardo sometimes spent his money on gifts for Fernando and especially for Juanita and Florinda, but if not for the money he earned from Fernando, he would have no pocket money in the first place.

Purchases in hand, Eduardo stepped outside Lawrence's store and appraised the sky. It was Friday in mid-November and the heavens were dark and heavy with the first snow clouds of the year. In the store Eduardo had heard some old men speculating about heavy snowfall by morning. He inhaled deeply to test the air; he hoped that they were right. He always looked forward to the first snowfall of winter.

Not long after he rounded the corner by Lawrence's store and was heading up the canyon, he heard the approach of a wagon behind him. The driver greeted Eduardo and slowed his team long enough to allow Eduardo to hop on the flatbed of the wagon. Eduardo thanked him and settled in to scan the headline articles. He read the front page articles and glanced through the rest of the paper. Then he set the paper aside, and enjoying the tingle of snow in the air, he began to think of the last months at Los Torbellinos High School.

After four months into the year, he felt at ease and sometimes even bored on the high school campus. The school was not as large as it had first seemed. By the end of the first month he knew the names of all of the students; furthermore, after he had adjusted to his new teachers and their class formats, he realized the work was not all that difficult. He was not a straight-A student, but he kept Bs and Cs in all of his classes, and he did have an A in gym and history. Also, he spoke English better and with less accent than he had before. At home, he spoke Spanish only to his mother and younger siblings, but he, Carlos, and Roberto always communicated in English now. Being on the boxing team was what he enjoyed most about high school because it gave him the opportunity to travel, and in the last few months he had visited more towns than he had previously seen in his entire life. Team travel had already taken him to Santa Fe, Albuquerque, and many smaller towns. As a substitute boxer, he sat on the bench most of the time, but that did not bother him. He felt he was not ready to be in the ring yet anyway, and he got to see all the fights. Still, aside from traveling and having more girls to flirt with, life at the high school had become almost as routine as it had been in Mr. Vigil's class, and certainly nothing at home was changing.

At length his family's pasture came into view. When the wagon was near his driveway, Eduardo collected his parcels and hopped down, saying good-bye to the driver. Instead of walking down his own road, he slipped through the fence into Fernando's pasture and headed across the field toward his friend's house. As he stepped under the eaves of the portal, Fernando opened the door, inviting Eduardo into the warm, cozy kitchen that smelled of cooked pinto beans and warm tortillas. Eduardo set his parcels on the table and walked to the stove to warm his hands. He opened the oven door quickly and looked inside.

"I thought maybe your cat was in the oven," he teased, closing the door again.

"No, no," Fernando smiled. "I think it's even too hot for Gatita in there now because the girls just finished cooking, but tonight, when the fire dies down, I'm sure Gatita will want to warm herself in there for a little while."

"That's a strange cat," Eduardo said, shaking his head and rubbing his hands together over the warm stove top.

"I see you brought the paper," Fernando noted.

"Yes, and the chocolate for you and the oranges for Juanita and Florinda."

Fernando smiled and picked up a chocolate bar. "That was thoughtful of you, Eduardo. The girls will be pleased, too. Would you like a cup of coffee and one of these?" he asked, holding up the candy bar.

"Well, I'd prefer a bowl of beans and a tortilla, if they're ready."

"Of course, of course, we won't eat till later, but you go ahead. Here let me get you a bowl." Fernando took a bowl out of the cupboard and filled it with beans from the pot on the stove; he set the bowl on the table and laid a spoon beside it. "You help yourself to the tortillas," he said, gesturing toward the stack of freshly made tortillas. Eduardo took a warm tortilla from the stack and sat down at the table. Fernando poured a cup of coffee for himself and one for Eduardo before taking his place at the table. He opened a candy bar, broke it into miniature squares, but then pushed it aside and pulled the newspaper toward him. First he glanced over the photographs and then read the headlines in his heavily accented English. "Have you read this article already? What's happening now?"

"Yes, I read it," Eduardo answered, "but there's nothing encouraging happening."

"Of course not, that's war and it's going to get much worse before the situation starts to improve. That is, if it's going to improve at all. You go on and eat. You can tell me about it later."

After he finished eating, Eduardo translated the highlights of the cover article for Fernando. He noted that Fernando shook his head and clinched his teeth at the news, none of it good. Eduardo did not like it when Fernando clinched his teeth like that; it made him look haggard and forlorn. News about the war always had that effect on his friend, so he was relieved to finish the translation and groped at any chance to change the subject.

Eduardo folded the paper and pushed it to the center of the table. At the same time, he glanced out the window.

"Look, Mano," he said, "it's started to snow. Look, it's coming down fast and heavy." They walked out on the portal, where they were joined by Juanita and Florinda. The women greeted Eduardo and all of them began to chatter at once about the falling snow, but after a few minutes, Juanita and Florinda went back inside their room.

"Don't stay out here too long, or you'll both take a cold," Juanita advised, as she closed their door to the portal.

"You know, the cold never bothers me," Fernando said. "I must have good circulation. I love the first snowfall of the year and I love winter." Then he laughed aloud. "What am I saying, I love all of the seasons equally, but winter is a special time with a spectacular beauty all it's own."

"Yes, I agree," Eduardo said, "by morning the valley will be covered in a beautiful, white blanket. There's nothing more beautiful and tranquil than a pure-white blanket of snow covering the landscape."

"Exactly, and even as old as I am, the first snowfall of the year never fails to awaken a deep spirituality in me, a feeling of cleansing and rebirth, like you said, a feeling of purity." Fernando smiled at the falling snow as if mesmerized. "But Juanita is right. We're not dressed for this weather. Let's go back inside and have some more hot coffee." In the kitchen, Fernando refilled their cups and sat down.

"I've never known anyone who loved the snow more than my son Alfonso. When he could barely walk, he'd go out and play in the snow until his little hands and feet were nearly frozen. Then he only came in the house long enough to warm up." Fernando unwrapped a second chocolate bar, broke it in half, and passed half of it to Eduardo before continuing. "Then one winter, when he was about twelve, he decided that he wanted to go into the high country and trap for pelts. I don't know where he got the idea from, but he was determined that trapping would be great fun. Well, since there's not so much work to do down here in the valley during winter, I agreed to go with him. I got snowshoes for both of us, and we built a sleigh to transport our gear up to the cabin." Fernando chuckled. "I warned Alfonso that he was going to be tired and cold and hungry long before we'd be able to reach the cabin, but he promised he wouldn't complain. We set off early in the morning before full sunrise, and the snow was deep so it was almost nightfall by the time we finally made our way up to the cabin. My hands and toes were nearly frozen and I knew that Alfonso was in pain, but he never shed a tear and never complained. I remember that I was very proud of him," Fernando sighed. "Anyway, we built a fire in the stove and the cabin was warm in no time. Then we had something to eat and both of us were so tired that we went to bed directly after dinner."

Eduardo was listening intently. He loved to hear Fernando talk about his past, though whenever Fernando talked about his son, Alfonso, Eduardo felt a disturbing conflict within. On the one hand, hearing about Alfonso made him feel helpless and melancholy for Fernando's sake because it was clear that Fernando loved his dead son immensely and missed him still. On the other hand, though he hated to admit it, Eduardo was jealous of Alfonso; jealous because Alfonso had shared a relationship with his father that Eduardo had never known with his own father and never would. He knew that Fernando loved him, too, and that he was important in the old man's life. However, when Fernando talked about what he had shared with his son, Eduardo became painfully aware of what was missing in his own life. To shake the disturbing thoughts, Eduardo blurted, "That must be something rare. I mean to see the high sierra in winter. That is something I'd like to see."

"Eduardo, I can promise you that there is nothing more beautiful. It's like a vision from heaven . . . so beautiful that you can't imagine it. As I told you, when we approached the cabin that first night, we were exhausted and it was nearly dark so we didn't properly appreciate the beauty. But early the next morning we awoke refreshed and eager to get outdoors. We had a good breakfast and left the cabin. The sun was up shining so brightly off the snow that we were blinded for a few minutes, but after our eyes adjusted to the brightness, we stood in awe. Both of us speechless from the beauty surrounding us. Everything, everything was covered in white, white snow, and there were crystal-clear icicles hanging off of the trees and bushes. The air was crisp and fresh, and there was a beautiful blue skyline against all the white snow that was sparkling like diamonds reflecting the sunlight. Finally, Alfonso said, 'Papá, I didn't know that anything could be this beautiful.'

"Well, then we set out with Alfonso's traps. I wasn't happy about him wanting to trap, but I didn't say anything. We put out five traps, two down at the beaver pond and the rest on the mountainside. The next morning, while I was cooking breakfast, Alfonso was so anxious to check his traps that he couldn't wait for me. He ran down to the beaver pond and was back in ten minutes with tears streaming down his face. There was a beaver in his trap, and I guess it frightened him to see the animal in so much pain. Alfonso begged me to go shoot the beaver to put it out of its misery. Well, I told him that he should have had pity on the animal before he decided to trap and maim it. I told him that it wasn't right to trap an animal and leave it to suffer and that he had to finish what he'd started. I gave him his gun and he went down to the pond and shot that old beaver. Then I watched him cross the river and walk up the mountainside. An hour later, he was back at the cabin with the rest of his traps. He'd sprung them all and brought them in, and he never trapped again. I didn't tell him, but I don't think I was ever more proud of him than I was on that day. We didn't talk about it, but I know he knew how I felt."

"After that, since he didn't want to trap anymore, did you come back down to the valley?" Eduardo asked.

"Oh, no. It was after that when we started to enjoy ourselves. We put the traps away and put on our snowshoes and wandered all over the mountains. It's another world up there in the wintertime, and we saw some beautiful sights. We saw snow fowl and fox and bobcats chasing hares over the snow. Once when we were standing on the mountainside, we looked down and saw a huge, graceful puma crossing the snow-covered meadow not twenty feet from our cabin. One day, we came across a herd of elk that were nibbling on spruce tree needles, and Alfonso shot his first bull elk. Of course, it's antlers had fallen away, but the meat was just as good. When we were dressing out the carcass, I asked Alfonso why he didn't cry when he shot the elk, and he said, 'Because he didn't even know he was going to die. He wasn't frightened and in pain like the beaver.' That was all he said.

"We were up there for over a week and only came home because I knew the women would be worried about us. The whole time we were up there we never saw another human being. There was peace and quiet and God's beauty all around us. The only sounds we heard were the sounds of nature—the cry of a snow hawk or at night the howling of the coyotes and the wind. It was lonely in a peaceful, comforting way. We enjoyed it so much that we went back for a week or two each year until Alfonso died.

"The winter before he was shipped overseas, we went up into the sierra for the last time. Those were some of the very best times of my life, those winters we spent together up in the high country." Fernando stopped talking long enough to sip his coffee and suck on a few pieces of chocolate.

"Unfortunately, I never have been able to bring myself to go up there in the winter since. There's no point because some things can never be repeated . . . except up here," Fernando said, tapping his temple with his index finger.

Eduardo saw that tears had begun to stream down Fernando's cheeks. He felt tears filling his own eyes. They looked out at the falling snow. Neither of them spoke. Eventually Eduardo glanced down at his watch. He stood up taking his coat off the back of his chair. "Well, Mano, I guess I'd better be leaving. I know my mother is going to be wondering where I am." He wiped quickly at his eyes with the back of his hand. "Tomorrow morning I have to help my brothers around our place, and then in the afternoon there's a boxing match at school. And tomorrow night there's a dance at the high school that I want to go to, but I'll stop by on Sunday to visit."

Fernando stood up to walk him out. "Very well, Eduardo. You know we always look forward to a visit from you. You're always welcome. Thank you for the gifts."

"It was nothing," Eduardo said, stepping onto the portal in front of Fernando. Fernando patted him on the back and said good-bye. Before walking out into the snow, Eduardo went to Juanita and Florinda's window. He peeked through the window and saw both of them sitting at a table crocheting by the light of a kerosene lamp. He knocked on the window and waved good-bye. The women looked up from their work, smiled and waved. Then Eduardo was out in the snow.

"Good-night, Eduardo," Fernando yelled. "Enjoy yourself at the dance." Eduardo stopped and turned to smile and wave at his old friend before he ran on.

Everyone was looking forward to Saturday night because dances were rare events in Los Torbellinos. Eduardo could dance a bit because Carmen had a Victrola phonograph that she taught him with when he lived in El Valle. But that was a long time ago and he had never danced to live music; he was nervous as well as excited about the high school dance.

The boxing meet went like any other. Most of the time Eduardo never got into the ring, but that was fine with him. He enjoyed watching Manuel and Carlos, the best boxers on the team, because he aspired to box as well as they did. Manuel's match was the last one of the day, and as usual, he won. In fact, the Mustangs won the entire meet, which put them in especially high spirits for the dance.

At eight that evening, Carlos, Roberto, Eduardo, and their friends met behind the high school campus. There were fifteen of them, and at least five of them had a bottle of alcohol. Roberto had a bottle of corn whiskey, and some of the other boys had bottles of red wine. They all wore their best clothes and had taken special care grooming. Eduardo was nervous about the dance until he took a few big swigs from Roberto's bottle. Then feeling high and reeking like a cheap cologne factory, they walked to the gym, where music was already blaring from inside the building.

Inside the band had set up in one corner of the basketball court. The floor was sprinkled with a fine layer of sawdust and streamers of multicolored crepe paper had been strung from the ceiling to the walls. The lights had been dimmed and a few couples were already sliding across the floor to the steady rhythm of the music.

By nine o'clock the gym was packed. A big group of girls came in together, and almost before they had time to settle on the bleachers, Carlos and Roberto had selected a partner and were leading a smiling girl to the dance floor. The music started up with a fast beat.

Both Carlos and Roberto looked like they had been born dancing. Carlos held his partner closely but respectably, and then he began to spin her around and around at his fingertip. Roberto clutched his partner so tightly about the waist that it looked indecent. His partner seemed not in the least offended and danced as gracefully as possible crushed into his pelvis like she was. Eduardo—a bit drunk—smiled and wondered how they had learned to dance so well. But in no time, one of the senior girls was pulling him onto the dance floor.

"Do you know how to dance?" she asked.

"Yeah, a little," he answered.

"Well, don't be nervous," she giggled. "I'll coach you." She was a good dancer and a good teacher. Soon he was actually enjoying himself. He danced through a number of songs with her, and then her friends took turns dancing him across the floor.

During intermission, Eduardo and the other boys went outside behind the gym to take another drink. Eduardo had not been in such high spirits since getting drunk with Fernando, Diego, and Nicolás in the sierra, but this was different. He was enjoying himself because of the girls and the music and the dancing and the lively atmosphere. Maybe he was only drunk, but he felt close to Carlos and Roberto like he never had before; maybe they had the right idea after all. At any rate, now he understood why they had always gotten so excited about going to dances. He had been missing out. He loved to dance, and he was feeling more relaxed each time he was out on the floor with a girl in his arms. He could not wait for the music to pick up again and said so. Carlos winked at him and smiled.

Back inside, he spotted María Archuleta dancing with Manuel. They danced every dance together. María looked sexier than ever. But Eduardo did not feel jealous, not tonight, because he was having too much fun. When the band announced the last song, Eduardo was disappointed. He was not ready to stop dancing, but after the last dance someone turned on all of the lights to signal the end of the evening. Eduardo and his group said good-bye to the girls they had been dancing with, and then there was nothing to do but go out into the cold night.

Outside they huddled together, puffing on their hands to keep them warm. They passed the bottles around. None of them wanted to go home yet, but there was nowhere else to go. They would freeze if they did not start moving soon. As they were about to break up and head off in separate directions, Manuel and María came outside and got into one of the few cars parked outside the gym. Manuel started the engine, and the couple drove off. The car belonged to one of Manuel's uncles, but Manuel drove it frequently.

"Shit," Roberto said, taking a drink, "that bastard has everything."

"He acts so tough with his uncle's car," one of them said.

"He acts so tough without his uncle's car," Carlos laughed. They all did.

"Well, muchachos, I wish I had me a car. Shit. I wish I had me María Archuleta," Roberto said wickedly. "Man, is he going to have some fun now."

"Don't worry. We'll hear about it on Monday," Carlos said. "We'll hear all about it just like always." And he took another drink to warm himself for the long walk home in the freshly fallen snow.

TWENTY-FIVE

"Manuel Lovato is a sonofabitch. Qué cochino," Eduardo spoke to himself as he walked through the barren fields toward home. He squinted to see better in the dusky light. The trees and fences were obscured by the muted gray and black tones that had come with descending darkness. "Damn," he exclaimed angrily as he ran into the strands of a barbed-wire fence. He felt his way along the wires until he found a stout post, where he climbed quickly up and over the fence. His coat snagged on the wire in mid-air and he heard the rip of cloth. "Sonofabitch!" he cursed. On the ground again, he felt the large rip in his good coat and continued talking to himself, "He thinks he's such a stud. Ah qué cabrón, ese Manuel, ese cochino."

Monday after the dance, Manuel was dressing in the gym locker room when some of the boys began to tease him about María Archuleta.

"Well, how was it?" one of them coaxed, though Manuel didn't need much coaxing to brag about his conquests with girls.

He pursed his lips, "Right there on the front seat," he gestured, "I had my hands all over those nice tits of hers." He clinched his teeth and grimaced, "It was good." Everyone was listening to him now, so Manuel thrust his pelvis back and forth. "Yeah, boys, it was good." The other boys whooped and laughed. Manuel was disgusting in the same way the men who liked to hear stories about Lydia Lepage were disgusting. Eduardo could not imagine why the girls were so crazy to go out with him; all of them knew, everyone knew, how he talked about girls after he dated them for a couple of months. It was disgraceful.

Eduardo moved more cautiously through the oak thicket and suddenly burst into the gypsy camp site, completely startled. They had set up in the secluded patch of forest on Fernando's property. There were five covered wagons in the clearing. A few small cooking fires were burning and horses were tethered to trees at one end of the camp. Four feet in front of him a tiny child wearing a long woolen gown squatted close to the ground warming herself by a fire; she began to scream when she saw Eduardo. Her mother, who was cooking over another fire a few yards away, looked up at Eduardo when the child cried out. There were other men, women, and children all dressed in layers and layers of bright clothing. The elusive gypsies that he had heard so much about were finally back in the valley, and he was stunned speechless at having ambled into their camp.

A scrawny dog rushed up from under a wagon and began to snarl and bark at Eduardo. He thought he might have to kick it to prevent it from attacking him but instead glared at the dog and then back at the woman who was cooking by the fire. Finally, she smiled and began to laugh; her laughter was strong and full, almost like a man's. Eduardo smiled and shuffled his feet nervously. The woman yelled at the dog, which promptly tucked its tail between its legs and slunk away. The woman had olive skin and black eyes, and she was taller than any woman he had ever seen. Her thick black hair was piled on top of her head in a loose bun. She stood up to her full height and moved gracefully toward him; her figure was powerful, somehow intimidating and appealing at once.

"What can we do for you, child?" she asked, in an oddly accented Spanish.

"Nothing, nothing," Eduardo managed to say. "I didn't know you were here. I was on my way home. I . . . I didn't know you were here. This is the shortest way to my house. I didn't know you were here," he repeated obsequiously.

"Ha, ha," she laughed, "No one ever knows where we are because we are everywhere but never for long." The woman stooped and gathered the squalling little girl into her arms. "Who are you?"

"My name is Eduardo Montez." For a strange second he wished that he were cradled in her strong arms like the child.

"Eduardo," she said familiarly, "we are only looking to trade a few things in your village before we move on." Her rich hair was held in place by a pair of ornate silver combs. She wore a pair of long earrings that had the same ornate design as the combs, and there were too many necklaces and chains around her neck for him to count. "You said you are on your way home, but you are out late, no? Where is your home?"

"Just there," Eduardo pointed in the direction of his parents' house.

"Ah," she sighed, nodding her head, "then tell your father we will visit him tomorrow. Perhaps he wishes to do some trading, and since we know you already, we will give him good bargains."

"My father is not home," he said, realizing his mistake too late.

"Ah," she smiled, "then tell your mother we'll visit her tomorrow."

"Yes, but I have to go now."

"Then go," she said coldly, flicking her hand in the air. Eduardo retreated around the perimeter of the camp. They had a way of taking over; he felt like the intruder. This was Fernando's land, not theirs.

"Excuse me," Eduardo said to a burly man who was standing at the edge of the camp. "I didn't know you were here," Eduardo said, hating the apologetic tone in his voice. The man nodded and grunted something unintelligible to Eduardo. The man's hair hung nearly to his shoulders in a jagged cut that looked like it had been executed with a dull knife, and he wore a bandanna around his neck. After he left the oak grove, Eduardo ran through the fields toward home.

"Mamá, Mamá," he yelled, rushing into the kitchen.

"Where have you been?" Elena began to scold. "For all I knew, you could have been dead somewhere. Where have you been?"

"Mamá, I was chopping wood for Mano Fernando, and then I had to chase some stray cows out of his fields. I told you I was going to do some work for him this afternoon so I could finish paying for my boxing boots," he panted.

"Yes, and what about your chores here? I suppose that Mano Fernando's business is more important to you than your work here, and all to pay for a pair of useless boots. Such waste."

"Mamá, you know that I always do my work here, but . . ."

"But what?" she interrupted impatiently.

"The gypsies. The gypsies are here in Los Torbellinos . . . nearby in the forest on Mano Fernando's land."

Elena's eyes widened and she lowered herself into a chair at the table. "The gypsies . . . are you sure?" she asked.

"Yes, like I said, they're camped across the river in the forest on Mano Fernando's property."

"Dios mío," she sighed, "what terrible, lazy people they are. They are filthy and a pack of thieves. How did you find them? You didn't speak to them, of course," she threatened, her voice angry again.

"Yes, I saw them . . . I spoke to them," he confessed.

"Qué estupido!" Elena said springing to her feet. "Qué estupido," she repeated, swatting him on the head. All of the other children had gathered in the kitchen by now. "What did you say to them? You didn't tell them where we live?"

"Mamá, I didn't know they were in the forest. I walked into their camp accidentally. I had no idea they were there. Then before I could leave, this woman was talking to me. I had no choice, but don't worry because I didn't tell them where we live." At least, that was a half-truth, he thought, for he had not told her exactly where his house was.

"What did you say?" Elena insisted.

"The woman asked me my name, so I told her. Then she asked me why I was out so late. I told her that I was on my way home and that I walked into their camp accidentally. After that I left. They don't know where we live." He thought it best not to mention that the woman said they would stop by in the morning to do some trading.

"Well, if they don't know, they'll find out. These people are not normal and have curious ways of finding out what they want to know. They are thieves, and they'll come here asking to trade something of no value for something of value. And . . . if we don't oblige, they'll return later and steal from us," Elena predicted grimly. She sighed heavily and went on, "They travel around the villages from house to house, and people give them the things they want so they'll go away and bother someone else. They'll be here tomorrow, and I don't want to be alone when they come," she spoke frantically now. "Carlos, Roberto, and Eduardo, all three of you will stay home from school tomorrow. Those people are everywhere at once and if we don't treat them well, they'll return and steal from us. Dios mío," she wailed, "these people are bad, and they are sly. We'll give them what we can. Hopefully they will leave after that."

Eduardo stared at the ground feeling guilty and stupid. He should have know better than to say anything to the woman. She was sly. She had twisted words out of his mouth. He should have known better because since he was a little boy he had been warned about the gypsies. Once when he was young, still living in El Valle, the gypsies had visited his grandparents' house. Carmen made him hide in the loft when they saw the wagons approaching because she said if the gypsies saw him they would return later and steal him. She said that gypsies often stole small children to sell or to add to their own clan. Those hours hiding under the bed in the loft had been terrifying, and for weeks after they left, Eduardo was always looking over his shoulder for fear that he would be stolen by the gypsies as Uncle Juan had been stolen by the Apaches. And even though he was almost a man now, the word gypsies still evoked fear in him. During their visit in El Valle, the gypsies had stolen a hand-carved crucifix off of the wall in the sala. No one had seen them take it, but it was gone when they left. Also, they had insisted on reading Fidelia's fortune, but none of the adults would tell Eduardo what the gypsy woman had said, except that it was nonsense and the devil's work.

That night after dinner Roberto told Eduardo, "We're going to the gypsy camp tonight. They can read your fortune and tell you how to get certain things you really want. Do you want to come? Carlos is coming with me."

Eduardo was immediately excited about the prospect of returning to the camp, for the gypsies were strange, alluring and frightening at once. At first, he hesitated to answer out of his old fear for the gypsies, but when he saw Roberto growing impatient, he made up his mind. "Yes, I'll go but it's late. They might be sleeping."

"Gypsies sleeping?" Roberto said doubtfully. "More likely they're having a party, and if we don't take the chance and go tonight, we may never have the chance again. If they do come here tomorrow, Mamá will never permit us to have our fortunes read. Then they'll probably move on tomorrow, so it's tonight, or never."

"Okay, okay, I'll go with you. We can go out the window after Mamá is in bed. It won't be long now." While they waited, they scraped together what money they had; it was not much but surely enough to satisfy a gypsy fortune-teller.

As they approached the camp late, the skeletal gypsy dogs began to bark. There was a single, large fire in the center of the camp. Many of the men and women were sitting around it on logs. One of the men took a burning stick and held it aloft while he walked toward them to see what the dogs were barking at.

"Who is it?" he called in Spanish.

"There are three of us here," Roberto called out. "We want to have our fortunes read."

"Um," the man grunted, "Wait here." He went back to the fire, and they could hear him speaking to the others in his language.

"They are probably Romanian or Turkish," Carlos whispered. "They say most of the gypsies are either Romanians or Turks, but sometimes I hear that Spanish or Indians travel with them." The boys heard laughter, and the man returned.

"I will take you to my woman; she gazes into the crystal and reads the hands. She will read your fortunes. Come." They followed him to the fire pit. "She will see you one at the time. Two of you must wait here; it's warm enough by the fire." The others sitting on the logs moved over to make room for them. "Who will go first?" the man asked.

"I will," Carlos said, following the big man. At his wagon the man spoke in his own language, and there was a reply from within. Soon a woman pulled back the heavy canvas and invited Carlos in. After half an hour, Carlos returned to the fire and sent Roberto to the wagon. Eduardo watched him scramble inside. Carlos took Roberto's seat, and the two of them listened to the gypsies speak their strange language.

At last, Roberto emerged from the wagon and returned to them quite solemn, not himself at all. Eduardo went to the wagon but hesitated for an awkward moment.

"Come in." Instantly he recognized the woman's voice. Somehow he had known that the woman he had met earlier would be the fortune-teller. He hoisted himself into the wagon. There was hardly room to move inside the wagon's narrow bed, and the place was cluttered with clothes and bedding. A kerosene lamp glowed dimly from one corner; their bodies cast eerie, giant shadows on the canvas. The sleepy-eyed gypsy woman sat smiling at him.

"So you told your brothers about us and you have returned as well. That is good. Sit here," she said, touching the vacant crate next to her. Eduardo sat on the crate noting the draped orb in front of him. It was surprisingly warm inside the wagon, and the woman's bright blouse was unbuttoned to her navel; she must have been nursing the little girl who now slept on the mattress in a bundle of blankets. For a few uncomfortable minutes, the woman stared at Eduardo with her sleepy eyes and placid smile. Finally, "You are a serious one, Eduardo," she said, not forgetting his name and still smiling. She pulled her blouse to. "I knew that from the time you stepped out of the forest. You do not take the time to enjoy the pretty things in life. That is a shame." She sounded far away, almost drunk. Her eyes were a bit glazed under the droopy eyelids, and a pungent, smoky odor permeated the air. Slowly she pulled the black drape away from her crystal ball. She lifted the crystal and spread the black drape over the crate before she set the crystal back in place. Eduardo laughed nervously, never having seen an object so strangely perfect as this crystal globe.

"Eduardo, place your hands on the crystal like this," she said curving her long fingers around the ball, almost caressing it. He did as she asked, shivering a bit from its iciness. "Now open your hands and look deep into the crystal," she instructed. Eduardo gazed into the transparent depths. "Please move you hands away from the ball now," she said. Eduardo glanced up at the woman's face and saw that she was squinting, glaring trancelike at the ball. Tears trickled from the outside corners of her eyes. "Yes, yes," she smiled and said something in her language.

"What? What?" Eduardo asked.

"Nothing important. I only said that the crystal never lies."

"What do you mean?"

"Be patient, be patient," she whispered, still gazing hard into the crystal. "Yes, three times tonight the crystal has shown me the same images. The very same images for all of you. That is indeed rare. I have never seen it happen before."

"What do you see?" Eduardo insisted.

At first, she ignored him. Eduardo fidgeted nervously. "Yes," she said at length, "soon you will follow your brothers on a long journey far from your home." She spoke calmly, but her eyes had widened, becoming more intense. She stroked the ball gently with her right hand. "Soon you will leave your village and travel long on the water. You, like your brothers, will fight in a war far from your home."

Eduardo felt his heart begin to pound faster and faster. Fernando had said the same thing many times in the last weeks; he had said it was inevitable. The gypsy stroked the crystal again with both hands; then shaking her head, she instructed, "Place your hands on the crystal. Sometimes my friend plays tricks, but he never lies." Eduardo cupped his hands around the crystal and stared hard into its depths once again. When he moved his hands, the woman stared at the crystal with her head tilted aside and her body leaning forward. "This is terrible," she said, returning to an erect position. Her voice sounded excited for the first time since they had begun.

"What?" Eduardo demanded.

"The crystal shows me that there will be a monster in this war. He shows me Lucifer up from hell . . . death and destruction!"

"Lucifer up from hell. That's stupid," Eduardo said, pouncing to his feet. The woman ignored him and continued to gaze intently into the crystal ball.

"This . . . this monster will end the war and change the world forever. Yes, Lucifer always wins when men's hearts are evil."

"And will I . . . will I and my brothers survive?" Eduardo asked, thinking of Fernando's son, Alfonso.

The woman gazed into the crystal for some minutes before answering, "Yes, you will survive, but none of you will ever be the same again." She stroked the ball delicately. "Here I see the anger and the fear and the pain of millions and millions of men, women, and children. Here I see death," she hissed. Suddenly she pulled the drape from under the crystal and covered it. "That is all that my friend will offer tonight, but sit down and give me your hand."

"But . . . you have to tell me more about this war," he begged, returning to his seat.

"I cannot. As I told you, the crystal will offer only so much, but I can read your hand, give me your left hand."

Obediently Eduardo extended his hand toward her. "You have good hands," she said, seductively caressing his hand with her long, slender fingers. Then she began to examine the lines on his palm. "Yes, the lines confirm that you will have a long life. There will be hardships. Hardships of the mind and body. Nevertheless, you will be prosperous and live a full life." Her voice had become hot and syrupy, making her words nearly unrecognizable. The warmth of her strong hands made him dizzy. "Oh, you are a passionate one." The words oozed smoothly out of her mouth, and she smiled warmly. "You will, of course, marry and have children," she said releasing his hand.

"Now give me something that belongs to you and only you." Eduardo fished in his pocket and handed her his rosary. The woman cupped it in her hands. "Eduardo, you may make a wish now, and I will be able to tell you if it will come true." Eduardo thought hard about all of the things he wanted. There was so much he wanted and wanted to know. "Eduardo, your mind is clouded. Give me your hand; I will teach you how to clear your mind." She took his hand and placed it over her heart. Eduardo's hand tingled against her soft warmth, and her chains and bangles softly tickled the back of his hand. "Now clear your mind and think deeply about what it is that your heart longs for most. Close your eyes and let pictures form in your mind."

Slowly two smoky images developed in his mind's eye. In one he saw his mother sitting in a field of grass; she was smiling beautifully; she was resting; she was happy. In the same field, surrounded by beautiful flowers, he saw Darlene running and laughing and smiling. Both of them were so beautiful. And then those images faded. Next he saw his dear friend Fernando, and then images of

Fernando's old house and the property began to flash through his mind. How could he choose? The gypsy woman removed his hand from her bosom and placed it over his own heart.

"Now think deeply and let your heart guide you. Make your wish." As she spoke, the images of Darlene and Fernando and the land faded from his mind. The other, the image of Elena sitting in the grass smiling, became more clear, more lifelike.

"I have made my wish," Eduardo said drowsily.

The woman closed her eyes and cupped the rosary in both hands. Eduardo waited, feeling as though he had just been awakened from hours of sleep. At last she handed the rosary back to him. "You are a compassionate boy. Will you tell me what you wished for?"

For some reason Eduardo was not embarrassed to tell her. "I wished for happiness . . . happiness for my mother."

"I see. That is a valiant thing to do. This woman, your mother, must be very powerful. I see that she has great influence over you . . . and your brothers. I wish I could tell you a lie, but I cannot. If you can believe me when I tell you that from now until the end of your life, you do not have, you will never have, the power to make another person happy, then there is a chance that you might find happiness for yourself. To believe that takes more strength and courage than most men have. I do not know if you will allow happiness to find you. I hope that you will, but you don't have the power to make other people happy . . . you are not God. You must first learn to recognize your own strengths, and you must realize that there are some things you can accomplish and some things that are beyond your power. If you do not learn to accept that, you will be unhappy and you will experience pain that is not yours. Perhaps, Eduardo, the next time we meet, you will have learned the difference between the things that lie within your control and the things that are not yours to control. Your mother's happiness, for example, is her own destiny, but now, Eduardo, it is time for you to go . . . unless you wish to stay with us forever," she laughed strangely and stared intensely into his eyes.

Eduardo rose slowly, taking his money from his pocket. "Here, take this and thank you," he said.

"Put your money away, Eduardo," said the woman with a lazy

smile. "I am already richer for having seen through your eyes. You are a strange young man . . . different than most. Oh, if you would come and live with us, the things we could teach you," she tempted, still smiling at him. "But your path, your destiny, is different than ours. You must find your own way, and you will."

"Thank you," Eduardo said. Backing out of the wagon, he moved slowly, wishing to linger in the woman's charm for just a few seconds longer.

"Remember us," she called to him as he jumped to the ground. He joined Carlos and Roberto at the fire. The three of them said good night to their hosts and walked home in silence.

The next day the gypsies did not visit their home. All three boys were somewhat disappointed and that night returned to the forest where the gypsy camp had been. Fire pits and trampled grass were the only evidence that the gypsy band had camped in Los Torbellinos for a night. No one else in town reported having seen them.

TWENTY-SIX

Carlos joined the army in June 1941. He had been stationed in El Paso for one year when Roberto came home drunk one night and announced that he also had joined the army. Elena screamed and cried the same way she had when Carlos signed up, but Roberto bluntly told her that he would have been drafted anyway. Besides, there were no jobs in Los Torbellinos, or anywhere else for miles around, and he had no desire to become a factory worker in some city. So after finishing high school, he went to basic training like Carlos had.

When Roberto came home from boot camp, he was more callous than ever. The broader shoulders and more tapered waist may have been the army's work, but the surly, swaggering cockiness was still intact and all his own. He wore his uniform well, carried himself with pride, and pretended to be undaunted by the fact that he was destined for an infantry unit overseas. Since the bombing of Pearl Harbor, America had begun mass mobilization of troops as well as mass production of machines and weapons for global warfare. So despite all of his brother's bravado, Eduardo sensed that Roberto had changed the same way Carlos had. Both had been tense after they returned from boot camp, but who could blame them. Elena did not help the situation by going into hysterical, tearful fits each time she looked at Roberto or each time Carlos's name was mentioned, or when they received a letter from him. She could not bear the thought that her sons would be shipped off to war in Africa, Europe, or the Pacific. Her hysterical outbursts made Roberto so edgy that he left the room every time she started up. But true to his nature, Roberto was determined to raise a bit of hell at home before reporting to his assigned duty station in North Carolina.

Two nights after Roberto's arrival in Los Torbellinos, he and Eduardo went to a dance at the high school. Roberto bought a bottle of whiskey before collecting the last of their gang, Victor and Vicinte. Roberto took a long drink from the bottle.

"This'll be like old times," he said, trying to convince himself that nothing had changed. "I promise you there was none of this in boot camp." He wiped his lips and passed the bottle to Eduardo.

"Is it as bad as they say it is?" Eduardo asked, taking the bottle.

"No, it's not so bad. Oh sure, I mean they scream at you every time you turn around, and they rough you up some, but it ain't no worse than what you already been through with Hansen. The only difference is that you never get a break from the bastards. It's all military discipline and shit. In basic you eat, drink, and sleep army, army, army all the time. You have to keep it in your mind that it's a game; that they ain't really going to kill you like they want you to think." He laughed sarcastically, "Well, I mean you ain't going to die in basic. Let's put it that way."

"Well . . . but I mean the war."

"Yeah, well? What about it?"

"Well . . . aren't you afraid?"

"What the hell do you think, estupido? Now will you quit talking like Mamá. When we go over there, I got a fifty-fifty chance like any other dumb bastard, and if I hadn't enlisted, tell me what I could do with my life? I sure ain't the Harvard type. Also, like I keep telling Mamá, if I hadn't enlisted on my own, in another month or so the draft would have caught up to me. Besides, I try not to think about the war, okay?"

"Yeah, okay," Eduardo said, feeling immature. They were silent for a moment.

"You know," Roberto looked serious for a minute, "this going to a dance don't seem right without Carlos. I think of him a lot and wonder how he's doing. For example, at this very second, I wonder what he's up to. What the hell. I bet that sonofagun is living it up down in El Paso."

As they walked into the plaza of Los Torbellinos, a shiny Ford convertible sped past, leaving them in a cloud of dust. The driver and his passenger looked back laughing. Both had short, greased hair and wore sports jackets. Roberto stared after the car. "Sonofabitches," he said. "Who the hell are those jotos?"

"Those guys come into town for every dance. They're seeing a couple of girls who live in the dorms."

Roberto's frown turned into the sneer that was so familiar to Eduardo. "I bet their daddies are good and rich. I bet they even know the governor and the president. That's why their asses are scot-free . . . no army for those college boys. We'll see them at the dance, no?" His eyes brightened. "Come on. Let's go find Victor and Vicinte."

By the time they found Victor and Vicinte, it was eight- thirty. When they arrived at the gym, they had already finished their first pint of whiskey and had bought another, which was now almost empty. The music boomed away inside the gym and made them eager to start dancing. They paid for their tickets at the door and went directly into the men's room to comb their hair. Roberto was talking slow like he did when he was drunk.

"Tonight I might have to beat the hell out of those jotos," he said breezily, adjusting the tie of his uniform in the mirror. "One thing for certain is that girls are crazy about a guy in uniform, especially out in this ghost town. Hey, muchitos," he said, as if suddenly becoming aware of his companions, "look at me. I look good, qué no? You boys look like shit," he laughed. "I ain't used to seeing civilians no more. Besides, once the girls see my uniform, they'll be all over me," he teased.

As they left the men's room, they passed the two young men from the convertible. Both of them were easily six feet tall, muscular, and looked to be the same age as Roberto, who deliberately stopped and glared at the two as they walked by. The driver of the car said something about a fresh shavetail and walked on, laughing.

Roberto kept a close eye on the two men from out of town and made frequent visits to the men's room to sip on his whiskey. He

danced nearly every dance, though he seemed to have more interest in watching the two men. When the band paused for a break,
Roberto sat on the bleachers scowling.

"Those goddamn jotos think they own the place. Before they
leave tonight, I'm going to give them a surprise that will make
them think twice before they come back to Los Torbellinos. I got
a great plan already, and we won't even have to fight them," he
said, nonchalantly including Eduardo, Vicinte, and Victor in his
scheme. He punched Victor playfully on the arm, "Hey, how good
is your throwing arm?"

"What are you going to make us do?" Victor whined, but Roberto
only laughed wickedly. Then the band kicked up again, and they
were all dancing. At one o'clock the band played the last song for
the night. When the lights came on in the gym, Roberto, Eduardo,
Vicinte, and Victor gathered in the shadows outside the gym to
finish off the last of their whiskey.

"So where's all them women you was going to get, Roberto?"
Vicinte taunted.

"Aw go to hell, man. I seen you try to grab a squeeze off of that
Julia you were dancing with. At least I felt up Juanita's nice ass
for nearly ten minutes while we were dancing. She's got some soft
tits, too. I could have taken her out to the bushes if I'd wanted, but
I got better fun on my mind for tonight."

"Oh shit," Eduardo said. "Here we go."

"So what is this plan?" Vicinte asked.

"See, los jotos are going to walk out of the gym any minute . . ."

"You're crazy," Victor interrupted. "Those guys could step on
you like a piojo, and they'd love doing it. They could kick the hell
out of all four of us together. Did you look at them?"

"Shut up," Roberto said angrily. "I ain't joking no more. I'm
going to go through with this, and if you don't want to be in on
the fun, then shut up and go home."

No one spoke for a few minutes. Victor pushed his glasses up on
his nose. "I'm with you, Roberto. You know, why the hell not," he
said, shrugging his shoulders.

"Me too," Vicinte said.

"For old time's sake. Sure why not," Eduardo laughed drunkenly.

In a few minutes the men left the gym with their dates. "Oh shit, here it comes," Victor said miserably.

"Now don't none of you have a heart attack, not yet," Roberto said exasperated. "See, those bastards will drive off with their girlies and park for a couple of hours. Then, of course, they'll bring the girls home and leave town down the main road the same way they came in. The difference is that we'll be waiting for them," he laughed.

"Exactly what are you thinking of?" Eduardo asked, remembering too many of Roberto's stunts in the past.

"Shit! Now you're starting to sound like Victor. Listen, when you make up your mind to do something, you have to go with it, qué no? I mean, we ain't going to do nothing that's going to kill no one, if that's what you're worried about." Eduardo felt slightly relieved. "We're going to make them madder than hell. Like I said, they'll think twice before they drive out this way again. See, we'll go to the edge of town and wait for them. All we're going to do is shower those fancy bastards and their fancy car with a good coat of gravel and sand. It's a perfect plan for a convertible. It'll be great. Come on."

They walked toward the edge of town under a half moon. "Let's spread ourselves out along either side of the road. When they drive past, we'll jump out from behind the bushes and let 'em have it good. They'll never know what hit them." Roberto laughed as he began to scrape up a pile of rocks and gravel with his feet. The others watched him dumbly. "What the hell! Vicinte, you go over there, and you, Eduardo, you go over there. Victor, you go down there by that tree," he issued the commands like a drill sergeant. "Let's move. Hurry." They followed his directions and spread out along the road. Then they crouched down behind the sage brush and sang songs while waiting.

After about an hour and a half the boys heard the hum of the car's engine and saw the lights off in the distance. "Here they come. Here they come," Roberto cackled with glee. "Throw as fast as you can when they're near you because they'll race out of here like lightning after I hit them." In a few seconds, the car was blaring down the road toward them carrying the jumbled sound of the men's voices. Roberto waited for the perfect moment. Then he began his assault with handfuls of gravel. When the first volley cascaded around his head and bounced loudly off the hood of the car, the driver swerved dangerously back and forth across the road nearly capsizing the car. Somehow he regained control and was driving into Vicinte's range. Vicinte let loose with his rocks. One of the men cried out in pain. Already both of them were cursing like demons while Roberto roared with laughter. Eduardo was ready when the car moved into his zone. The vehicle was definitely traveling faster now, but Eduardo decided to make his turn count. He fired several volleys before they were out of range. Next it was Victor's turn; he too made good on his assault.

The driver's initial shock had run its course. Now he was furious. The car came to a screeching halt before the driver executed a quick turn and headed back toward Los Torbellinos.

"Jesus Christ, Bob, drive on," the passenger yelled. "You don't know how many of them there are. There could be a whole gang of them." But his friend ignored him and growled, "I'm going to catch you and kill you, you stinking greasers. I'll make you regret the day you were born."

Howling with laughter, Roberto and company had already made their escape. They ran from the road taunting and teasing as loud as possible. "Yoo hoo, Bob, here we are. Bobby Boy. Yoo hoo, Bob, here we are." They could see the car patrolling the highway, but they were safe now and continued to yelp and howl to further infuriate the two.

"That stupid idiot," Roberto laughed. "We got them. We sure got them." They laughed the rest of the way home.

Three days later Roberto left Los Torbellinos in the mail truck. He was to report for duty in North Carolina, and the whole family was there to see him off. After saying good-bye, Roberto turned his back on them and tucked himself inside the truck. Naturally, Elena was wailing as if for a funeral. Eduardo saw tears in Roberto's eyes, as he was the last to embrace him. In fact, tears were flowing down Eduardo's cheeks and he did not fight them. For the first time in his life, Eduardo realized how desperately alone Roberto was. Sure Elena was crying and sad to see him go, as they all were, but she had never shown Roberto love, not the way she had always cared for Carlos. Though Elena was also cold to Eduardo, at least Eduardo had always had other people in his life. There had been Diego, Carmen, Rafelita, José, and even Fidelia. Now he had Fernando and the Indian women, and José and Carmen were still important in his life. For a short time, there had also been Darlene Lepage. But who did Roberto have; who had he ever had? With the one exception of Grandmother Rosita years ago, the grim, unbearable answer was no one.

The sudden realization made Eduardo feel tired and as heavy as stone. He wanted to go to Roberto one more time to tell him that he finally understood. Maybe to show him that he cared. He saw the back of Roberto's head and his shoulders through the rear window of the mail truck; somehow, despite the soldier's uniform and the broad shoulders, Roberto reminded him of, had always reminded him of, a little child. Eduardo tried to move, tried to go to his brother, but he was rooted to the ground. As he watched the mail truck pull out onto the road and head away from Los Torbellinos, tears streamed down his cheeks. At last, after all these years, Eduardo finally realized that a lonely, loveless existence had created Roberto. Maybe if he had understood sooner, maybe somehow he could have made a difference. He watched the truck until it disappeared, and long after it was out of sight, bitter tears of love, shame, and helplessness poured out of him.

TWENTY-SEVEN

Eduardo began the 1943-44 school year determined to keep busy. He knew that like his brothers he was destined for service in the United States armed forces and Eduardo had recently discussed with Fernando his plan to enlist. Of course, his friend had already guessed as much. They both knew that Eduardo ultimately had no choice, and so Fernando had calmly accepted the information and said in good spirit, "Well, Eduardo, that means that you'll have that monthly check, and before long this place will belong to you. Soon we can finalize our deal." Then reassuringly Fernando told him, "You'll see, it's all going to be alright in the end. It will. I have great faith that everything is going to be alright, and you need to have faith too."

For the fourth year in a row, Eduardo joined the high school boxing team only to relieve the monotony at home and now to provide a distraction from the grind of waiting for his day of enlistment. His grand ambition to become a champion on the boxing team had been dwarfed long ago by the beginning of the war. Eduardo, like millions of young boys across America, had been touched by the patriotic fever calling him to join the U.S. forces against the evil enemy. The war was an ominous lure, and he had long since given himself over.

By staying busy, Eduardo was able to keep his plans in perspective, able to keep the gnawing sensation of emptiness at bay. He constantly reminded himself of the purpose that had become the driving force of his life. If he was able to purchase his friend's land and house, Fernando would always be with him because Fernando

259

was inseparable from the property. And Fernando was right, if he kept his faith up, nothing could go wrong. When his fear about the war became overbearing, he thought also of the gypsy woman who had promised him that he would survive. In contrast to nothing, as silly as it seemed, that promise seemed all powerful. He also knew that to survive he must maintain the will of a survivor.

Every day, as always, he rose early to complete a few chores before school. He worked hard on his studies, and in the afternoon he trained rigorously with the boxing team. In the evening he often worked until after dark finishing the chores his younger siblings hadn't. Since his father was still away at the sheep camps, and Carlos and Roberto had both joined the army he was now the man of the house. He felt important because his mother no longer talked to him as if he were a child. But while she was dependant on him, she also had become even more pessimistic since Carlos and Roberto had left home. She was always worrying and complaining and frequently held candle-lit vigils in her room for Carlos and Roberto, whose companies could be shipped off to the war at any time. When she emerged from her room looking gaunt and terrified, Eduardo tried to console her, though his words never soothed her in the least. In fact, Eduardo felt no satisfaction from her dependence on him as he once thought he might. Her misery made him feel more helpless and empty than ever. At one time he had longed for the chance to show her how strong he could be and to prove that he could help her. But none of his support had pleased her, or made a difference in her chronically pessimistic disposition. She expected his support and gave him nothing. His plans were clear and he would fulfill his dreams with or without his mother's approval. At night laying in bed with his mind buzzing, all he could think of was surviving the war to buy Fernando's ranch. That was something to live for.

Carlos and Roberto wrote home once a month, and Eduardo answered all of their letters. Since the United States declared war against the Axis powers after the bombing of Pearl Harbor, thousands of U.S. troops had been sent North Africa, the Pacific, and most recently to Italy. Neither Carlos nor Roberto's companies had been called, though both wrote that it was only a matter of time.

Carlos had been transferred from El Paso, Texas, to a combat unit in Washington D.C. Roberto was still in a North Carolina combat unit. Their companies were under constant alert, and they held readiness drills around the clock.

Carlos and Roberto's letters never failed to send Elena into days of despondency. But after Elena received news of the recent Allied invasion of Italy, she was inconsolable. At night, every night, Eduardo and the other children heard her in her bedroom as she prayed innumerable rosaries and Hail Marys. She begged God to spare her sons. Eduardo often wondered what her trade-off was, because when he prayed he promised the Lord that he would forsake cursing or drinking or lying or saying bad things about people if only his prayers were granted. He wondered what his mother would sacrifice for the safety of Carlos and Roberto. He realized that he knew nothing about her. Besides his older brothers, he had no idea what was important to her. He saw worry deepening the lines in her face. Her anguish for Carlos and Roberto carried her deeper into prayer and further from the rest of them.

One cold morning in November Eduardo left the house eager to get away from his sorrowful mother. Since he could remember, worry and grief had been her life. As he walked past the post office on his way to school, he noticed that the driver of the mail truck was about to depart for his journey back to Santa Fe. On a whim, Eduardo asked the driver if he could catch a ride with him. The driver said that he always welcomed company on the long drive home. Eduardo pondered his decision for an instant. He was not prepared for travel; he did not have a penny in his pocket; he had not told his family of his plans. Shrugging his shoulders he accepted the driver's invitation and settled in for the long ride, knowing that the mail truck would not return to Los Torbellinos until the following day.

Eduardo wandered the narrow streets of downtown Santa Fe for an hour before he found the recruiting offices for the United States armed forces. He had decided long ago that he did not want to be an infantryman with the army. The stories his father had told about being an infantryman during World War I, and the death of Fernando's son as a foot soldier were dismal enough to direct him to another branch. And since Darlene's uncle had nothing but praise for being a sailor, Eduardo walked into the recruiting office for the United States Navy.

An hour later, he left the office a bit disgruntled. The navy recruiter said he could enlist, but there were a few problems that would prevent him from joining immediately. First of all, he was not yet eighteen. His eighteenth birthday was still two months away. At seventeen he could join the military but only with his parents' consent, and he knew that Elena would never sign the necessary paperwork. Eduardo was ten pounds underweight. The recruiter said that he must gain ten pounds before he could pass his physical examination for basic training with the navy. Nevertheless, the officer had supplied him with all of the necessary forms for enlistment. The recruiter secured Eduardo's mailing address and assured him that after he turned eighteen, he could be in boot camp in San Diego as soon as he gained the necessary weight.

After leaving the recruiting station, Eduardo walked the streets of Santa Fe for hours. His stomach was churning from hunger and nerves. He had made up his mind that it was pointless to spend another year in Los Torbellinos waiting for the draft to catch up to him. At least in the service he could begin saving his money to buy Fernando's land. He would rather take his chances with the war than spend another miserable year at home watching his mother grieve. He shuddered thinking of what she would do when they actually received the call to report to a battle line. He would leave now if it were possible, but two or three months had to be soon enough. He had always known that one day he would leave the valley, though he had never been so close. The papers he held in his hand were proof of the first steps that would change his life forever.

Eduardo wandered aimlessly in the streets until at four o'clock he realized that his throat was parched. He went into a drugstore and begged a glass of water from a girl at the lunch counter. In the end, after he told her his plight about leaving home without any money to visit the recruiting station, her heart softened and she gave him a big glass of milk and a ham sandwich. He wolfed down the food gratefully, and after thanking the girl, he returned to the streets. He thought briefly of trying to find Nicolás Martínez and

Diego, but he had not seen either of them since that coincidental meeting in the sierra nearly four years ago. Besides, he had no idea where they lived. The driver of the mail truck had invited him to spend the night with his family, so Eduardo spent the next two hours looking for his house. He was treated kindly by the family and given a good meal before bed. The next morning he and the truck driver rose at four o'clock and were headed back to Los Torbellinos with the mail bags by six o'clock.

Eduardo wished that he could postpone arrival in Los Torbellinos indefinitely. He knew his mother would have stewed herself into a rage about his rash overnight outing. But the mail truck pulled up at the post office in Los Torbellinos promptly at eight o'clock. He could go to school to put off the inevitable a bit longer, or he could go home and confront his mother. He decided to skip school and go home. After all, he was too nervous to be in school.

He found Elena busy over simmering pots in the kitchen. At first she ignored him, but Eduardo knew that she would not be able to constrain her rage for long, so he waited for the worst.

"You're disgraceful and make me ashamed to call you my son," she said, turning on him with a tea towel that had been draped over her shoulder. She began to slap him with the towel. "Do you think I don't have enough to worry about with your father and your brothers gone? Do you think that I don't have enough to worry about with the running of the house and the farm? Do you think that I don't have enough to worry about with the your brothers and sisters? Is this why you stay out all night . . . God knows where? Must I worry about you as well? Answer me. Answer me," she ordered. "How could I know that you were not lying under a tree beaten senseless by drunkards or your no good friends? How am I supposed to know these things? Where were you? Where were you?" She slapped him feebly before collapsing into a chair sobbing. "I know you weren't in school yesterday. What about your lessons?" she cried.

Eduardo stood in front of her. All of this was for him? "Mamá, I was in Santa Fe," he stammered.

"So you were in Santa Fe. Why did you go to Santa Fe?" she asked still sobbing. Then she realized. It had happened the same way with Carlos and Roberto. First the trip to Santa Fe and then the sheepish excuses and explanations for enlisting. "No," she said, "not you too. I forbid it. I forbid it."

"But Mamá, I'm almost eighteen. I'll be out of school in less than a year. Then what will I do here? There is nothing for me here. What will I do in Los Torbellinos?"

"You have nothing in Los Torbellinos?" she sobbed. "Then what am I? What are your brothers and sisters? Are we nothing? Is this land nothing? Who will work the land? Will you leave me here alone with all of these babies? Is that how little you care?"

"Mamá, the day will come in a year or less when I'll have to go. You know about the draft. It's war time. It's better to volunteer than to be called. They'll call me anyway within the months to come. It's already happened to lots of boys in Los Torbellinos who didn't volunteer on their own. You know that."

"No," Elena said, "you can't go. It's tragic enough that your brothers have to go into battle, but not you. We'll write the draft board and tell them that you're the man of the house and you can't go. We'll write that you are needed here to look after the farm and . . . and us." Suddenly she stood and left the kitchen. When she returned, moments later, her face was washed, her hair combed. "Go and feed the animals. The children didn't have time to feed them this morning."

Eduardo returned to his normal routine at home; there was nothing more to say to his mother. Three weeks before Christmas their father returned home for the holidays, which brought a spark of happiness back into their lives for a few weeks. Then one week before Christmas Eduardo received a formal Christmas card from the navy recruiter in Santa Fe. He was now eighteen, and he could enlist whenever he wanted. He was still underweight, but not because he was not eating enough. He ate like a horse but could never gain more than a pound or two before he dropped back to his normal weight. January and February raced by. They were a blur of school, work at home, a few out of town boxing matches that meant nothing to him, and some long comforting visits with Fernando and the women, though Eduardo was preoccupied with leaving the valley.

264

The first week in March he sent a letter to the navy recruiter. In it he stated that he was ready to take the physical examination for enlistment in the United States Navy. He was worried about his weight, but he thought he could gorge himself in the next weeks to get closer to the regulation. A week later he received a packet from the navy recruiter. It contained forms that had to be filled out and sent to the recruiter before he could return to Santa Fe and enlist. Eduardo completed the forms and mailed them back.

In four days, he received a letter that said he must be in Santa Fe on March 29, 1944, to take his physical examination. If he passed the exam, the letter stated he would be enlisted the same day. The following day, he would depart for San Diego. There would be no time to return to Los Torbellinos after the physical before he left for California. Eduardo's hands shook as he read the letter. He recognized the finality of his actions as he mailed a prepaid post card that told the recruiter he would be in Santa Fe on March 29 to take his physical examination.

The next week seemed like a few hours. There was no time left. Eduardo went about in a daze. Elena had seen it. She knew he was leaving before he told her. When he did tell her, there were no more tears, no more scoldings. Her face had hardened in the last weeks, but she did not try to stop him because she knew he was determined to go like Carlos and Roberto had been. Though he never knew it, she began to light candles for him in the church and at home, and she added him to her list when she said her nightly prayers and begged God to protect her sons.

The last weeks in March Eduardo haunted all of his favorite places in Los Torbellinos. One day he rode high into the hills and looked down on the village. He gazed long at the valley below, at his grandfather's house to the south, at his parents' house, and at Fernando's house and pastures. He wondered if the valley would be the same after he returned; he knew he would return, and though he rio longer wished for it, time pulled him to the threshold of his departure.

On March 28, 1944, he headed for the mail truck in front of Lawrence's store. He had said good-bye to everyone at home, but the image of his family standing in front of the house was still vivid in his mind. Half way down the driveway Eduardo looked back at them; it was as if he were seeing them through thick, cloudy glass. All of them, even his mother, were still waving. He turned and walked on, time pulling him to the instant of stepping into the mail truck and beyond until he was traveling south toward Santa Fe with the village of Los Torbellinos waiting behind him.

TWENTY-EIGHT

Eduardo sat on a stack of bricks in an alleyway a few blocks from the recruiting station. It was 8:30 A.M. and the Santa Fe streets were quiet. A few people moved around the sidewalks of the main plaza, busy opening shops or going to their jobs, but mostly the morning was gray, cold, and uninviting. Glancing at his watch, Eduardo saw that he had exactly thirty minutes to eat the rest of the bananas that he had purchased the night before. Even after gorging himself for the last two weeks, he was still eight pounds away from meeting the minimum weight requirements to pass his physical examination for the navy. Around 7:30 A.M. he began eating the heavy fruit, and now he was certain that he had eaten almost ten of the fifteen pounds. A thick scattering of banana skins lay around him as he sat with his knees drawn up to his chest to protect himself from the cold. He looked in the sack—seven bananas to go. He continued to eat, taking huge bites that he hardly chewed. Loosening his belt a few notches, Eduardo tried not to think about how uncomfortable he felt and hoped he would not be sick; he had to make the weight for his physical.

After finishing the last banana, he walked dizzily to the recruiting station, where other boys were waiting to sign in. At 9:30 A.M., all of them were taken by bus to a small clinic for their physical examinations. The doctor, a withered man with a wheezing cough and shaky hands, gave them medical forms to fill out and told them to indicate in writing if they had any "strange or unusual birthmarks, moles, tattoos, deformities, or otherwise identifying marks" on their bodies. They spent the remainder of the morning in their underwear and were prodded like cattle from one phase of the exam to the next. The doctor was accompanied by a nurse who scribbled furiously on charts in response to the doctor's dictations. She recorded the height, weight, blood pressure, and heart rate of each boy. When Eduardo stepped onto the scale, he was exactly half a pound over the requirement. The doctor took out his handkerchief, removed and wiped his glasses, the whole time staring Eduardo hard in the face. Then putting his glasses back on his face, he grunted and waved Eduardo on. One by one the boys went sheepishly behind a screen, where they were checked for hernias. Next their chests were x-rayed for tuberculosis. The final phase of the examination was a hearing and vision test. At one o'clock, they were loaded back into the bus and taken to a dingy cafeteria, where they ate lunch at the expense of the United States government. By two o'clock they were back at the recruiting station waiting to take the oath of loyalty to their country and sign the final paperwork for enlistment in the United States Navy.

Eduardo was out on the street by 5:00 P.M., thinking about where he could spend the night. The night before he had stayed with the Los Torbellinos mailman and his family, but they lived ten miles from the plaza, and he did not feel like walking out to their place. He had no idea where to go, a situation he had never confronted before; his plight made him alarmingly aware of how quickly time moved away from the security of home. Only two days before he had been chopping wood for the kitchen stove at five or six o'clock. Now, within hours, he would be on a train bound for San Diego, a town even more strange to him than Santa Fe. He felt a new vulnerability. He needed a place to spend the night. Sleep was not so important. He had always done with little sleep, but March nights were cold; he had to have a shelter for the night. He walked the streets surrounding the plaza for almost an hour wondering what to do. Passing the La Fonda Hotel he was attracted by the warm lights and the beautiful window displays. He hesitated and then pushed open the huge double doors and entered the hotel.

Once inside, he realized his mistake. He had only twenty dollars in his pocket and was sure that a room in this hotel would cost more than that. It would be even more humiliating to turn around and leave at this point. Instead, he moved forward, gazing at the brightly polished tile floors, the high ceilings, the glittering shops. In the main entrance people brushed past him, and Indian men and women were busy trying to peddle their jewelry and rugs to the hotel guests. Immediately Eduardo became aware of his shabby clothes and shoes. They were the best clothes he had, but in comparison to the suits and stylish dresses worn by the guests, his clothing looked worn and out of style. He squared his shoulders and tried to appear relaxed as he walked toward the receptionist's desk. All around him in the lobby sat well-dressed men and women engaged in seemingly important conversations. He clutched on the handle of his canvas travel bag more tightly and arrived at the receptionist's desk before he had decided what to say, or even thought about what might be appropriate to say. The woman behind the desk was Hispanic. She looked to be in her early thirties and was quite beautiful; her clothes and hair were elegant, and she looked comfortable, perhaps even bored, behind the desk. Eduardo knew that she had seen him enter; she had been watching him all the time and probably knew he was lost. After all, it was obvious enough.

Eduardo stopped in front of the desk and put his bag on the floor. With an air of boredom, the woman took a long drag on her cigarette and blew the smoke out through her nostrils before she spoke. Eduardo noticed that the bright red polish on her finger nails matched the red lipstick on her lips and cigarette butt.

"Yes?" she said in English. "What can we do for you?"

"I'm from Los Torbellinos. I joined the navy, but my train doesn't leave until tomorrow." He knew he was talking too fast and making no sense, but he wanted to get it over with. Regardless of what she might think, he only wanted it to be over. "I don't have a place to spend the night." The woman continued to stare at Eduardo, noting that he was more of a boy than a young man, a handsome, frightened boy. "Could you please tell me . . ." he tried to continue but she interrupted, charmed by his innocence.

"It's no problem," she said this time in Spanish and with warmth.

She crushed out the cigarette and looked around quickly. "Come with me. I can arrange for you to stay here tonight. You can stay in the room where the cook sleeps. He won't mind. There's an extra cot in his room anyway." She stepped out from behind the desk and led Eduardo past an opulent bar and through the dining room where the first meals were already being served by waiters wearing white jackets and black slacks.

Eduardo felt relieved when he and the woman pushed through a set of swinging doors into the haven of the hot, steamy kitchen. It was a huge kitchen filled with more pots and pans and cooking utensils than he knew existed. Enticing aromas permeated the air and reminded him that despite all of the bananas in the morning and the lunch at the cafeteria he was hungry again. There were five people working in the kitchen and they all looked up when he and the woman walked in. She led him to a short thin man who was dressed in white and seemed to be in charge. In a few minutes, she told Eduardo's story to a man who nodded and smiled while she spoke. He extended his hand to Eduardo with energetic friendliness.

"My name's Tito. Pleased to meet you, son. Sure you can sleep in the back room with me, but I hope you don't mind the smell of potatoes," he chuckled. "We stored three hundred pounds of potatoes in my room this morning." Then he laughed, "Besides, I can probably use an extra hand in here tonight."

Eduardo took Tito's hand. "Eduardo Montez from Los Torbellinos. Pleased to meet you, sir," he said, still a bit shocked by Tito and the woman's kindness.

"Okay. I think you're all set for the night," the woman said, smiling at Eduardo for the first time. "I have to get back to the desk, but Tito will take care of you. He'll probably even give you something to eat." She winked at them and turned to leave the kitchen.

"Thank you. Thank you very much," Eduardo said, but she walked on without turning back.

"You don't need to thank her," Tito laughed. "She likes to do nice things for people. Her only problem is she's spent too much time with them gringos, but under all that makeup she's still brown," he snickered. "Here, first let's get you something to eat. Then you can help me."

Eduardo was grateful to be in the warm kitchen, but he was more grateful for Tito, whose constant chatter helped him forget the empty feeling that had been gnawing at his stomach since he left Los Torbellinos. After a good meal, Eduardo peeled potatoes and diced onions by the tubful while the other cooks and Tito put out orders and made preparations for the next day. While they worked, Tito talked about his family who lived in Truchas, and he talked about his experience in World War I. He also talked about the current war and all of the people he knew who had gone away to fight it, and he said he was grateful that his own sons were still too young to be drafted. He told the story about how he came to be a cook, and he talked generally about anything that came into his mind.

When they retired to Tito's little room late that night, Tito fell asleep immediately. Eduardo lay awake for hours. In the morning, he only knew he had slept because he could remember an eery dream in which he was picking potatoes out of deep trenches in the earth, though in the dream he was a little boy of five or six again. He got out of bed feeling unrefreshed, and the gnawing, dancing butterfly sensation was back in the pit of his stomach stronger than before. He washed and shaved. Tito tried to give him a big breakfast in the kitchen, but Eduardo was too nervous to eat.

Tito walked with Eduardo into the alley off the kitchen's back door. Eduardo extended his trembling hand to Tito; the two of them watched his hand shake and then they made eye contact. Suddenly Tito pulled Eduardo close, giving him a strong embrace. Tears of gratitude flooded Eduardo's eyes and Tito stepped back, reaching at a chain around his neck.

"Here, son," he said, his voice cracking, "take this." He removed the chain from around his neck, placing it around Eduardo's. "It's my Saint Christopher medal. You know, he's the protector of travelers?"

"I can't take this . . ." Eduardo tried to protest. But he was cut off by Tito.

"I insist. He got me through the war. You take him now. I don't need him no more. Hell, I ain't doing no more traveling; I already seen all I want to see." Eduardo took Tito's hand again and squeezed firmly, reluctant to let go. "God bless you, Eduardo Montez, and you come see me when you get back," he said reassuringly. Smiling, Eduardo turned and walked to the recruiting station clutching the medal.